Unclaimed Bonds

A Game of Hearts Desire

Book 1

Lilinoe K. Russell

To all the readers who have watched The Bachelorette series, fallen in love with more than one contestant, and were seriously disappointed that the bachelorette couldn't choose more than one.

PLAYLIST

Unbreakable – Fireflight
Get Me Out (Orchestral Version) – No Resolve
My Arms – Ledger
Broken (feat. Amy Lee) – Seether
Villain – Rain Paris
Best Part of Me – Jeremy Renner
Easy On Me – No Resolve
Awake and Alive – Skillet
Come to This – Natalie Taylor
I Found You – Andy Grammer
Let Me Love You (feat. Lacey Strum) – Love and Death
Heavy (feat. Rain Paris) – Fame on Fire
What Have You Done – Within Temptation and Keith Caputo
Titanium – Charice
I Was Made for Loving You (feat. Ed Sheeran) – Tori Kelly
No Air – Caleb and Kelsey
Unstoppable (The Voice) – Brynn Cartelli
Badass Woman – Meghan Trainor
I See Red – Everybody Loves and Outlaw

Fall In Line (feat. Demi Lovato) – Christina Aguilera
Worth the Fight – No Resolve
I Hate Everything About You – Halocene and Violet Orlandi
Bring Me to Life – Evanescence

TRIGGER WARNING

This is a "why choose" paranormal shifter romance with some dark aspects that include triggers, such as murder, gore, graphic language, graphic sexual situations, child assault and rape (not depicted), toxic relations between the main characters, infidelity, child abuse and neglect, suicidal thoughts and ideations, human trafficking, drugs, and alcohol use. Future books in the series may also include kinks, such as bondage, blindfolded sex, breath play, agoraphilia, and BDSM. Because this is a "why choose" romance, there will be multiple partners (sometimes all at once).

Please proceed with caution.

— lilinoe k. russell

PRELUDE

Every story has a beginning. Every culture, every species, has a story to tell of how they came to be.

These stories become the foundation for who we are, why we look the way we do and why we behave and act as we do.

But as these stories are told from generation to generation, they change. Their truth becomes altered—even worse, forgotten.

Before corruption and greed came to the Luna Solar realm, the white wolf shifter species once existed. A rare species, unlike others known worldwide, it is said that the white wolves were never actual animals or humans but magical beings from the Fae world.

These intellectual beings possessed magic.

Those who migrated to the new realm believed they could harness the white wolves' powers if they had total control over the territory, as it was rumored that the powers of the land resided within its earth and waters. Soon, a band of shifters called the Resistance declared war.

The great war happened.

Genocide occurred.

There were no white wolf shifters left, and magic ceased to exist.

Time passed. New generations were born. Some remembered and carried on while others lived in total ignorance.

All hope is not lost. One day, when a new generation is born, they will harness the magic of their originals. Together, they will rekindle the traditions once forgotten, reunite our realm, and bring peace.

Then, and only then, will the white wolves return home, and the white wolf queen will reign again.

PROLOGUE

MAY 5, 2016

Through the haze of blood, sweat, and tears, I see him standing there, looking down at me as I am punched, kicked, and held down against my will.

"Stay down, you worthless bitch!" one of my tormentors growls right before he kicks me in the face.

Despite the wave of nausea and the darkness creeping in, I spit out the blood filling my mouth and push myself into a standing position.

I will not give in. I will not submit. Not today. Not ever.

A blow to the back of my head careens me back down onto my hands and knees.

"Submit!" a familiar voice shouts. I angle my head to glare at Kat, who used to be my best friend when we were younger. The bitter sting of betrayal tightens in my throat. She narrows her eyes and curls her upper lip in a sneer. Bending forward, she slams her fist into my cheek.

"So pathetic. Can't believe we're related!" my brother, Bart, snarls, kicking me in my side.

The air echoes with more laughs, more snickers, more shouts. "Pathetic!"

"Weak!"

"Ugly!"

"Submit!"

A forceful boot to my ribs knocks me onto my side. I continue to fight the darkness that wants to consume me. I don't know how much more my body can take, but I refuse to surrender. I roll onto my hands and knees again to stand.

Wavering, I shake my head, hoping to clear my blurry vision. I open my eyes, lift my chin, and angrily stare at the Young Alpha standing to the side, watching, waiting for me to submit, but I won't.

Another punch strikes my face. A crack sounds in my head, and blood gushes from my nose. I fight the wave of nausea and threatening dizziness. I widen my stance, and arms wrap around my waist.

"Aww, she thinks she's better than us." One of my tormentors chuckles, rubbing his nose along my cheek. "Maybe she needs a different kind of lesson." His hands roam to my breast and down over my abdomen.

Another male tormentor steps forward and runs his finger down the other side of my face. "I bet you will submit as I ram my dick into your tight pussy," he whispers in my ear.

I lift my chin, refusing to cower.

"When we're done with you, you'll submit and beg for more."

Strange hands tear at my school uniform, lifting my skirt, pull at my bra, cup my breast, and grab my ass. My lips tremble, and tears stream down my face. I hold my chin high, and I glare at the fucking future Alpha asshole still standing there, watching.

"We're going to make you the pack whore because that is all you're worth." A chorus of laughter ensues around me.

"Yeah, the ugly pack whore!" Kat barks.

"Enough!" A sharp command issued by the Young Alpha freezes the group in place. The air suddenly fills with an impenetrable silence. "I've had enough of this shit show!" the Young Alpha shouts as he turns to leave. His little group of followers release me.

"There's always tomorrow," one of them snickers.

"Or the next day," another one suggests.

"And the next," my brother adds.

Kat throws a knife at my feet. "Just do us all a favor and get it over with already."

I stand still, refusing to show any weakness or indicate they were so close to winning. I watch them follow the Young Alpha. My body shivers. Dizzying darkness slowly floods my senses. The ground begins to tilt. Unable to fight any longer, I slump to the ground as the world slips away.

I don't know how long I was unconscious—maybe seconds, minutes, or even an hour. I blink and realize the sky darkened slightly. It is now almost evening. Shit! I'm supposed to meet Ms. Fields for my music lesson.

I sit up, and nausea hits me. I close my eyes and take a deep breath, willing the sensation to pass. Slowly, I open my eyes, searching for the discarded backpack torn from me just before the attack. I emit a defeated sigh when I find it several feet away near a tree on the edge of the forest line, not far behind the school.

I gaze into the forest. I almost made it before the Young Alpha and his group of brainless bullying bootlickers found me. Sadness grips me, thinking about my attackers who once were my friends, but I immediately shake it off. I can't afford to feel any nostalgia toward broken relationships. It won't help me survive, and it definitely won't help me understand why I am the target of their rage.

I situate onto my knees and assess my injuries. Blood splatters trail down my front. My blouse is torn open. My skirt is twisted up around my waist.

I push my skirt down with shaky hands and gather the front of my blouse as I tentatively stand. Staggering forward, I reach for my backpack and retrieve my jacket. I delicately wrap it around my shoulders. Unlike some of the female pack members my age, I have yet to transition into my wolf. I prayed every day since I turned sixteen that I would shift, especially at times like these when I wish I could heal swiftly. As mad as I am at the moon goddess for my unanswered prayers, I can't entirely blame her. No doubt, the daily beatings and malnourishment contribute more to my inability to shift.

Sharp pain slices through me as I lift my arm. I wince, squeezing my eyes shut. Clenching my jaw, I zip the front of my jacket and pull the hood over my head. Kicking the dirt, I stumble over the knife Kat threw at me earlier. I bend down, sucking in a sharp breath, and tuck it into my waistband.

I make my way across the cracked and chipped walkway leading to Ms. Field's tiny cottage. As I approach, the screen door issues its familiar creak.

"Oh my god, Grit!" Ms. Fields cries, covering her mouth with her hand as she sees me approach.

I flinch at the sound of my name. I hate my name.

Tears well in her eyes. She whispers, "What have they done to you?" Motioning for me to enter her home, she closes the door as I step into her cozy living room. "Come sit." She gestures to the bench in front of her piano before disappearing down the hallway. She returns with a warm washcloth and some extra towels. Gingerly cleaning my face, she proclaims, "I'm going to speak to the principal and the Alpha's assistant. This needs to stop! They pick on you every single day."

I reach for her hand and shake my head. "No," I croak. "If you go to the principal or the assistant, you could lose your job. I won't allow you to do that. The school needs you. The students need you." Well, the good ones, anyway.

The Young Alpha issued an order at the beginning of my senior year. Any faculty who interferes with my "lessons"— more like punishments—will be subject to termination from the school and possibly even retribution by their own peers. They could face the same torment I face now.

Ms. Fields teaches music, one of my favorite subjects. She has always been kind to me. When I was ten, she caught me in the school's auditorium tinkering with the piano while hiding from my brother and his asshole friends. She didn't scold me or question why I was there. She simply sat next to me and began to teach me how to play the piano.

Now, I see her almost every day after school. These music lessons provide me with an escape from the torment in my life. They are also my protection. My hope.

Slowly shaking my head again, I study her. Her long, chestnut brown hair is tied in a messy bun. Instead of her school-issued blazer, she wears an oversized sweater and black yoga pants. Because of her small stature, she could easily be mistaken for one of the high school students. Her angelic face comprises soft features and a petite nose, but her spark shines in her big, light brown eyes with a blue ring around them.

I repeat, "No. I'll be fine."

Sadness reflects in her eyes. Grasping my hand in both of hers, she lowers her gaze. "I can't continue to stay on the sidelines and watch them attack you. This bullying has gotten worse. It's bad enough that you endure abuse in your own home. I have to do something."

I lean forward and whisper, "I'll be fine. I promise."

A single tear escapes, sliding down her left cheek.

Relinquishing my hand, I lift my backpack and pull out a slim wooden box. The moment I saw it, I thought of Ms. Fields. I snared hundreds of rabbits and sold their pelts to earn enough money to buy it. The box is handmade by one of our very own pack members, carved with an intricate design of lavender and daisies. Daisies are Ms. Field's favorite flowers, and lavender is mine.

I hand the box to her. "I want to thank you for the music lessons and for taking care of me."

"A gift for me? Grit, you shouldn't spend your hard-earned money on me." She passes the box back to me, but I raise my hands, refusing to take it.

"You never let me pay for my music lessons. You always feed me, clean me up when I'm a mess." I sigh. "You sew my school uniforms back together. Sometimes, you even manage to find me new ones. I saw this and thought of you. I wanted to give you something, to thank you."

Her hand glides over the cover of the box. Before she can lift the lid I cover her hand with mine.

I confess with a shaky voice, "I survived every day of this hell because of you. If anything happens to you because of me, I couldn't live with myself." I look up at her. "Please, let it be and take my gift." Leaning forward, I kiss her forehead and embrace her in a gentle hug.

Her shoulders shake as she cries, squeezing me gently. "I don't understand why this is happening to you," she sniffs.

I pull back from her and shrug. "Pack tradition. Only the strong survive." *And they're worried about what I will do to them once I transition into my wolf.* I keep that last bit to myself as I stand. Wincing, I pull on my backpack and head for the door.

"Wait. Don't go home. Stay here. Stay for dinner."

I shake my head. "I should go. The monster is with his friends, and my parents are out of the territory for some kind of business meeting. If I get home now, I can avoid him for the night."

Ms. Fields steps toward me, pleading, "Please, stay with me. I can petition for you to live with me. I can tell the Betas that I'll take their," she makes air quotes, "burden off their hands. Let me make this right."

If only it could be that easy. They won't release me. Letting me go would be admitting that they did something wrong, and that would make them look bad. Their image and power in this pack are all they care about. No, the Betas—my parents—will never let me go. They allow their own son, my brother, to torment me, beat me, and perhaps one day even kill me before they ever admit they are wrong.

"Grit, please. I know someone who can help. If I send him a message—"

"No! If you are caught, they'll execute you!" Swallowing, I lower my voice. "They will kill you, just like the others who tried to help me. Please, please, you've already done so much for me."

"Grit, they won't stop. They could kill you." Tears stream down her face.

I can't put her life in danger. I kiss her cheek, give her another hug, and then head for the door.

She follows me, holding the screen door open with one hand and the box I gave her with the other. As I reach the end of the walkway, I turn to look at her one last time and wave goodbye.

Night falls, and the forest floor turns into a tapestry of shadows as the moonlight filters through the branches of the trees. I listen to the rushing water from the Ruby Falls and the soft musical sound of crickets chirping. I sit on a jagged boulder in a clearing within the forest with my few personal items in a beat-up backpack and continue to pick at the frayed edges of my pleated skirt.

I left Ms. Fields' home three hours ago. He was supposed to be here to meet me, to help me. I replay the last conversation, or rather fight, we had a few days ago. He didn't feel my urgency to leave the territory was warranted. He promised he would be here today. But he isn't. He never showed. My heart breaks from disappointment and betrayal. Tears well in my eyes.

I try to shake off the pain and replace it with anger because I don't have time to grieve over a boy who broke his promises. I need to escape this territory before I end up dead.

We planned to breach the territory boundary into Territory One, the Emerald pack land. From there, beyond the pack territories, the city is a neutral area where I can hide. I can get a job, make some money, find a place to live. I can eventually go back to school and leave the LS for good.

And when I make it out of this territory, he better pray that we never cross paths again. Balling my hands into fists at my sides, I push to my feet with renewed determination. I advance through the brush and low-lying branches of the fir trees and blaze a trail to safety, to freedom.

Nervous energy vibrates under my skin. Soon I will be free of this horrible pack, of my abusive parents and brother. Halfway there, a cacophony of sound fills the air behind me—growls, snapping jaws, laughter, and whoops of joy. With a bone-jarring fear, I tear off my backpack and start to run.

My heart wants to leap out of my chest, and my lungs want to explode. The muscles in my legs burn. Fuck. Fuck! They're getting closer! A piercing howl sends shivers up my spine. Another howl emanates through the territory, then another.

My brother and his friends invented this signaling system. It's a red flag, a warning that they're coming for me. This time, they will make sure I don't survive. I know it. I can feel it. I need to get out of here, off this territory, and find sanctuary.

My steps falter, and I fall to my hands and knees. The beating earlier took a lot out of me. Gasping for air, I push myself up. I'm almost there, so close to the territory line. Hope and a renewed sense of energy burst through me. I sprint toward the boundary.

I tear through the brush, jumping over tree roots. But the crashing of the brush and the pounding of paws and feet behind me grows louder. Fuck! They're closer.

Then it hits me. Why the fuck am I running? Without slowing down, I scan for a low-hanging branch. If I climb up, I can jump from tree to tree. There, up ahead, I see one. Despite my body's protesting aches and pains, I push myself harder, faster.

I leap into the air with all of my might. Catching the branch with both hands, I hoist myself up. Just as my upper body makes it over the branch, a snarling wolf latches onto my leg. I hang on tightly as he jerks my body down. Desperately, I try to break the wolf's hold, ignoring the pain from the canines digging into my flesh. This wolf is relentless, shaking his head and growling. His teeth sink deeper into my leg. With my other foot, I kick his head repeatedly.

Another wolf comes, jumping up and raking its sharp claws down my back. I scream in agony, and my grip on the branch loosens. Together, they bring me down, tearing at me with claws and teeth. I whimper and press my lips together. I just want to scream or, better yet, die, but I won't give them the satisfaction.

Twisting, turning, punching, I thrash around to escape from under them. I kick hard, catching one of the wolves in the jaw. It squeals in pain, and I scramble to my stomach, hastily digging my feet and elbows into the ground to crawl away. I'm too slow.

The other wolf pounces, pinning me down with its weight. A chuckle echoes from somewhere in the dark, followed by a low growl.

Bart slowly walks forward. "Aww, poor little brat. You honestly thought you could outrun us? Where the hell do you think you're going, huh?" Crouching down, he grabs a handful of hair.

I grunt as his nails turn into claws and pierce my scalp.

"Even if you cross the territory line, no one will save you." He leans down near my ear. "This is pack business, and everyone knows that the other packs don't interfere with pack business, stupid bitch!" He shoves my face into the dirt. "Skunk, where the fuck is the rope?" he shouts. A wolf with a white stripe along its back emerges from the brush, holding a rope dangling from his mouth.

No, not Skunk—the only friend left among my peers. My eyes connect with his. His eyes reflect sadness and guilt. I avert my eyes. I don't need him to feel guilt over this. I rather he survive than end up dead, like the others who tried to help me before.

"I thought you chickened out on me, Skunk. Glad to know you're on our side." Bart snickers, grabbing my head again.

Skunk emits a low growl before he huffs and moves to stand by another wolf with blood—my blood—staining its muzzle. Bart yanks my head back. I squirm to fight despite the large animal sitting on my back.

He slips the rope over my head and around my neck. I study his face, looking for any signs of love or compassion, but all I see is rage. My parents never loved me. There was no coddling, no hugs or kisses. No kind words. Instead, I endured curses and slurs, slaps and punches. And Bart delighted in torturing me too. His eyes shine with cruelty and excitement. No love for his little sister.

"Why?" I whisper.

His face reddens, and a corner of his lip curls in a sneer. "Why? Because your very existence makes us sick. For generations, my family has done everything to wipe out your kind, and yet you still exist. Now I have to clean up their mess and get rid of you for them! Those ungrateful bastards!"

What the hell is he talking about? My kind? He's my brother, for fuck's sake. I mean, sure, he has brown hair and brown eyes like both of my parents, and I have blonde hair and blue eyes. I'm sure it's a throwback from some recessive trait generations back.

"But we're going to have some fun first." He nods at someone else in the pack.

Kat saunters over with a smug grin. She wields a new knife in her hand, waving it between her fingers like a prize. "This will be so much fun! I've been wanting to do this for ages!" She kneels in front of me. "Did you really believe him? When he said he would meet you tonight? When he promised to save you?" She snorts when I don't answer her. "It was all an act, Grit."

I stare at her knee, refusing to show any reaction to her words.

She cackles, leaning back to rest on her heels. "He told us, you know." My eyes move up to her face. "How he convinced you, how he made you believe that you were his true mate." Raucous laughter erupts from all of Bart's groupies and bounces off the trees. "Guess you wish you submitted now. Don't you, Grit?" She offers a cruel smile.

I don't want to believe her, but he isn't here. He never came.

"Shut the fuck up, and do it!" Bart yells. She cocks her head to the side, assessing me. The knife in her hand approaches my face.

She slices into my scalp, and I scream. Blood seeps into my eyes. Pain wracks my body, and when I just can't take any more, darkness consumes me.

I lie on the forest ground in a semiconscious heap. Bart stands over me, blood dripping from his hand. It isn't enough, wolves shredding me to pieces, cutting off my hair, slicing into my face. He has to beat me too. All of that isn't enough for these sick bastards.

I feel a tug. My heart freezes in my chest when I realize the rope is still around my neck. I reach for it—too late!

They drag me backward. The rope tightens, cutting off my air. I claw at my neck, trying to pry my fingers under the noose. I choke, sob, and kick my legs as my body slides through the dirt.

My upper body lifts into the air. No, no, no! My feet leave the ground. I flail for the rope behind me. I can't breathe.

Dots threaten my vision. The rush of roaring blood pounds in my ears, joined by a high-pitched ringing noise. My lungs are about to burst from lack of oxygen. I reach for the knife in my waistband. But my fingers are numb and soaked in blood. My hands tremble.

Don't give up! I yell at myself in my mind as I slowly saw through the rope. The knife slips from my grasp. My arms fall to my sides. My body stills, and my erratic heartbeat stutters.

It's over. I have no fight left in me. My heart stops. I. Submit. To. Death.

CHAPTER 1

THE LATE NIGHT SHOW

JESSICA
PRESENT DAY:
MARCH 24, 2025

With trembling hands, I fidget with the skirt of my dress and pull at my sleeves. My heart beats hard and fast against my chest. Beads of sweat start to form over my upper lip. I peak through the thick, heavy drapes, anticipating my introduction on *The Late Night Show with Sammy Cane.*

I watch her present her opening. I could have stayed in the dressing room and watched on the monitor, but my nerves forced me out here instead. Sammy is a pretty woman with dark blonde hair, warm brown eyes, and a beauty mark just above the right corner of her mouth. She was once a famous pop singer. The audience laughs and claps at her fun, energetic demeanor.

At the heart of the stage is a loveseat for the guest, an armchair for the host, and a rounded coffee table, where a mug of water or tea waits for me. A small band sits off to the side of the stage opposite me. My eyes shift to the open ceiling with large bright canned lights fixed to metal beams. Their warmth already blinds me.

Behind the filming crew and stagehands milling about are five rows of seats for the live audience. A tiny flicker of panic stirs in my gut, quickening my already erratic pulse, when I notice every seat in the studio is filled. I scan the audience for a familiar face, and my shoulders drop in relief when I find my mother sitting next to Sixes in the third row.

"I am so excited to introduce you to our special guest tonight. She is a singer/songwriter, the CEO of WP Corporation, and now the main star of our favorite reality TV show, *A Game of Heart's Desire: The Alpha Games*. Please welcome Alpha Princess Jessica Langhlan!"

The curtain parts, and the audience cheers as I make my way onto the stage. Still trembling, I force a smile, hoping it doesn't look scary or unnatural. I offer a little twirl to showcase my dress.

I promised my friend, Akiyo, that I would wear her latest design. The long, fitted, high-split dress, off-the-shoulder with long sleeves, features a green-and-gold gauzy Asian print, matched with high strappy heels I can barely walk in.

Internally, I pray I don't trip. Slow and steady, I tell myself, as my ankle wobbles. Finally, I reach the hostess. Relief fills my chest. Thank goodness. Sammy welcomes me with a big hug, and my nervousness melts away.

"Thank you, Alpha Princess Jessica, for joining us today. We are so excited to have you! It is such an honor to be in your presence!" She motions to the loveseat.

I wave to the audience as I take my seat. "What are you talking about? You're Sammy Cane, the first contestant to win *So You Think You Can Sing* in the very first season. You're the first and only music artist to have multiple number-one hits stay on the top ten pop music charts for months, not to mention the first female artist to own her own record label just one year after entering the industry. You paved the way for many young artists with a dream within the Northern A territories and worldwide."

She blushes at my own fangirling and drops her head.

"I have been a huge fan for years. It's an honor to be in the presence of the Pop Queen," I continue, pressing my still-shaky hands over my chest. The audience cheers. I raise my arms, pumping them in the air, encouraging them to applaud louder.

Her blush darkens with my praise, and she waves her hand to quiet the audience. "If I'm the Pop Queen, then you are the Queen of Rock!" The audience erupts with clapping and more cheering. Turning to the crowd, she asks, "Did you know that a couple of the top hits I sang when I first started, 'Unstoppable Woman' and 'Armor,' were written and composed by the artist formerly known as 'G'?" She points her thumb toward me. "Yes, everyone, if you haven't heard about it yet, the Alpha Princess Jessica Langhlan recently revealed that she is the mysterious artist famously known for hiding her features behind a mask."

I laugh. "When did I become the 'artist formerly known as 'G'?" Gasps and murmurs echo around the studio.

Sammy shrugs. "When the world found out who you really are, did you think that everyone would still call you 'G'?"

"Oh… I didn't think about it. I didn't exactly plan to, you know, come out behind the mask the way I did." I haven't even spoken to my manager since the whole thing happened. I just let my lawyer and PR rep handle it. "How have you been? It has been a long time since I last saw you," I ask Sammy, changing the subject.

She smiles. "I am great! Busy, between working and raising my little family, but I can't complain. My two little girls are growing up way too fast." The screen behind us displays her two children, one of them missing her two front teeth. The audience emits a collective "aww" in response to the picture.

"They are too precious!" I coo.

Sammy's head turns toward the end of the stage. A man wearing headphones with a mouthpiece makes hand motions. "Speaking of busy, underneath the mask and the title, I don't think anyone realizes how smart, talented, and hardworking you really are."

My mouth instantly dries at her insinuation. I casually reach for the cup filled with water and drink. I clear my throat before replacing the cup on the table. "How do you mean?"

She slips her hand between the armrest and the cushion of her chair and pulls out index cards with the show's logo printed on the back. "Well, for starters, at age sixteen, you challenged the LS territory's aptitude test and acquired a high school diploma. At eighteen, you earned a bachelor's degree in business, and at twenty-one, you finished your MBA overseas." She leans over the arm of her chair closer toward me. "Do you know what I was doing at eighteen? I was sneaking into karaoke bars and open mic nights."

I giggle. "And just look at where that has gotten you today." I motion to our surroundings.

She rolls her eyes. "If you only knew the half of it," she replies with a mischievous smile. "Anyway, we can talk more about that in private over lots and lots of cocktails." We chuckle before she switches gears again, glancing at her index cards. "You have practically built an empire of a multitude of businesses from hotels, restaurants, and clubs. Some of our sources reported that you have silent partnerships with wineries, whiskey distilleries, and other small businesses around the world."

Heat blooms in my cheeks, listening to my business accomplishments.

"And on top of all of that, you recently became the CEO of a worldwide business consulting company."

Shaking my head, I try to peer through the blinding lights, seeking out my mother and assistant. "I think you give me way more credit than I deserve. I have business partners, board members, hardworking management teams, and staff who helped me to grow these successful businesses. And my amazing assistant helps keep me in line. I didn't do it alone."

She fans the cards in front of her. "Oh, please! I for one know exactly how much work goes into starting a business. It's not easy, let me tell you. I'm just thankful that I went through all of the ups and downs of becoming a business owner before I had kids. Most people don't realize how much heart and soul you pour into a business—the sleepless nights, the tears. It's like selling your soul to the devil!"

"No, really, I—"

She places a hand on my knee. "You are amazing. It's okay to let the world see it. All the sources we inquired had nothing but wonderful things to say about you and your work ethic. Even those within the music industry said the same, and that includes me. My personal experience working with you was by far one of my most favorite memories."

I break into a bashful smile and incline my head. "Thank you."

She gently squeezes my knee before transitioning to the next topic. "You're here tonight mainly to promote the premiere of the show *A Game of Heart's Desire: The Alpha Games*."

I let out an audible breath and nod.

Before I can respond, she leans in, frowning, and says, "I don't get it."

I shrug. "What is there not to get?"

"Well, because you're you. For crying out loud, there have to be miles of men lining up who want to be with you. Why do you need this show?"

A man from the audience suddenly yells, "I'm single! Mate me!"

I offer a hearty laugh. Twisting my hands together, I contemplate my answer. I've been asked this question a million times. "I think you pointed out the obvious. I spent almost a decade trying to discover myself and make a career." I shake my head, disguising my embarrassment. "After a few mistakes, I convinced myself that I don't need a mate, that my career and family are all that I need. But as it turns out, there are rules—laws—I must adhere to when becoming a female Alpha. With that also comes personal sacrifices, not just to keep my role but to do what's best for my pack."

Still frowning, she responds, "I understand that, but again, why the show?"

I don't have an answer, at least not one I can honestly give. I recall the script I should say, according to my PR guy, but it just seems so... fake. But the show must go on. "Everyone thinks my life is so glamorous and romantic, traveling all over the world and meeting new people all the time. The truth is I haven't made many attempts to connect with anyone. Even though many of my friends are males, I simply can't make a phone call and ask, 'Hey, friend, are you still single? Great! How about you and I hook up and get mated before my twenty-fifth birthday?'" I jest.

That last part deviated from the script. My PR guy is going to have an aneurysm. Sammy offers me a sad smile.

Swallowing, I continue. "I know it's not the ideal way to find my mate. Trust me, I remember a time when I sat with friends watching the show, and I couldn't help but think, what's wrong with them that they can't find someone the normal way? I used to make rude comments and make fun of the female contestants," I admit with a snort. "I guess karma has a funny way of giving it right back to me because here I am, promoting the show."

Disappointment flickers across Sammy's face. "I hope you find your true mate." She looks at me thoughtfully, reaches over, and clasps my hand. "I always thought you were special. You write and compose music with so much love and emotion. You deserve to have a meaningful relationship in your life."

I look down at our hands. It is kind of her to say, but love, including a meaningful relationship, isn't in the cards for me. "Thank you. That means a lot to me, especially coming from you."

The man offstage with the headphones motions to Sammy again.

"Well, it's that time everyone!" The audience grows wild with whistles and cheers. "Let's play a game!"

My eyes widen. I was warned about this, but I honestly thought we took so much time already that I wouldn't have to participate. I glance over to see my PR guy's face. He shakes his head in caution. A part of me really wants to piss him off for his rude comments and annoying remarks throughout the week. This morning, he drank my coffee on purpose and then refused to stop to buy me another one.

Let's just say he's not my favorite person. I narrow my eyes and paste on my *fuck you, Gary* smile.

Turning my attention back to Sammy, I rub my hands together. "Let's do this!"

Finally, it's over. I make my way to my mother and assistant, Sixes, who moved from their seats among the audience to join our PR guy, Gary, and Anders, my head guard, backstage.

"Nice job. Cute act, by the way—playing all meek and innocent," Gary sneers in a hushed tone.

I lean closer to him and, in just as low of a voice, reply, "I'm in this mess because of your great idea in the first place. Besides, it was also your idea to act like a bubbly idiot to throw people off."

With a wide, fake smile, he looks around to ensure no one heard me. "No, you wouldn't need to pretend to be a bubbly idiot if you had just chosen a mate in the first place, Princess."

I roll my eyes, and he stalks off, letting my mother know he will meet us at my place later to discuss the plans with the production team.

My mother gives me a gentle smile and reaches for my hand when someone from behind me clears their throat. Anders takes a closer step toward me, and I put up a hand to stop him. A stagehand, or perhaps a cameraman, stands awkwardly nearby. This man isn't a threat.

"Uh, excuse me, Alpha Princess. I'm sorry to bother you, and I know you probably want to get going... You see, there's, uh... a little boy sitting over there." He points toward the audience. "He's asking if he can meet you. He... uh... he says he's a huge fan of yours." The poor guy is sweating as if I am going to bite off his head.

I smile to ease some of his nervousness. "A little boy?" I ask.

His shoulders relax. "Yeah. Cute kid. He made his nanny bring him here today. We don't normally allow children in, so I was surprised to see him sitting in the audience seats. He really wants to meet you."

I crane my neck. There he is—a little guy, not more than five or six years old, with jet-black hair, sitting next to a young, ash-blondee female.

Anders whispers in my ear, "I don't think this is a good idea. It could be a setup."

I watch the two. The little boy talks animatedly to his nanny, and she is intent on the conversation. They don't seem like much of a threat. I look around them, and they're alone. "It's just a little boy and his nanny. If you're so worried, come with me." Turning to the man who made the request, I add, "Or would it be okay if you bring the boy and his nanny backstage?"

"That won't be a problem. I can bring them now, if you like." I glance at Anders. "Will that work better for you?"

His face is stern, and he doesn't answer right away, probably calculating the risks to my safety either way. He finally nods, and the man leaves to escort the pair.

CHAPTER 2
A SON'S CHOICE

CONTESTANT #16

Reaching over, I gently remove the TV remote from my son's hand. He sits next to me in my king-sized bed as we watch *The Tonight Show* featuring the Alpha Princess Jessica Langhlan. He leans back, mirroring my posture, propped against the headboard with a couple of pillows against his back. His jet-black hair is smoothed down to perfection, and tonight, he sports a button-down, deep blue, pinstriped pajama set, instead of his usual favorites with cartoon characters. I smirk at his effort to dress up to watch a show on TV.

As the show is about to end, someone from the audience yells, "Sing a song!"

"Yeah, one of your songs!" a few more shout the same request.

"Sing?" the Alpha Princess asks.

The host suggests with his hands that the stage is hers. "Sure. Everyone's excited now that they know you are the masked singer 'G'. Go for it."

The Alpha Princess approaches the band and whispers to them. As they play the opening chords to a song, she closes her eyes and starts to sing. I'm instantly enraptured by her beauty and her voice, and when the lyrics of the song resonate, a deep ache envelops my heart. The camera shows the audience, capturing them swaying to the music, and the host offers a wide grin as he watches her perform. The camera focuses on the Alpha Princess, and it catches a single tear falling from the corner of her left eye.

Clearing my throat, I push down the building emotions and glance over at my son. He is also mesmerized by the princess, even though he doesn't quite understand the meaning behind her beautiful melody. When they cut to a commercial segment, signaling the end of the show, I turn off the TV.

He looks at me and says, "She's beautiful, Daddy."

I lean forward and kiss his head. "She really is, son."

He smiles. "Inside and out?"

"I guess you would have to be to write songs like that and sing with so much emotion that everyone around you feels precisely what you feel when you sing."

He nods before confessing, "I met her."

My smile flips into a frown. "What do you mean you met her?"

"Panny took me to watch her funny story. Panny's friend let us go behind the curtain to meet her."

"Penny," I correct him. Sometimes, I forget that he's six years old because he speaks like an old man. My fault, I'm sure. I speak to him like he's an adult.

"Penny," he repeats. "I told her, Dad."

"You told her what?"

He sighs, like I should already know the answer. "I told the Alpha Princess that if she meets you, she will know that she's your true mate."

Not this again. Ever since he saw her on the news, that's all he talks about. "She's the one, Dad! She's your true mate. I know it!" He crosses his arms and pouts.

I lean forward and tickle him. "Is she now?"

He squeals and giggles. "Yes! Yes!" he shouts.

"You know what I think?" I ask, gently hitting him over the head with the pillow. "I think it's time for you to go to sleep. It is way past your bedtime."

I lift him up and swing his upper body over my shoulder, carrying him to his room. Once he's in his own bed, I cover him with the comforter after he calms down and scoots lower in the bed. He groans.

"No! No negotiating. You agreed. We shook on the deal. I let you stay up past your bedtime to watch *The Tonight Show*. You said you would go to sleep as soon as it was over."

He scrunches his tiny nose. "Ugghhhh, fine."

I kiss him on the cheek. "Good night, son. I love you."

"I love you, too, Dad." He rests his tiny arms around my neck and hugs me. Then, he whispers, "She's the one, Dad. I can feel it. I felt it when I met her."

I pull back and search his pale blue eyes. "Son, I just don't think it will work. It's complicated. It's an adult thing. Don't ask any more questions, alright? Go to sleep."

"You have to fight for her. She's the one, Dad. Please."

I shake my head. "Go to sleep. We can talk about this later."

He mumbles under his breath, turning his back to me. Still, I don't want to have this conversation, especially with my six-year-old son, who shouldn't even understand the concept of true mates. Note to self: talk to my mother about limiting her rom-coms or whatever dramatic romance movies she watches in front of my son.

I make my way to the kitchen, where my nanny removes the dishes from the dishwasher. "What the hell do you think you are doing taking my son to a late-night show hosting the Alpha Princess?" I demand. She almost drops the dish in her hand. I scared her... Good. Honestly, what the fuck was she thinking?

"I'm sorry, Alpha. Your parents bought the tickets. I assumed you knew about it," she replies, looking down at her hand, trembling now.

"My parents bought the tickets?" She nods. Is that who put this whole stupid notion of the Alpha Princess being my true mate in his head? What the fuck are they thinking? I still want to ream the poor girl, but the truth is this wasn't her fault. I'll deal with my parents.

Pointing my finger at her, I instruct, "The next time my parents buy tickets to anything or tell you to take him anywhere, you clear it with me first. I don't care if you think I already know about it. He is my son! Is that clear?"

"Yes, Alpha. This won't happen again." Her eyes remain cast down. Shit, her face is red, like she's about to cry.

I turn to leave to check on my three-year-old daughter when my nanny says, "She's nothing like how I thought she would be. She was sweet, down to earth. She was good to Jackson, gave him attention, and made him feel... important, like the honor was hers meeting him for the first time." Fuck, fuck, fuck! Not her, too. "They bonded... I think Jackson is right," she blurts in a single breath.

With my back still facing her, I reply with a lethal edge in my voice, "I won't discuss this shit with my employees. Is this clear? We are not friends. If you want to remain an employee, I suggest you stay out of my personal affairs, including my conversations with my son."

"Y-Yes, Alpha. My apologies for overstepping."

Good, I think as I storm down the hall.

I need to talk to my parents. I know they treat their employees like family, especially the pack. I don't mind what they do, but I don't like it. It sometimes gives the employees and pack members the impression that they can talk to us like friends, give us personal advice, mind our fucking business, betray us. Like they have the right.

I'm a private person. I like to keep my life and my identity confidential. I don't want to be friends with everyone who works for me, including our pack. I'm their boss, their Alpha, and that relationship shouldn't have blurred lines. It's safer that way.

I sit heavily down in my office chair and lean forward, placing my elbows on my desk and my face in my hands. Growling into my hands, I flip open my laptop and take a deep breath. I open my itinerary for the next three days. What the fuck am I thinking? Why am I doing this? After that little rant in my head, I'm a walking, talking, fucking contradiction. This isn't who I am. I'm going against everything I believe. I'm going against everything I stand for. I'm taking an extended vacation from work. I can't remember when I last went on a vacation. I'm leaving my father in charge of the firm and the pack.

I turn my head and catch a glimpse of the photo of my partner and me, taken on our wedding day. It's one of the few pictures where I'm actually smiling. Our union wasn't based on love—well, romantic love anyway. It was an arranged marriage, but I was lucky to end up with my best friend in the whole world. The day she died, I almost lost myself entirely if not for my son and daughter. I almost reverted to how I used to be—an uncaring, heartless bastard.

Looking at the picture now in my hands, I recall that Emily never wanted me to give up on reuniting with my one true love. She always believed I still had a chance.

"I fucking hope you're right, Em. I hope you're right because if not, I will be making an ass of myself in front of millions of people."

CHAPTER 3
A PACK IN CRISIS

CONTESTANT #19

I glance down at the whiskey, neat, in my hand. I haven't touched it. This is my second glass. I filled the first glass with ice, and the ice melted, watering down the whiskey, so I chucked it. Determined to find some kind of peace to quiet my rampant mind, I made another drink, this time without ice, and I still haven't touched it.

I sit on my family home's balcony facing Ruby Falls. At any other time, the sound of the falls would welcome and calm me. It used to put me to sleep. But not tonight. So much shit whirls through my head.

"There you are, sweetheart."

I turn to face my mother. She has dark circles under her eyes. Her eyelids are swollen. A stab of guilt hits me in the gut. I made her cry. I haven't seen my mother for years, and when I finally come home, I break her heart. "Hey, Mom."

She runs her hand along the back of my head and rests it on the nape of my neck.

Gazing back at the scenery in front of me, I clutch my glass tighter in my hand. "I'm sorry for staying away for so long. Maybe if I came home sooner, none of this shit would have happened."

She clucks her tongue. "Stop doing that to yourself. Things have been bad for a long time. I'm glad you left when you did."

Recent events race through my mind, over and over on repeat. It wasn't supposed to happen this way. Nothing ever turns out how it should, not when it comes to her.

Now I need to fix everything that Dad and his asshole Beta fucking destroyed. How the fuck did Dad let this happen? I used to revere him. He was everything I believed in, until he wasn't.

"Our pack is in a state of crisis," I snarl. She remains silent, trailing her thumb back and forth at the base of my hairline. "I need to fix what they did to our pack. It has to start with this union." I squeeze the tumbler tighter, and the glass starts to crack. I throw it over the balcony. I wish I could beat the shit out of something. No, I want to beat the shit out of the Beta who my father trusted... and his son. I rub my shaking hand over my face and look at my mother. "She already rejected the betrothal contract. If she doesn't choose me in this stupid game..."

She shakes her head. "I'm so sorry, sweetheart. I wish I was stronger. I wish I had intervened in all of this."

I remove her hand from my neck and kiss it. "No, I... should have done something. Instead, I just stood there and watched them destroy her." The truth is I was a coward and didn't really try. I squeeze my eyes shut to block the memories of what I did... and didn't do.

My mother sighs and bends in front of me to meet my eye. Bracketing my face in both of her hands, she says, "You're a good boy. You remind me of your father, the young man I fell in love with."

I scoff. "No offense, but you're his true mate. You would love him and follow him, even if he was the devil reincarnated."

She tsks. "I'll let you in on a little secret, my son. Just because a woman finds her true mate doesn't mean we don't have free will. We can still make our own choices. We keep that to ourselves to let the males think they are in charge."

She shakes my chin, and I give her a tight-lipped smile.

"Like I was saying, you remind me so much of your father when he was young before the Betas corrupted him. You have a good heart, just like him. He cared a lot about this pack. He and his father built all of this just for them. And you, despite everything, have added to it for your... pack... Don't sell yourself short. You have come a long way since that time. You were just a teenager. There wasn't much you could do."

I shake my head. "I could have done plenty... I didn't have the balls. I tried to please Dad, even though it never felt right in my heart."

My mother grabs my face again. "Stop! You can't undo the past. All you can do is move forward, live in the present, and learn from your mistakes. It's all any of us can do right now." I try to pull away from her, but she holds firm. "Listen to me. Frederick can take care of things while you're gone, and business operations will run as normal. The Alpha King was kind enough to send some guards to help as well, and you still have me." She quirks an eyebrow, awaiting my challenge. "Sweetheart, I know you want to do what's right for the pack, but the most important thing is for you to do what's right for you. You'll win her back. Just let her see the real you and show her what's in here." She rests a hand over my heart. I place my much larger hand over hers.

Easier said than done. The real question is will she choose me? Especially after she discovers who I truly am and the part I played in her life.

CHAPTER 4

STALKER SYNDROME

CONTESTANT #20

I turn off the TV just before the Alpha Princess starts to sing. My phone rings, but I don't answer it. I'm too angry to speak to anyone right now. How can she do this to me? How can she even entertain the idea of another man, a man who is not me? I have been patient. I gave her space and time.

I walk over to the cabinet in my room and open the double doors, revealing pictures of my beautiful princess. I pick up a bundle of her hair, tied together in a knot, raise it to my nose, and inhale the lingering scent of lavender and honey. It instantly hardens my cock.

My phone rings again, and I return my precious one's strands of hair back to their place. I graze my hand over the broken pieces of a golden mask, one she once wore performing as "G".

"Soon, baby girl. I will have you soon, and once you're mine, I will punish you for running away from me." I run my thumb over a picture of her crossing the street in the city. I followed her for years, collecting her belongings—hair ties, panties, and earrings. I strategically placed hidden cameras in her home. I watched her every move. I watched her shower, masturbate, and fuck other men.

I gingerly close the doors to my cabinet and lock the door. For the third time, my phone rings, and I finally answer. "What the fuck do you want?!" I yell.

"I can't keep calling you. I have time limits."

"Not my fucking problem!"

"Stop being a baby. This is important. Get your head back in the game!"

I lean against the wall. "What the fuck do you think I'm doing?" Her voice annoys me. The way she speaks annoys me. Everything about her annoys me.

She hisses, "Everything is in order. All you have to do is win her heart, get her to mate you, and then kill the fucking bitch!"

I end the call and punch the wall, picturing her face.

These last couple weeks have been hell, dealing with my family, and I am not in the mood to listen to their shit. I may not be as conniving as my sister, but I don't need to be. I have charm, wit, and intelligence. She's the one in prison for life, and at twenty-seven, she will be there for a very long time.

As shifters, we can live until 200 years old. She was a miserable piece of shit anyway. She deserves to be in jail. Hell, she deserves the death penalty.

I can do this. I can win over the Alpha Princess, make her my mate, and convince her to turn over her business, pack, territory, and everything else she owns to me.

But I don't want to kill her so soon. I didn't waste years following her, loving her from afar, wanting her. Fuck them. I will do this my way, maybe after we have a couple of pups. Hmmm, that's a great idea, and after she shits out the last one, maybe by then, I will tire of her. I can blame her death on the birthing process. No one will suspect me.

I ball my hands into fists at my side. The truth is I don't think I want her dead. She is everything I ever wanted in a mate. She is tough, sexy as hell, and she fucks like an animal in bed. I hate weak women who cry and whine all the time, like my stupid sister. Women who can't take a good cock irritate me.

But I can't imagine having a problem with the Alpha Princess. In fact, I think she will put up a good fight. Thinking of her in my bed, fighting me, digging her nails into my skin as I force her to take my big cock, makes me hard. Fuuuckkkk... I want her. I want to pound into her and hear her moans and screams. I want to look into her eyes and see her hatred for me. Then, I want to see that anger turn into pleasure as she realizes how good the pain can feel for both of us. I want to feel that silky-soft pussy sucking my cock as she comes.

I groan as I push down on my hardened cock with my palm. I'm so fucking turned on right now just thinking about her. Soon enough, I won't need to take care of myself to the fantasy of the Alpha Princess riding my dick because she will be mine.

CHAPTER 5

LEAVING LOVE TO FATE

CONTESTANT #24

A knock on the door distracts me from my rapt thoughts. I clear my throat to call out, "Come in," and close my laptop.

"Hey. I just wanted to check in and let you know that everything is in place."

I regard my friend, rubbing my index finger under my lip.

"I want her guarded at all times, especially at night. She has a habit of getting into shit when she thinks the rest of the world is sleeping."

He smirks and shrugs his shoulders. "We already got it covered." I shake my head. She is so damn stubborn, too stubborn for her own good. She thinks just because she trained with the guards that she is invincible. She has found more trouble than anyone I ever met.

"Not good enough. I want eyes on her at all times."

He sighs at my request.

I can tell he's preparing to give me a speech or talk me out of my decision, but I already made up my mind. My future is set, and nothing will change it.

"You don't have to do this. You still have a chance. You just need to fight for her and prove that she will always be your girl."

I look down at my desk and rub my shoulder. "It's too late," I whisper. "She made her choice, and I made mine. I'm to be mated tomorrow."

He narrows his eyes. "Why are you doing this? My brother and I have stood by your side for years. In all that time, all you ever talked about was doing all of this for *her*." He gestures to the room, my home. "Now that you have a chance to fight for her, you hide behind political bullshit and tuck your tail between your legs. I never took you for a pathetic coward and a liar."

Slamming my fist on my desk. "Fuck you! She has made her choice!" I shout.

He glares at me. "Listen, you miserable piece of shit! I'm sick and tired of watching you go through the motions of your life like a zombie. Don't wake up lying next to a girl you don't want. Get your girl. It's not too late!"

I stand from my seat, so close to losing my shit, but I don't want to hurt my friend. I already lost too much. I can't afford to lose any more friends. There aren't many, and he is one of the few I trust with my life.

He shakes his head. "You're a coward. You claim to love her, yet here you are, being led by the balls."

I clench my jaw, and through gritted teeth, I growl, "She made her choice!"

"You keep saying that, but did she? You know what? I'm done. I'm not coming back when it's over. I'm not going to hang around and watch you live a miserable life. I'm going to do what you should be doing. I choose her." He shows me the finger and heads out the door.

I pick up my chair and hurl it at the door, where it splinters and shatters to pieces. I swipe the contents of my desk onto the floor. I kick and punch at the wall behind me. I turn to destroy my desk. Glass shatters around me. Smoke fills the air.

I fall to my knees and bring my bloodied, trembling hands to my chest. My breathing is ragged as I fight for control. My vision clouds with unshed tears, and I roar with rage and sorrow. I hang my head and cry.

A woman's laughter fills the silent room. "What are you doing?" she asks with a raspy voice.

I look around my destroyed office. Jessica?

"Stop what you're doing and come here." Her sweet, infectious laugh echoes across the room again.

"I'm capturing the moment, so I can remember this forever," I hear my own voice reply.

"Whatever happened to good old-fashioned memories?" she retorts.

I sift around the floor's contents and find her voice playing from my laptop. It opened when it crashed to the floor. The screen is cracked, but I can still see the video. I fall back, leaning against my broken desk and rest the laptop on my lap.

I remember we snuck off to make out. I caress her cheek with my free hand and kiss her, holding my phone above us. I smile, side-eyeing my phone to ensure the camera still frames us, and return my full attention to kissing her. The kiss is long, not sloppy or desperate, but full of passion, love, and desire. I finally pull back with a big goofy grin, run my nose along hers, and tilt her chin slightly so the camera catches sight of her beautiful face.

She turns back, attempting to play-bite my fingers. "You don't need to remember me with videos," she says, pouting. I lean forward to nibble at her bottom lip. I give her a playful growl. "I don't plan on going anywhere unless it's with you," she whispers against my lips, placing her hands on either side of my face. "I love you."

"Mine," I growl.

"Forever," she answers before kissing me along my jawline. I drop the phone as I reach for her.

I remember wanting to envelop her in both of my arms, feel her body pressed against mine. The last thing captured is a squeal, and we laugh before the video ends. I rewind to the part when I turn her face to the camera and pause it.

My heart sinks. Bile rises to my throat. Hot, burning tears sting my eyes, and I'm torn between wanting to punch another hole in the wall or throw up.

I want to smash my computer into a thousand pieces and destroy every reminder of her, but I can't bring myself to do it. Instead, I sit and stare at her face, frozen on the cracked screen.

This can't be how our story ends. He's right. I can't let her go without a fight, without her knowing the truth. I torture myself further by reopening the file I downloaded before my friend arrived. I complete the form and attach it to an email.

I will leave it up to fate. If I receive a response before my mating ceremony tomorrow, I will fight to win my girl back. If I don't, that's my answer, and I will let her go for good this time.

CHAPTER 6

BULLYING THE BULLY

CONTESTANT #25

My PR guy stares at me as I read through the contract. I review it one more time, and without hesitation, I sign the bottom. I slide the papers across the table toward him.

He shakes his head and sighs as he leans forward to collect them. "You could do so much better," he mumbles.

I narrow my eyes, daring him to continue.

He pinches his lips together. "All I'm saying is that this girl isn't worth your reputation or your time. I know some models, or, if you want a good girl, I have some friends."

I slam my palm on the table. "I don't want anyone else! If you so much as sneer at her name again, I will ruin your career so fast, you'll be living off the streets."

He holds up his hands. "Alright, alright. My apologies for stepping out of line. I just think you deserve better, especially after all the shit you've been through."

I look down at the wood grain of the conference room table

that has been in my family for generations. "What I deserve is a chance to tell her the truth, a chance to start over, a real chance at what was supposed to be ours. No more secrets. No more lies." I run a hand through my hair.

He rubs a spot on his forehead between his brows. "She will be the death of you."

I meet his eye. "That's a chance I'm willing to take. Now make it fucking happen. Get me in the lineup, or you will be out of a job."

He grimaces. "Getting you in isn't the problem. The problem is the Alpha Princess. I can get you in the door, but I can't guarantee you'll survive the first round of eliminations."

I study him, his usual greasy slicked back hair has gone slightly astray and his meticulously pressed business suit has wrinkles. He's traveled all over the Northern A and the LS, escorting Jessica as they promote the game. I should feel sorry that I forced him out here to meet with me, but I don't.

"Just get me in. I'll take care of the rest." I motion for him to leave.

He shuffles the papers into a neat pile before placing them in his briefcase. "She must have one hell of a magic pussy."

Rage rolls along my spine. I unleash my magic, wrapping it around his throat. I slam him to the ground before throwing him against the wall. I hold his body suspended in the air.

Slowly, I stalk toward him, my magic tightening around his throat. His eyes bulge slightly from his eye sockets, and his face turns a sickly shade of purple. "If I didn't need you, you would be fucking dead right now."

He croaks. I release my magic, and he crashes to the floor in a heap. Gasping for air, he crawls toward his briefcase. He slowly stands, and his trembling hand reaches for the doorknob.

Folding my arms across my chest, I glare at him. "Gary." He

turns his reddened face in my direction. "Consider this your last warning. One more degrading word out of your mouth—I don't care if you're talking to yourself, to anyone, or to her."

He vehemently shakes his head. "You won't. I will treat her with nothing but respect from here on out."

I grind my teeth, not trusting his word. I don't fucking trust anyone. I stare him down, looking for any clue that he's placating me just to escape my ire. "You're replaceable, Gary. Everyone is replaceable, except her."

He nods. "I understand, sir."

"Good. Now get the fuck out of my sight." Without another word, he's out the door.

I barely resume my seat at the conference table when heavy footsteps enter the room. "Hey. Was that Gary I just passed?"

I grunt at my cousin in response. He pulls out a chair and sits across from me.

"Okay. Was it not a good meeting?" He lifts his legs to rest on the table and tilts his chair back. I grimace. He smirks.

"It was fine. I just don't understand why my parents keep him around."

He shrugs. "He's an ass, but he is good at his job. Trust me. I went through a few of them. Gary referred me to mine, and I have to say I'm impressed. He highly recommended her, so he knows what he's doing."

I absentmindedly nod, not giving a shit about how good he is. He has been insulting the princess to her face and behind her back for years. I'm sick of it. I don't know why she agreed to work with him.

He snaps his fingers in my direction. "Did you hear me?"

I look up at him. "No, not a damn word."

He rolls his eyes. "Well, I just said you didn't need to go to Gary in the first place. I told you I had your back." He places a folded piece of paper on the table.

I pick it up and read it. There's an address and some room numbers scrawled on it. I glance up at my cousin, frowning. The address is for the hotel that I own. I raise a brow at him. He smirks. "What the hell am I supposed to do with this?"

"Pack your bags, and head into the city. That is where you will meet the production team's manager for your interview."

I instantly jump over the table and knock him out of his chair in a bear hug.

He laughs as he slaps my back. "Told you I had your back."

I squeeze his shoulder. "Thanks, man. This means a lot to me."

He slaps my back one more time before pushing me off him. "You better get going. Your interview is in three hours." I glance at my watch, noting the time. "Oh, and make it count because filming literally starts in two days."

CHAPTER 7

INTERVIEW DAY

JESSICA
PRESENT DAY:
MARCH 31, 2025

"**G**ood morning, Alpha Princess. I trust you slept well?"

I stand in my bedroom in front of my large glass windows, looking over my pack's houses. Daylight breaks through, painting the sky in beautiful shades of yellow and orange. I haven't slept. Too many thoughts swirl in my head, like I'm on a hamster wheel running for my life but going nowhere fast. I feel like I don't have control over my own life, and I meet the men—Alpha males I never met and know nothing about—tomorrow.

The production team insisted that their identities remain a secret. They need to capture my genuine reactions on camera.

The only ones who really know the identity of these men are my parents. They personally handpicked each one of them, based on who they felt would be the best match.

I sigh, thinking back to the day my father and I fought about this whole situation. I cringe. Did I make the wrong choice? Should I have simply chosen?

I tell myself I don't want or need a mate. I'm an independent woman. I don't need a mate for protection, financially or emotionally, and I'm not weak. I worked so hard to pave the way for myself.

"Alpha Princess?" I turn toward Carmen, the production manager. I think that's her title is, anyway. She moves behind the scenes, delegating, navigating, and basically telling me how to live my life for the duration of the show.

I offer her a small smile. "Good morning, Carmen. Sorry. I was lost in my thoughts." I sigh. "I didn't sleep—in fact, I don't think I left this very spot since I returned home last night."

She approaches me and awkwardly pats my shoulder. "Well, let's get you to hair and makeup so we can get started. We have the entire day to film your interview, take pictures, and showcase you with your parents. Whatever we cannot do today, if that should happen, we have tomorrow morning to catch up. Then, we will prepare you for your introductions with the men."

I nod, biting my tongue as I follow her out of my suite.

Two hours later, and with my mother's approval, Carmen gushes, "Aww, Alpha Princess, you look so beautiful!"

"Like I always said, it really does take a team to make me look this good," I deadpan. Carmen doesn't respond to my dry humor. Tough crowd.

Ignoring me, she claps her hands together. "Perfect. Now sit here, and we'll start your interview. When you speak, look directly at the camera. I will sit here and ask you follow-up questions as we go along. This is Christian, our main cameraman. He will be with you most of the time, catching your every move on film."

Christian glances at me from his setup and gives a warm smile.

I wrinkle my nose. "I hope there are limitations, especially when it comes to following me to my bedroom and using the bathroom. I kind of draw the line there."

He chuckles. "Ditto." At least *he* gets my humor. I assess him quickly. He's slim and stands just at six feet tall. He has reddish-brown, shaggy hair. As he looks through the camera lens, a stray strand falls into his eyes. He has a straight nose, brown eyes, and thick dark lashes. I frown.

"Have I met you before?" I ask.

"Nah. I have one of those faces. I probably remind you of a next-door neighbor, some guy you ran into at a bar, or a random person you went to school with and never talked to."

I laugh. "Those were some very specific examples."

He shrugs.

"You're stuck with me for the next six weeks, so please call me Jessica. It's too much, calling me Alpha Princess all the time. That goes for you, too, Carmen." She doesn't look up from her clipboard. Alrighty then, she is very focused on her job.

"Jessica, now here is how I want to approach this. Of all the interviews you did to promote the show, my favorite was *The Late Night Show with Sammy Cane*. I understand you went off script, but I liked it. You gave the viewers a glimpse of who you are and what they may see during the show. You were funny, sassy, different, and vulnerable—someone they can relate to or want to befriend."

I turn to Christian. "Are you recording this?"

He frowns. "Why do you ask?"

"Oh, I just want my PR guy, Gary, to hear this so I can tell him to shove it with a big, confident smile."

"Jessica, please focus," Carmen chastises me, still staring at her clipboard.

Does this woman ever laugh at jokes? I roll my eyes and scrunch my face at Christian. He shakes his head and chuckles softly.

"Okay. Start with introducing yourself, and then tell us how you came to be on this show. Look at the camera when you're speaking. Oh, and if it helps, just remember that the gentlemen will go through this same type of interview."

Why would that make me feel better? I flick my eyes upward before glancing at Carmen. She isn't paying attention to me. I glimpse my face projected on a set of monitors where she sits. Anxiety creeps into me, and my breath catches. This is really happening. I've been fumbling through the motions, but it didn't feel real until right now. I take another breath, trying to calm myself. I can do this. I have to do this.

"Jessica?" Christian questions. "Just look at me when you talk, like we're good friends just hanging out, swapping stories."

I nod. "Sorry. I, uh… I think it just sunk in. I don't usually like being the center of attention, especially when I feel so… exposed, which is odd—right? —because of my career. I spend a good deal of my life hiding out in the open, if that makes any sense," I ramble.

"What does that mean? Always hiding out in the open?" Carmen asks.

Still looking at Christian, I answer her question. "Have you ever played peekaboo with a child? After playing with them for a while, you realize that, for some reason, the child assumes you can't see them when they cover their own eyes. They know you are there, but because they can't see you, they think you can't see them. That's how I hide out in the open. As a music artist, I wear a mask and color my hair so no one recognizes me. My fans and music manager just chalk it up to being a little eccentric."

I laugh and smile at Christian. He grins back.

"I think no one can see me when I am up on stage, playing music, singing. I feel free. I share who I really am with thousands of strangers, sharing stories of anger, heartbreak, redemption, and courage. I close my eyes and do what I love. At work, I wear business clothing and glasses—another mask. I'm a no-nonsense woman, a force to reckon with, but I love that part of my life, too. My business isn't just about making money but about helping others to build careers and businesses of their own. Then, there's my role with the guards. I always feel a little more comfortable in that setting. Again, it's all about protecting others, but even so, I hide a part of myself just to fit in."

I pause. Everyone watches me, waiting for the next confession.

"Are you familiar with that superhero... Superman? During the day, he pretends to be a nerdy guy with glasses. He's sweet, clumsy, and nervous. Then, at night or during some kind of disaster, he transforms into Superman with superpowers. He protects those around him and defeats the bad guys. He either hides behind a pair of glasses, or he hides behind his insignia. Did anyone ever stop to ask him what his life would be like if he didn't have to hide? Would he even know? Anyway, I'm still figuring out who I am without the different masks. So sitting here with no mask, with no work to hide behind, talking about myself, is an unnerving experience."

"You're doing fine," Carmen responds from her seated position near the monitors. "Let's skip the introduction part for now and talk about how you ended up here on the show."

I chuckle. "Gosh, that is a loaded question. Where do I begin?" I glance down at my hands, collecting my thoughts for an appropriate answer.

"Just be honest, Jessica. This is the whole point of the interview. Viewers want to know the real you."

I nod, clear my throat, and look back at the camera. "Did you ever have one of those dreams where someone flips the channel? Suddenly, you're in a different dream, and it keeps changing from one dream to the next, like someone has control of a TV remote? Two weeks ago, to the day, that's kind of how my day started. I didn't have control over the remote, and I just found myself in one situation after another."

"Tell us more about that day," Carmen encourages.

"I could do that. Not sure how much time you have," I add with a smirk.

"Give it a go. We can take breaks in between, and I will guide you along with follow-up questions, if need be."

"Okay... But before I can explain that day, I need to fill in some details of my life over the past eight years. It might get a little confusing, but if you pay attention, it will all make sense eventually. I hope."

CHAPTER 8
WHEN SIBLINGS FIGHT

JESSICA
TWO WEEKS AGO:
MARCH 14, 2025: 5 A.M.
ALPHA KINGS MANSION

"So, this is what it comes down to, huh? After all these years, you three ganging up on me?" I say to my three brothers—the twins, Justin and Jeremy, and Luke—who slowly circle me.

I decided to come down to the basement of our family's mansion, which had been converted into a gym for an early morning workout. My brothers decided to ambush me. I take a stance, ready for a fight.

"Just tell us where you hid it, and we'll let you go," Justin offers with a sly grin.

"Yeah. No harm, no foul. We get what we want, and you're free to go," Jeremy adds.

I roll my eyes at the twins and turn to Luke. "And you? What part do you have in this?"

He shrugs. "You know me—anything for a good fight—and I always have my brothers' backs."

I cringe at his remark. Luke and I have a complicated relationship. I'm adopted, and he reminds me of that with snarky innuendos at every opportunity.

Over the years, I have just accepted what we are—a complicated train wreck of love and hate, friends and sometimes enemies. It sometimes drives pain deep into my heart.

"Just tell us what we want to know, Jessica," Justin repeats, cutting into my thoughts.

"I am not telling you anything. Besides, I can take the three of you, so bring it." I motion with my hand for them to advance. Luke's smile widens. Alright, tough guy. I will take you down first and shove your smug smile up your...

Justin dives, and Jeremy crouches to sweep my legs out from under me. I jump and turn just in time. Luke comes at me just as I land. Striking, I block him, grab him by the wrist, and pivot sideways, kicking him in the chest and sending him a few feet back.

Jeremy lunges at me. I don't try to avoid his line of attack. Instead, I take a few steps toward him. Justin sneaks up behind me, and I surprise both by jumping into a spread-eagle, kicking them each in the chest.

Luke's footsteps approach quickly so I drop to my knees and hit him in the stomach. I rock back on my heels and jab him in the knee, causing him to fall. Rolling into a crouch, I jump to my feet, swiveling around as Justin recovered from my kick.

I strike. He blocks. Justin is fast, but I'm faster. I keep striking, and he keeps blocking. Jeremy is on me again. I drop down to swipe his legs out from under him, but he moves before I can connect.

Tumbling out and away from the twins, I run toward the broom leaning against the wall.

Luke jumps into my path. "No cheating," he tsks.

"Oh, like three-on-one isn't cheating," I sneer.

He smiles, showing off his dimples—that fucker. I narrow my eyes and rush toward him. Gaining momentum, I jump and twist my body, clearing over his head and landing behind him, my back to his back. I slam my elbow into his kidney and back-kick his ass.

Pride swells inside me that I made that jump. Luke stands at six foot three or more by now. He's broad-shouldered and muscular. His arm reach alone could pull me down. Glowing, a little triumphant, I don't bother to glance back. I step into action to retrieve that broom.

But I don't get very far. Luke grabs my arm, pulling me around to his front, and holds me up against him.

He smiles again. "That was impressive, but I think I got you just where I want you."

Smiling back, I stand on my tiptoes, leaning in. His eyes widen as I progress even closer. I whisper, "I'm immune to the Luke Langhlan charm so I think... I got you."

Before he can respond, I jump, wrap my legs around his waist, and throw myself back. Twisting my body as we fall, I plan to wrench myself out of his hold. However, Luke grips me tighter and twists in the opposite direction. I initially land on top of him. He takes the impact fully from our fall.

In this position, being on top is not bad. I leverage my elbows to disengage his arms, push off his chest, and use my legs to backflip off of him, grabbing the broom just in time to hit Jeremy, advancing toward me. I strike him in the chest and then his arms and abdomen. Each strike is swift. He can't block them in time.

At the same time, I block Justin's strikes from behind me. I hit both of them so rapidly, it stuns them. In a final swipe of the broom handle, I take Justin's legs out from under him. Wasting no time, I put Jeremy down seconds after.

Stepping from between them, in case they try to grab my legs, I spin the handle of the broom, smiling jubilantly. Groaning and clutching at body parts, they make no further movement to fight. Pumping my fist in the air, I scream, "Yeah!", pumping the broom with my other hand.

Suddenly, Luke grabs the broom midair, tosses it across the room, and dives, pinning me to the ground. Damnit, I took my eyes off the other enemy. Shit! He yells to the twins, "Find whatever it is you need! I have her."

I squirm, buck, and kick my legs. He maneuvers, pinning both of my arms and trapping my legs with his own. The twins run out of the room, laughing.

"Nooo, don't! That isn't for you!" I shout. I narrow my eyes at Luke. "You idiot! I made those brownies for the Whitemore pack."

He laughs. "I hope you made a lot. Those two will probably eat two pans by themselves."

"Ugh, get off me!" I demand, but I know it's pointless because he's twice my size. I don't give up, though. In my pathetic effort, I continue to squirm and grumble.

Luke looks down at me, his expression serious. "Can we talk?"

"No. I don't want to talk to you, traitor! I have to stop the twins!" I spit. He leans his face closer, as if he is going to kiss me. My eyes widen. What the hell is he doing? I turn my head.

He whispers in my ear, "Stop doing that. You're turning me on, and I really need to talk to you."

What the hell did he just say?

He pushes his hips into me, and I feel his hardening cock.

Freezing in place, I keep my head turned, refusing to look at him. "If I let you up, will you stay and talk to me?" he asks.

I nod my head, but I don't intend to stay.

"Jessica," he growls. "This is important to me. Please."

I turn my head slowly. With those emerald green eyes, blond hair, and dimples, I see why women have such a hard time resisting him. Still, his expression shows sincerity. "I can't," I reply softly.

"You can't, or you won't?" He searches my eyes for the answer. His brow furrows, perhaps with pain, with remorse. My gut twists. "When will you be back?" he asks.

"I won't. I plan to head straight to the city after I am done at the Whittemore's. I promised Akiyo I would help her with the show."

He groans. "Jessica, you just got home last night." He brushes a strand of hair behind my ear. "It's been a long time since you and I talked. There are some things I need to say to you. For starters, I owe you an apology."

I frown. Where is this coming from and why? I shake my head. "Luke, I really need to get going. I don't want to be late."

He sighs. "You make it so hard to talk. Look, I don't want to fight. I want to make things right between us. I want... I want to talk, but I need you to listen first. Can we please meet after the show?"

I shake my head. "I'm not trying to be difficult. I just have obligations, and I promised Akiyo I would stay for the afterparty."

He gazes down at me intently. His jaw clenches, and he closes his eyes. "Tomorrow then?" Before I can hesitate or offer more excuses, he leans down and whispers, "Please, Jess. This is important to me." His face transforms with sadness.

I nod and softly comply, "Tomorrow."

He gives me a small smile before moving to help me to my

feet. I hurry to the training room door before the twins demolish all the brownies. I almost reach the door when Luke says, "Jess, I'm sorry if I hurt you."

What the hell? What is going on with him today? I toss a glance over my shoulder. Frowning, I reply, "What are you talking about?"

He hangs his head. "It hurt you when I said that I always have the twins' back." I shake my head to dismiss him, but he continues, "You may not think I do, but I will always have your back, too."

I don't know how to respond. I want to respond, but my words are not nice. I'm still deeply hurt by him, and I don't know if I will ever get over what he did. I take a deep breath and leave the room.

CHAPTER 9

FULL CIRCLE

JESSICA
TWO WEEKS AGO:
MARCH 14, 2025: 7:15 A.M.
WHITEMORE PLANTATION

The twins ate some of my brownies, but they were nice enough to leave a sufficient amount for the Whitemore Pack gathering. With brownies in hand, I make my way to the car waiting for me.

Anders, our family's head guard, stoically stands next to the car dressed in his formal guard attire. The deep hunter green of his suit contrasts with his pure-white hair and pale blue eyes. His youthful face might put him in his late forties or early fifties at least, yet rumor indicates he's in his eighties. I guess that makes sense because he has so much experience in his line of work. He has trained worldwide, especially in the Asian territory, in weaponry, hand-to-hand combat, martial arts, and then some. I overheard my parents say that he once was a Russian military spy. Rumors are rumors until proven otherwise, but from what I witnessed firsthand, he's an excellent fighter and guard, which is all that really matters.

I frown at Anders, unsure why he's here. Not that I don't want him to go with me. I'm sure he has more important matters to attend to than escort me to the Whitemore territory. Odyssey, my friend and fellow guard, stands next to Anders, also wearing his formal guard attire.

The driver door opens, and Ean pops out in uniform. I shoot Odyssey a questioning stare, but he schools his face, not revealing anything. Turning my attention back to Anders, I ask, "Where's Xavier? Is he okay?"

Anders grimaces. "Xavier is fine. I gave him the day off. I knew you would object to a separate car escort so the three of us will travel with you in the same car to the Whitemore territory."

Am I so difficult that I require two top guards, including himself? Odyssey offers me a cheeky grin. He must love this—he knows I won't argue with Anders. I roll my eyes at Odyssey and hand him a small package of dessert, keeping the larger one for the gathering.

His eyebrows raise. "What's this?" he asks.

"I made those for Xavier to thank him for being stuck with me all day and night. I guess you and Ean will have to share."

Hesitantly, he peers into the bag. "Are these your famous brownies?" I nod. "Shit. I have to share with Ean? He'll eat them all before I even get a chance," Odyssey grumbles.

I laugh in response. "Well, I guess it's a good thing he's driving then."

Anders scoffs, shooting me an irritated look, and opens the back passenger door. Without further delay, I slide in the car. Anders follows in after me. I notice the privacy glass is closed so we can talk in private.

"Thank you," I tell him. "I hope this isn't too much trouble."

He frowns. "I am here for two reasons. One is business, and the other is personal."

Personal? I have never really known Anders to do anything personal. He is always so dedicated to his head guard position.

"I haven't spoken to you for some time, and I wanted an opportunity to, umm…" he clears his throat, "discuss some things."

I study him. He avoids my gaze—so unlike him as he usually likes to maintain eye contact. He also perspires, despite the cool temperature in the car, courtesy of Ean, who likes it extremely cold due to his own internal warmth.

Anders clears his throat. Did he say something? He looks out the window and sighs, raking his fingers through his hair. "I would like to discuss my personal reasons first before we dive into business matters, if that will be okay with you?"

Nonchalantly, I respond, "Sure, whichever way you feel more comfortable."

"I don't particularly like discussing my personal business with anyone, but this is important to me. I would like to talk first."

Important to him? Wait. Isn't that what Luke said earlier this morning? He had something important to talk to me about, too. What is going on with this day? "Anders, if it makes you uncomfortable, you don't have to talk about your personal business. We can cover business, and you can slide it in somehow when you are ready. It's a two-hour drive."

He shakes his head and finally makes eye contact. "I'm worried about you. I just wanted to see how you're doing with the passing of Alpha Agnus. You two were quite close, and well, I know you don't handle grief very well."

I glance down at my hands, resting in my lap. "Thank you for your consideration, but I'm fine. I was with her the night before it happened." Anders watches me intently. "I'm fine, really. I know she was old. It's all a part of that circle of life. She left this world peacefully. She didn't suffer, and she wasn't murdered. I won't run away, if that's what you're worried about."

Anders places a large hand over mine. His warmth comforts me, and I welcome it.

"Speaking of the circle of life," I say, "we both have come full circle in this as well." He cocks his head, I smile. "Eight—almost nine—years ago, you and I sat in a car just like this one, except instead of going to Whitemore territory, we drove away from it, driving toward what turned out to be the beginning of my new life."

Squeezing my hand, he lifts and kisses it with fatherly affection.

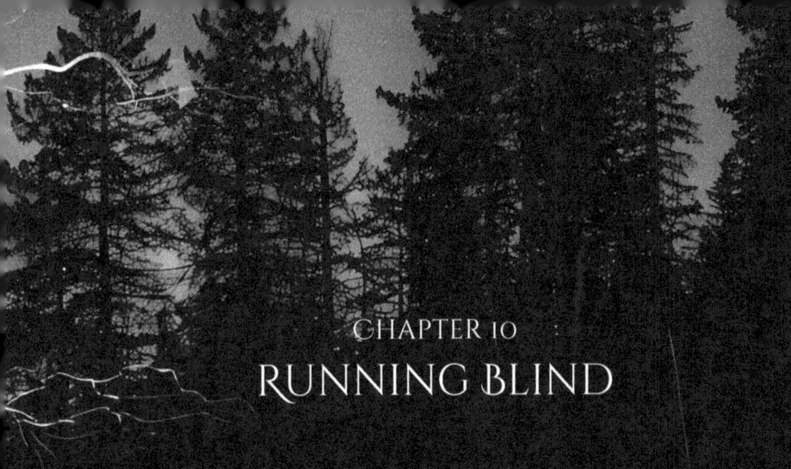

CHAPTER 10

RUNNING BLIND

JESSICA
EIGHT YEARS AGO:
MAY 17, 2016: 9 P.M.
EMERALD PACK CLINIC

I wake with a start and bolt up in bed. My vision is hazy, and I can't make out where I am. It smells funny, almost clean—so clean, it's sterile. A loud beeping noise pierces my mind, and a sharp pain shoots in my ears and my temple. I immediately cover my ears with my hands, but I realize my arms are attached to a monitor with some kind of small tube.

I'm scared. My brain screams for me to run. I need to get away. I need to be safe.

I pull at the lines attached to my body. Liquid pours from some of the tubes. It doesn't smell like blood, so I keep pulling, removing everything I find by roaming my hands over my torso.

I can't see clearly, which scares me even more. But I'm determined to get away. I need to protect myself. One last tube embeds in the center of my throat, held in place with a cloth strap. Feeling around my neck, I undo the strap and pull on the device.

Suddenly, I start coughing and choking. A slimy substance oozes from the gaping hole.

I want to cry. Who did this to me? Why? Without wasting any time, I slide out of bed. I hear footsteps racing around outside my room. The loud beeping and shrill piercing noises grow louder. Someone was alerted.

I slip outside my door into some kind of dark corridor. Relying on my instincts and other senses, I back against the wall, hiding in the shadows, and slide away from the oncoming footsteps.

I reach thick molding along the wall, a door, so I open it and slip inside. A clean antiseptic smell instantly hits my nose reminding me of the room I just vacated. I close my eyes wishing I could see my surroundings and take a deep breath. A vision of the room forms in my mind. The shelves are lined with some kind of cloth of varying shades of blue and sizes.

Cool air rushes against my backside. Grabbing at my back, I realize I'm partially covered. I grab for what feels like a pair of pants and slip them on, tying the drawstring tight and rolling the hem of the pant legs so I don't trip over them.

I tear off my gown only to discover another tube sticking out of my stomach. A sticky fluid drips from the line. Without hesitation, I rip it out. Instant pain and a burning sensation overtake me, but they pass quickly. Tossing the tube to the floor, along with the long gown, I find a shirt and pull it on. I need to get out of here.

Before I sneak back out the door, I hear loud, commanding voices. "Find her! She has to be here somewhere. She's hurt. She couldn't have gone far!" More footsteps echo in the hall, so I shrink back behind one of the shelves and crouch down.

All I can hear is myself breathing through the hole in my

throat. Air rushes in and out, mixing with fluid in a low rattling sound. Gross! I fumble through the items on the shelves to locate anything resembling a piece of cloth or napkin. When I find what I'm searching for I wipe at the slimy, slick... drool? Eww! I wipe it again and place my hand over the hole to quiet the gurgling noises I make when I breathe.

Fuck! Who did this to me and why? I don't have much time to think it over. The people outside pass down the hall. I tuck the cloth into my waistband and approach the door, slipping into the hallway.

I don't know where I am, but somehow, I can clearly see the layout of the building in my head. I find the exit and quietly, sticking to the shadows, still holding my hand over the hole in my throat, slink toward it. On my way over, I bump into a chair, filling the silence with a scraping noise against the linoleum floors.

Holding my breath, I stay very still, listening for anyone coming. It remains quite so I move forward, trying to avoid the chair in my path, when my bare foot brushes against something soft. I nudge it with my foot again. I gingerly bend down to pick it up and determine it's a hooded sweatshirt.

I put it on immediately. It's huge on me, but I don't care. It's perfect. I pull the hood to cover my face, and a distinct fragrance—a mixture of dirt, grass, and sunshine, paired with a clean-smelling cologne—assaults my senses. I also smell subtle hints of bergamot, melon, and cucumber.

The medley comforts me. I feel calmer, stronger. I smirk, thinking about when a superhero puts on their cape. Confidence takes over, and I feel more assured that I can escape to safety.

The cool night air blasts my face. I plaster myself against the wall of the building. My eyes are still closed. Did I not open them this entire time? In my mind, I saw my surroundings.

That's odd, right? I mentally shake myself. I don't have time to figure it out.

Ahead is a road that leads to a gate. From there, I can run and follow the road wherever it may lead. But I can't just run onto the driveway in front of the building. Someone will definitely find me and haul me back into the lab of doom.

With my free hand, I tug the hood to cover more of my face. Breathing in the owner's scent relieves the tension in my muscles. But what if he is one of the men holding me hostage and conducting all of these science experiments on me?

I slide along the brick wall and round the corner closest to the road. I hear crunching gravel headed in my direction, but instead of retreating, I run toward it. I make out the blurry outline of a tall, broad man. His large torso leads him to have a wide base stance. I push myself faster, and before he can react, I dive between his legs. Using the momentum of my slide, I jump to my feet and keep running toward the road.

Another man approaches from the right. I deviate from my path and rush at him. He bends low, bracing his posture, planning to grab me. I jump as high as I can, using my left foot to push off his shoulder, I reach for a low-lying tree branch above his head. I begin to climb. Slowly, I inch my way across the branch toward the roof of a building, and I leap.

I fall short. "Catch her!" someone shouts. Quickly shooting my arm out, I catch the edge just in time. I grip the ledge with my other hand and start to swing back and forth. My body swings closer to the wall so when I push against it with both feet, I flip myself onto the roof, landing on my back with a hard thud.

Bringing my legs toward my stomach, I push off the ground with a hand on either side of my head and stand back on my feet. I sprint along the roof, searching for the gate in my mind. I'm closer now.

To the side of the building, the two men I outsmarted earlier now run alongside me. I hear various orders yell through the air.

"Block the gate!"

"Don't hurt her!"

"If she falls, catch her!"

I stop abruptly at the end of the roof and almost fall forward. Waving my arms, I regain my balance. I need to get down so I decide to jump onto the closest man. Catching him off guard, we fall to the ground together. I waste no time pushing off his back and race toward the gate.

"Get her!" a man commands. "Watch her—she's a tricky one!"

Three men stand in front of me. One slowly approaches, expecting me to jump, so he keeps his posture upright. How does he know? How do I know what he expects me to do?

I fake an attempt to turn left, and when his body shifts to follow, I twist and head right. I jump-kick one man in the chest. He didn't see my attack coming. Honestly, neither did I. I acted on instinct. He leans forward, clutching his chest, so I plant my foot on his shoulder and grasp onto the iron gate.

I climb, swing my leg over, and freefall. Landing on my feet, I don't turn to take in my surroundings. The vision in my head disappear, but I keep running. Anywhere is better than here. Right?

I ignore the pain to my feet and legs as I dart over tiny pieces of gravel and sticks. I propel myself forward.

The gate squeaks as it opens behind me, startling me, urging me faster. Thudding footsteps follow. There are more of them now. The footfalls are heavier, louder, like a stampede of horses. That means they shifted.

Fear tingles up my spine. If they catch me, they will tear me apart. I hear growls, shouts, and curses in my head. What the hell? My body screams with pain, my lungs burn, but I refuse to surrender.

Get around her!

Cut her off!

Catch her from the right! I veer to my left. *How the fuck is she so fast?!*

Shut the fuck up and get her!

He will have all our asses if something happens to her!

Snarls penetrate my mind, and I sense their determination. I squeeze my eyes shut. I have no idea what lies in front of me. Tall grass brushes against my legs. Focusing on their directions, I do the opposite of everything they attempt.

Then, a vision of a wide-open space opens before me. Hope fills my chest.

Until I trip. Falling forward, I quickly scramble to my feet and keep going. The wolves are after me, even closer. How do I know they're wolves? I shake my head. I just know that I need to escape. They will hurt me, maybe kill me.

Fatigue threatens to immobilize my muscles. I'm not sure how much longer I can run.

Cut her off from the left. Don't let her get any farther away!

My heart pounds from equal parts exertion and fear. My feet pummels dirt, then gravel. Suddenly, I hit a wall. A literal wall. I hit the ground, stunned, breathless, on my back. Shit!

A sickening cold sensation creeps through my veins. I'm so fucked. I scramble to my feet, barely swallowing the threatening panic. I put my arms out to feel what is in front of me.

An image pops into my head of a house covered by overgrown weeds and vines. Gliding my hand along the siding, I walk around it. The wolves are closer still. Gaining speed in desperation, I stumble over bushes and other brush.

Eventually, I locate a recessed window, boarded over with

wood. I grip a panel and attempt to pry it off with my fingers, but it won't budge. I anchor my leg against the wall, and after a few tries, the board gives. A loud crack echoes in the night air, and yet again, I fall backward, landing on my ass.

Find her! She has to be here!

Gripping the windowsill, I squeeze into the opening and crash inside. I wheeze, pant, and hide in the room's shadow.

Retrieving the cloth from the waist of my pants, I wipe the disgusting fluid trickling down my neck and covering the hole. I crawl toward a rim of light—must be a door—and listen for the men and wolves chasing me. Yet, the rapid beating of my heart drowns out any other sounds.

I open the door slowly, praying it won't make a noise, and find a hallway. I have no idea if I am going in the right direction. It just feels right.

In my mind, a kitchen appears ahead. My tongue sticks to the roof of my mouth. I desperately need to drink some water. A cool surface brushes my fingertips, followed by the tangy smell of metal. I pat around and realize I found the sink. Grasping for the faucet, sickly wet air escapes the hole in my throat as I sigh. I wash my face and drink the cool water.

Immediately, I choke. Water spews from the hole in my throat. I slide down the cabinet to the floor, trying to catch my breath between coughing fits. Finally, after what feels like forever, I take a deep breath. I return to the sink to clean myself as best as I can. My mouth is still dry, but instead of drinking, I simply rinse my mouth.

The haunting howls of wolves forces me to crouch. I cover my head with my hands as their panicked shouts ring through my head. They all yell simultaneously, making it difficult to decipher what they say.

I crab-crawl away from the sink, in case they look through the kitchen window. My back hits a solid wall, and I slide my hands around to inspect it. It's another door. I yank it open, just enough to slide my body through, and gently close it behind me. My skin prickles from the darkness. The smell of cardboard boxes and aluminum cans fill the stale air.

I cringe. I'm in a pantry—a dead end. They will find me. When they do, I'm dead. I'm so dead.

I plop into a corner, pulling my hood over my forehead, as if it could make me invisible. My mind no longer offers clues to those outside, pursuing me. With my ears, I hear muffled talking. I can't understand specific words, but I know they're coming for me.

I don't know how long I have. Shifting quietly, I wrap my arms around my knees and rest my forehead on them. I stay there for a while, waiting for someone to find me, waiting to be caught.

CHAPTER 11
MAKING FRIENDS

JESSICA
EIGHT YEARS AGO:
MAY 18, 2016: 8 A.M.
WHITEMORE PLANTATION

The wolves chase me. Their jaws snap. Low growls emanate from their chests. My arms bleed from long, deep wounds. Pain infiltrates every fiber of my being. My lungs burn, and my heart feels like it will explode in my chest. But I must keep running. I can't let them catch me. They will kill me. Something stiff tugs around my neck—a rope. I fall backward, dragged. I claw at my neck to pry my fingers under the rope. I can't breathe. I throw myself forward, hitting my head... on a shelf?

I feel around me. I definitely hit a shelf. It takes a moment to recall where I am. I must have fallen asleep while waiting for my capturers to find me. I'm no longer in a curled sitting position, and a blanket drapes over me. Rubbing my forehead, I carefully sit up, avoiding the low shelf this time.

Grasping around my neck, I am relieved that there is no rope. I lift the sleeves of my hoodie to my elbows. There are no gaping wounds, no blood. I don't smell blood on me, either. The rough texture of my arm, though, indicates there once were wounds. Questions swirl through my mind.

Then, I remember the hole in my throat. Yep, it's still there. The front of my sweatshirt is wet. Disgusting! I find the cloth to wipe the mess and cover the hole with my hand.

I slowly stand and wonder, where did the blanket come from? I still can't see. Everything is a blur of shadows and light. How did I get here? How did I allude those men?

Panic rises from my chest. My heartbeat races. I press harder against the hole in my throat, quieting the sound of my rapid breathing. I smell him, the owner of this sweatshirt. I bring the neckline to my nose and instantly calm down. His scent makes me feel safe. I drop the fabric between my fingers as the heat of a blush enflames my face. Gods, I'm a mess. I'm swooning over a guy I never met.

I startle at a sudden voice. *Well, are you going to come out, or are you going to stand in there all day, talking to yourself?*

I stiffen, pondering my reply. *First of all, I am not talking to myself. I'm thinking. Secondly, the door is closed. How do they know I'm standing?* Tentatively, I step forward. Stretching out my arm, I feel for the door and push it open. Light fills the kitchen.

Well, aren't you a smartass. the voice mocks, breaking through my thoughts.

I look around the room to locate the person belonging to the voice in my head. I don't hear it with my ears. But that doesn't make sense. I rub my face and scoff. I am losing my mind.

I know what this is. I'm actually dead. Or am I dreaming? This must be a dream—a literal nightmare—because I have a gaping hole in my throat, and my bodily fluids are draining down my neck.

I hear a chuckle. Correction, the chuckle reverberates inside my head. *You're not dead, and you are definitely not dreaming. Now, come closer so I can look at you. My eyes are not what they used to be.*

I hesitate and turn my head, trying to recognize a shape or an outline. My left eye senses a little more detail if I turn my head to the right.

Several feet in front of me is a long table with several chairs. Someone sits at the end. A strange light surrounds the outline in an almost ethereal way, and fluffy hair haloes their head. Tentatively, I step forward.

Well, hurry it up. I am not getting any younger, the voice speaks in my head again.

Am I deaf, too?

Not deaf, dear, but maybe a little daft.

Daft? I now recognize the voice belongs to a woman, maybe an elderly woman. She called me daft, as in stupid. Keeping my head to the right, I quicken my steps, approaching the table.

No, daft as in silly, wiseass.

I proceed forward, furrowing my brow in confusion. How is this happening? I must miscalculate my steps because I collide with a person. Shit! I try to speak, to instinctively apologize, but air gushes from the hole in my throat. Before I can move, hands grab my chin, and with a firm grip, they shift my head from side to side.

"What you must have been through to get here," the woman says aloud because this time I can hear her and feel her soft breath on my face. "Now, take a deep breath and visualize your surroundings with your mind, as you did before."

Visualize my surroundings with my mind?

"Be quick about it. There isn't much time."

I don't know how I did it in the first place. Why is this woman so convinced that I can?

"Because you can. Now, stop overthinking and just do it."

Do what? Maybe I escaped from a nuthouse. Or I escaped *into* a nuthouse. Or maybe... Whack! A blunt object hits my right arm and then my left. My leg is struck next. Irritated, I take a deep breath, and the room blooms into sight with a little old lady holding a cane. She extends her arm to the side, attempting to hit me again. But this time, I snatch the cane from her.

"About damn time. Now, sit and have some tea."

Frowning at the old woman, I lower myself into the chair she indicates. She returns to the head of the table and scoots her chair a little forward. She's not much taller than I am, with all-white curly hair, and she wears an aquamarine tracksuit. I rest her cane against the table, so she can reach it when she's ready to stand again. On second thought, I move it to my other side so she can't hit me with it.

You don't miss much, now do you? She laughs.

Miss much?

She doesn't answer me—well, because her mouth doesn't move—and her voice reaches inside my head as she sips her tea. *Not only are you a wiseass, but you're also quite observant. You catch onto things quickly, when you don't overthink so much.*

I glance down at the cup of tea in front of me. I can't drink it, recalling my choking episode at the faucet last night.

Try again. You might be surprised.

How is she inside my head? I obviously can't talk with this stupid hole in my throat, and yet she's holding a conversation with me inside my head. I rub my forehead. I must be a ghost or maybe a zombie. I'm a walking dead carcass. That makes sense. I pat myself down to assess my body, and I feel a pinch on my thigh. Ouch! Seriously!

Not a zombie, after all. Another laugh emits from the old lady in my head. *And... I am not inside of your head. You are inside mine. Drink your tea.*

Rubbing at my thigh, I grumble and grimace at the cup again. I gingerly lift it as if it's full of poison and raise an inquisitive eyebrow. This won't be pretty. As I bring the teacup to my lips, I think, *can't say I didn't warn you.*

I take a small sip and wait for the choking and coughing to start, but nothing happens. I pull the cloth from my sweatshirt pocket and wipe at the hole. No warm liquid pours out. The hole is still there. I can hear myself breathing. But it's not as big as it felt earlier. I wipe my hand down my pants leg and try another sip. No coughing, no choking.

I don't like that you refer to me as an old lady.

I glance over at her. *Sorry. I didn't think you could hear my thoughts.*

My name is Agnus, or you can call me Aggie. You're on my territory.

I'm on her territory. I have to think about that for a minute, trying to remember exactly how did I get here? I don't even know where I am or where I came from. I try to think harder. I don't know where I live. I can't retrieve memories from my life before waking up as some kind of science experiment.

My hands begin to tremble. The china rattles, so I rest the teacup on the table.

Agnus reaches over to touch my hand. *Do you at least know your name?*

Staring at the tinted liquid, I focus on my name, but nothing seems familiar. I don't know who I am.

Finish your tea. It might come back to you. She pats my hand.

I'm surprised that no more choking episodes occur, and tea doesn't drip from the hole. Physically, it's impossible. But so was running away from a large pack of wolves last night.

Agnus collects my cup, peering into it and slowly moving it around. *Interesting*, she mumbles.

Turning my head to look at her, my vision blurs and refocuses like a camera. Her brows crease, as if she's solving a puzzle. She hums quietly and jots notes in a notebook next to her. What is she doing?

I'm reading your tea leaves, she answers. Studying whatever she sees in the remnants of my tea, she sits silent for a long time, writing more notes. Finally, she rests her pen down and closes her notebook. Giving my hand a reassuring squeeze, she claims, *All will be well, my dear. Now, the bathroom is down the hall. Wash up, and we will take a walk when you're all done.* She glances at my feet and adds, *No shoes? You ran all the way here with no shoes?*

I shrug.

Three doors down from the bathroom is my Marisol's room. She might have a pair she left behind in the closet. Have a look before you come out. Then, meet me on the porch.

Down the hall I approach the bedroom Agnus mentioned. The room smells musty and damp like it hasn't been used in a long time. I close my eyes, allowing the layout of the room to fill my mind. I see a little girl's room, with a full-sized canopy bed covered in a faded pink duvet, spiderwebs cover a lamp sitting on a nightstand near the bed. Disturbed dusty patterns near the window followed by bloodied footprints leading to the door, reveal a dark mahogany wood beneath the caked-on dirt and dust. I walk over to the boarded windows and find the missing panel I pulled off earlier. A quick glance at my feet covered in dirt and dried blood confirm that the footprints are my own.

In the closet, a line of shoes caked with dust sit on a shelf. A worn pair of Converse tennis shoes catch my eye I swipe away the grime and try them on. They fit perfectly. Smiling, I wiggle my toes.

As I head to the porch, I hear someone ask, "Alpha Agnus, is everything okay?" A tall, lanky, elderly man with salt-and-pepper hair approaches the house.

"Yes, everything is fine, Miller. I'm just taking my friend on a walk around the territory."

"Your friend, Alpha?" he inquires.

"Are you questioning my friends?" She rests her hands on her hips. I smirk at her sassy nature.

The man actually winces. "Uh, no, Alpha. It's just, uh..." He clears his throat. "You, uh, don't like people... or have very many friends."

She laughs and slaps his arm. "Yes, well, I like this Little One, which says a lot. Doesn't it?" She turns to face me and winks.

Miller holds out his hand to introduce himself. "I'm Miller, Alpha Agnus's right-hand man."

I first wipe my hands on my pant legs and shake his outstretched offering. I try to speak, but a breathy squeak emits from my mouth.

Agnus pats my arm and explains, "She's a little shy. Why don't you come with us and give her a tour of the place?" Embarrassed, I dip my head and reach to cover the gaping hole in my throat when Miller grips my hand tightly in his. His eyes narrow, scrutinizing my features. I don't blame him. I'm a teen who basically appeared out of nowhere.

"Does your friend have a name?"

"Of course she does, Miller," Agnus tsks. "It's Jessica," she proclaims.

His eyes widen before he once again masks his expression. He looks me over one last time before releasing my hand. Nodding, he says, "Very nice to meet you, Jessica."

I give a tight-lipped smile and nod as well.

Offering an arm to help Agnus off the porch, he continues,

"Your little friend Jessica wouldn't have been responsible for all that racket last night, would she?"

Agnus stops in her tracks. "Why, Miller, are you being rude to my guest?"

"Uh, no, Alpha. It's just... well... I'm just looking out for you... and the pack, of course."

"Just shut your ass and take us on that tour!"

I cover my mouth to stifle my giggles. Miller glances at me. Agnus is a feisty old woman. Then again, I guess she needs to be as an Alpha. I wonder why she never introduced herself to me as Alpha when she told me her name.

Both Miller and Alpha Agnus show me their little pack community—their homes, the small school, and even the tea plantation. Whitemore pack is known for its white tea. According to Alpha Agnus, the secret is their water source. It is believed that the water from Quartz Lake behind the plantation contains healing properties. The water is siphoned from the lake as a water supply to the plantation as well as the pack's general use.

At the end of the tour, they show me Quartz Lake. Alpha Agnus points to the other shoreline and says, "Beyond the lake is the seventh territory. Are you familiar with its history?"

I nod.

She stares into the distance—sad, wistful. "Good. It's important that you learn where you came from. It's important to learn the struggles and the sacrifices made by generations before so that you can have the life that you live now and in the future."

She speaks low, almost a whisper, but I hear her. I also notice the slight shine of unshed tears in her eyes. She blinks a few times, as if pulling herself out of a memory.

"You should sit and rest by the lake. Maybe take your shoes

off and dip your feet. When you're ready, return to the house, and you can make my lunch."

I almost nod in agreement but then pause, cocking my head in her direction. Why she thinks I can cook is beyond me. I simply shrug and turn back to the lake.

"You better figure it out. I missed breakfast this morning."

I shake my head, and a wheezy, fluid-filled laugh escapes from the hole in my throat.

CHAPTER 12

QUARTZ LAKE

JESSICA
EIGHT YEARS AGO:
MAY 18, 2016: 11 A.M.
WHITEMORE PLANTATION

Removing my shoes, I sit near the lake's edge, dipping my feet in the cool water. Peering at the other side, I think about the seventh territory. It's a large area of unused land so vast it is said to be one of the most extensive territories, compared to even the six significant territories of the Luna Solar realm, which form the LS territory.

The seventh territory once was known as the habitat of the white wolf shifter species. The history books claim that the great war occurred almost 200 years ago because of greed over land and power. So many innocent shifters died, and, in the end, it resulted in the extinction of the white wolf shifter species. No one has gained control over the seventh territory since the war.

Over the years, so many Alphas tried to lay claim, but the

land is protected by the Alpha King. Under a royal decree, the seventh territory will remain vacant until the rightful owner returns. Supposedly, only the Alpha King knows who that is—a name passed down over the generations from Alpha King to Alpha King. Because of this secret and others' greed, a small group of shifters, called the Resistance, plan to instigate another war and take over the monarchy and the seventh territory.

It's a rumor, but nowadays, you never can tell. Greed is a potent evil.

As I ponder the history of this land, I frown at the clear water before me. How can I remember all of that and yet nothing about my life before I woke up yesterday? I rub my eyes and rest my elbows on my knees.

I am exhausted, confused, and scared. What will happen to me now? Will I end up in an orphanage if no one claims me? Do I *want* to be claimed?

I listen to the harsh wet sound of my breathing. The more I think about my predicament, the more questions pop into my head. What have I done to deserve this? Am I a bad person? Did I commit some injustice? The thoughts circle endlessly. As the overwhelming sensations build in my chest and the threat of tears burns behind my eyes, a soft rustle stirs across the lake.

My body freezes. Directly across from me, on the lake's edge, sits a white wolf.

I don't move, afraid to scare her away. I tilt my head, studying the beautiful creature. I turn my head to the right. Am I seeing this clearly with my own eyes, or is it some weird conjured mirage in my head? My vision blurs, blinking and readjusting until it comes into focus. The wolf is still there, head cocked in the same direction as mine. I lift my hand to rub my face, and the wolf lifts her paw. She mirrors my movements.

I close my eyes, convinced I'm hallucinating. Opening them

again, I gaze into the lake's clear surface at the reflection of my hooded face. The white wolf's reflection is there as well, distorted by a ripple in the smooth water. As it settles, the white wolf is no longer alone.

I lean forward for a better look. In the reflection, four other wolves stand with her, two on each side. On her left sits a golden-haired wolf, fur as bright and warm as the sun, emerald-green eyes staring back at me. He reminds me of an empty field of lush grass bathing in the daylight. Eyes caress me, like a physical touch.

A chestnut-haired wolf with deep amber eyes sits next to him. As he stares back at me, his eyes change from amber to purple, red, and then black before returning to their original color. I could have sworn that his fur changed colors, too, reminding me of a chameleon. Despite an invisible barrier between us, his eyes convey a fierce protectiveness.

To the right of the white wolf sits a copper-haired wolf, fur glowing like flames in the sun. His intense steely grey eyes hold my own. A calmness settles over me, and the urge to run my fingers through his fur consumes me. I have the insane notion that he would burn the world down just for me.

Movement from the last wolf catches my attention. His fur is so black, it appears blue, and his dark blue eyes pierce me. He exudes a menacing, dangerous energy and a seriousness that supersedes that of the other wolves. The black wolf shifts his head, and a shadow lags behind. Turning back to face me, the blur takes shape. Is that a second head? His eyes are now a lighter blue color. Even his energy lightens, not domineering but just as intense. He is two souls trapped in one body. He should scare me, but confidence fills my soul instead.

Love, security, and strength flow among all five wolves. They convey a protective bond. I glance away from the reflection to see their physical forms at the edge of the lake, but there is nothing there. I drop my gaze back to the water's surface, and their reflection vanishes.

Astonished by my vision, I stopped paying attention to my surroundings. A low growl rumbles against my ear, and hot moist air brushes along my cheek. A horrible stench of rotten meat reaches my nose.

Slowly, I turn my head. All I see are teeth. I pull back to distance myself from the angry wolf's face. This isn't any of the wolves reflected in the lake moments ago. This strange, ugly wolf is half dull brown and half gray with a jagged scar along its muzzle.

The wolf snarls and lunges at me. I raise my arms to protect myself and fall backward into the lake. I stand, sputtering in waist-high water, frantically searching for the bicolored wolf. But once again, there is nothing there.

Choking from the water that had gotten into my lungs through the hole in my throat, I wipe my face and rub my eyes. I scold myself for daydreaming and force myself out of the lake before I drown. In the distance, just before the trees beyond the lake, I catch a glimpse of a white wolf running toward the seventh territory. Wiping my eyes again, even though my sight is not crisp, this time I am sure of what I saw.

A GIFT FROM A LITTLE FRIEND

JESSICA
PRESENT DAY:
MARCH 31, 2025

Carmen lifts the hand holding a pen, stopping me from continuing. "Was that a vision?" she asks.

"I'm not sure what it was exactly," I reply with a slight chuckle. "I was practically blind at the time and still recovering from extensive injuries. It could have been a hallucination or, like I said, a daydream."

"Hmm…" Carmen taps her pen on her clipboard. "I've conducted a lot of interviews in my career, and sometimes when someone wakes up from a near-death experience, they claim to see the other side or dream of angels or loved ones who passed. But I have never encountered anyone who experienced awakened visions. This is a first for me."

I laugh. "Are awakened visions a thing?"

"Certainly, it represents a state of increased awareness or a spiritual awakening, often accompanied by symbolic imagery. Take your wolves, for instance. Together they can symbolize something greater than yourself." She shrugs and jots down notes on her paper.

No one ever described what I saw that day as an awakened vision. Then again, I only ever told one person about it. "I mentioned to Alpha Agnus later on about what I had seen. She believed it was Quartz Lake, giving me a peek of what's to come. I honestly forgot about it until just now."

"What made you think of it?" Christian asks from behind the camera.

"It's silly, actually." I dip my chin as a blush warms my cheeks.

"You would be surprised what's considered silly in our line of business," Carmen counters without looking up from her notetaking.

I reach into my pocket and retrieve a folded sheet of paper. Opening it, I stare at the drawing that my new little friend gave me after my interview with Sammy Cane. He drew five wolves sitting near a lake.

Unlike my vision, where the wolves were behind the lake, his drawing places them in front of it, depicted as a messy glob of blue. He drew every wolf in the exact order I saw them so many years ago. Bright yellow for the golden wolf with green eyes. The chestnut brown wolf with two different-colored eyes, different-colored legs, and a circle around him. The red wolf like he is on fire. And even the black wolf with two heads. The white wolf with sky-blue eyes sits between them. He portrayed her much larger than the others. On the corner of the paper, he also included the ugly wolf with a scar on its muzzle, half gray, half brown, baring its sharp teeth.

I show them the boy's picture, and Christian zooms in on it.

"I made a new friend last week, and before he left with his nanny, he gave me this. His nanny said he's been drawing wolves since he could hold a crayon, but he's never done a group of them with so much detail before."

Christian motions with his hand, and I lean forward to pass him the paper. "Amazing detail for a little kid. How old is he?" He asks, studying the drawing.

"Maybe five or six, judging from his size."

Carmen hums, peeking over Christian's shoulder. "Did you get his name, by any chance?"

"Yeah. His name is Jackson—cute kid, smart. He kind of reminded me of an old man with his mannerisms and the way he spoke."

Carmen taps her finger on the arm of the chair. "What's this?" She points to a mark in the upper corner.

Christian shrugs. "If I had to guess, it looks like two angels —one with black hair and one with white." He smiles at me. "The one with the white hair looks like she's carrying a candy cane."

"Obviously, the one with the cane is your Alpha Agnus, but who is the one with the dark hair?" Carmen ponders.

I frown. I studied that picture so many times, but I never saw angels. Christian turns the paper around, showing me. They're so small. That must be why I missed it.

Christian passes the paper back, and I glance at it one more time. "Emily... she died a few years ago." I trace my finger over the tiny angels. "She was my best friend and just as important to me as Alpha Angus." I blink to stop the tears threatening to fall and clear my throat. "I guess this could only mean one of two things. I either made up the whole story in my head after seeing this, or it's confirmation that what I saw really happened."

Christian winks. "My instincts tell me it's the latter."

I nod as I carefully fold the paper and slide it back in my pocket.

Carmen reclines in her chair and clasps her hands together, resting them in her lap. "Okay. So let's take it back to what happened two weeks ago and the reason you're here."

CHAPTER 14

THE FUNERAL

JESSICA
TWO WEEKS AGO:
MARCH 14, 2025: 9:05 A.M.
WHITEMORE PLANTATION

"You've grown quiet. What are you thinking about?" Anders asks, pulling me from my thoughts.

I sigh. "I was thinking about the first time I met Alpha Agnus." I shake my head. "I was so upset with her when you came to take me. I felt like she ratted me out."

He laughs. "We chased you all the way from the clinic that night. You definitely gave those guards a run for their money, including me." He smiles. "I finally decided to knock on her door to let her know we were searching for you, but she was already on the porch. She said that she dreamed about you and wanted to get to know you a little more, so I should return the next evening after dinner. I tried to protest, but she dismissed me. I explained that I would return under the Alpha King's orders. She basically flipped me off and slammed the door in my face."

I giggle. "Sounds like her."

He shakes his head. "I don't remember why, but that entire day turned to shit. We couldn't pick you up until the evening anyway. When I returned, she explained that your name was Jessica and that I needed to raise you with the guards. She mandated that I bring you back regularly so she could spend time with you. She said that the two of you had become friends, and she liked your company." He raises his eyebrows. "I thought she lost her mind. Then she told me, 'Don't repeat the same choices of others. History doesn't have to be something we only learn from books. We also need to learn from those closest to us.' With that said, I brought you back to the clinic, as I was ordered to do, and had a long discussion with the Alpha King about what happened next."

I frown. "What did she mean by that?" I ask.

He runs a hand down his face. "I didn't know at first, but then I realized... much later." He falls silent and turns to look out the window again.

Why is he acting so odd today? I clear my throat. "She always played by her own rules. I mean, her funeral is by invitation only." I chuckle.

He smiled. "I know. I was invited. I would have been insulted if my own grandmother didn't invite me to her funeral."

My head whips up to meet his gaze. "Grandmother?"

He lowers his chin and nods. Anders doesn't explain further as we enter the Whitemore territory. My head still whirls from confusion and, well, plain curiosity. Stepping out of the car, Anders instructs both Ean and Odyssey to stand guard at the pack hall's main entrance.

Miller greets us. "I think we're ready to start. You are the last to arrive."

I smile apologetically, and Miller mirrors the gesture with kind understanding in his eyes. I hand him the package of brownies. "As requested."

He grins. "Oh, yes, these were her favorite. Mine as well." He squeezes my shoulder. "I remember the first time you made these, the first time we all met you."

I nod. "I made these for dinner every time I visited after that."

"A great tradition, one I will always treasure," he whispers hoarsely.

Sissy approaches and stands next to Miller. "Jessica." She hugs me and, pulling away, grabs both of my hands in her own. "Come. Alpha Agnus requested that both you and Anders sit in the front, opposite Marisol, Morgan, and Peter."

Anders simply nods. It makes sense that he would sit with the family, now that I know Alpha Agnus was his grandmother, but I'm just a friend.

Sissy guides us to the rest of the group, and I walk over to Marisol to offer my condolences.

She envelopes me in a hug. "Thank you."

Not sure of what else to say, I gently squeeze her hand.

Morgan and Peter stand on either side of me. Peter pats my back, and Morgan pats my arm. "Our Aggie loved you so much," Peter shares.

"I loved her, too. She was like a grandmother to me. I have a lot to thank her for. She was a large part of my life. I am who I am partly because of her influence. I hope you all know how much she loved all of you. She talked about you all the time. If I didn't know any better, I would never know you were her stepchildren. She always thought of you as her own."

Marisol dabs away fresh tears and replies, "I always thought of her as my mother, too." Peter and Morgan nod in agreement. Peter, the youngest of the three, spent the most time with Alpha Agnus. His eyes mist with the sheen of unshed tears as well.

Miller addresses the group, "Shall we start?"

Marisol nods, and I find my seat next to Anders. The funeral progresses exactly as Alpha Agnus planned—short and to the point.

When it ends, Miller clears his throat. "She requested that all five of you be present for the reading of her will."

He looks at each of us in turn, and we all agree. Of the three stepchildren, no one objects to Anders's presence. Do they know?

We follow Miller to Alpha Agnus's home and gather in her office. Miller sits behind Aggie's office desk and begins to read aloud from a stack of documents. "As the direct female descendant of Alpha Agnus Whitemore, Princess Jessica Langhlan will succeed me as Alpha of the Whitemore pack, and as the Alpha, she will become CEO of Whitemore and Parker Corporation."

Blood drains from my face. My throat tightens. I shake my head in protest before I find the right words.

Miller lifts his hand to stop me and continues. "I am reading verbatim from Alpha Agnus's will." He takes a deep breath. "Jessica, I see you starting to protest. Don't overthink this. Despite your feelings of incompetence and unworthiness, you are the next Alpha. I read your tea leaves many times over the years. I spent time with you, and in my own way, I prepared you for this role. This is your divine path. Miller will provide you with the appropriate documents for the plantation business, including my notebook. Morgan and Peter will give you information regarding all of the accounts and legal paperwork of the corporation. Take a deep breath, Jessica. Everything will work out in the end."

Miller hands me the worn notebook and scans over the paper. He glances at Anders. "Well, uh, there are a couple more things you need to know."

Anders stands directly behind me and places a warm hand on my shoulder.

Miller swallows. "You are aware that the Whitemore plantation borders the entrance of the seventh territory. What you are not aware of is that Alpha Agnus is the title owner of the seventh territory. She has been protected for many years through the royal decree that her mother before her established with the Alpha King at the time. Now that Alpha Agnus passed, the royal decree does not protect you as her successor."

Miller holds eye contact with me to verify my understanding.

"Not only are you the Alpha of Whitemore pack and CEO of her company, but you are also the landowner and ruler of the seventh territory, also known as Quartz territory. Because of the LS laws regarding female Alphas, you must be mated before your twenty-fifth birthday to maintain your position as Alpha of the seventh territory."

I stare blankly ahead, no longer distinguishing details or people, as my mind tries desperately to process what I hear.

Miller glances at me again. "In other words, to keep the pack and the territory protected and to prevent a direct challenge for your position, it is required that you are mated before your next birthday."

The room remains silent. My birthday is in less than eight weeks. I close my eyes shut, and my hands tremble. The fucking panic begins to take over, rising from my chest. Tears well behind my eyelids. I can't do this. I don't care what she thinks —I wasn't prepared for this role. And mated?! I can't...

Anders's warm hand squeezes my shoulder. "Breathe, Jessica."

I suck in a shuddering breath, open my eyes, and look up at Anders. Shaking my head. I turn to Morgan, Peter, and Marisol. "Why me? This isn't right. I think she made a mistake," I whisper.

"She's been coaching you for this role since you met her," Marisol says with an earnest smile.

Miller nods his head in agreement. He didn't even like me when we first met. Why is he agreeing to this?

"I'm sure you have questions. We are here for you, and we will help you. But Alpha Agnus has foreseen that you wouldn't need much of our help as you settle into your role and become mated."

Peter and Morgan offer additional encouraging statements, but they fall on deaf ears. One burning question flips over and over in my mind, and I need an answer now. I ask Anders, "What does she mean, I'm a direct descendant?"

"You haven't told her?" Miller snaps.

Anders clenches his jaw and then looks away. "You are the last surviving female of our family bloodline. According to our pack traditions, Alpha status is passed down from female to female."

Our family bloodline. Our family. Aggie is Anders's grandmother. "That means, you and I..."

He finally meets my eye, his shining with sorrow. "You're my daughter. I—"

Waving away any more of his words, I storm out of the study. I need air. My heart pounds loudly in my ears. I can barely keep any thoughts straight. All this time. All this time! Both Anders and Alpha Agnus knew who I was to them, and they never said a damn thing.

I pace near the edge of Quartz Lake. How the hell did they keep this a secret? If I ever thought my life was in danger before, this—all of this—puts my life, as well as the lives of the pack now in my charge, at so much risk.

Loud thunderclaps echo overhead. The sky darkens, casting a sinister shadow over the lake's cool façade.

I wipe at the tears streaming down my face. To my surprise, I discover I hold Alpha Agnus's notebook, the very same notebook I saw her write in since our first meeting after she studied my empty teacup. I don't even remember taking it from Miller.

I frown. Her tea readings were always accurate. I witnessed her predictions come true myself. But as many times as she read my tea leaves, I often wondered why she never told me about my path, my future true mate, or anything really. I never pushed because, sometimes, I didn't really want or need to know.

Over time, with all the stupid shit that happened in my life, I convinced myself that I didn't need tea leaves to foretell my divine path or my true mate. I made my own path. If she couldn't tell me when she was alive, then to hell with it.

I toss the notebook into the lake and watch it sink slowly down into its bottomless end. Angry tears continue to fall.

No, I don't need tea leaf readings or visions from a woman who is no longer here to answer my questions. And I definitely do not need nor want to read about the lies and secrets kept from me all these years.

I reach into my pocket for a tissue I stuffed in there earlier, and my phone tumbles out, landing on my foot. I pick it up, wiping dirt off the face against my dress. When I flip it over to inspect it, Emily's contact information flashes on display. The phone rings.

"This is Emily—you know what to do."

My heart breaks, shattering into a million pieces. I clutch the phone to my chest and stifle my sobs with a hand over my mouth. Emily... was my ride or die, my person. She knew when to give it to me and when to take me out of my head. She never held back what she thought, and I loved that about her. I didn't deserve her. I was a horrible friend, always caught up in my own shit. But she was always there for me. In times like this, I would have called her first.

I am such a selfish bitch. Here I am, wishing she was here to talk to when it's my fault she's gone. Guilt, regret, anger, and loneliness harden into my chest. She is the very reason why I can't be Alpha. My best friend in the whole world died at the hands of monsters, and I couldn't protect her. I couldn't stop it from happening. Still clutching my phone to my chest, I fall to my knees and scream. Lightning streaks the sky, and thunder booms, my scream lost in the sound.

My mind spins out of control. How am I supposed to protect a pack? How am I supposed to protect a territory that caused the deaths of so many innocent shifters? How many more people need to die because of me?

I can't do this. I'm not strong enough. I just want to fall apart.

Then, I hear it—a voice. My phone falls from my grasp, as if someone slapped it out of my hand. As I reach down, I realize I accidentally dialed someone.

"Jessica? Jess! Is everything okay?"

CHAPTER 15
DIVINE INTERVENTION

LUKE
TWO WEEKS AGO:
MARCH 14, 2025: 11:45 A.M.
ALPHA KINGS MANSION

I knock on my father's door to his study. "Jessica is on her way to talk to you. She's quite upset. I think she'll need to talk with Mom, too." I sit in one of the leather armchairs in front of his antique grand desk. Casting a quick look over his shoulder, I survey the towering shelves that stretch from floor to ceiling along the wall behind his desk, brimming with a blend of books on Luna Solar Territory Laws and photographs of our family. I am absent from every photo that includes Jessica. A pang of sadness causes my heart to ache.

"The funeral must have wrapped up by now. I still can't believe I wasn't invited to Alpha Agnus's funeral. It's not customary for the Alpha King to be absent from an Alphas funeral. I would have liked to be there for both the pack and Jessica."

I rub the back of my neck. "Alpha Agnus's passing isn't the sole reason for her distress—I mean, it's part of it." I exhale deeply. "Alpha Agnus named Jessica as her successor, and in doing so, the truth came out that Anders is her biological father."

My father frowns. "Let me guess. Anders hadn't told her before the reading of the will."

"Doesn't sound like it."

Through gritted teeth, he sneers, "Shit! We talked about this!" He grabs his phone, rapidly typing a text.

"Did you ever wonder how, of all places, she came to us? She literally ended up in Anders's backyard. She ran blind and broken into Alpha Agnus's home."

Without missing a beat or glancing up from his phone, he answers, "Divine intervention."

I huff and, under my breath, mutter, "Divine intervention."

His eyes lift to mine. "Or fate, whatever you want to call it. She ended up where she needed to be. I believe in that, at least."

I grimace. "Fate sure has a fucked-up sense of humor."

He smirks. "I take it you haven't talked to her yet?"

I shake my head. "No, and I think it will be even longer now before I have a chance."

Suddenly, the twins crash through the door. "Where's Jess?" Jeremy asks. "I could have sworn she'd be here by now. She's so loud."

"Loud?" I ask.

Justin shrugs. "She's freaking out. Her thoughts are shouting in our heads."

Jeremy straightens his posture, and a look of surprise crosses his features. "Holy shit! She's the Whitemore pack's successor?" He looks at Justin. "What the fuck? Anders—"

My mother enters the room and slaps Jeremy in the back of

his head. "Can't you wait until Jessica gets home so that she can tell us herself?"

Jeremy grumbles, "Did you have to hit me so hard?"

I chuckle. This is our family. It's like a circus, especially with the twins.

Jessica walks into the study. "Great! You're all here."

Her chest heaves, like she's out of breath. Her clear blue eyes, lighter than the clearest blue sky, appear bloodshot from crying. Her pale blonde hair, a bit disheveled, hangs to her waist. I swear her hair was a darker blonde this morning. She wears baggy gray sweatpants with a sports bra, and she pulls on a flannel shirt. My eyes naturally drift to her taut abs and full breasts.

My dick twitches, and I long to take her into my arms and fucking kiss her. I want to hold her and reassure her that she can do this. I want to make it clear that I will be here for her in any way she will let me.

She leaves the flannel unbuttoned and collects her long hair from underneath the collar. Maybe it's good that my brothers, Jessica, and I do not share a mind-link. I shift in my seat. Fuck, this isn't the time.

I rub my thumb over my forehead, hiding my reaction. Wait. Those are *my* clothes. They're from my stash in the barn for when I shift.

When I shift... I sit up straighter in my chair. "You shifted?"

The commotion stops. and everyone freezes. She looks at me for the first time since she entered the room, and a flash of annoyance crosses her face. "Of course I did. It was the only way to get here in minutes, instead of hours."

My father prods, "Jessica, you know that—"

She lifts her hand. "I know. I know. I was careful. No one saw me."

He sets his phone on his desk and then announces, "Anders is on his way."

Jessica rolls her eyes. "I don't want to talk to him right now."

Justin stands at her side and wraps an arm around her shoulders. "Can't say that I blame you, but he just might have a reasonable explanation for this."

Jealousy twinges up my spine. I want to be the one to comfort her, to wrap my arms around her.

Jessica turns to my father. Hurt and unshed tears shine in her eyes. She opens her mouth to speak but she closes it again. Cocking her head, she swivels toward the door just as Joe, our butler, appears.

"I'm sorry for the interruption, sir, but we have unexpected visitors."

Jessica's eyes widen. "It's the second territory Alpha and his Beta."

Fuck. She even has a connection with our staff. What the hell? A growl builds in my throat, and I run a hand through my hair.

My father stands up behind his desk. "Dammit. I told them in my last email that we would meet when we were available!"

"Sir, the Alpha and his Beta refuse to be turned away and insist they speak to you posthaste." Joe's face remains expressionless as he awaits further instruction.

My mother steps closer to Jessica. "Joe, bring them into the drawing room." She cups Jessica's face in her hands. "We'll go upstairs and change into something more appropriate for a meeting."

Jessica shakes her head. "He doesn't want to meet with me. He wants a meeting with the Alpha King to override my decision to refuse aid. Beta DuPont refuses to accept my role among the guards. He won't stop until he and his son get their way."

"That's bullshit!" Jeremy snaps. "You're a royal. You were given the role to oversee guard business by our father and Anders. Whatever you decide, he can't rebuke that. You ultimately have the final say."

She looks at me then, hitting me full force with the turmoil of emotions in her eyes. She's still all over the place. I don't need to hear her thoughts to know she's conflicted right now. I swell with pride that she turned to me for guidance and yet sad because it's only because she feels stuck.

Softly, I offer, "Go get changed. Dad and I can buy some time before you join us."

Glancing at her tiny bare feet, she admits, "I can't do this right now. It's too much all at once."

I stand from my chair and approach her. Lifting her chin with my finger, I stare into her beautiful clear blue eyes. "You *can* do this. I've seen you tear lesser men apart in meetings and on the field on a good day. I would hate to see what you do to an asshole on a bad one."

Her eyes search mine. My heart aches because she searches for sincerity. Can't she see how much I adore her? I smile.

She emits a slow breath and nods.

My mother ushers her toward the door, and the twins and I move to follow them. "Hold on, you three," my father directs. "Let them wait. In the meantime, Jeremy and Justin, gather the leads and a couple of guards. I hope Anders arrives in time."

Justin and Jeremy take their leave without question. On the other hand, I raise my eyebrow at my father in question.

After everyone else leaves, he says, "I don't have a good feeling about this. Jessica is on edge, and those assholes are up to something."

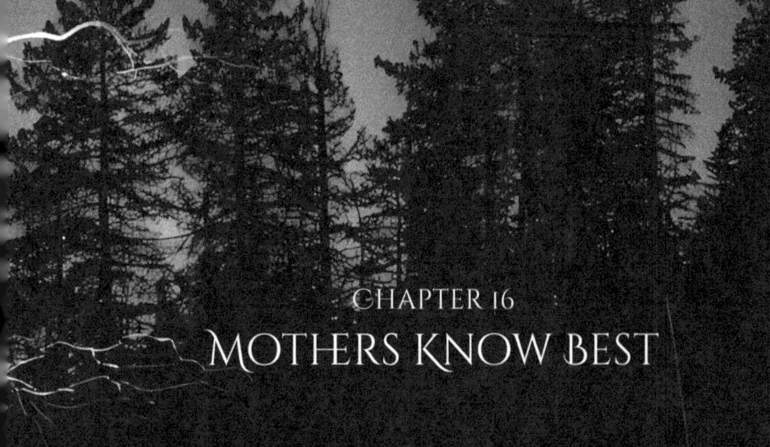

CHAPTER 16

MOTHERS KNOW BEST

JESSICA

TWO WEEKS AGO:

MARCH 14, 2025: 12:20 P.M.

ALPHA KINGS MANSION

My mother helps me decide on an outfit—a long sleeve button-down pale blue blouse with a collar and black capris. I pair the clothing with my favorite pair of chucks, instead of the black flats she placed near the bed. I smile as she shakes her head.

It's an unspoken compromise. As much as I would prefer to stay in my comfortable sweats and flannel, I can't face the Alpha of the second territory looking like a teenager who just stumbled out of bed.

The expression on my mother's face shifts as she contemplates what to say.

I take a seat at my vanity table and apply a little makeup. My mother brushes my tangled hair. It's been a while since I had it cut or styled. I tend to keep it in a bun or a ponytail.

Otherwise, it's all over the place. Occasionally, I color it to mask the pale shade with a darker blonde, sometimes brown. I just did it a few days ago, but when I shift, it reverts to my original color. Well, I certainly don't have time now.

I rarely let anyone see my natural hair color because the paleness sticks out like a sore thumb, especially against my tan skin. Most women, and men, with fair hair also have fair skin. But for some reason, my complexion is darker. The darker my skin, the more my hair seems to glow in comparison. Many women pay top dollar at the spray tan booths for a natural skin tone like mine. What a waste of time and money. It's easier to hide scars with fair skin.

I rest my foundation brush on my vanity and reach into my jewelry box for a choker to hide the scar on my throat. Ean has the one I wore earlier—my favorite. I handed it to him when I decided to shift and run, instead of ride in the car with Anders for another two hours.

I sigh and catch my mother's green eyes watching me in the mirror. She finally breaks the silence between us. "I'm sorry that your father and I didn't tell you about Anders and Alpha Agnus. Together, we decided that we would let Anders tell you when he felt the time was right."

I stare at my jewelry box. "I just don't understand why he would wait, and even then, he couldn't tell me when we were alone in the car on the way to the funeral."

She pursed her lips and nodded. "I understand why you are upset, but I also understand why he had a hard time. It's not an easy position for either of you."

I try to shake my head, but she has my hair in a vise grip to finish a French twist. "He should have told me—"

My mother snaps her eyes to mine in the mirror, causing me to stop in the middle of what I am going to say. "What difference would it have made if he told you today or eight years ago? Would this knowledge change your relationship with your father and me? With the twins? Would it have changed your relationship with Alpha Agnus?"

I frown. If I had known sooner that Anders was my biological father, would it have changed anything? Would it have changed me? Would it have changed the relationships I developed over the years?

CHAPTER 17

MAKING A GOOD IMPRESSION

JESSICA

EIGHT YEARS AGO:
MAY 18, 2016: 5:30 P.M.
WHITEMORE PLANTATION

I'm almost done with the final touches for dinner when Miller arrives. He doesn't knock but just walks in through the kitchen door. I hear his footsteps and recognized his smell.

He looks at me and smiles. "Smells delicious. I can't wait to try it." I smile back and nod as I make a place for him at the table. He then makes his way to the living area, where Agnus sits reading in a recliner with a crocheted blanket over her lap.

Agnus says loudly, "Miller, help me out of this death trap. I've been sitting in this chair for hours, and I can't seem to get myself out of it."

I frown. She never told me she wanted out of the recliner. I quietly meander closer.

Miller attempts to pull Agnus out of the chair, holding onto both of her hands and placing a foot on the footrest of the recliner. He almost clicks the footrest into place when it springs up, throwing Agnus back and dragging Miller forward on top of her.

I clap a hand over my mouth to hold in my laughter. Air squeaks from the hole in my throat. They don't notice me. Agnus is too busy pushing Miller off of her, while he attempts to stand upright.

Agnus swears, "Miller, you are a fucking idiot. Get off of me, and get me out of this damn chair!"

His face is flustered. He scrambles onto his feet and pushes the footrest with his hand at the same time that Agnus scoots forward, headbutting Miller in the process. Shocked, Miller falls onto his butt. Agnus growls. Using her legs, she tries to close the footrest, but it won't budge because Miller's knee is now trapped under it.

I place my other hand over the hole in my throat, disguising the noisy rush of air as I try not to laugh harder. But I can't help it.

Agnus hits Miller in the chest with her cane, creating some distance between the two. "Fucking smartass, get over here and help me."

Brushing my hands on my pants, I wipe tears from my eyes and approach with a wide grin. Miller finally moves his legs, I press the lever on the side of the recliner, and the footrest retreats into the pocket of the chair

Agnus hits me in the shoulder with her cane as she slides forward. "Smartass," she sneers.

Miller, red in the face, grabs for Agnus's hand, but she slaps him away and stands on her own. Still smirking, I return to the kitchen, wash my hands, and finish preparing the meal.

Dinner becomes an unplanned gathering. I'm glad I made enough food to feed everyone who came. Each visitor also brought a dish to contribute. I'm pretty sure the pack members, especially Peter, who came all the way from the city, are here to check up on me.

Throughout the meal, everyone's skepticism and hesitancy toward me lessen. I especially win them over with my brownies, topped with freshly made whipped cream and fresh strawberries. As some of the guests begin to leave, I receive compliments and hugs. After bidding their farewells to the others, Miller, Peter, and Agnus adjourn to her study for after-dinner drinks.

My body screams in pain. My vision comes and goes, but I am determined to finish what I started. I need to prove that I could be an integral part of this pack. I'm pretty sure no one misses me from wherever I used to call home. I really hope that Aggie, or rather Alpha Agnus, will keep me. I want to belong here, to her.

Gathering the dishes from the table, I hear a knock on the front door. No one is around, so I move to answer it. The second knock sounds a little more persistent. A man with all-white hair and a young face stands at the entrance.

He smiles. "Are you ready, Little One? It's time I take you back to where you came from."

I stiffen. He wants to return me to that place where they stuck all the tubes inside me. Hell no! I turn and run to the kitchen.

Alpha Agnus stands there. She clasps my chin and says, "No running. I asked them to collect you."

Hurt and disappointed, I yank my face out of her grasp and

turn away from her. I thought she liked me. I thought I did well enough for her to want to keep me.

She places her hand on my shoulder, spinning me to face her, and hands me my hoodie. "It's not the time for you to stay. You're a little early."

Too angry to acknowledge my confusion at her words, I snatch my hoodie, put it on, head for the front door.

Two cars are parked outside. Next to the first car stand two big men. I slowly approach them, pulling the hood of my sweatshirt over my head.

"No funny business," the tall giant warns. "We got you figured out. This time, you won't escape." He gestures to the second car, and four equally big men step out.

I shrug, disguising my intimidation. The slightly shorter one walks toward me, and I stagger backward, unsure of what he will do.

He introduces himself. "My name is Chris. I'm the third lead guard. This guy is Elias. He's the second lead."

Hesitantly, I shake his offered hand. Guards? Shit! I am in so much trouble. I close my eyes to hide my shame. When I open them again, Elias bends forward, eye level with me.

"You're not in trouble, Little One." He tilts his head, gesturing to the four others. "Those men are guards, but they are not important." One of them snorts at his statement.

A puff of air and a whistling noise emits from my throat.

Chris steps forward, and I step back. "How did you survive the day out here?"

I shake my head and shrug again. The movement creates a spinning sensation. My body sways slightly, and a large hand clamps over my shoulder.

"It's okay, Little One. We just want to take you back to the clinic so the doctor can look you over and help take care of you. You're safe with us."

Not sure if I believe his words or his intentions, I retreat another step. My knees buckle, but before my body hits the ground, large arms catch me. My vision blurs, and my body aches. I have no more fight in me. I let them carry and deposit me in the back seat. I can't push past the fatigue and weakness to prove my place in the Whitemore pack anymore. All for nothing. The tears fall, and I accept defeat.

Large hands wipe my face. "Don't cry, Little One. My name is Anders. I'm the head guard. You're not in trouble. I'm taking you home."

I turn my head to see the man who possesses the gravelly voice next to me and find the white-haired man. I grip the seat as anxiety rips through me, and the car pulls away from Alpha Agnus's home.

Home? I don't know where home is. How can he ensure I will be safe? Look at me.

My mind whirls with horrible thoughts and visions of what home will be like once I return. My heartbeat starts to race. My harsh, raspy breathing gasps through the hole in my throat. I want to jump out of the car.

A hand rests over my own, startling me. I didn't hear anyone else climb into the car and sit next to me. I sense a blurry shadow, an outline of a man. I face forward with a grimace.

The large hand over my own caresses my skin with his thumb. He leans close to my ear and whispers, "I got you."

My panic ebbs. I lay my head back against the car seat, close my eyes, and allow the soothing hand to lull me to sleep.

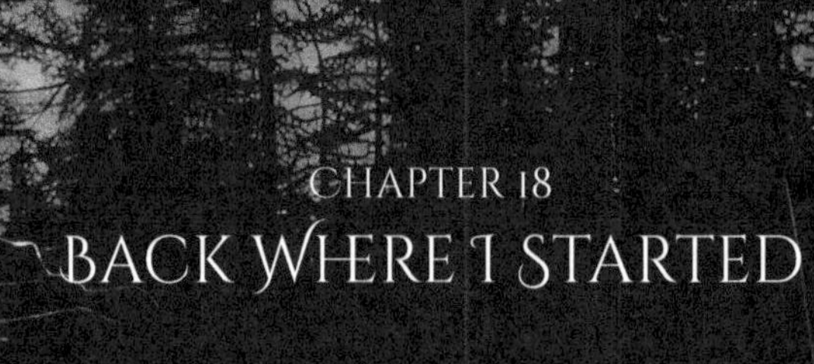

JESSICA
EIGHT YEARS AGO:
MAY 19, 2016:
EMERALD PACK CLINIC

The glint of a blade reflects the moonlight as it comes straight for my face. A high-pitched, manic laugh echoes around me. The knife slices into my cheek, my scalp. Screaming with every slice until my throat is raw, it aims for my eye.

I raise my arms to protect myself. *Stop*! *Please stop*! Breathing harshly, I open my eyes and assess my surroundings. My vision distorts the shadows and light. I sit up in bed slowly, recognizing the smell of the sterile room.

I remember the man named Anders collecting me from Alpha Agnus's house. I fell asleep in the car. I remember the man named Chris explaining they had wanted to return me to the clinic, where the doctor could take care of me. But I also remember Anders saying he planned to bring me home. Is this the clinic?

My heart rate accelerates, and the sound of my harsh, wet breathing bounces around the room. I close my eyes to calm myself. A warm palm holding my right hand, and another gently rubs my back.

"Shhhhh. You're safe, sweetheart. No one will hurt you," says a soft, soothing female voice. I can't see what she looks like, but I detect a hint of mint accompanied by a delicate flowery scent of jasmine and vanilla. She continues to rub my back. I roam my hands down my body. A tube sticks out in my stomach, and another line runs into my arm. I wear that weird dress thing that only covers my front. I reach for my throat—no tube this time, but the hole is still present.

The woman makes a shushing noise and continues to rub my back. "The tube in your stomach feeds you. The line in your arm hydrates you. It's to help you, not hurt you." She pauses before apologizing, "I'm so sorry I wasn't here when you woke up the other day. You must have been so scared. Between myself and my boys, we have been at your side since they brought you here. But my oldest son had to return to school. We all reluctantly left your side, not thinking you would wake up. You've been in a coma for almost two weeks."

My shoulders drop, and the tension in my body relents.

"I'm here now. I won't let anything bad happen to you, Little One."

I nod and squeeze her hand.

She guides me back to recline in the bed. "My name is Shakti. I know—it's a bit of a strange name, especially for someone born and raised in the LS. I can tell you how I was named, if you like?"

I nod again, encouraging her to continue.

"My father was a businessman who met many people

overseas. One day, he met a beautiful shifter princess, a daughter of an Alpha King, in India on one of his travels. He met her only once. She was a little girl, no more than four or five years old, but he couldn't get over how beautiful she was for a child. When he met his true mate, and they finally had a daughter after four sons, he was adamant on naming his daughter Shakti because he felt his daughter was the most beautiful girl he had ever seen and his daughter would forever be his princess. I wish he was still alive today. I think you would have liked him."

I reach out to find her hand and smile at her story, imagining how beautiful she is. I just wish I could see her, this woman who stayed by my side and comforted me. I worry I've lost my vision completely.

Without a voice and no vision, how will I survive? What kind of life could I possibly lead? Feeling sorry for myself, tears well in my eyes. What a mess. No one wants a weak person in their pack. A crybaby is weak.

A commotion outside my door diverts my attention. I can't hear much with my ears, but inside my head, two male voices grumble with each other. The words are too fast, much faster compared to someone speaking out loud.

The door of my room bangs open. *Great job, dumbass! You nearly woke the dead.*

The funny thing about these voices, as I pay closer attention, is they sound exactly the same in my mind. Yet, the intonation and personality behind the words help me to differentiate the two.

Shut up! You're the one who shoved past me as I opened it, Voice Two snarks.

Shakti leaves my side. "What the hell are you doing? I told you two to stay outside in the waiting area until she woke up and the doctor looked at her," she issues firmly. Ah, this must be two of the boys she mentioned earlier.

I told you we should wait, Voice One says. I picture an elbow hitting someone in the chest.

Pshhh. Like I'd listen to you anyhow. She needs us. You heard her thoughts, just as I clearly did, Voice Two responds, and again, another elbow jabs back in my head.

How are they doing this? It's almost like when I heard Alpha Agnus's voice in my mind. She told me to use my brain to visualize my surroundings.

You met Alpha Agnus? Voice One asks.

"Well, are you two going to explain yourselves?"

"Sorry, Mom, but... we, uh... ouch! What the hell was that for?" Voice One speaks out loud.

Shut up! Maybe Little One doesn't want anyone to know, Voice Two hisses in my head. I grow confused and overwhelmed as the banter between the two occurs at lightning speed.

"Sorry, Mom. It's just that...." Voice One stops mid-sentence. In my head, he asks if it's okay to tell my secret.

I hesitate, worried she won't like me anymore, especially if she thinks I'm weird.

She's our mother. You can trust her, just like you can trust us.

Trust. I contemplate the word. It feels like such a foreign concept. Even though my instincts tell me I probably could trust them, I'm not sure it's safe. Fear blooms deep in my chest.

You can trust us. Our mother knows that we communicate to each other in our minds. If you ever meet our big brother, you'll learn that he's special, too. It will be fine.

Caution still stirs in my heart. But I want her to know. I guess, if something happens or they kick me out on the streets, it's better to find out now, rather than later. I nod.

"Oh, for fuck's sake, we can communicate with her the same way we communicate with each other," Voice Two blurts.

"Jeremy, language! How many times must I remind you?"

Shakti scolds, not really reacting to what he just said. Personally, I would have freaked out.

"Nah, my mom's cool. I'm Justin, by the way." Voice One says to the whole room. "The abrupt one is Jeremy. I love how you picked up on the differences in your head." A slew of images flash through my mind of someone receiving a beatdown. I assuming those stem from Voice Two, or Jeremy.

"Mom, she can't see or talk. It was really bothering her. We just want to let her know that she's not alone, and we can help." Justin is cordial when he speaks. Maybe that's just the way he talks to his mom.

"She's scared and sad," Jeremy admits softly this time.

An image populates of a tiny person in a hospital bed, attached to tubes. She's thin, and frail, and her face is hollow and sunken in, akin to a skeleton. A woman dressed in a smock and matching colored pants works to rearrange lines and reposition the body.

Is that me? He's showing me what I look like. Wow. I look like death lingers closely. With each images, I experience their fear, concern, and sadness. They don't even know me, and they are worried about me.

"The doctor should be here shortly. He went to one of the pack members' homes to help with a birthing. I usually go, but I wanted to be here when you woke up," she explains.

I think it's strange. I only just met her, and I really feel like she cares about me, in such a short time.

She does. We all do. One of the boy's voices enters my head again.

"Mom, she's wondering why you care about her," Jeremy tells his mother.

A hand grips my own, and her floral perfume wafts closer. "Because the moon goddess brought you to us. I will care for you as if you were one of my own."

No words, no thoughts, can express the feeling that blossoms in my chest. Even without my memory, my instincts claim that I have never known this kindness. Two hands touch my feet.

"Hello, Little One. You're awake," a man's voice greets from the doorway. "I'm Dr. York. We haven't officially met." A shadowy figure stands off to the side.

"She can't see, Dr. York, and with the hole from the tracheotomy, she can't speak yet," Shakti proclaims, addressing Dr. York.

The smell of blood permeates the air around him, and I immediately tense. I shift in my bed, anxiety swelling in my throat.

"Uh, Dr. York, why do you smell like blood?" one of the boys asks the doctor.

He chuckles. "Occupational hazard. A patient bit me. I thought I cleaned up well enough before entering the room."

"I can, uh, still smell it," Jeremy shares. He is the more vocal of the two so far. Justin mainly addresses me through my mind.

I hear water running, and then paper crinkles.

He washed his hands. You're fine, Justin narrates. I nod.

"If you boys don't mind, I'll have you leave the room while I examine Little One." Footsteps shuffle across the floor.

Anxiety seizes me again. I don't want to be left alone in the room with him.

Relax. Mom is here. She and the doctor will explain to you out loud what he is doing. You're perfectly safe. Jeremy and I will be outside, listening. Footsteps leave the room, and the door softly closes.

We're right outside, Justin reassures me.

"You've made a connection with the boys already, I see. That's good. You need support. It will help you heal."

I nod my head, listening to their shoes scuff the linoleum floor in the hallway.

"I'm just moving out of the way, sweetie. I'm right here," Shakti says and rests her hand on my foot.

The doctor approaches the side of my bed.

"I'm going to start examining you now. My hands are a little cold. I just washed them."

I nod, indicating that I'm ready.

"So, Anders informs me that your name is Jessica. I originally assumed your name started with a G. Perhaps it's an initial of your last name," he declares.

"Dr. York, where did you find that information? I wasn't aware," Shakti asks.

"Oh, I wasn't completely sure so I didn't mention it. The letter G was written on the tag of an article of clothing she wore when she arrived. It was barely legible," he replies.

The letter G seems familiar. It feels almost right. It also feels like I hated it.

A chuckle echoes in my head. One of the twins teases, *Little G, I like it. I think I'll call you that, instead of Jessica.* I roll my eyes.

"I'm sorry. Is everything okay?" the doctor inquires.

Startled, I quickly nod. *Great! I almost got into trouble. Thanks a lot, dude.*

I hear laughter from both of them this time.

The exam lasts only a few minutes. The doctor asks yes or no questions so I can easily communicate with him. I have difficulty concentrating on the doctor, though, because the boys' thoughts overwhelm me. I can't filter them out.

Shakti and Dr. York discuss the various surgeries I will need. One to repair the hole in my throat. Laser eye surgery to fix my vision. Orthodontic surgery for my teeth. I try to pay attention, but I don't quite understand all the words he uses. Shakti seems to have everything under control. She asks questions and agrees or disagrees with his suggestions.

I feels like her child, not some stranger who just appeared out of nowhere. However, I am afraid to hope that I could stay with her, especially after the disappointment from last night.

Four weeks pass, and the surgeries don't go as well as everyone hoped. I am severely anemic from losing so much blood. The doctor mentions my body is malnourished so healing also takes longer than for any standard shifter, especially one who hasn't transitioned yet.

Although the hole in my throat was repaired, the initial incision damaged my vocal cords, and scar tissue developed, preventing me from creating sound. They sought out a specialist to determine if they could rectify the damage. Otherwise, I won't be able to talk ever again.

The laser eye surgery didn't go as planned either. The injuries were so bad that I needed to repeat surgeries and a special lens implant was inserted. Even so, my vision is not 100 percent, and I need to wear glasses.

Surgery after surgery, setback after setback, I fall into a mild depression, but the twins, Jeremy and Justin, don't give up on me. I'm not sure why two sixteen-year-old, nearly six feet tall, blond-haired, green-eyed teen boys want anything to do with me. Still, they visit every day, usually after school. Sometimes, they even stay the night. If they don't have school, they won't leave me alone, always acting as my interpreter and making me laugh at their stories and their pranks.

Before I could see, I imagined Shakti to be a beautiful woman. And she is. She's tall, at least five foot nine, and slender. Her big green eyes and long blonde hair match her boys. She also never leaves my side, unless someone is with me.

Anders visits daily to check on me and talk to Dr. York. Even Chris and Elias stop by to see how I am doing. The never-ending visitors help with my internal battle of despair, but it creeps in when I am left alone, especially at night when everyone sleeps.

The nightmares continue to haunt me. I gave up on sleep altogether. To make things worse, I finally gain the courage to look at my reflection, really look at myself. Standing in front of the bathroom mirror, I turn my head to inspect the left side of my face. I examine the scars. A long, puckered, angry, red, jagged line trails from the corner of my left eye to my chin, and another one starts at the corner of my mouth and sweeps up toward my ear. The whites of my eyes are blood red, contrasting the paleness of my light blue eyes. They make me think of vampire eyes. My lashes are slowly growing back in short little stubs, and my right eyelid has a pink scar.

Turning my head back and forth slowly, I examine the rest of my face. The too-big glasses hide most of my face, drawing the focus more than the scars. I rub my recently shaved head. Shakti attempted to salvage what was left of my hair, but in the end, I asked if she could just shave it all off. Angry pink and red bald spots dot my scalp. I lift my chin to see the freshly healing surgical scar at the base of my throat, where the hole had been. A faded pink line circles my neck just above it. I trace it with my fingertip. I hope this one fades. It's a little harder to hide.

Sighing, I undo the ties at my neck and back and remove the clinic gown, looking down at my chest. Dr. York seems to think that I am about twelve or fourteen years old. Cupping my breasts, I think I am about a full B cup. Would a twelve-year-old have boobs?

I graze my fingertips down my arms along the linear pink-

and-white scars, stopping where horizontal scars weave in, creating a tic-tac-toe pattern on my wrist. Turning to view my back in the mirror, I discover the worst of the wounds.

Jagged markings run down my back all the way to my right and left calves. It almost looks like I was mutilated and sewn back together. Facing forward, I find only one faded pink scar on each thigh, rectangular shaped about an inch long. No scars adorn my chest or stomach. I still have the feeding tube, though, because of my teeth.

I stare at my face and pretend to smile. My teeth are broken in half, some down to the gums, and several of my bottom teeth twist and jut out crookedly. The orthodontic specialist tried to salvage my original teeth, removing the ones he just couldn't save. He applied braces to straighten the ones still present, using spacers to account for the missing ones. Shakti promised that they would insert implants once everything else was fixed.

I'm not an idiot. Implants cost money, and good ones that stay in place when you shift cost more than a fancy condo in the city.

I know it's silly and probably vain to feel upset about my appearance. I know I should be dead. I eventually want to meet a boy, someone I could one day fall in love with. But who will want to kiss me with fucked-up, ugly, missing teeth? Who will want to touch me with scars all over my body? How many times will I have to explain myself when someone asks about them?

I look worse than a street junkie or a boxer, like someone threw me in a meat grinder, pulled me out, and pieced me back together. Opening my mouth, I examine my teeth again, smiling once more. I study all the wounds and scars. When I can't stomach my reflection any longer, I remove my glasses, slide to the floor, and quietly sob.

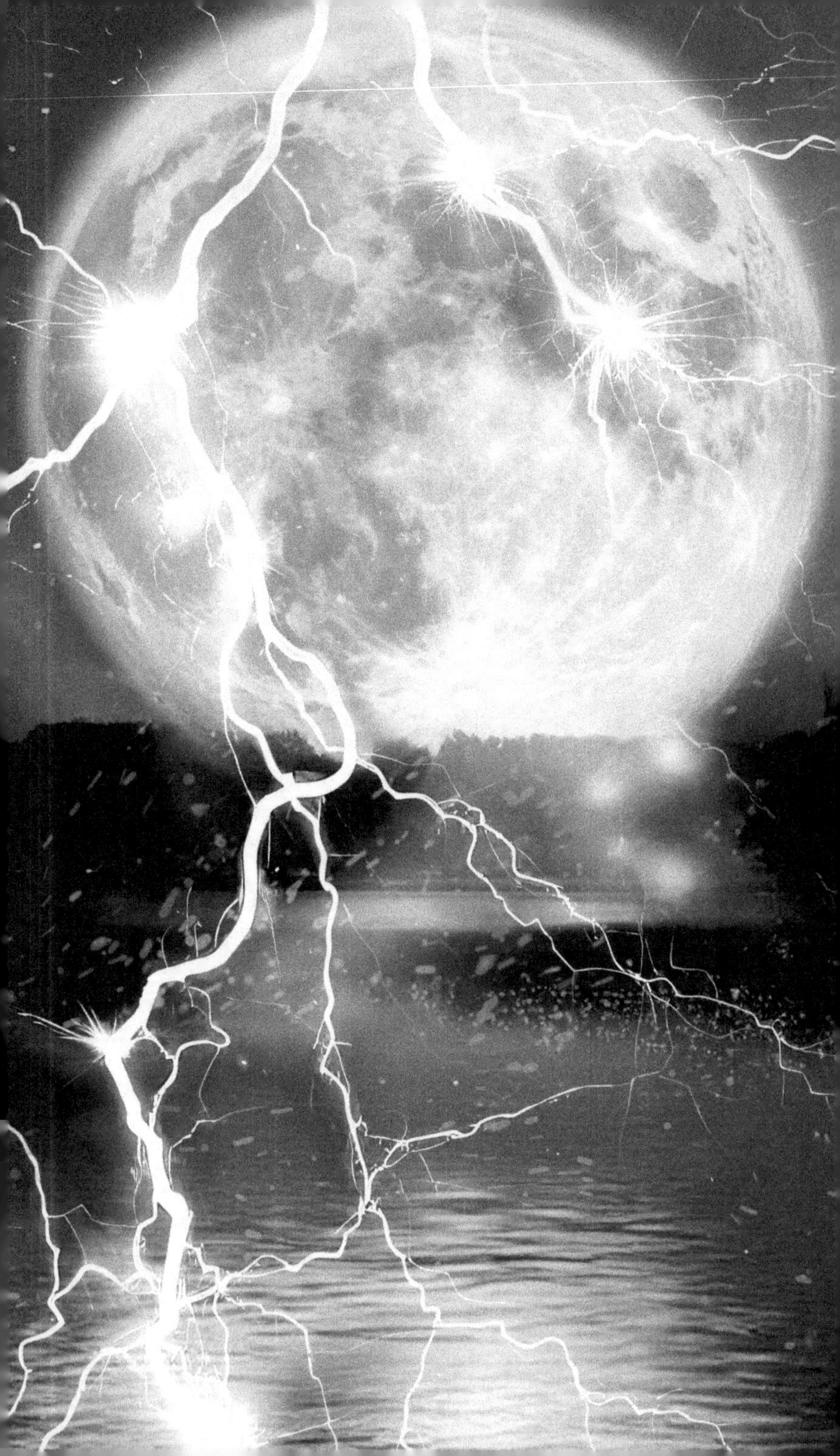

CHAPTER 19

GUARD DETAIL

JESSICA

EIGHT YEARS AGO:
JUNE 25, 2016: 9 A.M.
EMERALD PACK CLINIC

The twins gets into trouble at school, and Shakti grounds them. Their punishment includes their visits to me. Royal business requires Shakti to leave the territory, but she promises to remain in constant communication with Dr. York. She also assures that someone will stay with me so I am not alone. She will return as soon as she can.

Since last night, I haven't seen anyone other than Dr. York and my nurse, Mimi. A sharp knock at the door makes me jump, and four large men enter my room.

"Anders sent us," a deep baritone voice announces. I adjust my glasses on the bridge of my nose. The tallest one, with wide shoulders and black hair, spoke. He looks like Elias with dark brown eyes, so dark they're almost black, a square jaw, strong brow, and broad nose. His muscular frame tapers to a skinny waist, and he stands with legs slightly apart. "I'm Ean," he introduces himself with a smile.

I scrunch my face as I study him. Then, it hits me. I slid between his legs the day I escaped from the clinic.

I look around at all of them again. These are the four guards I ran from, but... I thought there were five of them—two I outran and three by the gate. My eyes widen. Were they the four men by the car when Anders came to collect me?

Ean bursts with laughter. "You remember us now, do you?"

I give him a tight-lipped smile and nod.

"What's wrong, Little One? Cat got your tongue?" a blond-haired guard asks. His green eyes sparkle with mischief. He isn't as broad-shouldered as the twins, and his blond hair is a couple of shades darker. He is leaner, with long muscular arms. I notice that his right forearm is slightly bigger than his left, making the veins more pronounced.

I quirk an eyebrow and point to my throat, still bandaged from my most recent surgery.

He raises both hands and shrugs. "Right. Sorry about that." He stretches out his right arm to shake my hand. "I'm Charlie. You jumped me, by the way, from the roof." They all chuckle.

Keeping my lips shut tight, I smile and blush, gingerly place my small hand in his much larger one. I hold up two fingers on my other hand. I actually jumped on him when I used him to grab onto a tree branch.

Another round of laughter circles the group. "Alright. Alright," he mumbles and lifts my hand to his mouth to kiss the back of it.

Heat flames in my cheeks. I quickly draw my hand back, causing more snickers from the others. I turn to the guard on Ean's other side.

"I'm Sodie. I was by the gate. You kicked me in the chest," he explains that, rubbing his shirt where I kicked him as he speaks.

I hang my head, silently apologizing. Ean claps him on the back.

Sodie is nearly as tall as Charlie and as broad as Ean, but he doesn't have that heavy-on-the-top look. His hair is a dark reddish-brown, and his brown eyes are lighter than Ean's.

Suddenly, another voice speaks up from the back of the room. "I'm Liam," he says, giving me a two-finger salute. He is the shortest of the group, but not by much. He has rich copper-colored hair, closely shaved on the sides and longer on top, which falls on his forehead just above his matching-colored brows and golden skin. His dark lashes surround steel gray eyes, burning with intensity as he scrutinizes me in return. Light freckles dance across his nose and cheeks, and he wears a diamond stud in his left earlobe. He leans against the wall, one leg propped up behind him. His muscular arms fold over his chest, and carved muscular biceps flex against the sleeves of his t-shirt. I catch a glimpse of chiseled abs beneath the raised hem of his shirt. I scan down the rest of his body and notice his sweatpants stretch over his muscular thighs.

He looks irritated, almost like he wishes he were anywhere but here. He is different-looking compared to the rest of the guards but still very handsome. He makes me blush a little as he continues to look me over.

Quickly, I look back at Ean, who adds, "The other one is Shadow. He's not here. I'm sure you will meet him soon." He bends at the waist so we're eye level. "I hear you've been cooped up in this room. Want to take a walk?"

Leaving the room sounds amazing. I nod enthusiastically.

"I checked with the doc, and he thought it would be good for you."

I glance around the room and then down at myself, grateful

for my baggy sweatpants and an oversized t-shirt. I complained to myself about my behind hanging out for everyone to see in that clinic gown so Shakti brought some clothes for me.

Without a second thought, I shoot out of bed and grab my shoes, the hoodie I found that first night I woke up, and a baseball hat Jeremy gave me to cover my bald head. Scrambling to put everything on, I move toward the door.

"Slow down, Little One. Where's the fire?" Ean jokes. I grin. I desperately need a change of scenery.

"Geez, you're fast. Are you sure this is a good idea?" Sodie asks, his expression filled with concern.

"Nah, she won't go anywhere. We're friends now," Charlie claims, resting an arm around my shoulders. Shaking my head, I slip from under Charlie's arm and shove Ean closer to the exit.

Ean laughs. "Alright, Little One. Don't get pushy."

I have never been more excited to take a walk in my life. I continue to urge Ean out faster, and chuckles follow me from the rest of the guards—well, except Liam.

I flick a quick glance at him over my shoulder. He looks irritated as hell. I wonder if this is some kind of punishment, being here, or if I crushed his ego when I ran from them. I shrug at the thought. Maybe he just sucks at being a guard, and it pisses him off that an untrained teenage girl like me got the best of him.

"I'm glad you brought a sweater. The weather has been a bit unpredictable lately. It's either gloomy as hell with small peeks of sunshine, or storming, especially at night. Never seen the weather quite like this before," Ean chats as he leads me out of the building. Sounds fitting, like my mood. As we step outside, the weather offers clear skies and sun. Perfect for a walk.

"Well, I'll be damned. It was gloomy just a few minutes ago, and I swear it was going to rain," Sodie remarks, frowning and looking up at the sky.

"See? That's what I'm talking about," Ean moans.

We start our tour at a statue of three wolves in front of the clinic. The clinic sits at the heart of the Emerald territory, combining both the Emerald Pack and the Guards. At the beginning of their time here in the LS territory, the guards were known as the Black Obsidian wolf pack, which came from a long line of warriors from the original Northern A territory before it was divided. When the small group of Black Obsidian wolves arrived in the LS territory, the White Wolf Alpha granted the Alpha a territory of his own next to the Emerald Pack territory. In appreciation, the Black Obsidian Alpha swore their allegiance to the white wolf Alpha and offered their services as protector to the white wolves. During the last great war, many of the guards died lending aid.

When the Emerald Pack Alpha was named King of the LS territory, the Black Obsidian Alpha swore their allegiance to the Emerald Pack Alpha, now known as the Alpha King of the LS territory. Because so few Black Obsidian wolves survived, they merged with the Emerald Pack, and the Black Obsidian Alpha resigned himself to head guard.

The Alpha King and the head guard worked to rebuild the guards. Over time, with still so few guards available between both packs, they decided to allow recruits to join from other packs. Because both territories merged, the Black Obsidian Territory became the training grounds for the recruits and home to some of the guards. The statue represents the original White Wolf Alpha, the Black Obsidian Alpha, and the first Emerald Pack's Alpha King.

Ean grins. "My family carries the original Black Obsidian bloodline. For generations, we have either been in the guard or had a hand in leading it."

"Thank you, kind sir, for the brief history lesson. For a moment there, I thought I was back in orientation," Liam mocks. There's a subtle accent in his speech. I wonder which area of the LS he comes from?

"Watch it. You're still a recruit, and I am your commanding officer," Ean sneers.

With a smirk, Liam shakes his head and continues to walk alongside Sodie, shoving his hands in his pockets.

Charlie bumps my shoulder. "Don't worry, Little One. You'll get used to the overabundance of testosterone around here." He winks and smiles before turning his attention back to Ean.

I blush, not used to this kind of attention. Seriously, has he seen me?

"Don't you have an off switch?" Liam grumbles. Charlie just laughs and throws his arm around my shoulders.

It leaves me feeling a little uncomfortable, so I grab his arm and place it back at his side, patting his muscular arm so he leaves it there. Another bout of laughter erupts from the group, including Liam. I silently chuckle along with them.

"Guess you found someone immune to your charm," Ean snarks. I simply shrug.

The training grounds are impressive. Money is not spared when it comes to training weapons and weightlifting equipment. The dorms are designed like a luxury hotel and include everything from a miniature movie theater with couches to a rec center with a pool table, dartboard, ping pong table, and an area to play poker. Their cafeteria comprises an all-out buffet fitted with round dining tables covered in white linen, silverware, and crystal glasses. They even have a spa and an indoor heated swimming pool.

The only thing missing is the guards' academic area. I thought I would find myself in an extensive library filled to the gills with books, many classrooms with teachers, a lab room with dead animal specimens, beakers, and chemicals used for science experiments, or a music room. None of that is present.

There is only one classroom and one teacher, and after everything else, I can't help but feel a little disappointed.

At the end of the tour, I stand in front of an obstacle course. It's vast, sporting quintuple steps, a rope swing, barrel role, what Ean calls a jumping spider wall, jump hang, spinning logs, curtain slider, and swing circle. I can't retain the endless names Ean gives them all. He says that no one makes it through the obstacle course on the first try, and even then, only one person completed it within sixteen minutes.

I stare, imagining myself progressing through the obstacle course. I bet I could, or would at least like to, give it a try.

Nudging my shoulder, Charlie smiling down at me. "What's going on in that head of yours, Little One?"

I shrug.

Sodie stands next to me. "I bet this Little One would give any of the recruits a run for their money." I beam.

Liam interjects, "Nah. It's a little more than jumping onto trees and roofs and climbing up a gate."

I cock my head toward Liam and mirror his look of annoyance. I hope my nonverbal statement shuts him up. Instead, he breaks into a grin.

Ean claps me on the back, thrusting me forward. "I would put my money on this Little One. She's definitely got grit."

I flinch. That word—grit—makes me want to grind my teeth and pull out my hair, if I had any. Surprised at my knee-jerk reaction, I shake it off and elbow Ean in the stomach. I gesture toward the obstacle course, asking if I can try it.

Ean shakes his head. "Hell no, Little One. I was given specific instructions to keep you occupied and safe, which means there is no way in hell that I'm going to let you run this obstacle course." I pout. "Come on. I told Anders I would bring you by his office."

I fold my arms over my chest. Ean narrows his eyes and

leans forward. Without saying a word, he grabs me by the waist and hefts me over his shoulder, knocking my hat and glasses off.

I pound his back with my fists and kick my legs. The roar of laughter follows us to our next destination.

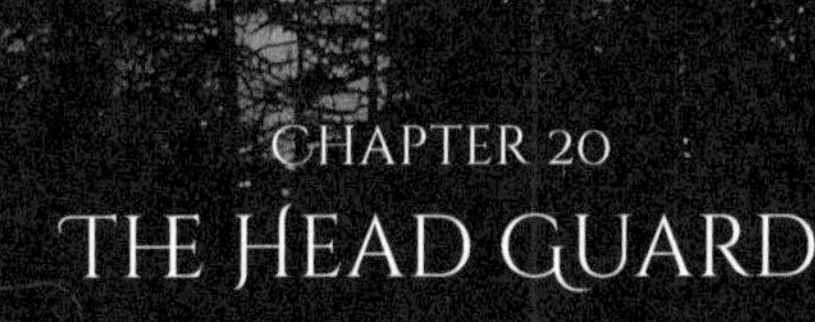

JESSICA
EIGHT YEARS AGO:
JUNE 25, 2016: 11:16 A.M.
EMERALD GUARDS TRAINING FACILITY

Ean pushes through the door of Anders's office. My glasses sit askew after he harshly placed them back on my face. I push them up the bridge of my nose with my index finger and adjust my hat so the brim faces forward, instead of the haphazard way he plopped it on my head.

Anders watches me without saying a word. I study his stern expression, his rigid posture, the way his arms rest stiffly on his desk. I have never visited Anders's office, and our interactions in my room at the clinic have been brief. But we are now in his domain.

Curiosity swells within me, and I glance around the room. Floor-to-ceiling shelves contain leather-bound books. Forgetting myself, I walk toward them and trail my fingers along their spines, reading titles as I pass.

Over the past couple of weeks, studying with Justin and Jeremy, I discovered that history is one of my favorite subjects. I especially love reading. Reading has been my solace since my vision returned, especially at night. Anders's office offers its own little library, something I hoped to see on our tour earlier. I would love to read some of these books, everything from sonnets and classic novels to history books from all over the world on the art of war and weapons. For me, this is so much better than any clothing or makeup store.

On the far wall before Anders's desk, a five-tier shelf holds books of various sizes and shapes. The spines are worn, cracked, and peeling from overuse. I gape at the numerous volumes, retrieve a small, slender leather book, and carefully open it. On the very first page, scrawled in neat cursive, is a name, while the second contains a date and a handwritten entry. These are not printed books but handwritten journals.

Staring at the journal in my hand, I smile. My heartbeat races with excitement. It's like finding treasure. I want to know who wrote these. There are so many of them. Were all these written by one person? A strong urge compels me to start with the very first book. Would Anders let me read these?

Anders stands from his desk and strides toward me. "So, you like to read?" He gently lifts the book from my hand and returns it to its space. Before I can protest, he reaches for the first book on the top shelf and hands it to me. "These are journals from the original Obsidian Pack Alpha, who we now refer to as the original head guard. Of course, while most shifters can live over 150 years, many of the head guards, due to war, have not lived as long. These journals are passed down from head guard to head guard. They detail a series of events that you will never read in history texts and accounts of their personal lives."

I wonder if Anders keeps his own journals. Where would he keep them?

Anders laughs. "I do keep my own journals but in a secret place. Only my replacement will have access to them once I pass or leave my position, as is tradition. Many Alphas keep the same tradition. It's a way for the former Alphas to leave their legacy behind and help guide the future Alphas in their current role. It was once thought of as a way for the future Alphas to understand the foundation of how the pack came to be and hopefully to prevent the current Alpha from repeating mistakes from the past."

Anders pauses. Emotion crosses his features, but he quickly masks it and offers me a small smile.

"History lessons are designed to teach future generations how to analyze and solve problems in the present and understand the past leaders and previous cultures. They're supposed to strengthen our critical thinking skills. Today, with social media, technology, and, well, just the basic understanding of history being manipulated, we have forgotten who we are and where we came from. As shifters, we forgot how to rely on our basic animal survival instincts." He turns to the shelf full of journals. "As the head guard, I try to teach the recruits the importance of who we are, what we protect, and what we represent. That is why the history of the LS territory is the most important lesson the recruits learn."

I look down at the journal. I could learn so much, not just from these journals but also from Anders. I hand the journal back to him. I don't want to ruin it, and I don't know where I will go once I heal. Maybe, one day, I can return, and he will let me read these precious artifacts of our history. We can sit and have meaningful conversations about the past.

Anders finally takes the journal after studying me for a moment and places it on the top shelf. "It will be here when you are ready to read them, although I prefer it doesn't leave my office."

I furrow my brow, unsure how to interpret his words. I don't want false hope, so I glance at the floor and nod.

He rests his hand on my shoulder. "All this talk about journals and history gives me an idea." Returning to his desk, he opens a drawer and passes me a leather-bound book. Imprinted in the leather, filled with gold overlay, the cover depicts an emblem. A dark green emerald sits in the center, and diamonds embellish each corner of a triangle.

I delicately trace my fingers over the design, loving the way it feels. I open the cover to reveal a blank page. I arch my eyebrows. What is this?

He clears his throat. "I know that you can't remember anything prior to waking up in the clinic, but I think this might help. Journal writing isn't just about documenting events. It's about reflection. You could write about your experiences, discoveries about yourself, maybe even your nightmares."

I run my hand over the emblem again. This looks expensive. I can't accept this. I shake my head and give the journal back to him. But he doesn't take it.

"The emblem on the cover is the guard's crest designed by the first head guard. The emerald represents the Emerald Pack. The white diamonds represent the white wolf species. I think this was meant for you, Little One."

Hanging my head, I fight the tears that threaten to fall. I fidget, unsure why Anders is so invested in my wellbeing. When the doctor decides to discharge me from the clinic, I will most likely be sent to an orphanage. With my memory gone, I cannot aid Anders in investigating my attack. Because I'm not from this territory nor belong to the Emerald Pack, there really is no reason to investigate it, unless someone reports a missing child to the guards.

Anders narrows his eyes. "You are definitely not going to an orphanage, and because you're still recovering, according to Dr. York, you will be here for a while." He chuckles softly. "You're quite observant, aren't you?"

I scoff. I don't have a choice. My vision sucks. I can't talk. My only option is to listen and take note of my surroundings. I never know when someone will attack or betray me. So, I must be prepared. One can never be too sure, and I won't repeat the mistake of assuming I will stay with a pack when I am not asked. The memory of Alpha Agnus returning me to the guards still stings.

"On second thought, you're not as observant as I thought," Anders counters, forcing me out of my internal rant.

My eyes widen. Anders is talking to me as if I spoke aloud. I cock my head to the side. How is he doing this?

He laughs. "It's not me. You are doing it. It's quite a neat little talent. I have not encountered many shifters who can mind-link outside of their animal form, including very powerful Alphas."

I shake my head. Alphas? I am no Alpha. How does a mind-link actually work? Did I do it on purpose, or does it just happen? Like the twins, they can communicate only with each other through their link.

"You think too much. It makes me wonder, when you find your voice again, if you will talk nonstop, like you do in your head."

I snort. *Can you blame me, if the only conversations I can carry occur in my own head?*

Grinning, he replies, "Alpha Agnus warned me you were a bit of a wiseass."

CHAPTER 21

FALLING INTO ROUTINE

JESSICA
EIGHT YEARS AGO:
JUNE 30, 2016: 6:45 A.M.
EMERALD PACK CLINIC

The guards and I adopt a comfortable routine. Ean visits in the morning and takes me for a walk around the training facility. Then, I meet Anders in his office, where I sit with him for a couple of hours. If a situation happens and needs his attention, I curl up in one of his chairs and read the journals of the original head guard. I take his other books to the clinic and pore over them every night.

Charlie picks me up at Anders's office to walk me to my room. The first time he stays with me, he brings his guitar and sings. I become mesmerized by how he moves his fingers over the strings and simultaneously fingers the keys, intrigued by the coordination required to strum, change notes, and sing simultaneously. The music causes the pain in my body to subside. My heart doesn't ache. My nerve endings don't jump. I feel safe. When I close my eyes, I feel whole again, alive—not broken, scarred, and stuck in a clinic room. After a few songs, I ask Charlie to teach me how to play. Giving me his flirty smile, he obliges, and now, he teaches me every day.

Sodie visits in the evenings. He teaches me how to play poker, trumps, and blackjack. He promises that once I improve, he will show me how to gamble. I think about playing cards with the twins and test my ability to beat them at some of these games.

Liam takes the night shift. He enters with that same pinched expression. He sits in the corner of the room at an angle, where he can see both my bed and the door, all night reading, never once checking on or speaking to me. He never uses the bathroom, takes a walk, or moves just for a break. Sometimes, when I'm sure he isn't watching, I study him over the pages of my book. When contemplating his own reading, he rubs his lower lip or plays with the diamond stud in his left ear. He sighs and runs his long fingers through his hair when he seems frustrated. Occasionally, his mouth twitches, trying to prevent a smile. I can't help but wonder if he silently studies me, too. The heat of a blush rises from my chest to my cheeks so I bury my face in the page. If he even notices me at all.

Maybe because of silence at night, I can't help longing for the twins. Usually, by now, they fall asleep over their textbooks or recline nearby, snoring. Although I appreciate the quiet, especially whenever they're around, I miss the chaos. I miss them.

A dull ache throbs in the middle of my back as I sit in my clinic bed. I set my book down to stretch and twist, but the twinge remains. It doesn't move. I assess whether I have pain anywhere else. It's so hard to tell. My body hurts all the time. This ache is new... and persistent. Ignoring it for now—it's tolerable—I return to reading.

Leaning back against my pillow, I stare out the window. The sky lightened, indicating early morning, but a dreary grayness looms. A light drizzle starts, reflecting my mood.

"Hey. You feeling okay?" Liam asks.

I forgot he still sat in the corner. I perform a quick internal check. Yep, all the everyday aches and pains are present and accounted for, especially in my back. I contemplate that dull ache—it's not worse, just still there. I shrug it off, pushing myself to the edge of the bed, and nod.

Liam looks at me, running his index finger below his lower lip.

Heat creeps into my cheeks. I turn my head and continue to stare out the window.

Right on schedule, Ean arrives, breaking me out of my reflection. I welcome the distraction. "You ready to start your day with all this awesomeness?"

I glance first at Liam, who frowns still studying me, and then watch Ean walk into the room with his usual smile.

"Alright. You know the routine. Breakfast first, and then we can get you out of here." Ean places a cup of my meal replacement shake in front of me. The sight of it makes me want to puke. In fact, I don't think I finished the one from last night. The cup sits on my nightstand... empty. Huh? I don't remember finishing it. I turn toward Liam, but he already left. Did he drink it?

Shifting back to eat my "breakfast," a sharp pain rips through me, forcing me to lean forward. I squeeze my eyes shut for a moment and open them slowly as the pain fades to a dull ache.

"Everything okay?" Ean asks with concern.

I nod, lift my shake, and drink it as fast as possible. A change of scenery will help with my mood and my pain.

We don't take our usual path this time. Ean speaks, but I

don't listen today. My stomach hurts, and nausea threatens to take hold. I probably drank my shake too fast, so I just breathe and ignore it.

Using my surroundings as a distraction, I glimpse Liam leaving a building. With a book in one hand, he casually strides onto the grassy area, likely heading toward the dorms. A group of three guys exit the building after him, walking faster.

One of them shouts, "Hey, Fitzpatrick. I'm not done talking to you!" Liam maintains his casual pace, not even glancing back to acknowledge the guy.

The other two increase their pace. The one with curly, dirty-blond hair knocks the book out of his hand and sneers, "You think you're better than the rest of us just because you got the VIP assignment."

Liam stops walking, only to pick up his book from the ground.

I grip Ean by the shirt and point at Liam. He shakes his head. "This is the way things are. If he's going to be a guard, he needs to learn to stand up for himself." Facing the group, Ean crosses his arms over his chest and watches. I mimic Ean's stance and fold my arms over my middle.

All three guys now surround Liam. The one who shouted first runs a hand through his dark brown hair. He is slightly bigger than Liam, but I can't see his face. "You know what I think? I think you have a thing for her. I hear she looks like a boy," the guy with the dark brown hair taunts.

Liam doesn't respond. He pushes past the guys. The third guy, the silent one, wears a hat. His build is similar to Ean's, but he isn't anywhere as tall. He grabs Liam by the shoulder and forces him to face his friend.

"I bet it must bring back some great memories. Doesn't it?" The dark-brown-haired guy steps closer to Liam. The curly-haired one whacks the book out of Liam's hand again.

"Maybe I should pay her a visit and show her what a real man can do."

Liam yanks his shoulder away from Hat Guy and walks away.

"Come on. Fight me! I know you want to."

Liam retrieves his book for a second time. They won't leave him alone. Two of them snatch him from behind and hold his arms down.

The ringleader cocks his arm back to hit Liam, and I tug on Ean's shirt. *Stop them. Stop them please!* Thunderclaps and dark clouds roll in overhead. *Ean, stop them!! It's three against one. This isn't right!* I motion with my hands, but my efforts are futile. If he won't do anything, I will. Pushing away from him, I take three steps before Ean drags me back by my hoodie.

"It's okay, Little One. Watch." Thunder claps again. My heartbeat races. When I turn back to the fight, Liam somehow manages to release himself from their hold. I watch in frustration as all three guys punch, hit, and seize Liam.

He blocks each kick, each punch, and strikes back. Liam puts one of the attackers on the ground and lands two punches to his face when another jumps him from behind. Liam rolls out of the way just in time, jumps up and kicks him in the face. He clutches the one who started this whole ordeal by the throat and mercilessly hits him again and again.

Blood spews everywhere, and an image flashes in my mind. I no longer watch Liam hit his opponent but rather see myself receiving blows to the face. In slow motion, a fist punches me, and someone—a teenager with brown hair, not much younger than these guys—yells, "I fucking hate you!"

Stop! I scream in my head as lightning streaks through the sky. Liam halts mid-hit and turns toward me. I stare back. *Please, stop!*

He looks down at the guy in his grips, leans forward, and,

with a snarled expression, grounds out, "If you go near her, I will rip your fucking head off!" He releases his grip, and the guy flops to the ground. Liam strides over to his book lying open in the dirt, picks it up, and walks away for a final time.

All three attackers lie in a bloody heap. My stomach curls, and nausea upheaves my insides. I scurry to the nearest bush and lose all of my stomach contents.

Ean pats my back. "Whoa, there, Little One. I think I should get you back to the clinic. Too much excitement for the morning."

Still dry heaving, I shake my head. Another streak of lightning flashes in the sky, followed by a crack of thunder.

Anders isn't happy with me. His pinched expression stares straight ahead. Even though he is busy and needs to follow up with Liam, he insists on escorting me to the clinic. He finally glances over and asks, "What was it about the fight that made you sick?"

I replay the whole fight in my head, the flashback I saw, and the look on Liam's face as he hit the other recruit.

Anders abruptly stops and meets my eye directly. "Do that again." Confused by his request, I shrug. He claims, "It was like watching a movie. Replay that whole incident in your mind again, especially that flashback of the person hitting you. I want you to hold that memory."

It's no use. I never see faces. Even if in my line of vision, it's too blurry or distorted by shadows.

He leans down, resting his hands on his knees, to be eye level with me. "Just give it a go. Plus, I want to see and hear what you saw." I do as he asks. When he is satisfied, we return to my room, where he leaves me so he can attend to the recruits, promising someone will come by shortly.

Charlie arrives sometime after lunch. He shows me a notebook with thin scrawled handwriting. He says that I inspired him to write a song. Reading the lyrics, I give him a tight-lipped smile and point to his guitar.

With his sinfully charming smile, he obliges and plays some chords, but it just doesn't fit. Charlie wants it to be a slow song. To me, though, my instincts scream the lyrics fit better with a faster tempo, more upbeat, one that matches his personality and his style. Together, we change the music chords and rearrange the lyrics until it finally all clicks together.

Charlie chucks my chin. "You got some real talent, Little One. It makes me wonder if you ever played before."

I lift my left hand and wiggle my fingers.

He rubs his thumb over my fingertips. "No calluses," he confirms, gazing at me with a serious expression. "I hope you get your voice back. It would be nice if you and I could sing a duet together."

I huff and wrinkle my nose, pushing my glasses up simultaneously.

He raises his brow and smirks. "Don't give me that look. Call it intuition. I think you are musically inclined." He shrugs. "You know everything and could probably sing, too."

I roll my eyes.

"I'm serious. I think we could make a great duet. Look at what we just did in a few hours." I stare at him blankly. "I guess in time we'll find out." He winks, and just like that, he resumes his flirty, joking ways and begins to pack up his belongings. "I can't wait to show the guys what we put together," he gushes, clapping his hands together. "I will see you tomorrow and let you know how it went." He leans over and gives me a hug. "Get some rest, Little One." He kisses my cheek.

Liam walks in just as Charlie pulls away. Wearing his regular sour expression, he lifts his chin in Charlie's direction and retreats to his usual post.

Charlie smirks, watching Liam, before collecting his guitar and notebook to leave. Liam is earlier today. I assume Sodie will stay with me tonight then.

Sighing, I gather my bag of toiletries—a gift from Shakti—and head to the bathroom. When I return, I put everything back in my nightstand drawer. On the bedside table sit a little medicine cup full of vitamins and supplements and a tall glass filled with my meal replacement shake.

"The nurse just came. She said she will be back with your injections in a few minutes."

I nod without turning to look at Liam. I grab a beanie from my nightstand and notice a notepad and pen next to it. Sliding the beanie on my head, I don't disturb the tablet.

"Charlie returned not long after you went into the bathroom and brought a notepad. He said in case inspiration hits you and you want to write more song lyrics." Smiling to myself, I pick up the notepad and pen.

Liam rarely talks—this is the most he's spoken to me since I met him. I like the sound of his voice. That slight accent—wow. It's soothing, sexy even. If he talked more, I wouldn't mind listening. I blush and quickly scribble a question on the paper, holding it up for him to read.

Slowly, he reads the paper and then looks at me, then back to the paper. "No. You're stuck with me until morning."

I offer okay sign and walk away to my bed. Nervously, I glance at Liam in the corner of the room when Mimi enters with the injections. She asks to see the wounds on my back and the surgical incision on my throat, and I freeze.

I forgot about dressing changes. Usually, Sodie is here for this part. With his expressed interest in the medical field, he tends to help the nurse. It never bothered me for some reason with him around for my regular check-in. Mimi passes her wound care kit to Liam and chastises me, discovering I haven't taken my meds yet.

Embarrassment warms my cheeks. I have to change into the clinic gown that exposes my backside.

Dr. York arrives shortly after Mimi leaves to conduct his routine assessment and ask his questions of the day. I probably should tell him about the new pain in my back and the stomach discomfort. But I don't want to endure more tests, scans, and another treatment plan. I'm sure, with a short nap, I will be fine. I've been pushing myself, which Dr. York warns me about.

With another cross over my heart, I promise to sleep tonight after I finish my shake. I really can't wait to get this stupid tube out of my stomach. Maybe it is causing some of the discomfort. If it's still there tomorrow, I'll tell him then. After Dr. York leaves, I lift the glass and drink.

Frowning at the pale-yellow concoction, I only manage to swallow a third of it. I already feel full.

"You have some of it on your upper lip." Jumping at the sound of Liam's voice, I look over at him. I swipe at my lip with my fingers. He chuckles, stands, and pulls a paper napkin from the dispenser on the wall near the sink. Dragging the chair Dr. York sat in earlier closer, he straddles it and resumes reading.

Seriously, is he going to sit there in front of me while I drink this crappy-ass drink? But he doesn't move, nor does he look up from his book. Looking down at my hands, I don't know what to do with myself. Even if Sodie can't hear my thoughts, he talks to me about various topics. Glancing around the room, like I haven't done it a million times already, my mind wanders back to Liam's fight.

Did he learn how to fight in the program? Gods, to think I tried to stop it myself because Ean wasn't doing a damn thing.

Like I could ever protect someone like Liam. I didn't exactly do a stellar job protecting myself, obviously. I wonder if I will be able to stay here? Would Anders teach me how to fight like Liam. If whoever hurt me found me again, then I could fight them off, or at least defend myself.

I chance a peek at Liam, only to find him staring at me. Shit! Quickly searching for a distracting task, I attempt to finish my shake. Making sure I wipe my face with the napkin, I set the glass down and scoot into bed, feigning interest in my book.

"I worried that I scared you off, after you watched that fight," he confesses.

I frown. I was overwhelmed at first but mostly concerned about him. I was more frustrated with Ean for not interfering. Swiveling around to face him, I shake my head, dropping my gaze to my lap.

"I heard you went straight to Anders, and you shared what you witnessed to him."

Still averting my eyes, I nod.

A soft laugh escapes him. I blush at the sound. "I also heard you tried to stop the fight, and Ean stopped you."

I want to bury my face in this mattress and suffocate myself with the blankets right now. Gods, hearing him say it makes me feel like a complete idiot.

His large hand rests on my knee. "Thank you for having my back. I don't encounter that very often. It meant a lot to me that you would even try, especially knowing what you've been through."

Nodding briskly, I stare at his hand. His thumb gently brushes the fabric of my pants a few times before he removes it. An uncomfortable silence surrounds us. I shift back, leaning against the mattress, and take a final sidelong look at him before picking up my book again.

"You should get some sleep," he proclaims.

The clock on my wall indicates it's barely eight o'clock. I narrow my eyes. I don't intend to fall asleep this early.

He sighs, stands from his chair, turns on the lamp near my bed, and switches off the overhead light. Returning to my bedside, he holds out his hand. "Book."

I shake my head. He motions with a "gimme" gesture. Pouting, I plop the book in his open palm. He places it next to his on the table. Hmm, he's reading *The Art of War*. I read that two nights ago.

"Glasses."

I cross my arms over my chest and wrinkle my nose.

He chuckles and repeats, "Glasses."

I roll my eyes, remove my lenses, and hand them over. He presses the button that lowers the head of my bed, grabs his book, and returns to his chair.

Lying flat on my back is uncomfortable, but I don't want to turn my back to him or face him. Why is he sitting there? My face feels warm. I like it better when he isn't so close. I squirm, trying to find a more comfortable position, but I can't take it. Finally laying on my side, I avoid looking directly at him.

"Most people close their eyes when they sleep," he mumbles.

I sigh. Suddenly, a sharp pain tears through the center of my body. I tuck my knees up to my chest, but this time, the pain doesn't dissipate. I squeeze my eyes closed and will the pain away. That doesn't work either.

A warm hand grasps my shoulder. Before I can open my eyes to look up, a wave of nausea hits me. Pushing myself up into a sitting position, everything starts to spin. I feel myself fall forward or sideways, unsure which direction is up or down.

As the dizziness starts to recede, I slowly open one eye. Liam stands in front of me, holding me upright. Another sharp pain rips through my body, more intense than the first. Resting my head on Liam's chest, I attempt to regulate my breathing, but the pain is unbearable. Nausea overcomes me, and my stomach clenches. I try to push Liam away, but it is too late.

I cover my face, mortified, when another rush of pain and nausea begins again. It feels like someone is stabbing me through my back into my stomach.

Liam rubs my back. "Breathe. Just breathe. I got you. The doc or the nurse should be here any minute."

My head spins, and the sound of rushing water fills my ears. Muffled voices murmur around me, but I can't decipher their words. Then, I succumb to silence and darkness.

CHAPTER 22
SODIE'S SECRET

LIAM
EIGHT YEARS AGO:
JUNE 30, 2016: 8:25 P.M.
EMERALD PACK CLINIC

Where the hell is the doctor and the nurse? I pressed the emergency button what feels like an eternity ago. Jessica slumps forward in pain. I should probably rush out and call for help, but I don't want to leave her alone. She doesn't make a sound, but her face contorts and scrunches in agony. It's so intense, I can almost feel it myself. She tries to push me away, but I refuse to move in case she falls over.

She pukes all over me. And I don't care. Her safety matters more.

Shit, why didn't she tell the doctor what happened this morning? I sat in the corner of the room and watched her downplay all the answers to the doctor's questions. It wasn't my place to interfere or call her out.

At the same time, she didn't really lie. He didn't ask her if anything new started today or last night. I *knew* something was wrong and didn't do anything about it.

I glance down at my vomit-stained shirt and pants. Instead of a sickly yellow color, though, bright red blood mixes with what looks like dark coffee grounds. I rub her back, murmuring to keep her calm. I don't even know what I'm saying. I just try to hold onto my own control as anxiety threatens to take over.

My heart hammers against my chest. Control my breathing. Keep it together. Fuck, I need to *do* something. If the doctor doesn't come soon, I will take her to him. Sodie arrives.

"Get the doctor or the nurse now!" I bark.

His steps stutter, and he rushes out the door. His quick footfalls disappear down the hall, and he shouts for help. When he runs back through the door, Jessica slumps over in my arms.

"Where the fuck are they?" I growl.

Sodie looks me up and down. "She's vomiting blood," he claims.

Anxiety squeezes around my heart as her body goes limp, her lips turning white. "I'm fucking carrying her."

Before I can gather her in my arms, Sodie grabs my shirt. "Wait. Let me try something."

"We don't have time!" I shout, ready to punch him if he tries to stop me again. Her breathing grows shallow. Her heart rate slows to a dangerous rhythm.

He looks at me with wide eyes. "Trust me, please." He climbs into her hospital bed and, reaching between us, places one hand over her abdomen and another on her back. A bright white light emanates from his hands.

Finally, footsteps approach from the hall. The doctor and nurse rush into the room, and they stand in stunned silence.

The doctor takes in the sight of my clothing and the puddle on the floor. Turning to the nurse, he tells her to call for more staff and prepare the small operating room.

Despite the fear in Sodie's expression, he continues to hold his position. Jessica starts to stir. Her breathing slowly returns to normal. Her heartbeat accelerates slightly, and color returns to her ashen-colored lips.

The doctor comes forward. The light emanating from Sodie's hands fades. He releases his hold on Jessica and backs away. I don't move.

"Liam, I need to take a look at her," the doctor demands.

I hesitate, still clutching her to my chest, but then shuffle to the side to make room. The doctor glances at Sodie warily. Then, he gives Jessica his full attention.

Anders races into the room, along with the nurse. The doctor announces, "I need to get her into surgery right now." Jessica hasn't opened her eyes or regained consciousness. I don't want to let her go. "This is life or death. We need to go now."

We spend two days and three nights in fucking hell. Jessica had some random, spontaneous internal bleeding, the cause of which the doctor can't determine. She lost so much blood, her organs start to fail. The doctor begins a blood transfusion, and she reacts horribly to it. He can't tell if it is a bad batch of donor blood or if she built an immunity from before.

When the medical team stabilizes her, they ask everyone to get tested to see who is a match. The only one who comes close is one of the recruits named Darwin, and thankfully, he donates blood to her.

Still, even with the blood transfusions, her body won't heal. The wounds she sustained from her initial injuries break open, and she develops an infection. It is one thing after another. I overhear the medical team say over and over how they have never seen anything like it.

Her body endures so much. She was doing so well, but now she took one giant leap backward. She's back on a breathing machine, this time with a tube down her throat. Heart monitors beep at us, and IV bags hang from a pole. No one can figure it out.

I think the only piece keeping her alive is, at every chance, Sodie uses his healing magic on her. Even he can't understand why it isn't enough.

I sit at her bedside and hold her hand, just like I did when we brought her home from the Whitemore plantation, internally praying for some kind of miracle. Is it too much to ask for another one? She already survived the first time.

A loud argument starts in the hall. I kiss the back of her hand before standing from my chair to check outside.

"No!" Jeremy shouts.

"I'm sorry, boys. I think we have done all that we can. Without the machines..." Shakti's voice breaks.

The doctor gently squeezes Shakti's shoulder. Anders turns around, swiping both hands through his hair. Fat tears fall down Ean's face. This must be fucking bad if Ean is crying. I can't even look at Charlie or Chris. I might lose my shit if I do. Elias tilts his head back, staring at the ceiling.

"You can't. Mom, please," Justin whispers. Shakti breaks down into tears, turning into the doctor's embrace.

Jeremy's face turns an angry shade of red. His breathing is labored, and his hands ball into fists at his sides. "Are you going to call Luke? Will you to tell him that all his efforts were for nothing because we gave up on her?!"

I can't listen. She is not dying! I feel like someone stabbed me in the fucking chest. Heat radiates off my body. My chest heaves. My vision goes red, and I'm on the brink of losing control. But I don't fucking care. I'll burn this whole fucking place down if she dies.

A giant hand wraps around my throat, and my body slams against a wall. I roar in anger. My fist hits a solid object, but it doesn't budge. Their hand squeezes harder, cutting off my air supply.

"Get it together!" a harsh voice whispers in my ear. "We have enemies here. I will not lose you, too!" My rage blinds me, and I grasp for anything to grab a hold.

The hand loosens, and I'm pulled into a strong bear hug. I succumb and wrap my arms around a large body, gripping the back of his shirt. "She can't!" I sob. "She can't die." As soon as I let myself fall apart, I recognize Ean.

Sodie is the last one to hear the news. He loses it as badly as the twins and I, if not worse. We hang our heads, silently crying, as we witness one more person who cared about Jessica lose faith. It's amazing how much of an impact she made on all of us in such a short amount of time.

When Sodie calms down, we follow the doctor into the room. We solemnly watch as the nurse, with shaky hands and flowing tears, unhooks the IV lines, shuts off the breathing machine, and removes the tube from her throat. However, the doctor stops her before she turns off the heart monitor.

Shakti's mate, Nathan, wraps his arms around her, gently kissing the top of her head as she sobs into his chest. He also rests his hand on Justin's shoulder. Justin in turn reaches for Jeremy's.

In sixteen hours, there have been no changes in Jessica's vital signs. The rhythmic beep of her heart echoes around the room. Nathan convinces everyone to take a breather. Sodie and I volunteer to stay and notify the others if anything changes.

Earlier, we pulled Jessica's bed to the middle of the room and situated chairs around it so everyone could sit with her. Sodie occupies the chair across from me. He looks like crap. I can only imagine I must look the same.

Emily strides into the room, her long black hair tied in a high ponytail, arms crossed over her chest, lips pursed, like she's ready to tackle anything in her way. Her dark eyes, nearly as black as Elias's, roam over Jessica's body. Her eyes widen in shock before they soften and then shine with unshed tears.

"Why didn't anyone call me sooner? I had to hear about this from Luke, who is in another country. My own brothers are here every day, and I didn't receive a single phone call or text. You look like shit, by the way. Do you need a break? I can sit with her and let you know if anything happens."

She sighs, and I squeeze my eyes shut. I don't have the energy for Emily's ramblings, but the irritation brewing inside of me isn't her doing. I open my eyes to meet her questioning gaze and release a long breath.

"You hadn't met her. And you were at summer school in the city."

"That's not fair. I wanted to meet her as soon as I heard she was here, but every time I asked, I was told it wasn't a good time. I drove here as fast as I could without getting another speeding ticket."

My heart softens. Knowing her, she must have dropped everything as soon as she heard from Luke to be here. "I'm sure your dad appreciated it."

She nods and plops herself in a chair next to Sodie. "Yeah, except this is the one time I think he would have been a little more forgiving," she jokes.

I offer her a halfhearted smirk. Sodie hasn't looked up or

acknowledged Emily since she walked in. He just sits there, eyes vacantly staring at Jessica's still form.

Emily gently nudges his arm with her shoulder. "I'm Emily, by the way."

He slowly rotates his head and tips his chin. "I'm Sodie, one of the recruits."

"I assumed so. It's nice to meet you. I heard you're one of the highest ranking recruits, aside from this guy." She points her thumb at me. "The leads are quite impressed with your work ethic and perseverance. They have high hopes for you as a guard. That's why you were assigned to VIP detail."

He flinches at her words. His eyes glass over and shift over to meet mine. Without saying anything, he asks if he can trust her. I nod. He hovers his hands over Jessica's abdomen and her heart, infusing her body with his healing magic. Emily gasps.

As the minutes pass and nothing happens, our hope dwindles further. With a heavy sigh, Sodie drops back into his chair. Despair grows heavy in the room.

Emily rests a hand on Jessica's leg. "I read somewhere that magic healers can pull energy from other magic wielders to strengthen their magic. I'm not a magic wielder, but some generations back, we are rumored to carry white wolf shifter blood. Maybe if you pull from my energy and tap into Liam's, we could help."

Sodie scoffs. "You read that somewhere, like from one of those damn romance novels girls like to read."

Emily glares. "If you must know, asshole, I read it in a journal of my great-grandfather's, who happens to be the son of the original head guard. And for the record, I don't read romance novels."

Sodie's eyes widen. Right, he had no idea that Emily is Elias's daughter.

"Just do it, numb nuts, before everyone returns," Emily

sneers, leaning over the bed and placing a hand on my shoulder. I rest my hand over Jessica's heart. With a tilt of my head, I encourage Sodie, who eventually places one hand over mine and another on Jessica's torso.

Together, we give Jessica everything we have.

When Shakti and Chris's mate, Tater, return, we are exhausted. But there is still no change. Sensing the weariness deep in our bones, Shakti forces the three of us out of the room.

"You three need a break. We'll take over and call if... anything happens." Shakti promises with a break in her voice. Tater rubs her arm, turning her own head away to wipe at the moisture around her eyes. Tater, like Emily, hasn't met Jessica officially. And yet she already mourns her.

My gut twists at the sorrow on both of their faces. Both Chris and Elias's family have been in and out to support Shakti and the twins. They are a tight-knit family and why solidarity and unity are instilled among the guards.

We all nod. Sodie is the first to stand. I give Jessica's hand a final squeeze and reluctantly walk toward the door.

JESSICA
PRESENT DAY:
MARCH 31, 2025

Carmen gawks at me with wide eyes. "How the hell are you alive?"

I smirk. "I ask myself that same question all the time. At this point, I should have died twice."

She shakes her head. "On top of the trauma you already suffered, you survived internal bleeding, anaphylaxis, sepsis, and organ failure. I mean, the list goes on. How?"

I laugh softly. "Dr. York couldn't figure it out either. He called in specialists, and they didn't understand it. No one really knows how it happened in the first place. I mean, there were theories." I lift my hands and shrug.

"So just like that, you got better and woke up."

"Not exactly. After I they took me off life support, I didn't die, as the medical team and specialist predicted. I spontaneously started breathing on my own, and my heart rate remained slow but steady. After about twenty-four hours, maybe... Sorry. This is all secondhand information. My timeline could be wrong. My vital signs improved, and I began to heal. Apparently, there was only one donor from which I could receive without a negative reaction, so they gave that a try, monitoring closely for any signs of rejection. When there were none, they moved forward and gradually incorporated other treatments. It was very limited because my body just healed on its own, like a normal, nontransitioned shifter should. It took about a week or so before I woke up."

Carmen purses her lips. "Did you experience other medical emergencies?"

"Yeah. Near-death experiences seem to be my forte." Licking my lips, I gaze around the room. "My brothers and I have a running joke, you know, because I'm adopted without any recollection of where I came from. They used to tease me that I was part feline."

"Feline?"

Christian and I bark with laughter at Carmen's question. Clearly, she doesn't understand.

"You know, cats have nine lives. I think I'm down to my last one."

CHAPTER 24
SHADOWS AND LIGHT

SHADOW

EIGHT YEARS AGO:
JULY 25, 2016: 10 A.M.
EMERALD GUARDS TRAINING FACILITY

Anders blows out a harsh breath and places a single fist in front of his mouth. He's stressed, like the weight of the world rests on his shoulders.

"If you tell me what's going on, I can offer some advice." Not sure how great my advice will be, but if it's guard related or legal counseling, that I can do.

He shakes his head. "A lot has happened since you last checked in. I didn't want to involve you because there wasn't much you could do, and I wanted you focused on school."

"I see. Obviously, you're experiencing some kind of internal war. Normally, you look more put together."

He scoffs. "I take it that's an idiom for you look like shit," he deadpans.

I stare at him blankly.

He sighs and replaces that mask I'm accustomed to seeing him wear—the "head guard" mask. "Actually, there is something I wanted to run by you. A few weeks ago, there was another incident between Marcus, Dustin, and Boris."

"Let me guess. Liam was their target?"

Anders grunts. I'm not surprised to hear this. From the moment Marcus Greystone stepped foot on training grounds, he has been gunning for Liam. I tried everything to prevent Greystone and his two cousins from the Northern A territory from becoming a part of the recruit program.

"Alpha Greystone got involved?" He most likely pulled a political card, which is how his son and his two nephews from his Luna's side were able to get in.

"You know he did. He coddles that punk, even when he does something wrong. I also suspect that they're here for other reasons. We've been keeping a close eye on those three and divulging very little guard information, which is a disadvantage to the rest of the recruits."

"Sounds like you have everything taken care of."

He pauses and shakes his head. The guard program has been threatened before. He and the other two leads have this under control. Unfortunately, with Alpha Greystone involved, this isn't a legal issue. This is more of a political problem, and once politics enter the arena, the situation is not always black and white. But Anders knows this already. He doesn't need my advice on this situation. I wait for him to continue.

"Marcus verbally threatened Jessica in a sexual manner. It was probably just a barb or a taunt. With Liam's history with the Greystones, though, he responded to his threat physically. My concern is that, in retaliation, Marcus will make good on his threat."

"Jessica?"

"She's our VIP... case... for lack of a better word." Before I can inquire further, Chris and Elias walk into the office.

"Shadow, been a while. How are you doing?" Chris asks as I stand from my chair and dip my chin in greeting. Chris mirrors my gesture and sits on the edge of Anders's desk. He comes across as friendly and a little charming, but don't let that fool you. He is one hell of a guard and one hell of an interrogator. I've seen him rip apart shifters who thought they were tough and make them cry.

"Doing well. Thank you for asking," I reply. Took me years to respond to a simple question in less of a formal way. I dip my head to Elias as he takes the seat opposite my own. After everyone else is situated, I return to my seat.

"I hear you just wrapped up your bachelor's degree. Heading into law school?"

"I actually am finishing up my last year in law school now."

Chris frowns. "I thought you were Charlie's age?"

"I am. I finished my bachelor's degree early." My lips twitch into a forced smile.

Chris nods. "Yes, now I remember. Must have heard the information wrong." Chris rubs his hands together. "So, we are all here. What do you have for us, Shadow?"

"It took me a while to gain permission to enter Territory Two under the guise of a recruiting officer looking for potential recruits. Fortunately for me, Alpha Rhineheart's PA was the one who responded to my most recent email. Unfortunately, too much time passed, and my attempts at an investigation came up a little short."

Anders steeples his hands and rests his fingertips against his lips. "Well, let's see what you discovered."

Reaching down, I retrieve the items I brought with me and place them on the desk. "There is no missing child reported throughout the entire territory. I didn't even come across a fresh grave or a headstone in their pack's cemetery. I hacked into the school's database, and there is no female child listed with a first or last name starting with 'G'."

Anders frowns. Then, he asks, "The school uniform—was it a match?"

"Yes. All the students wore the same standard uniform as the one you gave me." He doesn't respond so I continue. "I did meet with one of the school staff—I believe she was a music teacher. She was the only one willing to speak with me, not that I got much information from her. This is pure speculation, but there was something terribly off about the entire pack, especially at the school. If I had to guess, everyone was... well, mourning mixed with a sense of fear. Except for a bunch of punk-ass teenagers who could use a lesson in manners, especially the punk who leads that group."

"Let me guess—the Alpha's boy?" Elias theorizes.

"I didn't sense he was an Alpha, just some punk with a mouth. He only caught my attention because he had a new scar on his left cheek."

"Like from a fight?" Anders asks, studying the two bags I placed on his desk. One contained the uniform from the girl they call Little One. "What's this?" He lifts up a backpack.

"After coming up empty-handed, I decided to walk through the forest, in case I could find anything on my way to the territory border, where she was found. I found that under some bushes."

Anders opens the backpack and passes items to Chris, who flips through the pages of a notebook.

"I also discovered a shredded jacket with a hood. It's in the bag with the uniform. Oddly enough, the tag is still intact, with the letter 'G' written on it. I found some markings on a tree not far from where I found the jacket. Several hundred yards away was the tree she was hung from."

Anders looks to both Chris and Elias. "What grade do you think this textbook belongs to?" He tosses it to me.

A slip of paper falls out. It's a photograph of a teenage girl with a heart-shaped face and platinum blonde hair tied in a long ponytail. Her striking dark eyebrows and thick, dark lashes contrast with the paleness of the rest of her hair. Full lips form a smile, showcasing straight white teeth. But her smile doesn't reach her eyes, clear and ice blue with a dark ring around them.

I'm mesmerized by her beauty. My heart rate increases, and I squirm in my seat. Huh, it's not like me to respond this way to anyone, let alone a picture of a young woman. The deep rumble of a distinct voice tries to push forward in my mind, but I force it down. Not now. Don't do this now.

Elias bends to look closer at the picture and then passes it to Chris. Chris inspects it, and a sad smile crosses his lips. He reads the words on the bottom of the picture. "Ruby Falls High School, class of 2016." He flips the photo over, but no inscription is written on the back. Class of 2016 means that girl should have graduated this year. She looks a bit young to graduate so soon.

Anders receives the photo, and I watch him intently. "Did you see a girl at the school who looks like this?" he prompts.

"If I saw a girl like that, she would have stood out." All the pack members, including their children, shared the same characteristics—chestnut brown hair and brown eyes. Like most packs, you can tell who belongs. Nowadays, though, packs intermingle, leaving their territory for school or business. The Ruby Falls Pack is a very traditional pack. They keep to themselves, and people rarely leave.

A firm knock interrupts us. Ean ushers in a short student wearing a baseball cap, glasses that cover most of his face, a large t-shirt, long gym shorts, and a worn pair of chucks.

Suddenly, a deep emotional ache fills my chest. My vision

tunnels. A burst of white light knocks me back into my chair and steals my breath.

His aura consumes the entire room, shedding the darkness and shadows that engulf me, realigning my soul. The light calls to me. I want to leap out of my chair and embrace it, embrace him. I grip the armrest, rooting firmly in place. Mentally, I shake off the strangeness of this feeling that formed deep in my chest. But this ache runs deeper than anything I have experienced before. The light curls around my heart and embeds itself in my soul.

"What did I tell you about your hat?" Anders teases.

What the fuck just happened? My head whips toward Ean, who hovers protectively. He nods at me in greeting and turns back to the student with a goofy grin. Confusion clouds the rational part of my brain.

The young man removes his hat, and Ean ruffles the already-disheveled hair—white-blonde hair. The student scrunches his face and brushes Ean's hand away before hugging Chris.

"Hello, Little One. Did you enjoy your walk this morning?"

Little One? Little One... Wait. Is this...?

Elias's booming voice fills the small office. "Why does he always get the first hug? What am I? Invisible?"

He, or rather she, nods at Chris, releases him, and walks toward Elias, who stands, dwarfing her already small stature. She hugs him, too.

"Did you get some sleep last night?" Elias asks. She nods. Elias gently touches her face, inspecting it like a doting father. His thumb trails the scarring along her left cheek. Satisfied, he drops his hand. "Good. Glad the boys are looking out for you."

Elias talks to her with so much tenderness. My heart squeezes. What is that? I rub my chest. Maybe I ate something recently that doesn't agree with me. No, I eat the exact same foods every day, at the same times. I never stray from my biological schedule.

Guiding her by the shoulders, Elias turns her to face me. "Little One, this is Shadow. He's one of our best guards, or he was. He lost his title since you outran him, too."

Ean scoffs. "Best guard? What the hell am I? I'm the one busting my ass training the newbies, while this one goes off to a fancy college."

"I don't see you doing any training now. Besides, I'll earn my title back eventually," I counter, lifting an eyebrow at Ean in a challenge. He's been training his whole life to become a guard. Then I arrived, and it all came naturally to me without trying. It frustrates him to no end, made worse when I don't respond to his jabs or his competitiveness.

His brows rise in surprise, assessing me. I realize my facial expression is not practiced. I don't usually banter with anyone. What did she do to me?

Little One timidly steps closer and holds out her hand to shake mine. Elias reaches out to stop her.

Normally, I don't shake hands or hug. I don't like being touched. Yet as I take her dainty hand, a burst of white light and a tingle of electricity snake up my arm and embed themselves into my chest. I study her face, her breathing. She doesn't appear to have the same response to me. Furrowing my brow, I bend forward slightly. How can this be? "Can you remove your glasses?" I ask.

She jerks back just a little, like I slapped her in the face.

"I didn't get a good look at you when we first met, watching you run away," I joke with a genuine smile. I don't want to intimidate or scare her away.

Reluctantly, she removes her ridiculously large glasses.

It's her—the girl in the picture. Same heart-shaped face. Dark contrasting eyebrows. Her eyelashes aren't as long as they were. I see the scars much clearer on the left side of her face, like someone deliberately cut into her flawless skin. A white puckering scar sits in the hollow of her throat. White scars run along her arms and across her wrist.

What the hell did they do to you?

Anger spreads through my entire being. I want to kill the fucker who hurt her. I swallow the emotions that flare up in my chest and clear my throat. "I trust you are doing well?"

I wince. I sound like an asshole. I feel eyes staring at me. Everyone in the room scrutinizes me.

She offers a tight-lipped smile and a nod. Then, she turns away from me to face Anders.

"Yes. I received your application. We can discuss it when I'm done with this meeting," Anders says to her.

I look around the room. Was I so lost in my thoughts that I didn't hear her speak?

Chris laughs. "Little One, girls are not allowed in the guard." She swivels toward Elias. "Don't look at me. I don't make the rules, Little One. You know that." She stares at him for a moment, then at Chris, and back to Anders.

Anders raises a hand. "Jessica, I promise we will talk about this later. No more arguments." She emits an irritated sigh, and Anders smiles. "You have my word."

She nods and rounds the room, giving Elias and Chris hugs. Walking behind Anders's desk, he receives a hug and a peck on his cheek.

He blushes. "'Bout time. I was starting to feel left out."

She pats his shoulder and leaves the office, taking her light with her. She doesn't look back at me or say goodbye.

I feel a little—what? Miffed that she dismissed me so easily. Especially when I can barely hold it together. "Did I miss something?" I ask. "I swear I didn't hear a word utter from her mouth."

Anders clears his throat. "My apologies, Shadow. I should have explained while she was here. She doesn't speak because the tracheostomy caused some complications. This past week, she's managed small sounds and short phrases but nothing substantial. She's also used to not speaking so she doesn't. Initially, when we brought her back from Whitemore plantation, she bonded with me and the Langhlan twins, and we could communicate through a mind-link. Recently, she mind-linked with both Chris and Elias. She doesn't know how she does it, and she can't seem to do so on command. Her mind-link is also one-sided. We hear her, but she cannot hear us."

"Mind-link? A mind-link usually works only when in wolf or animal form and with members of the same pack. Only a true Alpha can communicate with pack members in human form through a mind-link. Even then, that's rare. Obviously, she's a magic dweller. I could sense her magic surrounding her. It practically enveloped the whole room."

Anders frowns. "I'm sure there's more to it, but without knowing her origins..."

I stare at Anders. As clear as day, I see it. "I'm sorry, Anders. What is your relationship with the young woman?"

Chris smiles, and Elias chuckles. "You see it, too. Don't you?" Chris asks.

"What is it you see?" Anders grimaces.

I issue a crooked smile. "Other than the similar characteristics you both share? The eyes and nose? And, if her hair was any lighter, it could be almost white." He maintains my gaze without replying. "She has strong magic, stronger than anyone I encountered, including you."

Anders reclines in his chair and wipes a hand over his face. "This can't be," he whispers.

"Where's the paternity test?" Elias asks. "The results should have arrived by now. It's been a few weeks."

Anders pulls an envelope from the top drawer of his desk. "I didn't have a chance to open it."

"Or maybe you wanted to convince yourself you didn't need to," Elias suggests. Anders passes the envelope to Chris, who gives it to Elias.

"Why would you request a paternity test?" I ask.

"She needed a blood transfusion when she first arrived. The doctor asked everyone to get tested to find a more direct match."

"Anders was the only one who came close," Chris adds. "The doctor only asked Anders out of desperation."

"Then, a few weeks ago, Jessica reacted to the blood transfusions using Anders's blood," Elias explains. "One of the specialists asked if Anders was a direct blood relative. Of course, he denied it."

Anders looks away. "I don't have a daughter. I would know," he mumbles.

"That you know of," Chris argues. "Look, you can stay in denial all you want, but you know deep down that it's a possibility. Otherwise, you wouldn't have agreed to the paternity test."

Anders drops his chin to his chest, looking at the photograph in front of him. A crimson flush creeps from beneath his collar. "Aside from the hair and eyes, she looks just like her mother," he finally admits softly.

"It's a 99.9 percent match," Elias informs Anders. Elias shows me the test results.

I think Anders already knew, even before the blood typing. He didn't want to face the truth, especially given the way she was found.

His shoulders tense, jaw clenches, and the flush turns to an angrier red. He slams his fist down on the desk. "Dammit! I can't believe she would do this!" He looks over at Elias and Chris. "Was this some kind of retaliation against me?" he shouts. The two men stare at him, unblinking. "When I find her, I will fucking end her!" His breathing becomes labored, and the temperature in the room drops dangerously low.

Chris hops off the edge of the desk. "Wait! You don't know the whole story. You're jumping to conclusions. At this point, we still don't know what really happened or how."

"What really happened?!" Anders yells. "You saw what she looked like when she arrived at the clinic. You heard the doctor! Years of abuse and malnourishment. She was tortured. Her back was filleted. They cut off her hair and marred her face. She was beaten, strung up, and hanged from a tree, barely alive! Multiple failed surgeries, and even after all of that, she still nearly died only a few weeks ago."

Standing, I lift my hands to distract Anders before ice shards start flying. "Chris has a point. We don't know what happened. We can't storm into a territory and start killing people without any proof of who attacked her. All we—I mean, you—all you can do is focus on right now. That's what we—you—can do for her right now."

Why the hell do I keep saying we? This isn't about me right now. This is about Anders and the young woman, and as much as I am on board for killing the fuckers who hurt her, we need to keep our heads. I mean, his head. Shit!

Anders glares at me, chest still heaving.

"We can figure out the rest later," I assure him.

He stands, leaning forward with both hands planted on his desk. Frost forms on the wooden surface, and his harsh breaths puff into clouds.

I turn toward Chris and Elias. Worried expressions mirror my own. I have never seen Anders like this.

Still hunched, he closes his eyes and takes several slow, deep breaths. The room temperature begins to return to normal. "I will kill the asshole responsible for hurting my daughter, and not one of you better stand in my way," he promises with a deathly calm.

"I'll stand by your side, my friend," Elias commits.

Chris nods. "No one deserves what she endured. We need to be logical about this and develop a plan. A plan to take care of her right now and keep her safe."

Once calm, Anders slumps into his chair. "What the fuck am I going to do? I can't have a daughter. I just can't. Every female in my bloodline carries a curse." He sighs and rubs his temples. "Pretty fucking obvious—the curse is already affecting her."

Chris begins to pace. "Technically, it's not a curse. It's a bunch of greedy bastards who think they can gain something by hurting others. Just so happens the females in your bloodline are their main target."

"I have to take her to Ryuku. I don't have a choice." A pained expression crosses Anders's face. "She'll never forgive me, if I take her away from here and dump her at the school in the Asian territories, the same way my boys were dumped, the way I was dumped, away from the bonds she has developed here." He closes his eyes and shakes his head.

Chris interjects, "Save that as a last resort. You saw the way Ean and Charlie are with her, not to mention the twins. Don't forget about us. We have all formed some kind of bond with her as well. And if Shakti hears about this..."

Anders hesitates. "If I am completely honest with myself, I want her here. But who the hell am I to raise a daughter? I have only ever raised sons—well, here anyway."

"Why can't you do it all?" I ask.

"What?" three voices respond at once. When I look around

the room, three pairs of eyes gape at me, like I grew an extra head.

I shrug. "You said that Shakti formed a bond with the girl. She's a woman. I'm sure there is some womanly instinct there that can help you raise her. So have an honest conversation with the Alpha King and the Luna Queen and ask them to adopt her. That way you can still be a part of her life and stay involved with pertinent decisions that affect her."

Chris snaps his fingers. "Like hiding her out in the open. No one will question the Alpha King about an adoption."

Elias slowly nods.

"No one outside of us and the Alpha King and Luna Queen need to know of her true origins. As far as anyone knows, she's just a teenager found in distress, and we rescued and took her in. From what I overheard, she wants to be in the guard. Let her. You can train her yourself, keep an eye on her. She won't be far from home. The Langhlan twins are in the next group of recruits, so she will still be around them, as well as Charlie and Ean working full time with the recruits and their training. Once her magic comes in fully or after she finishes the recruit program, whichever comes first, then send her to the Asian territory."

Anders eyes me wearily. "Jessica... Her name is Jessica. I can't allow a female into the recruit program."

I laugh. "That little person who walked through your office door just moments ago looked like a young man to me."

Elias shrugged, and Chris smiled. "That just might work actually," Chris agreed.

"Will it?" Anders snaps. "What the hell will you tell your daughters when they find out? Some of them wanted to be in the guard, and we flat-out said no. How many other girls have we denied? Remember the protest we put up with when one of their mothers turned out to be a journalist?"

Elias shrugs. "Fuck it. If anyone finds out she's a woman, we can always say it was a pilot program."

I shake my head. "Actually, you don't need to lie. The Guard bylaws state that the recruits are to be male. However, a section states that all royal heirs need to participate in the guard program. With Nathan as the Alpha King and Shakti the Luna Queen, that would make Jessica a princess. Even though she is adopted, it won't change her given title. The royal clause does not specify male or female. Even if you were sued or had a huge protest, that clause alone protects the guards."

Anders runs his hands through his hair. Elias laughs. "This is why you are the best guard we ever had."

"And a soon-to-be badass guard lawyer," Chris adds.

I see the wheels churn in Anders's mind. "I need to speak with Nathan and Shakti first, make sure that this is what they want. I can't force them to take on my responsibility."

"Do you honestly think it will be a problem? I wouldn't put it past Shakti. She already had a plan in place once Jessica is discharged from the clinic. Faith hasn't asked me once to bring her home, and you know how she is. She kicked me out of my own home when I told Eugene I wouldn't take his boy in. Did Tater say anything to you?" Elias looks at Chris, who stops pacing.

"Actually, she hasn't." Chris snorts, facing Anders with a smirk. "Talk to Shakti. I think it's already a done deal. Little One isn't going anywhere."

Elias chuckles. "You may want to take him," he says, jerking his head in my direction. "Chris and I can hold up shop here."

"Before you all leave, I have one more topic to discuss— Sodie's placement with the guards."

I lean forward. "What's going on with Sodie?"

"Nothing bad. He asked to stay on as an active guard. He wanted to be personally assigned to Jessica. I initially had no problems with it. However, given the circumstances, I think it will be best for Sodie to attend Ryuku for more training."

I frown. Not everyone with magic needs to attend Ryuku. "Did his magic become stronger or change?"

Chris cocks his head. "You sensed his magic?"

"Yes. I wasn't very concerned about him revealing himself. Most light manipulators don't often bring attention to themselves and remain under the radar. Unless I am wrong..."

"I think there is more to him than maybe even he realizes, or he's really good at concealing it. Either way, he saved Jessica's life. As a thank you, I want to help him."

"How did he save Jessica?"

"He's a healer. If he wasn't there, and did what he did, she wouldn't be here right now, giving us hell to admit her into the recruit program."

Chris's face brightens. "He mentioned an interest in the medical field in his interview. Now I know why. Let's give him every opportunity to make it happen." Elias nods in agreement.

"I was going to mention this later, but we're here so... I may have a potential candidate in mind who I want to discuss with you. I came across this candidate accidentally when I was in Territory Two. He was a little elusive, but I can't blame him. He doesn't exactly belong to a very forgiving territory, particularly when it comes to magic. He reminded me of Liam—a little broken, untrusting, bit of a loner. He is past the recruiting guard age. I would like to send him to Ryukyu."

"What can he do?" Chris inquires.

"He can manipulate water, which is how I found him, messing with the water element near the falls."

"Okay. So what's the big deal? We've encountered a few shifters in the past with that ability."

"Have you ever met someone who can manipulate the water element, shield kinetic energy, and neutralize magic?"

Elias's eyebrows raise, and he leans forward. "You found a shield? That's like finding a needle in a haystack."

"It gets better. There's something else he can do. I've seen it in his aura, but he hasn't tapped into it yet."

"A triple threat?" Elias asks incredulously.

I smile. "Imagine having someone like him as a guard."

Chris whistles, and Anders nods. "Okay. If you trust him and he is on board, I'll get everything ready. I will send you the details for you to pass onto your recruit. I really wanted to send Liam with Sodie, but this is the second time he declined."

"Why?" I ask Anders, who simply shakes his head.

Elias answers instead. "He won't say. I really wish I could break down some of that barrier he constructed so tightly around himself."

CHAPTER 25
WELCOME HOME

JESSICA
EIGHT YEARS AGO:
JULY 25, 2016: 1:30 P.M.
EMERALD PACK CLINIC

Dr. York sits in front of me, legs crossed, with my medical chart on his lap. His posture is relaxed, face devoid of creases, especially between his brows. When he finally meets my eye, a soft smile touches his lips.

"Everything looks good. Your hair has grown at least three inches. Even your eyelashes are coming back in. All of your wounds have closed. Labs have almost returned to normal levels. I am pleased with how well you're healing these past few weeks. I admit you gave us all quite a scare. I'm happy everything turned in your favor."

"Me, too," I rasp.

His smile widens. "Your voice is slowly coming back, too, which reminds me. I submitted a request for speech therapy. As soon as I hear back from them, we can start that." Nodding, I watch Dr. York jot a note in his scrawling, messy handwriting. "Do you know what all of this means?"

A sense of dread creeps along the back of my neck. Do I know what all this means? Is he referring to my labs? No. He looks too happy to be thinking of my bloodwork.

"You no longer need constant medical supervision. The rest of the treatments can be done outside of the clinic."

Yep. I was afraid he would say it. My hope to remain here long enough to enroll into the guard recruit program crashes and burns. Shakti hasn't mentioned anything about taking me in. I guess that means orphanage here I come.

My lips tremble so I press them together and put on a brave face. I can't cry. This is supposed to be good—no, great—news. But it makes me so sad, knowing I must leave. I refuse to cry in front of Dr. York. I'm not his problem anymore, and I won't make him feel guilty or sorry for me. I offer a small smile and nod.

He pats my knee before standing. "I'll tell Anders." As soon as he leaves, I reach for the journal under my pillow and pour my disappointed feelings onto the blank pages.

I haven't seen Anders in a few hours, and other than Ean, the rest of the guards were absent all day. Maybe Anders told them not to come, now that I am awaiting discharge.

Sighing, I look out the window. Dark clouds roll overhead, and large raindrops slide down the glass pane. I stopped crying about an hour ago. It looks like the weather decided to cry for me now.

"Everything okay, Jessica?" Facing Anders, I nod and smile half-heartedly.

Anders crosses the threshold to my room and sits at the foot of my bed. Over his shoulder, I see that strange man I met earlier, Shadow, lurking in the doorway.

Wait. Is this the same guy? He looks different somehow. He

removed his suit jacket and tie. Some of the buttons are undone, exposing his throat. Slowly, my eyes return to his face. His jet-black hair almost seems blue. He styles it shorter on the sides and a little long on the top. He has a widow's peak, and it curls into a slight wave that rests on his forehead just above his dark brows. Thick lashes surround dark blue eyes—well, they were dark. Maybe the lighting is different here because they appear lighter now. The corner of his lip twitches with amusement.

That's what it is. He's amused. His expression has softened. When I first walked into Anders's office, he acted like a life-sized cardboard cutout of himself. He was stiff and void almost. Now, he is animated. His face reflects—I don't know—life.

"I'm sorry I took so long. My meeting went a bit longer than originally planned."

I understand.

"Thank you," he replies, reaching for the book in front of me. I planned on reading it after my journal writing. I guess I won't finish it now. "Weapons of martial arts. Hmmm, this wouldn't by any chance have to do with you wanting to be in the guard?"

I glance down at my hands and answer him with my thoughts. *It was in your office. I thought I would familiarize myself with some of the weapons.* I wrinkle my nose.

Anders smiles and shows Shadow the book's cover. "Is it alright if we table our discussion for the moment? I would like to discuss something else first."

Well, that's a polite way of saying no. My heart sinks. The rain taps harder against the windowpane.

"I didn't say no, just yet. I need to think about it, and I need to discuss it with Chris and Elias." Hope flickers in my chest. "Shadow is our recruiting officer. I gave him your application. He will review it, and depending on our collectively decision, he will notify you."

It's not a definitive answer, but I can look forward to a response, at least a small possibility that they won't write me off completely.

Anders chuckles. "Don't think too much about it. I haven't made up my mind yet, but it's a start. We can talk about it more a little later."

I lean forward and wrap my arms around Anders. "Thank you," I rasp, using my voice. Then, I jump off my bed and bound over to Shadow. As I wrap my skinny arms around him, a tether of sorts tugs at my heart.

He tenses, with a quick intake of breath. Am I hurting him? Maybe he doesn't like being touched.

Shit. I loosen my hold on him when his arms slowly, awkwardly embrace me. The tension I felt earlier softens. I peer up, expecting to see his chin. Instead, striking blue eyes gaze down at me. A clash of light and dark alternate before settling on a lighter shade of blue.

He stares at me for a few more seconds before looking to Anders, frowning. "It stopped raining," he claims.

I drop my arms and face the window. The sun shines in all its warm glory.

"So it seems," Anders whispers.

Shadow asks, "Does the weather always match your feelings?"

I shrug, looking to Anders to interpret for me. *Not that I've noticed.*

Anders shakes his head. "Jessica, why don't you mind-link with Shadow and tell him yourself?"

I don't know how to.

"You've done it with Chris and Elias. Why don't you just—I don't know, humor me—give it a try?"

I clasp my hands in front of me and fidget with my fingers. I don't know how to connect willingly. With Chris and Elias, it just happened, the same way it did with Anders and the twins.

I angle myself slightly and stare straight at Shadow's forehead, pretending for an instant that I can break past the invisible barrier that lies between his skull and brain. Feeling ridiculous, I eventually lower my gaze. His features are soft, and a slight smile touches his lips. At least when he smiles now, he doesn't look constipated or like he's holding in a fart.

Shadow bursts into a hearty laugh, and my eyes widen. "That's too bad. To think this entire time, I thought my smile looked genuine," he commented.

Nope. definitely looked like constipation. I press my lips together to prevent my growing smile.

"I'll keep that in mind. Thanks for the tip."

Yeah. Sure. Any time. Heat rises, coloring my cheeks. I don't like the idea of him hearing my thoughts anymore. It's too much like an invasion of my privacy. Regaining my composure, I clear my throat. *So, in answer to your earlier question, no. I haven't noticed whether my moods correlate with the weather.*

Shadow's smile fades, and his expression becomes serious. "Maybe you should pay attention." His eyes shift from my face to Anders. "Well, I really should be going. I'll keep in touch and let you know when I will be by again."

Anders nods farewell.

Before Shadow turns to leave, he says, "I look forward to our next meeting. I'm interested to see what else pops through that mind of yours."

I stand by the door and watch his retreating back, still trying to make sense of him. He's peculiar; that's for sure. As he strides down the hall, I notice how tall he is—at least six foot two—with wide shoulders that taper to a narrow waist. I admire his backside, for a few more seconds. His girlfriend is a very lucky girl. I shake my head to clear it of his image and turn back toward the room.

Anders narrows his eyes. "Please don't tell me you look at all the guards like that."

I blush, glancing down at my hands. *Oops.* I forgot he could still hear my thoughts. I wrinkle my nose and smirk.

"Oops? Do not make me lock you in our dungeon until you're 100," he threatens.

I cock my head to the side. *We have a dungeon? Did I miss that part of the tour?*

"Stop being such a wiseass." Anders's phone rings. "I need to answer this. You'll be discharged within the hour, and I'll return to collect you." He raises the phone to his ear and walks out of the room.

I guess he lost the nerve to tell me that I'm going to an orphanage.

Mimi arrives with an injection and a medicine cup full of supplements. I thought I was done with those. I haven't taken any since I woke up from that whole ordeal, almost dying and whatnot.

Shakti isn't here to question it, and the twins can't interpret for me. My voice is still too weak to murmur more than a word or two. So, I simply take the medicine.

After Mimi leaves, I pack my belongings. I don't really have much. Everything fits into two shopping bags, mostly clothes Shakti brought for me. Left alone with my thoughts, I decide to clean my room, make it presentable, as if no one was here. I just need to stay busy. I don't want to cry.

I hope while I am cleaning my room that the guards stop by. Even when Shakti and the twins resumed their daily visits, the guards continued our routine. I began to think of them as friends, family even. Especially Liam. I thought we had gotten closer. He even started reading to me at night, so I could fall asleep. All in my imagination, I suppose.

Time creeps slowly by, and my heart aches. The twins don't show up, and neither does Shakti. It hurts they didn't say goodbye. Outside, rain pummels the earth.

It feels like forever by the time Anders returns. He retrieves my two bags and asks. "Is this everything?"

I nod, pulling on my favorite hoodie, the one I found that first night. Anders leads me out of the room and walks down the hall. I stall, turning to look at my room, my home, one last time.

My chest constricts, and my throat closes. I tug at the neckline of my hoodie. I can't breathe. Tears fall, fogging my glasses. My whole world is changing again, and I don't know what to do.

A warm arm wraps around my shoulder, and a large hand cradles my head, resting it against a warm chest. I take a deep breath, drawing in the fresh smell with a hint of campfire smoke that permeates my senses. I squeeze my eyes closed in relief and cry into Liam's shirt.

"Shhh. I got you. Breathe."

I wrap my arms around his waist and cry harder. His other hand rubs my back in small circles. Slowly, my throat opens again, and I can breathe. I feel safe.

Another hand caresses my shoulder, and any lingering panic melts away.

Liam kisses my temple, and I pull back to find Sodie standing beside me. More tears fall. I thought they weren't coming. I hug Sodie, removing my glasses to bury my face in his chest.

"Don't cry, Little One. You will like your new home. I promise," Sodie assures me.

I nod and, pulling back to see his face, offer him a smile. I reach for Liam again and squeeze his arm.

"Come on," Liam says, clasping my small hand in his much larger one. "Anders looks like he's ready to murder us. We're the reason he's late."

I wipe my face with the sleeve of my hoodie. Sodie chuckles behind me as Liam leads the way.

Anders waits next to a car. He opens the back passenger door and motions with his head for me to climb in. My heart sinks that I didn't get to say goodbye to Ean or Charlie. Anders stands by the door, waiting, but I take one last look around before I do.

"I really do hope you're not contemplating running," Anders says.

Snorting, I shake my head. If I did, wouldn't he know? I step toward the car and then stop.

"If it makes you feel better, these two are riding along." Sodie approaches the front of the car, and Liam rounds the back to enter from the other side.

I sigh and finally get in myself. Anders follows as I scoot across the back seat. As the car pulls away, I look behind, watching the clinic slowly disappear. Anders pats my knee, and Liam reaches for my hand, gently stroking the back with his thumb.

After only five minutes, the car turns into a long driveway with a tall iron gate. A paved roundabout circles a gorgeous fountain in front of a large mansion. My heartbeat races, and the blood drains from my face.

Is this the territory's children's home? I knew it! I knew they would take me to an orphanage. The tears well in my eyes, and I want to puke.

"Jessica, this is not an orphanage. Relax. This is your new home."

The car stops, and Liam squeezes my hand, bringing me back from my panicked state. He whispers in my ear, "Breathe. No one will hurt you. We won't leave until you're settled."

Anders offers a slight smile. "I promise you will be pleasantly surprised." I exit the car and follow Anders to the front door. He knocks while I try to hide behind him.

A man with thinning black hair, bushy eyebrows, and a thick mustache answers the door. He nods at Anders and holding the door open for us to enter. Reaching for me, he ushers me through the door. "Joe, this is Jessica. Jessica, Joe works here. He is also a trained guard. If you ever feel unsafe or need help, you can trust Joe."

Joe raises his right hand, showing me the large ring tattooed on the back of his hand. The ring depicts the guard crest, with an emerald and a diamond in its center.

I stretch out my hand, and he shakes it, bowing. There's something about Joe that instantly resonates with me. *Very nice to meet you, Joe. I wish you could hear me say it because I think I already like you.*

Joe pulls back his hand sharply, eyes widened. He stoops forward to meet me at eye level. "It is very nice to meet you, Jessica. I think I like you already, too." I smile. He stands to his full height and offers, "Here, let me take those." He gestures to both Liam and Sodie to hand him my shopping bags. "I'll have these taken to your room, but first, let me show you where everyone is anxiously waiting for you."

He ushers us in to close the front door and leads us deeper into the mansion. We pass a grand staircase that leads to a second floor, as well as smaller rooms I can barely peek inside. Then, it hits me—I will work here. I wonder if I'll be part of the cleaning staff or the kitchen staff.

Joe abruptly stops in front of me, and I almost bump into him. He turns to look at Anders.

Anders chuckles. "You're not here to work as a servant or on the kitchen staff. Stop dragging your feet, and you'll find out exactly why you're here." He pushes me gently forward as Joe continues down the hallway. Peeking over my shoulder, I see Liam and Sodie close behind.

Familiar voices tickle my mind. The twins. They're here! Justin and Jeremy are here!

"Surprise!" a group of people shout.

I grab my throat and step back. Anders grasps both of my shoulders and encourages me forward. Ean, Elias, Charlie, and Chris all gather, along with some unfamiliar faces. A large banner hangs on the back wall that reads, "Welcome home, Jessica!"

Shakti walks up to me with a huge smile and gives me a hug. "Welcome to your new home and family, sweetheart."

I look around the room at all the faces staring back at me, and I want to turn around and run. It is all so overwhelming. I don't deserve any of this. Everyone has been so nice. I feel guilty for not showing them any appreciation. I have nothing to give in return.

Fear consumes me, instigating another panic attack. I will be punished soon, for making a fool of myself and embarrassing them.

My body trembles. I need to hide. I recall the rooms we passed. Would they mind if I slipped into one of them?

CHAPTER 26

MY FAMILY

JESSICA
EIGHT YEARS AGO:
JULY 25, 2016: 5:30 P.M.
ALPHA KINGS MANSION

Two hard bodies—Justin and Jeremy—crash into me.

Why does she think she's in trouble? I hear Jeremy ask in my head.

You're not in trouble. You don't need to hide, Justin reassures me. *You're our sister now. Everyone here is your family.* Jeremy assesses me, seeking reassurance that I won't run. "Come meet everyone. We're all excited that you're here!" Justin smiles.

I hesitate, glancing at Anders, who nods in approval. I smile at the twins. I'm still uneasy and itch with the need to run, but with my two...

Wait. They said... sister? I frown and turn toward Elias.

"Little One, I want to introduce you to my family. You already know my oldest, Ean." I nod. "This is my beautiful mate, Faith." He wraps his arms around a tall, beautiful woman with long dark hair and kind eyes. Her face is round and feminine.

She quickly pulls me into a hug. "I'm so happy you're doing well." She squeezes me before letting me go. "You also know Liam. He is the newest member of our little family. We unofficially adopted him a few years ago."

Liam stands next to Ean, smiling at me.

"Elijah is our youngest."

Not nearly as tall as Ean, Elijah has the same dark hair and dark eyes. His features are softer, not as broad as Elias's and Ean's. He takes more after his mother. I offer a little wave, and he jerks his chin in greeting.

"Why am I introduced last? You even introduced Liam before me. It's because I'm a girl, isn't it?" A mirror image of her mother steps around Elias. "I'm Emily. I'm not the youngest— I'm actually older than Elijah by like two years. I wanted to visit when I first heard about you, but Ean wouldn't let me. It's not like I would bother you. I go to the private school in the city so I'm only home on the weekends." She quickly pulls me into a crushing hug. "Oh, wow. We need to work on finding you some better clothes."

I grimace and look back at the twins.

"Don't worry. Between Sixes and I, we'll have you looking so good, the boys will have to lock you up. Do you talk? No? Not much? That's okay. Elijah doesn't talk much either, and everyone knows I can talk enough for every—"

Ean clamps a hand over Emily's mouth. "He doesn't talk because you don't let him. Geez, calm down. You're going to... Ouch! Did you just bite me?"

Everyone in the room laughs, and I cover my own to stifle my raspy wheeze.

Emily winks and whispers, "You and I are going to be the

best of friends." She gives me another hug, and just as she releases me, I'm dragged over toward Chris.

"My turn," he claims with a smile. "Little One, this is my beautiful mate, Tater." Chris's mate is not as tall as Faith or Emily, but she is just as beautiful, with dark blonde hair and big hazel eyes.

"I'm also the head of the household staff. If you need anything, you can usually find me in the kitchen."

I smile and nod. She also hugs me. So many hugs!

"This is my daughter, Sixes. She also works here, and I personally assigned her to you. If you need absolutely anything, don't hesitate to let us know."

"Yes, Emily is right. We need to do something about your style. Not to worry. You're in good hands," she declares with a wide smile.

I glance down at my baggy outfit. This is as good as it gets.

"Give it a rest, you two. She's not a doll," Charlie teases, winking at me. "She looks perfectly fine, just the way she is."

Chris clears his throat, giving Charlie a sideways look. "You've already met Charlie. Tater and I have four more girls. Two of them are away at school. And the other two had prior commitments, but you'll see them around."

I smile and nod. I guess I will be smiling and nodding a lot as my words are so limited.

"This old man is my father, Duck. He's also the main ranch hand and manages the dairy." I look up at an elderly man with dull gray hair and kind green eyes. His skin is deeply tanned and slightly leathery, likely from working out in the sun, his smile reaches his eyes.

"Hello, Little One. It is a pleasure to finally meet you." He reaches out to shake my hand.

Instead of clasping his, though, I turn his over. They are large, weathered, and callused. I rub my palm over his fingers.

"I hear you're learning how to play the guitar?"

I nod enthusiastically.

"If Charlie gets too busy to work with you, I don't mind stepping in. Some of the dairy hands and I put together what we call a garage band. We would love to have you come around and maybe one day join us."

I lunge forward to give him a hug. Chuckling, he pats my back.

"Dad, maybe you can take her to visit the ladies when she's settled," Chris suggests.

Ladies? I look to the twins, and they laugh.

"He means the cows," Jeremy explains.

I blush. *Please tell him I would love that.* Justin interprets for me.

Scanning the room, I find Shakti next to a regal man of at least six foot five. My eyebrows raise. He looks exactly like Chris. Are they twins?

Justin chuckles. "You've already met our mother. This is our father. No, he and Chris are not twins—they're cousins. Duck and our grandfather were twin brothers."

I peruse the room. I don't see another elderly man anywhere.

Where's your grandfather? I ask Justin through our link.

He passed away before we were born.

I'm sorry. I didn't mean to ask.

It's okay. We would have told you eventually. You're family now, Jeremy declares.

The regal man wears dark jeans and a long-sleeved, plaid shirt. His energy is so huge, powerful, very... My eyes widen, and I step back. My mind whirls.

I am in the biggest house in the territory. The two lead guards are family. I take another step back. The twins said sister. I'm their sister. No, no, no... He's the Alpha King. And Shakti... is the Luna Queen.

Anders places a warm hand on my shoulder. "It's okay. You're not in trouble," he whispers in my ear.

I shake my head. *I don't deserve this. What if I'm a bad person? What if I was attacked because I did something wrong? What if... What if whoever did it comes after me and hurts the Alpha King and his family? I can't stay here!* My glasses fog, and tears spill from my eyes.

Anders spins me so I face him. Chris and Elias stand on either side of him.

I can't put the Alpha King and the Lunar Queen's family in a position that can hurt them. I remove my glasses and openly cry.

"Jessica, look at me. Do you think I would bring you here if I had any doubt that you would put their lives at risk?"

I sniff. *You don't know me. I don't know me! What if I did something that caused this whole situation? We don't know anything!*

Anders leans forward to meet me at eye level. "I will never let anything happen to you or the royal family. It's my job to protect them, and that includes you."

I rub my nose with the back of my hand and shake my head. *I don't deserve this. I don't deserve to be here.*

"Why do you feel you don't deserve to be here?" Chris asks, rubbing my back.

I just don't. It's a feeling deep in my bones.

"Little One, you didn't deserve what happened to you," Elias adds. His hand gently squeezes my other shoulder.

"Everyone deserves a second chance," says a deep voice from behind me. "We want you to be a part of our family, of our pack. Look around you. Everyone here wants to know you and give you a better life, one you deserve."

Pressure clenches around my heart, and I look at Anders.

"I will never let anything bad happen to you ever again. You are mine to protect, Jessica. You are here because we want you here. I want you here," Anders confesses.

Tears threaten again at his sincerity.

"As much as I appreciate your concern for me and my family, it is also my job to protect them, as well as you. Besides, there is one other person who feels this is where you belong. If she had anything to say about it, she would have been the one to convince me otherwise." The Alpha King points to the back of the room.

Sitting in a chair, holding her cane, is Alpha Agnus. "Well, it's about damn time I got some attention. I was beginning to think I made the two-hour drive just to be ignored," she huffs, and everyone chuckles. "Jessica, this is where you belong. I know for a fact you're not a bad person. What you've been through is not because of anything you did. You were just in the wrong place with the wrong people. You need everyone in this room, and whether they realize it or not, they need you."

The Alpha King laughs. "You better listen to her. She's a little scary," he whispers. "Even I'm afraid of her."

"Now, come give me a hug. Or are you going to just stand there and cry over what-ifs?"

I wipe my face with my sleeve, clean my glasses, and walk over to Alpha Agnus.

"There's my girl," she says as I embrace her. "Well, do we get to eat, or will everyone just stand around and watch this poor girl take it all in?"

"You heard her. Let's eat," the Alpha King announces to the room.

The room erupts with laughter and talking as everyone gathers around the buffet arranged along one wall.

Shakti wraps her arms around my shoulders from behind.

"Thank you for joining our family. I knew you were mine from the moment I met you." She kisses the top of my head.

The Alpha King speaks with Chris and Anders while they stand in line to fill their plates. When he catches me watching him, he winks and continues his conversation.

I grab Justin's arm. *Can you tell him I'm sorry for making such a fuss? I'm sorry if I embarrassed him.* He walks over and repeats what I said to his father.

The Alpha King approaches me, leaning down to meet my eye. "I'm not embarrassed at all. You're entitled to how you feel. In fact, it is our fault for putting this on you. We should have approached this with a little more caution, talked to you, explored how you feel. We were excited and jumped in without thinking of your needs. We're the ones who owe you an apology. I promise we won't make this mistake again." He lifts his little finger.

Justin explains, *It's a pinky promise. It's something we do in this family. Along with voting. I'll tell you all about that later.*

Holding up my little finger, he entangles his large one with mine. My heart swells with an unknown emotion. I feel safe and cared for. Dropping my hand, I gaze around the room. I have a family now.

The Alpha King wraps his arm around Shakti's waist and leads her to a large table, sets a plate of food in front of her, and kisses her forehead before returning to the line. No one serves him or stops what they're doing to let him go first. He talks to everyone. He claps Anders on the back as if they're old friends. And Shakti talks to Tater, Sixes, Faith, and Emily. It's so casual —no airs, no hierarchy.

Justin and Jeremy chat with Liam and Sodie, like they always did in my clinic room. Nothing changes now in their own home. I like it. It feels right.

"Jessica." Alpha Agnus crooks a finger at me. "I expect a visit from you at least once every other month."

I thought you were done with me.

She scoffs, "Don't be a smartass. Just because I knew you belonged here for now doesn't mean I abandoned you. Besides, I need you to come back to make me those brownies. Miller had everyone make me brownies since you left, and they just aren't the same."

I cover my mouth and giggle. *You made everyone bake you brownies?*

She raises an eyebrow and whacks me with her cane. "Miller, how many brownies have we gone through?"

He grimaces. "I lost count. Please come back, Jessica. She's driving everyone crazy."

I burst into another raspy laugh and shake my head. *They're just brownies. I don't know what's so special about them.*

She frowns. "Just tell me you'll return and make them again. Give Miller a list of what you need. I'll make sure we have everything in stock."

I shrug. *Here, I thought you wanted me to visit because you wanted my company.*

"Don't be a wiseass!" she growls.

I wrinkle my nose and offer her a tender smile. Behind Alpha Agnus, I glimpse a piano in the corner of the room. I hesitate at first and then decide to look more closely. It is a baby grand piano, shiny black as if someone polishes it regularly.

With the pad of my index finger, I touch it. But I feel guilty for leaving fingerprints so I wipe the smudge with the hem of my hoodie. Sliding onto the bench, I lift the cover, revealing the piano keys. A music book sits on the sheet holder. I thumb through the pages, and some of the music titles seem familiar.

Play something, Alpha Agnus urges in my head.

Play what?

Just close your eyes and play something. It will come.

I hover my fingers over the keys, and they begin to move. In my head, colors take shape in a kaleidoscope. Behind closed eyelids, a yellow-white light radiates from my heart through my fingers. With only a few notes of sound, I make music.

The song is slow and haunting at first and then softens. It matches the way I felt a few minutes ago—sad, worried, fearful, relief, and then acceptance. Even with so much uncertainty in my future, it will be okay. I will be okay.

I play the last few notes, ending the song. I open my eyes to look down at the keys and my fingers. Flipping my hands over again and again, I check. Are these really mine? I can't believe I played. Where did that even come from?

The room is quiet. Everyone stares at me.

Oh, gods, am I in trouble? Why do I keep screwing up? I wait for the yelling, for the punishment. Instead, Shakti raises her hand over her mouth, and tears streak down her face. She slowly approaches me. I wince.

"That was beautiful!" she exclaims, resting her hands over her heart. "Can you play another one?" I hesitate, and she adds, "It's okay. Give it a try. It's okay if you play the same one. It was beautiful."

I don't want to disappoint her. Swallowing, I take a deep breath, close my eyes, and place my hands over the keys once more. and another song flows through me.

With the final notes still lingering in the air, I slowly open my eyes. Shakti stands between to Anders and the Alpha King. My parents, my chosen family.

The party lasts for a couple more hours before everyone slowly begins to depart. Alpha Agnus is the first, complaining that her old bones must endure a two-hour drive back to her territory. She makes arrangements with Shakti and Anders for my next visit to her territory then leaves.

Emily promises she will return to hang out often. Ean grunts. "You're going to wish I kept her away longer. Trust me."

I shake my head. I like Emily. She talks a lot, so much so that the twins don't need to interpret for me at all, but she has charisma and charm. She makes Liam laugh.

He's different around her, more social, and for the first time since I met him, I see a playful side to him as he teases Emily and banters with Ean and Charlie. When the boys gang up on Elijah, Emily jumps in and basically hands them their asses. I just met her, but, in my heart, I know she's right. I can already feel a bond between the two of us forming.

Anders approaches. "You'll be okay. I won't be very far, and I'll see you regularly. Besides, I haven't forgotten about our pending discussion. We'll talk more later. For now, get acquainted with your new home and family." He pulls me into a quick hug. "Liam will check the perimeter. When he's satisfied everything is in order, he'll return to the training facility. Don't run... Promise?"

I won't go anywhere. I cross my heart.

"Good." He squeezes me one last time before turning to leave.

Sodie hugs me next. He is the only one here tonight who doesn't have family. I want him to know that I think of him as my family. I point to his chest and then my own.

He smiles. "Are you adopting me?" I squeeze his hand and nod. "Good. I already think of you as my family, too. See ya around." He touches my chin before heading for the door.

Liam stands off to the side. He doesn't move at first. Frowning, he scans the area and grabs my arm. "When you find your room, flick the light on three times so I know you're okay and settled in for the rest of the night. There is no rush. Take your time." Then, he disappears into the night.

Returning to the foyer, my new family waits for me. "Ready to see your new room?" Shakti asks.

"Tomorrow, we can give you the grand tour. You're free to go wherever you please, and you can play the piano whenever you like. This is your home now. I want you to think of it as your own," the Alpha King adds.

"You can call him by his name," Jeremy offers. "You don't have to call him the Alpha King," he snickers.

I elbow him in the ribs. When we reach the top of the stairs, the Alpha King says, "It's okay to call me Nathan. In time, when you are comfortable, you can call us Mom and Dad, if you want." Glancing at my toes, I'm unsure how to respond to his kindness. He puts his hand on my shoulder and make a gesture to follow Shakti.

Shakti indicates the various guest rooms as we pass down the hallway. She notes the twins' bedrooms and Luke's room on the opposite side. Then, she opens double doors to a room at the end of the hall.

"This used to be the boys' playroom, but they've outgrown it and spend most of their time in their own rooms. I thought you might like it. It has better lighting and more space."

I peek behind her. Large floor-to-ceiling windows frame the expansive territory beyond the grounds. A hearth centers a sitting area, and a desk and series of bookshelves situate across the room. Shakti walks farther into the room, and I follow her toward a huge canopy bed with lavender bedding and gauze curtains. The furniture is white with an antiqued look. The desk and shelves match the décor.

"I wasn't sure what color scheme you would like. I thought pink was too girly and blue too boyish so I chose purple. If you don't like anything, we can always change it."

I spin in a slow circle. I love everything about the room. It's perfect. The small couch features a sage green fabric, with a matching chair. Above the hearth hangs a large flat-screen TV.

I notice the centerpiece on a coffee table. A rectangular planter holds succulents and sprigs of lavender. I smile. I love lavender, and purple has always been my favorite color. The green is a perfect combination. I pause at that thought...

"She loves it," Justin says out loud.

"You nailed it, Mom. Apparently, lavender is her favorite," Jeremy shares, picking up another pot with sprigs of lavender in it. "Is lavender a flower or a bush?" Everyone laughs at his question. "What? I'm serious."

Shakti opens a door into a private bathroom with a walk-in shower, clawfoot bathtub, water closet, and double vanity. Why would I need two sinks?

Justin chuckles. "It's just the way the bathroom layout was designed."

"I noticed you liked the lavender and honey soap collection I got for you so I stuck to that. We can get you something else if you like," Shakti says.

At the very entrance of the en-suite, where we passed double doors before entering the full bathroom, she pulls it open. It's a walk-in closet, already stocked with some clothing, but not enough to fill it.

"I picked up some clothes for you, but I thought we could go into town one day soon and you can pick out your own. I think you might like some of the cute little boutiques there . If not, we can order anything online."

She walks out of the closet and stands in front of the glass French doors and steps out onto a balcony. A small wrought-iron table with two chairs and a lounger face the beautiful vistas beyond.

"You can sit here and eat breakfast or study if you get too cooped up indoors." When Shakti returns inside, she hits a button on the wall, which activates heavy drapes drawing closed. "The curtains block out the light if you decide you want to sleep in during the day or just feel the need for privacy." Pressing another button, she reopens the curtains. "Anders told me you like to read. He gave me a list of books he thought you might like to start your own library collection. And the boys have an extra laptop and an iPod they don't use, but I can get you your own."

I shake my head, overwhelmed by the room, by the items, by the care she put into it, all for me. This is more than enough. If I didn't know better, I'd think I'm still in a coma and this is all a dream. This can't be real.

Just when that nagging feeling that I don't deserve any of this echoes in my head, Jeremy sets his arm over my shoulder and pinches me.

Ass! I slap him in the chest.

He grunts and laughs, rubbing where I made contact. "Did that feel like you're in a coma?" he taunts.

"Jeremy! That wasn't nice!"

Nathan laughs. "Shakti, leave them alone. It's what siblings do. Besides, I think she can handle it."

The twins stretch out on my bed and turn on the TV. Shakti and Nathan position in my sitting area and check in with me before they bidding me good night. This is more than I could ever want. Eventually, they wrangle the twins out of my room to give me some peace and let me settle in.

When everyone leaves, I remember Liam's request. He left a long time ago. Running onto my balcony, I look for him, but little good that does. I can't see anything. I listen intently, but I hear nothing. He may have gone, but I walk inside and flip the light switch three times.

JESSICA

EIGHT YEARS AGO:
JULY 25, 2016: 11:45 P.M.
EMERALD PACK CLINIC

I know I promised I wouldn't run away. But does it count if I run back to the place where it all started?

I turn on the light of my room in the clinic. It looks like I was never here. The bed is stripped of sheets, but I climb onto it anyway and sit in the middle. Being here makes me feel better. This feels like what I deserve more than the luxury of my new home.

I just sit in silence, lost in my thoughts when a knock startles me. Liam stands in the doorway, leaning against the frame with his arms crossed over his chest. My breath catches at the sight of him.

He offers me a crooked smile. "I followed you back here." I avert my eyes. He probably thinks I'm an idiot. "How about we take a walk?" I hesitate, preferring to remain in my safe place.

"No one's in the clinic. I don't think it's good for you to stay here alone."

Sliding off the bed, I follow him out of the room. I don't know where he's taking me, but I trust him. I wish I could talk to him. I wish he could hear my thoughts. I wonder... maybe he could. I did it with Shadow, but I don't really know how.

I reach for Liam and gently touch the back of his arm.

"I can already hear your thoughts," he admits.

I snatch my hand back. *How?*

He shrugs. "Not sure. It happened that night you ran from the clinic. At first, I thought I imagined it. Then, when we returned to pick you up and your thoughts, your voice, was in my head. I knew you weren't feeling well, trying to fight it. I felt your panic... and then I stood guard outside of your door every night after you returned."

Why can't I hear your thoughts?

"I'm not sure. Maybe because I'm built different. The twins are happy and secure with their lives. I tend to shut people out. I spent my entire life erecting a wall, probably to protect myself."

I frown. *What happened to you?*

He stops walking. When I look around, I realize we're standing in front of the obstacle course. He takes me around and motions for me to climb up this wall. I hesitate at first, unsure why he wants me up there.

"You'll see."

I step back, and with a running start, I jump and grab onto a peg. I smile as I start to climb. This is what I need—to feel something, to feel... alive. Liam climbs after me. I almost reach the top of the wall when I glance down at Liam.

My foot slips. My heart flutters with panic. I'm too high. A fall could break my neck or crack my head. Either way, I definitely die. I grasp for another peg, but I miss it.

"Hang on. I'm coming," Liam calls.

I will my racing heart to slow. Then, suddenly, air—no, wind—surround me. As my grip falters, I let go. I open my arms and allow the wind to take me. I stop falling. The wind pushes me back up the wall, and I perch my feet on the top.

Slowly, I turn toward Liam, just below me. I offer him a hand, but he doesn't take it. Narrowing my eyes, I wonder... I picture air around him boosting him forward.

A gust of wind carries him, and he lands in a heap. My eyes widen and laugh, covering my mouth.

He dusts himself off. "H- how?" he stutters. He quickly pulls me to him. "Shit," he breathes, his warm breath caressing my cheek. "How long have you known you could do that?"

I shake my head. *I didn't.*

He holds me away by the shoulders, meeting my eye. "The lightning, the rain, that's all you. You're doing that," he says.

I'm not sure. I replay the conversation with Shadow before I was discharged. I hadn't really noticed before.

Holding my hand, he crosses to the other side and sits, letting his long legs dangle over the edge. Chuckling, he asks, "You were checking out Shadow?"

Huh? How did we get from *I didn't fall to my death because the wind saved me* to *I was checking out Shadow?*

"I saw it in your conversation. You replayed it in your mind."

I was merely making an observation. I cringe. That's the second time I was caught doing so.

"Sure, like you weren't checking out Charlie that first time we came to your room," he deadpans.

I was not checking him out. If I was checking anyone out, it was... I clear my throat. I need to think of something else. Liam glances down and rubs his lip. I wish I knew what he was thinking.

Sitting in silence, I relish the feel of the night. The sky is clear, and I can see the stars. Liam trails his thumb along the back of my hand. He said he could hear my thoughts that night they came to get me from Whitemore plantation. He could hear the panic in my head. The panic started in the car.

I close my eyes. He was in the car with me that night. It was him, the man who calmed my fears.

"There are two places I like to go when I need to think," he confesses. "Here and a place near the edge of the territory, near the cliff. You can see all of the seventh territory from there. I can show you the next time. It's much prettier during the day."

I see why he would seek such a peaceful refuge.

"When I learned that you couldn't remember your past or what happened to you, I envied that—your ability to forget all the bad and horrible things, your ability to start over with a clean slate. But after watching you, hearing your thoughts, seeing your reactions, not fully understanding why you feel the way you do, reliving the nightmares that haunt you, I realized that it's actually more of a curse than a blessing. You can't work through your feelings if you don't know why they exist in the first place. If I had to guess, you were made to feel inferior to them, made to feel like you had to earn everything, including feelings. If you showed any signs of weakness, you were probably punished for that, too. I know because that is how I was raised. I may not have the scars on the outside. All my scars are here." He taps his temple.

Unshed tears fill my eyes. I squeeze his hand. He understands me, even though I don't really understand myself.

How did you come to live with Elias and his family?

"I ran away from home. Anywhere was better than that hellhole. Then, I met an old man when I was living on the streets. He took me in and gave me shelter, food, a warm place to sleep at night. He educated me and taught me how to redirect my anger, how to fight. He became my best friend, the only person I could trust. Right before he died, Elias Blackguard showed up. After Eugene passed, Elias returned and brought me here."

He sighs, releasing what sounds like the weight of the world. I briefly rest my head on his shoulder before he continues.

"When I first came to stay with Elias and his family, it took a while for me to open up. Even though I made one good friend, it was still hard for me to believe there were other good people in this world. I've lived with them going on three years, and I still can't let them in completely. I tell you this because these are good people. You can trust them. They already love you like you are family. They will accept you as you are, maybe even love you harder because you are different."

He releases my hand and holds it palm facing the sky. A ball of fire forms. When he closes his hand, the flames extinguish.

"Between my shitty ass-attitude, all the baggage I came with, and the magic I wield, they never once pushed me away. They still love me and protect me. They will do the same for you. So will I."

Questions about his magic spin in my mind. Liam patiently answers them and keeps hold of my hand. Eventually, Liam decides it is time to take me back, but I don't want to return to the mansion. I'm not ready yet. We agree to visit Anders.

We repel down the wall using the ropes. Liam touches the ground first. When I dangle only feet away, he lifts me off the wall. As he sets me on my feet, I feel the heat radiating off his body, his warm breath on my face.

His lips are close. If I lean just a fraction closer, I could feel them press against mine. Then, I remember my braces and broken teeth. I remember the scars and my glasses so big they nearly cover my entire face.

I squeeze my eyes shut and turn my head, embarrassed by my thoughts. Any teenage boy who looks like Liam would never find me attractive.

I quickly turn, pulling the hood of my sweatshirt over my head and shove my hands into my pocket. Liam follows me to Anders's office, and I try desperately to divert my thoughts from wanting to kiss him.

When we arrive, Anders studies me. "Why don't you find something to read," he suggests. "Liam, may I speak to you outside?"

I step in front of Anders, not wanting Liam to get into trouble. *Wait! I ran away from the mansion back to the clinic. We just talked. He helped me understand what I'm going through. He didn't do anything wrong.*

Anders smiles. "He's not in trouble, and neither are you. I just want to speak to him. That's all." He raises his eyebrows. "I'm worried that I've selfishly kept Liam on the night shift, and I want to ensure that he can keep up with his final training regimen."

I release a breath. *Okay. He's a good person. He deserves to be here. I don't want anything to jeopardize his position here, especially because of me.*

"That won't happen." Reluctantly, I move aside as Anders and Liam walk out the door.

Not that I don't trust Anders, I want to ensure he isn't reprimanding Liam for taking care of me tonight. I press my ear flush against the door. Their voices are a low murmur, and I can barely decipher their words. I close my eyes and concentrate on their surroundings. Just like that, both of their voices infiltrate my mind.

"Did you see any sign of Dustin, Marcus, or Boris when you went back to the mansion?" Anders asks.

"No, but I found a few of their tracks, definitely Marcus's

and Dustin's. Boris is too smart and sneaky to leave any traces behind."

"It's good you followed your instincts. I'm not too sure on the exact timeframe, but Sodie and Darwin saw Boris lingering near the clinic."

"Yeah. I got Sodie's text so I took her somewhere safe and made sure we weren't followed."

"Good. Thank you. I got it from here. Why don't you get some rest?"

"Sir, Marcus is after her because of me. I'm sorry for my part in this mess."

"No one blames you, son. These assholes were raised to be criminals."

"Sir, if they hurt her, I can't promise you that I won't—"

"If either one of them touches a hair on her head, you have my full fucking permission to end them. No questions asked!"

"Yes, sir."

I hear the shuffling of feet. In a panic, I shove away from the door, grab a book, and plop in one of the chairs.

When Anders returns, he doesn't ask why I ran back to the clinic. "Are you warm enough? Do you want some water?" We fall into our comfortable modes—him working, me reading. When the light of dawn breaks, Anders stands from his seat and stretches. "Let's take a walk."

I pull on my hoodie and follow Anders. We walk in silence. He doesn't say where we are going or what we are going to do. When he stops. I notice a group of men running toward us. Tugging my hood down, I cover my face and lower my head after I adjust my glasses. The group gets closer, shouting and glancing sideways at us. Anders folds his arms watching them in turn.

Charlie and Ean lead. Ean shouts another command, raising

a hand in salute. Charlie smiles and winks. I try not to grin as Anders groans.

The rest of the men follow, saluting Anders and facing front as they pass, except for three. I feel their eyes on me. I lower my gaze, as if I could make myself invisible. I only glance up to catch the back of the group. Sodie smiles, but Liam doesn't look my way at all. Does he regret telling me about his past and showing me his secret?

I peek at Anders, and he resumes our stroll. I follow Anders into a clearing. No one can see us here. He sits on the ground and waits patiently as I lower myself next to him. He rests both hands on his knees. "Close your eyes. Keep your mind blank, and focus on your breathing."

I observe him for a minute, just sitting there, breathing slowly with his eyes closed. Then, I take in my surroundings before mirroring his behavior.

I lose track of time and awareness. Wind swirls around me, caressing my face and rustling my oversized hoodie. It whirls stronger, yet I don't open my eyes. Rain begins to fall. But it doesn't rain on us.

I listen in to the sounds of nature. The rain pounds heavier. The winds grow stronger, whistling and moaning as it whips around. Thunder claps, shaking the ground beneath me, and behind the thin lids of my eyes, I see a flash of lightning.

Don't lose focus on your breathing, Anders says inside of my head. Through all the chaos surrounding me, I sit there. Without any hint of the storm slowing, the rain and thunder evaporate. No more flashes of lightning, and the wind dies. Silence, there is nothing more but silence.

The birds start to chirp, and I slowly open my eyes. The sky is clear. The ground is dry, no sign of the raging storm.

Anders stares at me. Not sure how to respond, I smile and

shrug. He simply grunts and proceeds to stand. I follow his lead, but we remain in the clearing.

Dipping his chin and bending slightly at the waist. When he's back in an upright position, he slides a foot forward and lifts his arms. His body sways in a slow, even rhythm. I watch in curious fascination. His movements are deliberate and fluid, moving his arms out then back in, moving on the balls of his feet so his body sways in tune with his arm movements. Then, he switches sides. His movements remind me of water, languidly rolling over smooth river rocks.

I want to move like him, but I'm not sure how or where to start. I commit each movement to memory. Finally, he holds the last position, brings his legs and arms back to center, and bows.

"I do this every morning, if you would like to join me," he remarks.

I would like that. Thank you.

Turning on the balls of his feet, he begins to walk back the way we came. "I would like to talk about what happened while you were meditating."

Did you see it? The storm?

"No. I didn't see anything, but I could hear it in your mind —the rain, the thunder, the whistling of the wind."

No flashes of lightning?

"You saw flashes of lightning?"

I nod. *Then I heard your voice, telling me to focus.*

"I didn't say anything out loud. You heard my voice?"

Yes, in my head.

"Have you ever experienced anything like this before?"

I start to shake my head but recall my fall from the rock wall. *Well, actually, last night or early this morning. Don't get mad, please, and don't punish Liam.* I wait until he gives me his full attention. He doesn't make any promises.

I show him my memories on the wall.

Shock, rather than anger, registers on his face. "You pulled Liam up with your magic?" I nod. "Did Liam show you or tell you what he can do?"

I glance down. It's a secret. I try to clear my mind.

"Jessica, I know. It's okay. He's not in trouble."

I turn my face away, unsure of whether to reveal the truth, but I trust Anders. *He showed me.*

"Okay. Do you think you can keep your magic under control?"

I don't know. I didn't know I had any.

He nods. "Fair point. Do you still have the journal I gave you?"

Yes. I've been writing in it.

"Good. Keep track of anything else that occurs. We can work on control and building on your capabilities. It's important we keep this to ourselves, except for Nathan and Shakti, of course. I want you always to be honest with them. Is it okay if I tell them?"

I hesitate. *What if they don't want me, once they find out?*

"Trust me. That will not happen." Anders guides me toward the mansion. Instead of using the front door, we enter through the back.

Tater greets us and fusses over me, placing a smoothie and my supplements in front of me at the table where I sit. She's in charge of giving me my injections now. I thought I forgot them at the clinic. She places a small bowl of scrambled eggs in front of me.

I smile. I haven't been able to eat real food. Her smoothies have real fruit in them, disguising the taste of the supplement I was given in the clinic.

"I think you'll like my special diet a whole lot better than what they served you in the clinic. I'll think up different things we can try until the doctor says we can introduce you to regular foods again."

"Thank you," I rasp. My voice is stronger today. I wonder if the meditation helped.

"Oh, and Alpha Agnus insisted that I cook all your meals with water from her territory. Don't tell her, but I'm only going to use it in your smoothie." She sets a glass of water next to me. "Of course, I'll also make you drink it as plain water."

Joe strides into the kitchen. "Good morning," I croak out.

"Good morning, Princess. The Alpha King will join you shortly. The Luna Queen took the boys into the city for some school event. They look forward to seeing you later this afternoon."

I smile. *Were they worried I wasn't here this morning?* I ask through my mind-link.

"Anders notified them you were with him. All is well, Princess."

My tension and anxiety over disappointing them ease. I can focus on eating my breakfast. Anders and Nathan enter the kitchen, and after bidding Anders farewell, Tater lays a plate of breakfast in front of Nathan. He sits at the breakfast nook with me.

"So today is my favorite day of the week. It's the one day I follow up on business with the pack. Would you be interested in tagging along with me."

I nod enthusiastically.

"Great. Duck will join us, and he can share all about the pack's history and how we came to be in the dairy business."

We spend the entire day together. I fall in love with the territory, the pack members, the dairy, and the farms. I love listening to the two men share their beloved history of the pack business and its expansion into sustainable agriculture. By the end of the day, I also fall in love with two more men, who accept me and love me as if I am truly one of their own.

JESSICA
PRESENT DAY:
MARCH 31, 2025

My father sits next to me and squeezes my hand.

"I remember that day as if it was yesterday," he says, eyes shiny with unshed tears. He looks back to the camera. "I must admit, I wasn't sure what it would be like adopting a child, especially an older one. Both the twins and my mate were so adamant that I would love her like she was my own. Even though I agreed to it, especially since she won the hearts of the three toughest men I know, I was still apprehensive. Maybe some of it was my ego, and I worried that she and I wouldn't bond as well as she did with the others."

He looks down at our intertwined hands and smiles.

"At the end of that day, when my mate and I left your room that first night, all my reservations and fears evaporated. My heart swelled with so many emotions, the same ones I felt when I laid eyes upon my boys—love, fear, excitement, and protectiveness all rolled into one big ball. When you hugged me good night, it hit me right here." He brings his hand, still holding onto mine, and rests it over his heart. "That's when I knew—even though I didn't create you—you were mine."

I let go of my father's hand, lean over, and give him a hug before wiping the tears from my eyes.

Carmen lifts her hands, forming a T for time out. "I have a few questions." She glances down at her notes and then at Anders. "For you." She points a ballpoint pen in Anders's direction.

He frowns. Somehow, Carmen convinced him to join us for this portion of the interview. She wanted all of my parents, including Anders, to be present. He protested at first, insisting that he didn't need to be involved.

My mother wouldn't hear of it and insisted, along with my father, that he join us. I agreed with them. I hadn't known all these years who he really was to me, but he has always been there, just like a father, legal papers or not, blood or no blood. I always thought of him as a father figure. I want him by my side, secrets and all, because that is where he belongs.

Carmen raises her pen to her lips and hums. "I think giving the viewers a more in-depth look into your position as a head guard and how is it that she is your biological daughter is a more intimate approach. We already covered the relationship and the bond she made with the Luna Queen and Alpha King. I want to learn more about you, Anders."

Anders sits stiffly next to me, hesitating. He stares at Christian, who in turn watches Anders. Do they know each other? He finally takes his eyes from Christian and looks at me.

"You don't have to. I know that you like to keep your personal life private. Carmen, I don't want—"

Christian interrupts, "I think Jessica should hear your side of the story. You never really gave her much of an explanation from the sound of it. You can't just drop a bomb, a big one in fact, and then expect her to fill in the blanks on her own."

Anders remains silent. Finally, my father speaks. "Anders, it's time. I have been telling you for years that your secrets will eat you from the inside and will catch up to you one day."

Anders squeezes his eyes shut and sighs. "Fine. What do you want to know?"

Carmen beams like she won a prize. "How did you become the head guard? It's obvious from the history books that a Black Obsidian guard was the original head guard, but now he's second lead. How did you earn your position?"

Anders turns his head to look at my father. He nods, giving him permission to share his story. "In order to tell you that, I have to start with the beginning. After the great war, many of the white wolf shifters fled the LS territory. Some stayed under the protection of some of the packs, and some became rogues. My grandmother, Alpha Agnus, was a baby at the time. She lost her mother in the war. It was her father who fled the LS territory, raising her in secret.

"The resistance formed a white hunt after the great war, searching for any survivors and killing them. Then, they killed anyone who showed signs of either magic or white wolf characteristics. Even though the history books claim this period passed, it didn't. The Resistance just became more secretive in their dealings, especially after the new monarch was established. When my grandmother was a young adult, she met her true mate, another white wolf shifter, and they had a daughter. The white hunt caught up to them. Her mate was killed, and my grandmother, protecting her only child escaped.

"The risk was too great to keep her child and stay hidden and alive. She had met a family in the Asian territory and sent her daughter to be raised by them to keep her safe. My grandmother set out to find the white wolves in hiding to figure a way to return home.

"Her daughter grew up and met her true mate, another white wolf shifter raised in the Northern A territory. They also had a daughter, and a couple of years later, they had me. I was two, maybe, at the time—too young to remember any of it. Our home was broken into, and my parents were murdered. My sister, just five years old, was killed in her sleep.

"I was taken and spared. I'm not sure why. My grandmother eventually tracked me down by discovering the group of men who killed my family and saved me. Instead of bringing me to her new pack, she sent me to live with the family who raised my mother."

He pauses, glancing first at me and then back at Christian. My father squeezes his shoulder.

"I was an angry kid. I felt abandoned and hurt that my own grandmother wouldn't take me in, so I acted out. I started fights and even joined an underground fighting ring. My adopted family didn't know what the hell to do with me. Finally, my grandmother sent for me to return home. By then, she mated with an Alpha who had children from a previous mating, and together they returned to the LS territory. I was still so angry with her, more so because she mated a man who had children. She raised them as her own, yet she didn't raise me or my mother."

My heart breaks for him. I picture a young boy with anger and hurt from feeling abandoned.

He runs a hand down his face. "I didn't make it easy for her. I hated her façade of being an older woman who mated a younger man, of being weak. I wanted revenge on the ones who killed my family, who killed her mate. She tried to talk me out of it and said that things would fall into place, but I refused to listen. I left our territory. Not caring if I put myself at risk, I went in search of the Resistance. Instead, I found a group of rogues with the same goals as me—to take down the Resistance and the monarchy so that the white wolves could return and seize what was taken from them.

"I was almost seventeen at the time. On one of our runs, we encountered a fight. From my standpoint, I immediately recognized the guards—outnumbered and losing. I didn't know who they were fighting, though. But I knew for sure it wasn't the rogues, even though people usually blamed us for every random killing that occurred.

"I was tired of it—tired of being labeled as the bad guys— when we were the ones searching to defeat the Resistance. I made the decision to assist the guards, to prove everyone wrong about us. I motioned to my group to help.

"As we approached, I saw three shifters in wolf form surrounding a woman huddled on the ground, using her body to protect a little boy. I ran, zeroing in on the three shifters. I attacked them, using my magic to build a wall of ice in front of the woman to shield her and the boy. I killed the shifters, ripping out their throats with my teeth, and more of them attacked me and the other rogues. When the guards realized we were on their side, they changed tactics and focused on the ones they were there to protect.

"The rogues and I killed many shifters that night. Slowly, the others understood they wouldn't win, so they retreated. I brought my wall of ice down, but when I got close enough..."

Anders closes his eyes briefly and clenches his free hand into a fist. Turning toward my father, I read grief and sadness in in his expression.

"I was too late. The woman died protecting her son. We were also too late to save the head guard. He was killed in the attack. We helped the guards collect their own party, and without a word, we disappeared into the night. For days, I couldn't rid myself of the image of the mother huddled around her son, bleeding to her death. I replayed my actions, my decisions, over and over in my mind. If I had reached them sooner, if I hadn't delayed in my decision to join the fight, I could have saved her. Her son would still have a mother. That boy was now like me, without a mother, all because of the Resistance. After that, I pushed and trained my group of rogues harder. I was even more determined to take down the Resistance."

I clear my throat. "How did you know it was the Resistance?"

"One of the rogues investigated them. He learned of the origins of the attack. They planned on overtaking the Alpha King and his family."

I gasp and clap my hand over my mouth. "That little boy you saved..."

"It was me," my father answers. "That night, he saved my life. His group saved my father, as well as Duck. My father sustained many injuries. He never quite recovered to his normal state, but he and my uncle survived. I lost my mother and grieved her loss, but I still had my family. I will be forever grateful for Anders and his group. We lost our head guard, Elias's father, that night, but he was killed before Anders's group even arrived. The Resistance was smart. They eliminated our strongest guards first, weakening our defenses, to ultimately reach my family."

Carmen quirked a brow at Anders. "Okay. So you saved the Alpha King and his father with your group of rogues, but that still doesn't explain how you came to be the head guard."

My father smiles. "Anders wasn't the only one who knew how to obtain information. Duck tracked the rogues. He trusted someone in the group. He discovered that a teenage boy led the rogues to aid us, and he and my father traveled to Whitemore plantation, known as Parker territory back then, and spoke to Alpha Agnus. When my father learned of Anders's situation, he decided he wanted to bring Anders into our home, offer him guidance, serve as a role model, and fill in as a father figure, which he felt Anders needed. Anders is a natural Alpha. It was obvious he needed another Alpha to help him understand himself.

"Anders came to live with us a few days later. At the time, the head guard and Duck's family also lived in the mansion. He was close to Elias and Chris's age. Over time, he grew close to the pair. I was ten and maybe a little bratty, before life circumstances changed me. Chris and Elias usually ignored me, even though I looked up to them. But Anders was my hero. Still is."

My father smiles and slaps Anders on the back. Anders smirks, lowering his gaze.

"I was a pain in the ass, following him everywhere, copying everything he did. I wanted to be just like him. But he never made me feel like I was a bother. He never told me to leave him alone. He talked to me all the time and taught me how to fight, to protect myself. So, I became his shadow. In my eyes, he was my big brother."

Anders grunts. "You're still a pain in my ass."

My father laughs. "I love you, too. Anyway, Duck took over as interim head guard. He and my father decided to recruit the rogues, who fought alongside the guards."

"Who are the rogues?" I ask.

"You've met them. In fact, two of them work as part of the household staff," Anders clarifies.

"Joe's a rogue?"

Anders chuckles. "He's a guard now, but yes, he once was a rogue. When he learned that I came to stay at the mansion, he took a job on the staff. He was the first friend I made when I moved to the LS territory. He became protective of me, knowing I didn't make the best decisions, considering where my head was at, at the time. He wanted to keep an eye on me. He also became very protective of Nathan. When he completed his training, he decided to remain as staff in the household. He served as both guard and butler. Xavier took the chauffeur position."

I smile, thinking of Joe and Xavier. "They're older than you. You just jumped into their group and bossed them around?" I tease Anders.

He grimaces. "I didn't boss anyone around. They had a goal, one I shared, so I used my training from the Asian territory, even though I wasn't done yet, and taught them."

My father adds, "Even at a young age, Anders was quite skilled. Both my father and Duck were pleasantly surprised to see the rogues in combat training, even more so because, in a short time, they learned to fight, strategize, and work together as a unit. All their training came from a young teenage boy. They allowed Anders to oversee some of the training, under their guidance, of course. It became pretty evident what Anders was meant to do."

"Yes, but wasn't that a role meant for Elias?" Carmen interjects.

Anders nods. "I didn't want the role. I wasn't born into the family, and I wasn't officially adopted. So they created a hierarchy of sorts—a head guard position with a second and third lead role. They would determine each role later when we came of age. I was perfectly fine with the second or third lead position.

"You must understand, for the first time in my life, I had friends and a family. I didn't want to disrupt anything meant to be theirs. I was open about how I felt, and I didn't begrudge Chris or Elias anything. In fact, I decided to join the military.

Chris and Elias wanted to come with me, but their other obligations required they remain at home. So I went alone, hoping that when I returned, Elias or Chris would fill the head guard position.

Anders pauses, gazing intently at Christian. What is he trying to convey? He reaches for a glass of water on a nearby table. I smile at him in encouragement to continue.

"I was nineteen when I left for basic training. I met my true mate a couple of weeks before I was due to leave. I tried to fight the bond. It wasn't safe for her to be with me. It haunted me, knowing her fate would be that of my parents and grandfather. I tried to stay away until I couldn't anymore.

"I kept my relationship a secret. I didn't want anyone to know. I wrote to her every chance I could under a fake name. She wrote back. After basic training, I returned home for a short vacation and snuck off to meet her every chance I had. I loved her. I wanted to keep her safe and protected, even if it meant protecting her from me. So, I didn't hesitate when I received new orders for a job. I finally confided in Joe and Xavier and asked them to keep an eye on her, to make sure she was safe.

"A short while later, after I returned to the military, I received word that she was pregnant. Between Joe, Xavier, and I, we moved her to the Northern A territory under the ruse that she planned to attend college. She did go—I made sure of it after. When my twin boys were born, I relocated them to the Asian territories to be raised by the same family who raised me. By then, my mate hated me. I refused to tell her where they were. She lost her children... and me. I paid for her education and kept tabs on her until she returned to her family. I stayed in the military, and between deployments, I visited the boys from time to time. I know it wasn't enough. I needed to protect them. I... I... would rather see them alive, safe, even if I couldn't be in their lives completely.

"I wanted it to be different, especially when Chris and Elias met their mates. It killed me to see how happy they were. When I came home five years later, I had a crazy idea that maybe we could make it work. I lived with the Alpha King and became part of the guard. I found her again and pleaded with her to forgive me. She sent word that she wanted to see me and talk, so I had hope. As we left our secret meeting place, I had gotten word of another deployment. I promised that when I returned, I would find a way to become a family again.

"My deployment extended for years. I couldn't write or call anyone. When I finally returned to base, Joe notified me that the Alpha King wasn't doing well. I needed to return home as soon as possible. I arrived in time to sit at his bedside and say our final goodbyes. It was the worst day of my life, and it worsened by the minute.

"I found a letter from my mate, dated two years prior, claiming she didn't want to see me anymore. She didn't want me to find her. I planned to find her anyway to explain why I was gone for so long. But the doctor called for a family meeting. They found traces of poison in the Alpha's blood.

"Everything happened at once. I lost a man whom I called a father, and I lost my mate. I was enraged that the guards allowed this to occur. I lost sight of everything else and made it my personal mission to find the asshole who killed the Alpha King. When I found him, I made sure he knew exactly why he was dying. My grief, anger, and regrets consumed me after that. I reverted to my original thinking, that I couldn't risk being involved with my mate or my sons. I convinced myself that who I was, even being with the royal family, wasn't safe. So I decided to dedicate my entire life to protecting those right in front of me, my brother, because every time I looked at him, I saw the ten-year-old boy who lost his parents, like me, to the Resistance. I promised his father—"

"Our father," my father corrects in a hushed tone.

"Our father," Anders repeats. "I promised I would protect him with my life. Between the four of us, we built the guard recruit program so that nothing like that would ever happen again."

My father clears his throat. "I named Anders head guard after my father died. Elias and Chris agreed."

Anger swells within me that Anders gave up so easily on his mate and his sons. But I understand, more than he may think. I guess history has a way of repeating itself.

Anders turns to me. "When I learned you were mine, I wanted to find my mate and ask her what the hell happened. I had no idea you existed. At the time, I couldn't trust myself not to hurt her, for hurting you." He swallows hard. "After some time, though, I realized your mother would never allow such a travesty to happen to you. I know her better than that. I know in my heart she never told me about you because she wanted to keep you. I couldn't be the man she needed, and she at least had you."

He leans forward in his seat, resting his elbows on his knees, and covers his face with his hands.

"Anders," my father whispers.

"Don't, Nathan," he mutters.

I rub his back. His despair breaks my heart. I wonder if there is some way, through this stupid show, I could find her, find some answers.

Anders drops his hands and gazes at me. "I haven't seen your mother in twenty-five years. Every time I look at my boys, I see her… and you. You have my eyes and my hair, but so many aspects of you remind me of her."

"Anders," my mother whispers from the end on the couch. "Maybe it's not too late," she offers.

"She will never forgive me for what I did. After twenty-five years, she's likely moved on by now. I don't blame her, if that's her choice and she's happy. That's all that matters to me."

Swirling small circles on his back with my fingers, I feel his pain behind his words. "You love her," I declare.

He drops his head, hiding the pain that flashes across his face. "I never stopped."

We take a much-needed break after Anders's confession. My parents want to consult with each other in private, and I answer emails and some text messages. We all return at the allocated time.

Carmen breezes into the room as I take my seat. "We are missing one of your family members."

I glance over at my mother on my left, my father on the far end of the couch, and Anders still seated on my right. "I don't understand. I'm pretty sure I covered everyone."

"You haven't really spoken about Luke."

I clear my throat. I don't want to discuss him. "Well, that's easy. He was away at school. I didn't really know him that well."

She narrows her eyes. "I don't believe you. I think it's important you talk about him so the viewers know your *entire* family."

"Uh, isn't the whole point for viewers to watch a bunch of men fight over me to win a contest?" My mother jabs me in the side with her elbow. Her smile doesn't falter, but I catch her motherly side-eye, the one she usually reserves for the twins. I roll my eyes. Fine. "Let's see. I can't remember where I left off." I try to evade her question, but Carmen is too perceptive.

She reviews her notes. "You spent the day with your father. Anders explained his position in the royal family. You started talking about the incident that led you here, but I cut you off. Let's jump in with how you met Luke."

I pinch the bridge of my nose. I really don't want to, especially with my parents here.

My mother reaches for my hand. Concern crinkles the corners of her eyes. "Did something happen between you and Luke you don't want to talk about?"

A lot happened that I don't want to share. How much do I say? It's complicated, and I don't want to portray Luke poorly on national TV.

Sighing, I shake my head. I peek at my father, who mirrors her look of concern. I lick my lips. "It took me a few weeks to acclimate to my new home. I got along well with everyone, but it was hard to accept all I was given. I continued to feel like I didn't deserve them. So, my parents decided to give me chores. I worked with Duck at the dairy, and Tater gave me tasks around the house. I also went with Mom on her pack rounds and pretended to be my father's secretary when he worked in the office. On occasion, I dusted and cleaned Anders's office."

My parents all laugh, remembering those days.

"It was the only way she would accept her allowance and other gifts we gave her," my father admits with a smile. "I don't think I ever met a teenager so unwilling to accept free money. Even when we gave her an allowance, she returned half to invest in stocks and to pay off her medical debt."

Carmen frowns. "You had medical debt?"

My mother shakes her head. "No, she didn't, but she insisted she pay for time and treatments while at the clinic."

I blush, shrugging. "I just felt it was the right thing to do."

CHAPTER 29
ACCLIMATING

JESSICA
EIGHT YEARS AGO:
SEPTEMBER 18, 2016: 10:20 P.M.
ALPHA KINGS MANSION

After the first few weeks, I finally start to settle into my new home. Chores give me a sense of accomplishment, like I earned and deserve to live in my luxurious room. Everything feels right. I begin to feel like I belong, among the pack, with my new family. My parents decide that I am sixteen years old and declare the date when I was found as my birthday.

Professor Hocson, the recruits' professor, proctors me while I take various academic tests to determine my education level. He frowns when I pass all of them and accuses me of cheating. Liam sits in the room with me. The professor knows of my link with the twins and believes I linked to Liam for the answers.

He's wrong. Liam can hear my thoughts, but I could never hear his.

Anders intervenes on my behalf, but Professor Hocson isn't easily dissuaded. He makes me retest with Ean in the room. Afterward, my test scores satisfy him. Everyone agrees I can test out with the recruits during their examinations to receive my high school diploma. Professor Hocson even volunteers to enroll me in core college courses in the next term.

I still want to escape my room some nights, and I revert into insomnia due to the nightmares. I never had them when Liam sat next to my clinic bed. Even though Emily and the twins try piling into bed with me to help me sleep, I still experience them. So, I just don't sleep.

I eventually begin referring to Shakti and Nathan as Mom and Dad. The first time I used the more familiar term, they beamed with happiness at my acceptance.

Some nights, I find my father awake at his desk. I'll pop into his office and talk to him for hours about the history of the LS, how some laws were created, and why—no topic is off limits. We debate the issues facing the territory. I particularly enjoy these nights. When we tire each other out with debates and talk, we both retire to our rooms.

One night, my anxiety spikes. The recruits count down the time left in the program. Ean and Charlie are two of the trainers, so I will still see them, especially if I am accepted into the next recruit class. But both Liam and Sodie plan to move on after graduation. Sodie will continue guard training somewhere else, and Liam—well, Liam never says anything. In fact, Sodie is the one to tell me Liam is leaving after graduation.

I try to push down the hurt that builds behind my heart. Liam doesn't owe me an explanation. I might have a crush on him, but he doesn't feel the same way. Every evening, Sodie visits after their training. Then, Liam relieves him for the night shift. Even though I no longer need it, Anders wants them to finish their assignment before graduation.

I won't argue. I actually miss them when I don't see them.

Some days, Liam behaves like he had when he first came to my room—silent, distant—wearing his pinched expression. Other days, though, he's friendly, sweet, chatty. I swear on the nights he walks me back to the manor from guitar/band practice with Duck, he bumps into me deliberately, grazing my hand and holding my pinky for the briefest of moments before tucking his hands into his hoodie's front pocket.

But no matter his mood, he always makes me flip the light switch three times before I prepare for bed. My heart sinks when I think about him leaving, but I don't have a choice. Besides, he doesn't want someone like me—broken, ugly, with no future.

Roaming the halls that night, I find myself standing in front of my father's office door. It's slightly ajar. I can hear him talking then, another voice, more distant, replies. White static surrounds the voice, distorting their words, making it hard to hear. I think they're on speaker phone.

"What the hell do you mean, you're adopting her?" the voice shouts. "What happened to equality in the family and everyone getting a say?! I didn't vote. You never gave me a chance to voice *my* concerns. What the hell are you two thinking?"

My father responds slowly, "I'm sorry you feel that way, Luke. I admit I'm a little surprised with your tone at the moment."

"We know *nothing* about her. What if she's pretending to have amnesia? What if she's working for the Resistance? How do you know we can trust her? What if the Resistance planted her in our home to kill all of us in our sleep? What if she—"

"That's enough!" My father booms, his voice loud, commanding, stern. "Where are these conspiracy theories coming from all of a sudden?" he asks. "You were on board when we talked about bringing her into our home. You were on board when your mother wanted to redecorate the room for her."

"There's a difference between letting her stay with us and adopting her," the voice growls.

"I want to know right now where this is coming from!" my father prompts. "Luke, you better think long and hard about how you answer me."

"I don't want her in our family. I will never accept her as a sister."

I heard enough. I pull away from the office threshold and race out the back door. With no idea where to escape, I want to run and find Anders. But I don't want to cause anyone to take a stand over a conversation I shouldn't have overheard in the first place.

I decide to head toward the barn. I find Queenie's stall, wrap my arms around her neck, and cry. Queenie nuzzles me with her nose.

I would never hurt anyone. Why does he think I would?

"Hey, Little One. What's with all of this?" A large, warm hand strokes my back.

I turn and bury my face in Duck's buttoned Western shirt. Too many words circle my brain, so I use my mind-link to recapture the conversation I just witnessed.

"I see," he says. Queenie nibbles at my ear when I don't pay her attention. "Luke's a good boy. I'm sure once he gets to know you, he will feel bad about his reaction. This family doesn't have a good history with trusting newcomers. I'm sure he's just looking out for his parents and brothers. It's hard because he's so far away. You'll see."

I shake my head. *He sounded so angry.*

"Let me tell you a story, then, about Charlie and Sixes. When Charlie was born, he was the only boy in the entire house. Luke hadn't come along yet, and the four eldest girls had the run of the house. When Charlie arrived, the girls loved him. Everyone doted on him, like he was the prince."

Duck chuckles. I smirk, thinking of a young Charlie.

"He charmed all the girls to do his bidding and got away with the devilish things, I tell you. When Tater announced another baby was on the way, Charlie was initially on board. He nuzzled his mama's belly every chance he got. He talked into her belly and told the baby he couldn't wait to meet her. But, when the baby came, things changed. Everyone's attention focused on Sixes, instead of him. He received scoldings when he acted out or disturbed the baby. He got jealous. He once stole Sixes right out of her crib and buried her in a stack of hay. Another time, he gave her to one of the dairy workers and told him to take the baby home."

I giggle, picturing a toddler Charlie giving away Sixes.

"Eventually, he accepted his new baby sister. When she got older, he grew into an overly protective big brother, and the two have been thick as thieves ever since. My point is that once Luke gets to know you, he'll get over his insecurities, too, and I can see him becoming another overly protective brother. Just wait and see."

I smile up at Duck.

"Feeling a little better?"

I nod and lean in to give Duck a hug.

"Good. Now let's get you back inside. A growing girl like you needs her rest."

Shoot, I can't remember if he likes strawberries or blueberries. Maybe I can make both. It's been weeks since I eavesdropped on the call Luke and my father. Luke is coming home this evening. I'm really nervous. I already know he's not a fan of mine. I want to make a good impression.

So, I decide to make him dinner—well, everyone dinner.

This week marks six months since I was rescued. I use both Luke's homecoming and my anniversary with the family as an opportunity to say thank you. I also hope Luke will see that I love his family and would never deliberately hurt them.

I gnaw on my lip. I'll ask Dad. Shutting off the stove so I don't burn anything, I walk toward my father's office. I review my notes on the way. He likes roast beef and roasted potatoes, not mashed. Soup is okay. He doesn't really have a preference.

I crash into a hard wall and fall backward to the floor. Wincing, I look up to find Charlie standing in the hall. He glares and doesn't offer to help me stand. Okay, then. I've never seen this expression on Charlie's face before. He folds his arms in front of his chest.

I pick myself up and rub my tailbone. "Sorry, Charlie. I wasn't paying attention to where I was going." I adjust my glasses and tap the bill of my hat, both of which went askew in my tumble.

"I guess we have a thief in the house," he spits.

His tone sends shivers up my spine. I squint. The arms folded over his chest are even. Charlie's right arm is slightly bigger than his left. This guy has a grim set to his lips, and dimples indent his right cheek. This isn't Charlie, but holy shit, it could be his twin. I step back and swallow. This is Luke.

He snatches the hat from my head. "This is mine," he says. I blink at him in dismay. I never expected this level of hostility. "This is also mine." He pulls on the strings of my hoodie.

I found this hoodie, my lucky hoodie, the night I ran away from the clinic. I thought I could use some luck to cook and serve a perfect dinner for... this asshole right in front of me. I lift my chin. I won't let him intimidate me. I didn't do anything wrong. He steps closer, and closer still, but I refuse to back down. I return his glare.

"What else have you stolen while I was gone? Should I start locking my door or put an alarm system on the valuables?"

What the fuck is his problem? Fine. If he wants his sweatshirt, he can have it. I shove the piece of paper into the front pocket and remove my glasses. Pulling my arms through the sleeves, I remove the oversized, comfortable garment and shove it into his chest. I stand there, seething, in only a sports bra and lounge pants. I need to go upstairs and get another shirt.

He catches it. "Thanks. I'll have this laundered. It stinks," he sneers.

Anger shoots up my spine. A clap of thunder erupts over our heads, shaking the entire mansion. I jump. Shit! I didn't mean to do that. I spin around and race up the stairs to my room.

Resting my glasses on my desk, I pace and shake my arms. *Deep breath. Deep breath*, I repeat to myself. Just like Anders taught me. *Calm down*, I scold myself. Anders explained that my magic is connected to my emotions. I take another calming breath and think of things that make me happy.

Luke's angry face pops into my mind. Thunder rumbles from a distance, and heavy rain pours outside. *No, no, no. Calm down. Calm down.*

My bedroom door crashes open. "What the hell was that?" he asks, accusing.

A flash of lightning streaks outside of my window. I face him as I slowly back toward the French doors. He needs to get away from me.

My hands tremble from the buzz of electricity in my fingers and palm. I back up the cool glass of the doors hits my back. I grasp for the handle and slip onto the balcony. Rubbing my thighs, I urge, *Calm down. You can do this.* I take several deep breaths. The flash of lightning and thunder appear farther away. The downpour soaks me in minutes, but I don't care.

"Are you doing this?"

Why can't he take a frickin' hint and stay away? I'm not bothering him. I'm trying to retreat.

He grabs my shoulder and forces me to look at him. "Are you doing this?" he snaps.

Instinctively, I raise my arms, palms out to protect myself. A force of wind slams him into the outer wall. Lightning and thunder explode around me.

He slowly stands and approaches me again. "Get it under control before you hurt someone," he commands through clenched teeth.

"Then get away from me," I squeak. Moving away from him, my back hits the railing. But he prowls closer. "Stay away from me!" I try to shout, but my voice fails me, emitting only as a rush of air.

His menacing, haunting demeanor causes tingles of fear to spread within my body. He places his hands on either side of me, resting them on the metal barrier, trapping me in his space. "I swear if you don't get this under control and hurt my family..."

The wind howls around me loudly, reflecting my hurt and anger. "I would never hurt your family!" I whisper-scream. The wind whips around us.

The balcony quivers from an impending earthquake. I'm not doing that. My eyes widen, but he still doesn't move, his eyes narrowed, lips curled in anger. I push him, hard, loosening his grip. The balcony shakes more intensely, knocking me backward. I wince, and the railing breaks under my weight.

I fall, contorting my body to find the ground rushing up to meet me. I raise my arms in front of my face, anticipating the impact.

The wind catches me just in time, hovering me a few feet above the earth. Pain sparks in my abdomen as a loose part of the railing stabs through me. Using the wind, I levitate away from the flying projectiles, press my hand over the wound, and plummet to the ground. Something slides from my waist and slithers away. What the hell is that? But I can't see clearly enough to figure out what it is.

Luke stands over me, eyes wide. "Are you okay?"

What the fuck is his problem? One minute, he's trying to kill me, and the next, he's as white as a sheet with... concern? *No, I am not okay. I'm angry, you piece of shit for brains.*

A bolt of lightning slaps the ground, close enough to send Luke flying toward the house. I get to my feet and see blood on my hand. The wound, thankfully, isn't very deep. Fucking asshole! Thunder booms, and Luke jumps. I prowl toward him with as much menace and threat as I can muster. He appraises me, swallowing.

Since I can't speak loud enough to make my fucking point, I force my voice into his head. *I would never hurt your family!"* My chest heaves. I press a hand into my side and clench the other into a fist so I don't lose control of my magic. *But if you ever come at me again, I promise, I will hurt you!* Another bolt of lightning strikes the ground near him. He rolls out of the way and covers his ears at the booming thunder.

I use the wind to lift me onto my balcony. The cute little table and chairs fell over the side from the earthquake. I walk into my room, close and lock the doors, and draw the heavy drapes. For good measure, I also lock my bedroom door.

I don't understand. Why would he attack me that way?

If dinner was for Luke alone, I would dump everything, partially cooked and raw, in the middle of his bedroom. I wanted to prove to him that I wasn't the monster he thinks I am. My heart aches, thinking he won't appreciate any of it anyway.

But it's not just for him. All of them are coming for dinner tonight, and I want to thank them for accepting me into their family. So, I will finish what I started.

I don't bother to reread the list of Luke's likes and dislikes. He can kiss my ass. I hope the dinner turns out so well that he chokes on it when he learns I made it. I hope his guts twist in knots and he becomes ill for at least a week. Maybe not that last part. He will no doubt accuse me of poisoning him and try to kick me out of my home.

Downstairs, I set the finishing touches on the dining room table and take one final look.

"It's perfect," Joe says from the doorway. I walk over to give him a hug. "I think the family will be impressed. It's nothing like Tater or I have ever done before."

I offer a tight smile. He's just being nice. We return to the kitchen, and I focus on the last-minute details.

Joe reaches for the serving trays on the upper shelves when he asks, "Jessica, what happened to you?" I glance around and shrug. "You're bleeding. What happened?" he asks again.

Glancing down, my shirt is covered in blood. All the moving around must have reopened the wound. "It's just a scratch," I whisper.

"Show it to me."

"It's nothing, Joe. Just a scratch," I rasp.

"Then, show it to me."

Stepping away from the counter, I lift my shirt. The bandage I placed earlier is soaked through.

Joe peels the bandage away from my skin and frowns. "This is not a scratch, Jessica. This looks like you were stabbed."

Sidestepping away from him, I replace the blood-soaked dressing and lower my shirt. "It's nothing, really. I'm fine." I avoid his eyes and desperately think of anything but what happened earlier. I'm surprised no one thought to look for us with all the noise and earthquake.

He retrieves a box from a nearby cabinet. "Go upstairs and change. Here are some dressings you can use." I look around and vow to clean my mess before Tater and the rest of the staff arrive. "I got it. Go," Joe says firmly.

Thank you, Joe. I'll make it up to you.

"Jessica." I stop on my way out of the room but don't turn around. "I don't care who he is, if he hurt you..."

No, Joe. It was an accident. All good. Like I said, just a scratch. I've had worse. I leave the kitchen before he responds. I don't like lying to him, but I can't tell him what happened. I don't need Luke accusing me of being a snitch as well.

I run up the stairs, hurrying before everyone arrives. Justin and Jeremy stand in the hallway talking to Luke, smiling, laughing, patting each other on the back.

I clutch the box from Joe close to hide the blood on my stomach. I consciously think about the various ingredients I used in the meal preparation and make a list of tasks, confirming I accomplished them. Just so the twins don't pick up on my thoughts.

"Hey, Jess. Did you meet Luke yet?" Justin asks.

I lift my head and quickly glance at Luke. He plasters a fake smile on his face. When the twins turn to look at me, he drops it. I close my eyes and take a deep breath. Ouch, that burns. Returning the tight-lipped smile, I shake my head.

Jeremy places an arm around his shoulders. "This is the best big brother you will ever meet, besides us, of course."

I give a curt nod and wave. Another burning sensation rubs over my wound.

Justin frowns. "What's burning?"

"Hmm?"

He steps toward me. "Why do I smell blood?"

Oh, I was helping in the kitchen and spilled blood on my shirt.

I'm going to get changed. No big deal. I'll meet you downstairs. I push past them.

Jeremy grabs my arm. "You're trying to hide something," he proclaims.

Justin grabs the box out of my hands. "Why do you need the first aid kit?"

Pulling my arm out of Jeremy's grasp, I snatch the box back from Justin. "I'm fine. Just a scratch," I explain.

Jeremy narrows his eyes. "That's not from a scratch!"

Justin pulls me closer and lifts the hem of my shirt. "What the fuck happened? And don't try to hide it."

I shake my head, trying to inch my way to my room. *I'm fine, really. Go spend time with Luke, and I will meet you downstairs.* I back into my bedroom door, but the twins hover in front of me. Luke leans against the doorframe to his room, smirking. Bastard.

The twins frown and turn toward Luke. "Did you see the blood on the front of her shirt?"

Luke tilts his head for a better look. For a brief moment, concern crosses his features. He stalks over and reaches forward to lift my shirt. His eyes widen. "Why didn't you say something?"

"What would you have me say?" I grit, staring into his emerald-green eyes. Does he want to tell them what happened? Because I'm not.

"Tell us what, Jessica?" Justin asks. "What are you hiding?"

"You're working really hard not to think about your injury. Why?" Jeremy observes.

I lower my eyes. "I'll meet you downstairs," I whisper. I don't lie to the twins. I don't lie to anyone. But they're so happy to see Luke. I won't cause a family rift because of Luke's insane notion that I am out to hurt everyone.

Justin rests his hand on my shoulder. "Let me help you clean it."

I shake my head, and he turns to Jeremy. I push my door open enough to slide into my room and quickly move to close the door.

Jeremy blocks it, pushing it wide open. "I'm not letting this go. Tell me right now! After everything you've been through, you got hurt again, and I want to know how."

Sighing, I walk across the room and open my drapes. "It was an accident. I fell off the balcony."

The twins peer through the window. "Shit! We're three stories up," Jeremy exclaims.

"It's embarrassing. Can you please let it drop now?"

Jeremy frowns. "Are you okay?" I nod. "You never lied to us before or hid anything. It just made me worried that someone hurt you." He pulls me into his embrace. "Don't make me worry like that." I nod again against his chest, and he releases me.

Justin joins me in the bathroom. "Let me see." He shakes his head. "You need stitches, or it won't stop bleeding. How long ago did this happen?"

I shrug. "A few hours. I needed to finish making dinner."

"So stubborn," he grumbles, placing butterfly bandages to keep the wound closed. "I'll take you to the clinic."

I shake my head. *Have dinner with Luke. I'll go after dinner is served. You missed him, and I can tell he missed you guys, too.* I push at his shoulder so he stops fussing over me. *Go! I'll finish cleaning up and meet you downstairs.*

After I throw away the old bandage and wipe down the counters, I leave the closet wearing a dark maroon blouse and dark jeans. Staying here may not work out after all. Luke never once spoke up and admitted how I fell over the balcony He just let me stand there and lie to my brothers. I hate him for that. Heading downstairs, I pass Luke's room.

"Why didn't you tell them the whole truth?" I stop and turn toward his voice. He's leaning against the open door.

"What's there to tell?" I glare.

"It was my fault you got hurt. The first person you should have run to is my father."

I step toward him. *It's not like you admitted your part. Goddess forbid you show your true colors to your brothers!* I snap in my mind. I grind my teeth and take a steadying breath before I lose control again. *Look, I don't know why you think I'm this horrible person, but I am not here to steal from or hurt your family. I love them. I didn't run to him, and I didn't tell the twins because they love you. They missed you. I don't want to ruin your reunion. You don't want me here? Fine. I'll leave. I didn't ask your family to take me in. I appreciate everything they have done for me.* I glance down. *But if my being here will ruin your life and your relationship with your family, then I'll go. No one needs to know we even had this conversation.*

I leave him standing in the hallway, mouth hanging open as I walk away.

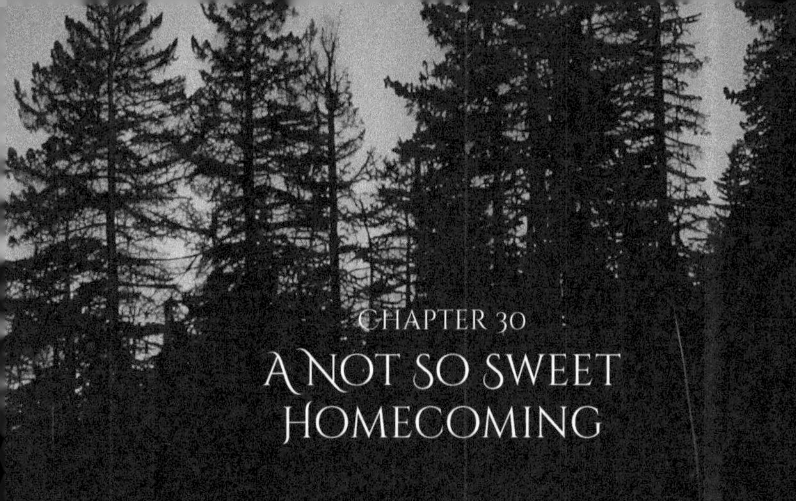

Chapter 30

A Not So Sweet Homecoming

LUKE

EIGHT YEARS AGO:

November 7, 2016: 6:45 p.m.

Alpha Kings Mansion

Aunt Tater has outdone herself. The aroma of roast beef fills the air. The dining room looks like a photo in one of those fancy living magazines. I can't believe it. I've never seen the room look so professionally and elegantly decorated. Hell, it doesn't ever look like this when we have a special guest over. I hug and greet everyone. Being with my family takes me out of my foul mood. Despite the little feud between Jessica and me, I think I can ignore her for the rest of the night. Or, well, try to.

My mind keeps replaying her little speech in the hall, where her raspy voice magically cleared. Yeah, right, she'll leave. She has too much to lose. Who the hell would give up being a princess, not to mention free money, a luxury home, and an elite education? I know she won't leave. I know it. She knows it.

All her brave talk is just that—talk. I'm onto her. She isn't the first woman to use me to become the future Luna Queen or, in her case, a princess. I won't let that happen, especially not after Sherise.

A sharp pain in the back of my arm brings me back to the present. Spinning around to face my attacker, I find Emily—all five foot nine, long, glossy black hair, and dark piercing eyes that gleam with the promise of murder in them.

"Ouch! What the hell was that for?" I whine, rubbing my arm.

"For being a douche canoe! I hope you can live with yourself after what you did."

Great. Jessica must have told her or Sixes about earlier. The twins mentioned that Emily and Sixes are friends with her. Their girl trio has apparently been inseparable since she moved in. Why am I surprised that she'd sic Emily on me? Emily's like a bulldog, overly protective and loyal to a fault. Fuck with her or those she cares about, and she attacks first, asks questions later. Now she's using Emily to fight her battles. I grab Emily by the elbow and pull her to the side so no one can overhear our conversation. "It was an accident. I didn't mean for her to fall off the balcony. She just made me so angry, I lost control of my magic."

Emily's expression transforms from a murderous glare to... shock? She raises a hand. "Wait. Who the hell did you push off a balcony? Elaine? Damn. I wish I was there to see that."

What the...? I frown. She's not mad because of Jessica? "Wait. What the hell are you mad at me for, then?"

"You ignored my phone calls and texts for the past few weeks. I hope your insides rot from guilt and... No, don't change the subject. Who did you push off a balcony?" I glance around the room, avoiding her direct gaze, when she grabs my face.

"Who did you push off the balcony?" she repeats slowly, like I'm a child who can't follow directions.

I swallow. In my peripheral vision, the spiky platinum blonde hair flits around the dining room, mingling with my family. I shift my gaze for a millisecond before focusing on Emily, but she figures it out.

Her jaw drops, and she hisses, "You didn't."

"It was an accident," I hiss back.

"Lucretius Jacob Langhlan, I am so going to kick your fucking ass, and then when I am done with you, I will tell Liam so he can finish you off, cut you up into pieces, and feed your body parts to the pigs!"

I desperately glance around the room. Everyone is so busy talking to each other, they don't mind Emily's outburst. "Keep it down! Like I said, it was an accident!" I whisper harshly.

"You! You of all people should know better. After everything she's been through, how could you?"

Her words hit me like a knife in the back. "You're not even going to listen to my side? Am I the only one who thinks her being here is a bit suspicious?"

"You know what, Luke? Not everyone is Sherise or Elaine." She folds her arms in front of her. "I'm so mad at you right now —I can't even look at your face!" She spins around, whipping me with her long hair as she stalks away.

I want to follow her to plead my case when Joe whistles for everyone's attention. He announces that everyone has arrived and asks us all to take our seats. Usually, family dinners are held in the music room, and food is set up on a table against the wall in warmers. I wonder why tonight is so different, so formal. It can't be just because I returned home.

The staff serve us first with a soup. Jessica sits next to Anders. Nothing is placed in front of her, though. She stands and walks over to Joe. She inclines her head for him to sit at the table.

Justin, on the other side of her, says, "Come on, Joe. Join us."

He blushes and shakes his head. Anders motions for Joe to take the chair that Jessica vacated. She pulls Joe by the hand, and he finally concedes. Jessica pats his shoulder and kisses his cheek, making him blush even more.

"You will always be family, Joe." I raise my glass to him, and everyone follows suit. I glance in Jessica's direction. I want her to hear so she understands I accept staff as family over her any day. I quickly glance toward Emily and tense from her immediate scowl. A heaviness weighs down my chest.

My father clears his throat and stands from his seat. "I know we usually have a more casual get-together. But tonight, Jessica asked if she could make a special dinner. She worked hard these past weeks, doing chores to earn money to pay for all the food and decorations. She kicked Tater and Joe out of the kitchen to prepare everything all on her own. It was important to her to welcome you home, Luke. She wanted to make a good impression. At the same time, she wanted to thank everyone for accepting, loving, and welcoming her into our family."

I look around at the table. Everyone smiles, eyes brimming with emotion. Was I wrong to assume that she was some gold-digging, manipulative person? No. No, this is part of the scam. I know it! How can every single person at this table not see what she's doing?

My father's eyes shine with pride. Gazing at my mother, she wipes at her tears. He places a hand on her shoulder. "Before the soup gets cold, how about we eat?" he encourages us with a nod.

I almost issue a snarky comment, warning everyone that we might get poisoned. Then, I think better of it. It seems everyone except me genuinely loves her. She must be a very good actress, pretending to be shy and to hate being in the center of attention. No one comments on the fact that she hasn't returned to join the rest of us.

I can't stifle my curiosity so I finally ask, "Why isn't Jessica eating with the rest of us, especially since she went to all the trouble of making dinner?"

Justin looks at me from across the table, but Jeremy answers, "She doesn't eat in front of anyone. She's a little self-conscious about her teeth. It's also why she doesn't talk much."

I frown. She spoke to me. I hadn't really paid attention to her teeth.

Emily elbows Jeremy. "That's not why she doesn't talk. Her voice is still hoarse from the tracheostomy. The initial cut damaged her vocal cords. She's been working with a speech therapist to strengthen her voice."

Bile rises in my throat. The hole in her throat makes her unable to speak?

Jeremy adamantly shakes his head. "She won't eat in front of others or talk because of her teeth."

I snort. "A little vain, don't you think?"

Justin retorts, "It's more than that. You weren't here when she finally saw what she looked like, after she woke up from being in a coma. That beating she took damaged her teeth. When she looks in the mirror, she thinks... she thinks she's ugly," he admits with a blush.

I have to admit that when I first saw her with the large glasses and the baseball cap hiding her face. I didn't see past the camouflage, but when she removed her glasses and glared at me with those pale blue eyes, striking dark brows, and thick dark lashes. I nearly forgot what I was saying, which made me angrier. I assumed she deliberately used her looks to manipulate me.

The staff brings in the main course, removing our soup

bowls. Jessica is among them. For the first time since being home, I study her. She doesn't fully smile, careful not to show teeth. She gestures a lot with her head or hands, like she's mute. She covers her mouth when she laughs. Silver glints in the light. She wears braces. Big deal. The glasses cover up most of her face, partially hiding the long scar down the left side of her face. If I look carefully, I notice bald spots where hair hasn't fully grown in yet.

She seems comfortable with everyone here, but she still hesitates, keeping her distance. Charlie flirts with her, and I roll my eyes. He flirts with everyone. But she doesn't blush or drop the plate she holds, as some women do around Charlie when he cranks up the charm. She murmurs something that makes Ean roar with laughter and Liam chuckle. Then, she just walks away without looking back.

Emily reaches for her arm and whispers into her ear. Jessica presses her lips together. Why? To stop a smile? Emily wraps her arms around Jessica's waist in a hug before releasing her. Jessica kisses the top of Emily's head before leaving the room.

Elias leans forward to speak to my parents. "Those two are inseparable. I hope Emily's not being a pest. She never comes home anymore."

My mother scoffs. "Elias, you know your kids are more than welcome here any time."

"Yeah, except Emily's a bit of a—well, for a girl, she's not the tidiest person."

"Hey, I heard that!" Emily grumbles. Ean, Elijah, and Liam laugh. Emily throws a roll at Liam, but he catches it and takes a big bite. My parents chuckle as well.

"Yeah, well, after Jessica cleaned the twins' rooms, I'm pretty sure she can survive anything," Aunt Tater chimes in.

"I had to pay her double and give her a bonus after she finished," my father adds.

I personally wouldn't clean the twins' rooms, even if they paid me a million bucks. That doesn't mean anything. She's just hard up for money.

Jessica returns to set the main course in front of me. Offering a tight-lipped smile, she whispers, "I heard this was your favorite. I hope you like it." She moves away before I can reply.

Emily raises a brow at me. "Go on. Try it. She worked her ass off, putting together this five-course meal with all of your favorites. She even paid the staff tonight with her own money, so everyone can enjoy dinner and spend time with you. Just thought you should know." Emily stares while I cut into my meal and watches me take my first bite.

This is the best roast beef I ever tasted, better than some five-star restaurants I have been to. Emily isn't done with me, not yet anyway. She starts talking about Jessica and all the little things she has been through during her short time here. Hearing all that Jessica has experienced, how everyone around me knows her so well, makes me feel worse for assuming the worst of her. She should have struck me down with lightning earlier today. I would have deserved it.

As dinner continues, enjoying my meal becomes more difficult. Guilt sits heavy in my gut. By the time dessert comes, I notice Jessica is absent. I want her to be at this table, to be with her family. I prepare to stand, to apologize for being such an asshole, and ask her to join us.

Emily barges into the dining room from the kitchen. "Hey!" she shouts. "Where's Jessica? I can't find her anywhere."

Justin and Jeremy both frown, looking at each other with concern.

"She's not in the house. I can't hear her thoughts," Jeremy states. He can't hear her what?

Justin turns to our father. "Before dinner started, I told

Jessica she should have her wound assessed. She might need stitches—it was bleeding so badly. I totally forgot about it and meant to check in with her."

Anders stands from his chair, pulls his cell from his pocket, and leaves the room. Liam retrieves his own phone, retreating to the farthest corner of the room. Anders returns, glowering. "She hasn't been to the clinic. The doctor will call if she shows up."

Liam ends his call. "Sodie's been keeping an eye on Dustin and Marcus. They're currently in the rec room. He assumed Boris was in his room since he last spotted him a little over an hour ago. He's checking now and will text—" His phone buzzes. "He's not there."

Anders immediately barks orders to Ean, Charlie, and Liam. Duck calls all guard pack members within the territory to begin a search. I run out the door, following them.

Liam turns to say, "Sodie is gathering the rest of the recruits to secure Dustin and Marcus, and then they'll join us to look for Boris."

"Aren't we kind of jumping the gun, just a little?" I ask.

Liam sighs. As we join the other recruits, he explains about his fight with Marcus, Dustin, and Boris, as well as Marcus's threat. One of the recruits overheard the three of them talking, making plans to kidnap the VIP, and informed the leads.

Unfortunately, Anders couldn't dismiss the three recruits because of Alpha Greystone's political pull. He increased security, but he didn't want to draw unnecessary attention. He employed the recruits, claiming it as part of their training.

Joe, Duck, and Xavier are also on high alert. Some of the dairy hands, who are also guards, watched over Jessica. Unbeknownst to her, Jessica was never really left without a guard... until now. If Liam revealed this story to anyone outside of the guard, it would sound farfetched and maybe even a little overprotective.

Among the three, Boris is the worst. Evil oozes around him. When I first met him, my skin crawled. I dug into his background. Like Dustin, he is from the same pack in the Northern A territory. Several reports from the school he attended before coming to the recruit program include incidents of bullying and fights. He put two other teenagers in the hospital.

One report turned my stomach. This girl not only went to the school administration to file a complaint against him, she also sought out the authorities. He harassed her for months. I have a copy of the report. In her own handwriting, she wrote in detail how she suffered by his hand for months. After she reported the rape, she mysteriously disappeared. Not long after he arrived in the LS territory, her body was found. She was raped, mutilated, and decapitated. I showed the reports to my father and Anders. They both tried to remove him from the guard program, but the Sixth Territory Alpha made a fuss and pulled some political bullshit. Since there was no proof that Boris murdered the girl and official charges were not made against him, he got to stay.

What if Jessica left the mansion to run away, like she told me. What if I sent her straight into the arms of a psychotic rapist and murderer?

CHAPTER 31

ONE SET OF TRACKS

LIAM

EIGHT YEARS AGO:
NOVEMBER 9, 2016: 4:00 P.M.
GUARD TRAINING FACILITY

We searched the entire area. She's gone. We tracked her as far as the forest, where she left a faint trace of fresh blood behind. I squeeze my hands into fists. *Where the fuck is she?*

Some of the pack men found Boris naked, beaten, and bound with zip ties. He just came to and started healing by the time we joined them. He admitted that he followed her and planned to coerce her back to his room. Of course, Ean and Charlie resorted to beating the shit out of him to obtain that bit of information. He claimed he didn't get very close to her when he was attacked.

"Boris says five men attacked him," Charlie reports, pulling my attention to his debrief. We all gather in the conference room at the training center.

Anders paces back and forth. I study the room. Everyone looks exhausted and subdued. Justin's eyes are red-rimmed. Luke and Emily looks the worst. She sniffs and wipes her face. She refuses to leave. Same as the twins, Sixes and Elijah.

I rub her back, offering comfort. She murmurs, "I shouldn't have left her alone. I should have eaten with her in the kitchen."

"Beating ourselves up over what-ifs won't change what happened," I tell her.

"She's my best friend, and I left her alone. She did all that work, and no one bothered to keep her company. I'm a horrible friend." She starts to cry.

I massage her quivering shoulders. If anyone is a horrible friend, it's me. I haven't been the greatest friend to her either. I know my behavior confused her.

I've been trying to keep my distance to keep Marcus and the other two assholes away from her, especially if they are after her in retaliation. Also, I'm leaving after the graduation ceremony.

But I am not handling it well. I don't want to leave my family or her. The more time I spend with her makes it harder to leave.

Charlie slams the table with his fist, cracking the wooden surface down the center. We all snap to attention. With a murderous glare, he blasts, "Did anyone hear what I just said?" He sighs. "I get it. She's my little buddy, too. Sitting here feeling guilty and beating ourselves up won't bring her back. We need to keep our heads clear and focus on finding her. Now, Pops was the best tracker in his day. He thinks Boris is full of shit. He found one set of wolf tracks near where Boris was found and one set of shoe prints in the forest. He thinks this was a one-man job. Whoever took her is clever. He left just enough of a scent to confirm she was there. He carried her out. Hence, one set of tracks."

"Why take Boris's PT uniform?" Jeremy asks.

Charlie shrugs. "I'm guessing to hide his own scent and throw off the trackers."

"How does all of this information help us figure out where to look for her?" Emily inquires. "We still don't have any leads. Has anyone heard from Shadow?"

Anders stops pacing. "He's been searching, with no results. He thinks she's no longer in the LS territory."

Emily drums her fingers on the table. "Has anyone checked the airport security system? The cruise ships? What about the shipping docks?" Everyone stares blankly at her. "What? You already did that? It's just a suggestion because we all are beating our heads against a wall."

I stand. "No, we haven't thought of that. We were stuck focusing within the LS territory. Elijah, come with me."

Anders frowns. "Wait a minute. What are you doing?"

"No offense, Anders, but the guards lack basic technology skills. However, we have a few recruits who are very capable of hacking into system databases."

Emily squeals. "Can I help?! I can crack some codes!"

"Because I taught you," Elijah grumbles.

Elias glances at his children. "Should I be worried?"

Jumping up with renewed enthusiasm, Emily pushes me out the door. "Not if it helps get Jessica back!"

LUKE

EIGHT YEARS AGO:

NOVEMBER 11, 2016: 8:30 P.M.

ALPHA KINGS MANSION

We search every pier, every airport. For hours on end, we search every security system we can hack into. Shadow, wherever he is, looks everywhere. If something happens to her, I will never forgive myself.

My parents are beside themselves with worry, and my brothers... blame themselves. I head over to my father's office. I need to tell them about my fight with her. I need to explain that maybe she isn't missing after all because she ran away, because I chased her away. They should know the truth.

The door to the office is cracked open, and I lift my hand to knock. Anders's voice travels into the hallway. "Don't tell me to calm down, Nathan! She's my daughter!"

"I understand, Anders. She might not be of my blood, but I think of her as my daughter, too."

"I made a mistake. I should have sent her to Ryukyu as soon as I found out. This is my fault!"

"It's not your fault. We don't know anything. We can't jump to conclusions."

"What if it's the same people who tried to kill her before?"

"It could be, but we don't know for sure."

"Nathan, stop trying to sound reasonable!"

"What should I say, Anders? Gather all your men and storm a territory without any proof? Start a war on guesses and possibilities? I want to find her just as much as you do. I want everyone responsible to be punished. My hands are tied unless I have actual proof."

I hear a crash inside the office. "She's a good girl, Nathan. She never asks for anything. She works harder than any man I know. She's smart, beautiful. I'm supposed to worry about horny teenage boys chasing after her, not about who's trying to kill her next," Anders laments. "She doesn't deserve to live like this because she carries my blood."

"We will find her, Anders, and we will take better precautions when she returns. Isn't that the whole reason why we agreed to adopt her? So we could protect her better?"

I close my eyes and lean my forehead against the wall. I want to puke. I had it all wrong, so wrong. And I might be too late to make it right.

WITHOUT A TRACE

SHADOW
EIGHT YEARS AGO:
NOVEMBER 12, 2016: 3:33 A.M.
LUNA SOLAR CITY

The guards, recruits, and even some Emerald Pack members search endlessly for any traces of her. There are no leads. I look everywhere I can imagine, but nothing.

My phone buzzes in my pocket. "Emily, I don't have anything new to tell you."

"Nothing on our end either," she replies, sighing.

I hate to say it—it hurts to even think it—but I don't believe we will find her. She could be anywhere. The only certainty I cling to is that she isn't dead.

"Shadow, are you still there?"

"Yeah, I'm here."

"Do you think... is she... Did she—"

"She's not dead."

"Okay," she whispers before sniffling. "I *have* to find her. She's my best friend," she croaks.

"I thought I was your best friend," I deliver in a monotone voice.

"You are... but she has a personality."

I emit a breathy laugh. "True."

"Did you just laugh at me?"

I smile, a genuine smile. I have been doing that a lot more lately, as well as laughing, since I met Jessica. "I did."

"She changed you, too. Didn't she?"

She has. I saw the changes in Charlie and Ean before they even knew it. Liam's magic has strengthened, as has Sodie's. I'm not sure how or when she did it. I am not even sure she knows she did it. Charlie and Ean's magic were always there, just dormant. So were Emily's and Elijah's. Somehow, she awakened them all.

As for me, she realigned my soul and gave me a piece of myself back. There is so much more to Jessica than even I can understand, which is why I am driving myself crazy looking for her. If anyone knows half of what she can do, they will kill her or, worse, keep her prisoner and use her as their own personal weapon.

My phone beeps, indicating another call. "She did, Em, which is why I am doing everything in my power to find her. I have to go. Someone is calling."

"Okay. You'll call me if you find anything?"

"You will be the second one I call, after Anders."

"Okay. I love you."

"I love you, too. And Em? Get some rest. Okay?"

"Okay." She disconnects the call.

I never said those words to Emily before. I thought them, but I never felt them, until now. Emily has been my best friend since we were kids. Even when I lost who I was, she never stopped being my friend.

"Strap?" I answer the second call.

"Shadow, you still looking for that girl?"

My heart races. "Yes. You find something?"

"Not sure if it's who you're looking for, but a young woman washed up on shore near Pier 22. Almost fits your description, except she has long hair."

Long hair? "Did you notify anyone?"

"No. I told the boys to hold off until I spoke to you."

"Continue to hold. I'll be there shortly." I end the call, immediately send a text to Anders, and slip into the shadows. It must be her. I know it, like a pulsing feeling in my chest, like a second heartbeat.

I approach Strap from behind. "Where is she?"

He jumps. "Holy fuck! Where the hell did you come from?"

I smile. "Exactly."

He shakes his head. "She's right over here. She washed up on shore about five minutes ago. I called you as soon as my boys described her. She's, uh, naked. We covered her up as best as we could."

I clench my jaw. Time slows as we approach the pier. I should have just transported there, but I try to limit exposure to my abilities. But I know Strap. I don't necessarily trust him, but I scare the crap out of him enough to know he won't fuck with me. We finally reach the area. A bunch of men standing around, restless.

White-blonde hair floats in the waves. Her bare feet poke through a covering. The men part, letting me through, and I look down. Her lips are pale and cracked. Mouth slightly open, I can tell she's breathing. Thick eyelashes shadow her cheeks.

I crouch and touch her cheek. She's cold. Despite some confusing changes, without a doubt, it's her.

Standing, I reach into my pocket and hand Strap a wad of cash. "Pay your men and keep your mouths shut."

I scoop her into my arms and walk back the way I came. When I'm sure no one is around, I slip into the shadows and take Jessica home.

CHAPTER 34

SO MANY CHANGES

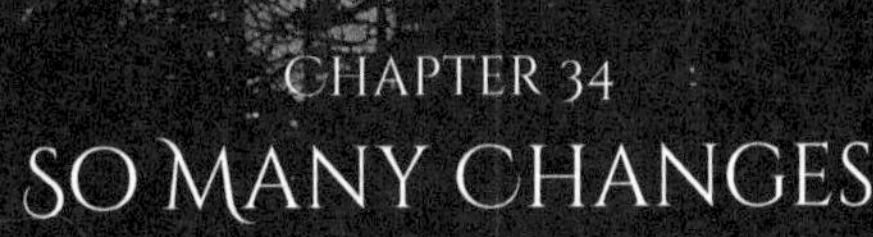

JESSICA

EIGHT YEARS AGO:
NOVEMBER 12, 2016: 7:16 A.M.
EMERALD PACK CLINIC

I wake up to the bright light of the morning rays streaking in through the window. I blink a few times and realize this isn't my bedroom. I'm in the clinic. Slightly confused at how I got here, I survey my surroundings.

No machines beep, and as I roam my hands over my body, no tubes or needles protrude from anywhere. I instinctively reach for my throat. There is no hole, just the puckering of a scar where once was.

My mouth is dry, like I swallowed sand. Pulling myself into a sitting position, my hand accidentally bumps a head with long black hair. Emily. I smile and gently massage her scalp with the tips of my fingers.

She groans. I roll my eyes. This girl can sleep like the dead, heavier than the twins. If we were ever under siege, the attackers would think they were dead and leave them alone. I apply more pressure.

She moans, briefly lifts her head to squint around, and plops her head back onto her arms.

I shake my head. My tongue sticks to the roof of my mouth, and my stomach gurgles. I guess I'm hungry, too. I press the call button and to rub Emily's head while I wait.

My door flies open. Ean barks, "Emily! This isn't room service. We don't—" He stops when he notices me sitting there, eyes open, stroking Emily's long hair. "Little One," he whispers.

I start to laugh, but it sounds like a wheeze before I cough.

He turns and closes the door, leaving me coughing and choking to death while Emily continues to sleep. He finally returns with my nurse, Mimi.

Ean wakes Emily. When she awakens from her sleepy haze, she lunges at me in a strong embrace and begins to cry. "I'm so sorry! So sorry! I shouldn't have left you alone."

I rub her back. "I'm fine," I whisper. When she pulls back, I wipe the tears from her face.

"What happened to you? You look *so* different." She lightly tugs on my hair.

I glance down at the strands of blonde hair in her hand and run my fingers through the long strands, as I just did to Emily. Definitely mine, attached to my scalp. I lift the strand closer to my face to examine it.

Emily watches me. I simply shrug.

Dr. York enters the room. "Jessica, you're awake."

I'm still holding my hair when I turn to him and ask, "Can hair grow like this overnight?"

He rests his forefinger over his lips. "No, not usually. The length of your hair typically represents about a year or two of growth." Reaching behind my back, I find that my hair hangs to my waist. "As shifters, our hair does grow rather fast. In the past six months, if I had to guess, your hair grew about four inches. Of course, if you slept regularly, it probably would have grown a bit more."

My hair isn't the only thing that changed. The wounds on my body closed. The scars don't look fresh anymore. I no longer have a straight boyish figure. My breasts grew a whole cup size, at least. I am even taller, now hitting the five feet marker, and my feet are also a size bigger. My body is toned and muscular, like I work out or train regularly. I can see without glasses, and my voice, once I have drunk enough water, no longer resembles a teenage boy's hormonal rasp. There is some rasp to it, don't get me wrong; it isn't perfect, but it is clear. When I speak, I no longer struggle to be heard.

The best part of all the bodily changes are my teeth. The braces are gone. I have a mouth full of healthy, white, straight teeth. Mentally, I feel different, too.

After rushing into my room, my parents, Anders, and Dr. York sit, bewildered at my transformation. Anders explains that I was missing for five days. I can't believe it.

Chris arrives and questions me. Over and over, he asks if I was hurt or if I saw the man who took me, assuming it was a man. Was there more than one man? Did they touch me? How did I escape? Where did they take me? The questions repeat, on and on.

But I have nothing to share. My last memory is leaving the dinner party. I knew Dr. York stayed at the clinic late on Fridays to finish his charts. I planned to catch him before he left to stitch the wound on my stomach. Even though it was dark, I had walked from the mansion and training grounds to meet Anders every morning so I memorized the path. I wasn't worried that I couldn't see well at night.

"Jessica," Anders mutters my name. "Talk to us. What's going on in that head of yours."

I frown. "You don't believe me? Why? You can hear my thoughts. You would know if I was hiding something."

My mother shakes her head. "We haven't been able to hear your thoughts." Chris nods in agreement.

I look to Anders. "I kind of miss knowing what you're thinking," he says with a sad smile.

"I'm so confused right now. I keep replaying everything that happened yesterday in my head. None of this makes sense," I huff. "Now, I'm broken." I rub my forehead.

"Not broken. Maybe you need time to process everything," Dr. York suggests.

I nod as a thought sprouts in my mind, like I forgot to do something important.

"Can I visit Alpha Agnus's place?" I ask. "I just... feel like I need to see her. Maybe a few cracks with her cane will put things into better perspective," I joke.

Visiting Alpha Agnus helps me sort through my feelings and hone some of the magic I thought I no longer possessed. She says that my mind matured during my absence, and now I have better control of it. This is why no one can hear my thoughts anymore, unless I allow it.

By the time Xavier picks me up early Friday morning, I feel better and look forward to returning home.

"I was told you were scheduled to take the academy exam this morning with the rest of the recruits."

"Right! I guess I forgot." I wince. Will memory loss be my new thing? Great. Now I have holes in my head.

"Don't worry about your bags. I will take care of them when I return to the mansion," he comments, opening my door.

"Thank you, Xavier." I hug him.

"My pleasure. It's good to have you back, Little One." He squeezes my arms before letting me go.

Ean waits by the doors and smiles when he sees me. "You ready?" he asks.

I wrinkle my nose. "I forgot to study."

He pats my back. "I'm sure you will do just fine." He knocks on the classroom door and playfully pushes me inside.

"If you're looking for the head guard's office, it's farther down the hall," Professor Hocson instructs in his English accent, peering at me with his dark beady eyes. He's an eagle shifter. I remember that.

"I'm here to take the exam, Professor."

"You what?" he asks sharply.

I remove the hood covering my head. "I'm Jessica Langhlan. We agreed I would take the exam with the rest of the recruits."

He stands quickly from the seat behind his desk. "Oh, goodness, Princess. My apologies. I didn't recognize you." He motions to an empty chair.

I cross the room without looking at anyone.

"You will need to remove your hat and jacket."

I start to unzip my hoodie but hesitate when I remember what I'm wearing underneath. Crap! My borrowed bra is a little too snug, and Sixes gave me a pink tank top and yoga pants. My hair hides inside my sweatshirt because I don't know how to braid it. Maybe it's long enough to cover my backside.

"Hat and jacket," Professor Hocson repeats.

I slowly remove the hat and set it on the table. Taking a deep breath, I pull off my hoodie, hang it on the back of the chair, and drop into my seat. Someone whistles from the back of the room, and heat burns my cheeks.

Professor Hocson approaches and places a pencil and an exam booklet in front of me. "You sure you want to take the exam today? It's not too much, considering everything you've been through?" he asks in a low voice.

"Thank you for your concern, but I feel better and would like to take it today."

"Okay. Well, the exam clock started fifteen minutes ago. If you need extra time, I can make an exception since you arrived a little late."

I offer a small smile and open the exam. I'm not there very long when I hear the rustling of papers and a chair scraping along the floor.

"Thank you, Mr. Fitzpatrick. You may leave. Grades will be posted in two hours." I glance up as Liam passes. He smiles and winks at me.

I furrow my brow. I didn't expect that from him. I thought he would avoid me or stare with his usual pinched expression.

Then, Luke stands. He offers me a big smile, showing those damn dimples. I frown and look back down at my exam. What the hell is up with them? Sodie is the next one to turn in his exam. When he passes me, I give him a huge smile. His friendship never wavered. I am really going to miss him when he leaves.

It doesn't take long for me to finish. I turn my booklet into Professor Hocson. "Done so soon? You sure you don't want extra time?"

"No. I'm confident with my answers."

"Alright. I'll let Anders know how you did. Have you thought about what you would like to major in before we start your core college courses?"

"I haven't made up my mind yet."

"Well, that's okay. We have about a month before you need to decide."

I nod and turn to gather my things. Marcus and Dustin

watch me from the back of the room. I hurriedly grab my hat and head out the door.

Sodie, Luke, and Liam stand at the end of the hall, talking amongst themselves. As I continue to walk out of the building, they all follow me. What is with them? The last time I saw Luke, he treated me horribly. And Liam? Don't even get me started. His hot and cold demeanor always makes my head spin. Now he's being attentive and nice.

I ignore them both and turn to Sodie when he asks, "How do you think you did?"

"Not terrible, I think. How about you?"

He shrugs. "As well as I could."

Guilt spreads in my chest. Did I somehow mess up his studying time... by going missing? I hope not. Sodie deserves to graduate.

He bumps into my arm. "I'm not a good test taker, but I had good study partners." He tips his head toward Liam and Luke.

Heat tingles along my bare arm. I glance over to see Liam's hand fall back to his side.

I'm not wearing my sweatshirt. I immediately stop. "I forgot my hoodie. I'll be right back." They all follow me. "I don't need an escort." They just stare at me, unbudging. I pivot specifically to Liam and raise my eyebrow, daring him to reply. He doesn't, simply inclining his head.

I hurry inside to the classroom, which has since emptied. My sweatshirt is gone.

"Forget something, Princess?" Marcus asks as Dustin holds up my hoodie and waves it at me. Marcus sits on the desk closest to the door. Dustin remains by the doorway, leaning against the frame and crossing his arms over his chest. "Tell me, Princess. Did Liam set up my cousin to take the fall for your little escape plan? Hmmm?"

What the hell is he talking about?

"Did you two have a falling out, and you planned to run away? I saw that look he gave you, but you ignored him. Is that why you showed up here looking all sexy, instead of like a boy for a change? Trying to show him what he's missing?"

This guy is crazy. I glance over at Dustin, who grins and licks his lips, like I'm some special treat he wants to devour.

"My cousin took the fall for your little game." He bolts off the desk and looms over me. "He was kicked out of the guard, beaten up, and humiliated because of you!"

With pure instinct, I intercept his hand before he grabs my throat. His other hand raises to hit me, I block it and move back.

Marcus chuckles. "Oh, my beautiful princess has some fight! Is that how you like it? Fight first. Does that turn you on, Princess? I can play along. When I win and pin you under me, you're going to enjoy what I give you." He steps closer, and I take two backward. "Don't run, Princess. It's obvious that you and I were meant for each other. I can give you so much more than that worthless bastard."

I laugh, catching Marcus off guard. "You seem to be quite obsessed with Liam's sex life." I roam my eyes down his body. He's aroused. When I gaze back at his face, I smile and wink. "Is he the one who does it for you?"

He scowls and darts for me. Instead of backing away this time, I run for him. I jump, twist, and wrap my legs around his neck, pulling him to the floor. I leap up onto my feet, lift my leg, and plant my shoe into his face. Rage sings through my blood and distorts my vision.

Dustin moves away from the door. I kick him in the chest once, twice. I spin to kick him a third time with all my might, sending him crashing into the wall.

Marcus stands, dazed but upright, so I turn my attention back to him. I kick him in the stomach, shoving him into a desk. He recovers quickly and charges me. I strike him in the chest and then in the stomach. When I get in close enough, I kick him in the groin.

He falls to his knees, and I lean forward and fist his dark brown hair and pull. In a low breathy whisper, I taunt, "Is this how you like it? Rough enough for you, handsome?" He growls. "No? I guess I'm just not your girl." I punch him in the temple, knocking him unconscious.

A hand grabs my shoulder, I plow my elbow into something solid. I lift my other arm to punch, but my arm is blocked. I lift my leg to kick, but he grabs my leg and pulls me into him.

"Fuck, Jessica. It's me." Liam releases me and wraps me in his arms, crushing my face into his muscular chest. The scent of a crisp, clean cologne with an underlying hint of campfire smoke fills my nostrils. "Shhhh. I got you. It's okay."

My heartbeat starts to slow, and my vision returns to normal.

"Shit. I thought I was running in to save you. Didn't think I would need to save these assholes *from* you." He chuckles.

I don't reply, simply clinging to him as if he's my air, my calm in the storm.

"Bring her to my office," Anders commands. "Get these fucking pricks out of here. I've had enough of their crap to last me a lifetime."

CHAPTER 35

SUBMISSIVE

JESSICA
PRESENT DAY:
MARCH 31, 2025

Carmen lifts her hand. "Did you ever figure out what happened to you during the time you were missing?"

"No. I honestly can't remember. Like I said, one minute I was walking in the dark to the clinic. Then, I woke up in the clinic bed."

She nods. "Did you and Luke make amends?"

"That's just the beginning of our very long and complicated relationship. It kind of needs to start here to make sense. I know I barely scratched the surface. If you like, I can pick back up from two weeks ago to answer your original question."

"I'm quite intrigued, actually. Did Luke intentionally try to hurt you?"

I glance down at my hands. "No. I don't think it was intentional. He was angry. I was angry and scared, too. We were young and didn't have control over our emotions. The balcony incident was an accident. Neither of us could have known that balcony railing would break the way it did. Now, I know he tried to save me. At the time, I didn't."

I swallow, pausing to choose my next words carefully.

"My conflict with Luke is ours. It doesn't paint the right picture of who he really is or what kind of an Alpha King he will become. I want to make that very clear. Luke is a good man. He's hardworking, generous, and kind. Unfortunately for him, his title and the responsibilities he was born into put a lot of pressure on him. He sometimes has to think about those first, before he can think about himself."

I clear my throat, unsure of what more I really need to say.

"I just don't want anyone to judge him for what I say because they are *my* feelings, *my* views. I wish things were different, but... it is what it is."

"That's very kind of you to say," Carmen responds. "Can you tell me—because I am just dying to know— were you and Liam a couple? You talk a lot about him. Did something develop between the two of you?"

"I think it's pretty obvious that I had a crush on Liam from the very beginning." I lower my gaze, thinking, *Please don't cry. Don't cry.* "I... It... We weren't meant to be." I look up at Christian, instead of Carmen. "I wouldn't be here now if we were."

Christian holds my eye. "I guess we need to find your true mate, then."

Grateful for Christian's reply, I nod and stare directly into the camera. "Hard to fill the role, especially when I have two amazing fathers that I placed on a pedestal. Not to mention some really awesome uncles."

My parents chuckle softly. I pat Anders's knee and turn toward my father.

"They raised the bar tenfold, and they expect me to find a mate who could compare." I smile at them.

Carmen hums. "Well, your parents selected a variety of men whom they felt were compatible for you. We also selected some men that might be just as compatible. I'm confident you will find someone by the end of the show."

My mother's head snaps up. "What do you mean, you also selected compatible men?"

Carmen coughs into her sleeve. "The producers insisted that, even though the timeframe is much shorter than any other season, we maintain our number of contestants. Twenty..." Her eye contact unwavering, she continues, "We selected additional men yielded as a possible match in the algorithm."

"Algorithm?" My mother raises an eyebrow.

Carmen nods. "Jessica took a compatibility test when we first started. We received applications when word spread, and we also had a list of other men who wanted to be on the show from previous seasons. We chose men who demonstrated high percentages that matched Jessica's from our database." She pauses, watching my mother. "It wasn't something I had control over."

My mother's eyes narrow. "Perhaps, but it was something that you could have brought to our attention sooner."

Anders swears under his breath. "Were any of these men vetted?"

Carmen looks to my father, avoiding Anders's deadly stare. "They were vetted by our standard protocol."

Anders and my father both immediately stand. "Not good enough. I want their names."

"I... we... can't. It's too late. Filming starts tomorrow evening."

My father glowers at Carmen. "This is our daughter's life, her safety. Who do I need to call?"

Carmen pales. "It's out of our hands. The men are already here, currently being interviewed, and—"

My mother holds up her hand. "If anything happens to our daughter, I am warning you right now, not only will I take your company to court for breach of contract and personal harm inflicted on my daughter for the company's own personal gain, I will disband it and sell it off piece by piece, and everyone, including your producers, will never recover."

Carmen slides off her chair to her feet. "I can show you our protocol, how we vet all of the contestants. I will call the producers." She straightens her shoulders. "You realize that if you stop production now, you also breach contract, and the company can sue Jessica. She signed and agreed to be here. We agreed to your terms of bringing on the men you chose, but the producers have a right to make changes as they see fit."

My mother raises her chin. "I will need to review it, then. My understanding was that changes would only be made in the actual filming, not the men selected for the competition."

Carmen shrugs. "You can take it up with our production's lawyers."

My parents argue with Carmen as they all exit the room. They won't let this stand. I look to Christian, and we both laugh. He shakes his head.

"So do we continue, or do we wait for Carmen to return?" I ask him.

He checks the camera. "I'm still filming. We can continue, if you want. Who knows when they will return. Doesn't sound like your parents will back down."

I chuckle. Carmen doesn't know what she's up against.

He smiles, studying me for a few seconds. "I don't get it," he finally admits.

"You care to elaborate?"

"You, sitting here. You seem so—I don't know—for lack of a better term, submissive."

My eyebrows raise. "Submissive? I'm anything but submissive. Trust me."

He cocks his head to the side and narrows his eyes. "When you talk about what happened to you in the classroom, you took down two trained recruits. It seems you gained more confidence. But now, you sit here, letting your parents fight with the producers. You always appear so nervous. You looked like you might have a panic attack when we started."

I sigh. "I did have more confidence for a period of time. Losing my best friend, Emily, brought back the panic attacks, feeling insecure, hiding. She wasn't supposed to die. It should have been me."

He looks at me thoughtfully and exhales. "How about we resume with what happened two weeks ago? You were getting ready for the unannounced guests who demanded to be seen."

CHAPTER 36

STAYING THE COURSE

LUKE

TWO WEEKS AGO:
MARCH 14, 2025: 12:30 P.M.
ALPHA KINGS MANSION

"No matter Jessica's reaction, I need *you* to stay the course."

I nod as we walk down the hall toward the conference room. Three gentlemen at the table stand as we enter. I immediately recognize Alpha Rhineheart, a tall man with dull chestnut brown hair and a rectangular face. I haven't seen him in several years. I remember him as a strapping man, but now he looks beaten down, far too old for his age. I can't help but notice the blankness in his eyes.

To his left is Beta DuPont, a short man with thinning brown hair, a round face set in a pale pallor, crooked yellow teeth, and a gut that protrudes over his belt.

To the Alpha's right is a young man, the spitting image of what the Alpha once looked like. He's young, maybe around my age. The only difference in comparison to his father is his eye color. They are much lighter, more of a golden brown than the bland, lifeless hue of his father's.

"Gentlemen," my father acknowledges as we approach the table.

Alpha Rhineheart shakes our hands with less vigor than I expected of an Alpha, almost as if he functions on autopilot. However, the Beta's handshake is firm. I glance over to my father, and he nods as he takes his seat. We all follow suit.

"Thank you for agreeing to meet with us, Your Majesty," the Beta says, settling into his chair.

"Yes, well, it appears that I wasn't given a choice in the matter as you refused to leave," my father replies bluntly.

"I apologize for the intrusion, but it is of the utmost importance that we meet with you. I have been trying to get your attention for several months. My pack is in a state of crisis, and it's all due to your daughter."

My father raises an eyebrow. "My daughter is the sole reason for your pack's critical state?"

"Yes, Your Majesty. She has been attacking us for years, financially and physically. It seems she has a personal vendetta against us."

What the fuck is this bullshit?! The Beta wastes no time jumping to his agenda.

"Your Majesty, wine sales have considerably decreased over the past five years, putting our pack in a financial situation. A reliable source informed me that your daughter, through an affair with the world-renowned chef, Jacques Gattefosse, persuaded him to stop purchasing our wines. Because he is popular and sought after, many restaurants follow his trend."

My father catches my eye and then asks the Beta, "Who is your credible resource linked to the famous chef?"

"Well, uh, Your Majesty, I cannot divulge that information.

But I assure you my source is a close friend of the chef and has worked alongside him for many years."

My father chuckles, and I laugh.

Young Alpha Dimitri snorts, adding, "I didn't realize that Jacques Gattefosse had any friends. He's known for being a bit of a loner. The last I heard, the longest employee to work with him lasted six months."

Beta DuPont's face reddens. He gnashes his yellowed teeth together. "Whose side are you on, boy?"

He laughs, not intimidated by the Beta. "Just stating a well-known fact to those who work within the restaurant business."

Beta DuPont leans forward. "Your Majesty, our territory has been attacked repeatedly by rogues. We have requested aid. When the guards came to the territory, they took advantage of our female members, refused to train our young. Most recently, one of your guards attacked our pack members, leaving them no choice but to defend themselves against him. Your daughter crossed our territory lines, attacked and killed two of our pack members! We came here to inform you. I'm sure your daughter has invented lies to gain your favor, but—"

"I hope you have concrete proof and substantial documentation to support these allegations, Beta," I sneer at DuPont.

"I- I, well, yes. I...."

My father turns toward the Alpha. "Well, do you?" he asks in a commanding voice. The Alpha doesn't flinch, simply staring straight ahead. Slowly, his gaze shifts to meet my father's. "Alpha, I asked you a question! Do you or don't you have substantial proof to support these allegations?"

Alpha Rhineheart opens his mouth but falters.

"Your Majesty, I have several witnesses who can attest to these attacks," the Beta claims.

"I am asking your Alpha. You better have a damn good

reason for wasting my time," my father growls. "You come into my home unannounced, refuse to leave, and accuse my daughter without proof—"

Beta Dupont stands. "Your Majesty, please, if you will just listen!"

"Is there a reason why your Beta is taking a stance, as if he's the one in charge of your territory?" my father asks the Alpha. But Alpha Rhineheart doesn't answer, nor does he look at my father.

The Young Alpha assesses his father, concern overtaking his features.

"Your Majesty, I speak for both the Alpha and Young Alpha because I have been the one in charge of these affairs. The Alpha has not been doing well, and the Young Alpha was away attending school and addressing business afar over the years."

"I wasn't made aware of Alpha Rhineheart's health condition, Beta DuPont," my father responds, eyeing Alpha Rhineheart as he speaks.

The Young Alpha leans forward to look at Beta DuPont. "Neither was I," he states pointedly.

Beta DuPont continues to protest and pleads to be heard, but I stop listening. He and his son are fully responsible for the destruction of their winery and pack business. Everyone knows this, and all of the LS territory refuses to conduct business with the Ruby Falls Pack. No formal reports have been filed of rogue attacks on any other territory—only theirs—but as usual, there are no witnesses. I can safely assume those are lies as well. But why the hell target Jessica?

"Alright! Enough!" my father shouts. "This is all hearsay, Beta. There is no proof to support your accusation without a paper trail, written statements, or actual witness stating my daughter's direct involvement to sabotage your sales."

"Your Majesty, what about the attacks? Our territory has

been attacked repeatedly by rogues. Just a few weeks ago, your daughter refused to send aid."

"Where is your report?" my father roared. "My head guard requested your territory report on that incident for several months now, and he has not received one to date."

"But, Your Majesty, I did send one, not once but twice. I'm sure your daughter intervened in our email communication and destroyed the copy."

My father turns to the Alpha. "Where is the report?" Alpha Rhineheart swivels toward Beta DuPont.

Beta DuPont continues, "Your Majesty, sir, I told you. I sent the report."

"Alpha Rhineheart, your Beta is crossing a very fine line with me. I personally sent you an email and a handwritten letter asking for your pack's account of what took place. I asked for a detailed report, along with accounts from firsthand witnesses. You have not responded. Then, you come here accusing my guards and my daughter of personally attacking your pack. How do you answer for this?"

Again, Alpha Rhineheart turns to his Beta. "I am not asking your Beta, Alpha! I am asking you!"

Clearing his throat, Alpha Rhineheart finally answers, "Your Majesty, all of the accounts my Beta relays are true."

Growling, my father gets to his feet and slams his fist on the table.

Young Alpha Dimitri immediately stands. "Your Majesty, I apologize for their behavior. I didn't come here to accuse your daughter of anything, and I am quite familiar with how Beta DuPont and his son operate." He glances between his father and the Beta. "While it is true I was away from the territory for some time, finishing my degree and seeking out other business opportunities to sustain our pack financially, I came here for answers, as I am sure there is a reasonable explanation for the princess's actions behind these allegations."

The door suddenly opens, cutting off Young Alpha Dimitri. Joe clears his throat and announces Luna Queen Shakti and Princess Jessica.

Alpha Rhineheart and I rise with the announcement. My father's face is red with rage, he looks over at my mother as she approaches the table.

She smiles and gently pats his arm. "Gentlemen." The three men bow their heads in respect. She glances at the table, offering, "I'll see to the kitchen staff and bring in some refreshments."

My father glares at Beta DuPont. "Not necessary. They will not be staying much longer."

The Beta flusters, scowling at the Young Alpha.

"Well, in that case, I will leave you all to it, then." My mother places a gentle kiss on my father's cheek and turns to leave.

Taking her cue, Jessica steps out from behind my mother, placing herself between my father and I. "Gentlemen." She dips her chin in acknowledgement.

I study the men's reactions to her entrance. Alpha Rhineheart stares blankly. Beta DuPont frowns. But the Young Alpha's jaw drops. His eyes wide, like he's seen a ghost. Mouth slightly agape, he pales.

He stammers, "Grit?"

"This is Alpha Princess Jessica Langhlan," I interject. Jessica turns her smile toward the Young Alpha.

He shake his head and runs a hand down his face, collecting himself. "I guess the allegations are true, then?"

Schooling her features, Jessica glances at the other two men. Then, giving her full attention again to the Young Alpha, she asks, "Allegations?"

CHAPTER 37
ALLEGATIONS

JESSICA
TWO WEEKS AGO:
MARCH 14, 2025: 12:45 P.M.
ALPHA KINGS MANSION: CONFERENCE ROOM

The second territory leaders are notoriously known for their disdain toward successful women. The Ruby Falls Pack is traditional pack and views women beneath men. According to their traditions, women belong in their beds or in subservient positions, such as housekeepers or cooks. Despite how the world around their territory evolved, they strongly maintain their beliefs.

Naturally, Beta DuPont's correspondence has clearly conveyed his disdain for my position.

Even though my intention was to show him that I desired peace, his reply only reinforced that women like myself would only bring downfall to those around me when I try to fulfill a leadership role. Of course, I won't let him make me feel inferior to his status. Alpha Agnus taught me better than that.

My mother turns to leave the room, and I step around her to give the gentlemen my attention. The group is tense with an interrupted confrontation. I just wish it wasn't happening today, of all days.

The young man standing next to Alpha Rhineheart stares at me, his mouth hanging open. He stammers, "Grit?"

"This is Alpha Princess Jessica Langhlan," Luke interjects. I glance at Luke and return my gaze to the young man.

Frowning, he shake his head. "I guess the allegations are true then?"

My brow furrows in confusion. "Allegations?"

Beta DuPont laughs, and Alpha Rhineheart joins him. "This all makes sense now—the attacks on my pack's winery, the drop in sales for the past five years, the personal attack a few months ago from you and one of your guards." Beta DuPont points a finger at me. "Has this been your plan of revenge all along?"

"I have no idea what you're talking about, Beta DuPont." Beta DuPont turns to Alpha Rhineheart. "After all this time." Alpha Rhineheart nods. Speaking to my father, the Beta continues, "Your Majesty, I am not sure what she told you over the years, but I can assure you, it is all lies."

What the hell is he talking about?

My father places a hand over mine. "You better start making some sense, or I will—" my father starts when Luke cuts in.

"Actually, I want to hear all about these lies. I always had my suspicions, the way she ran into our territory, begging the guards for help, manipulating her way into my family, into my pack all those years ago. Not to mention how she ruined my relationship with my mate."

A sharp pain pierces my heart from his words.

"I think it's time for the truth to come out finally. Don't you think, Jessica?" He gives me a cold smile.

My eyes widen, and tears burn the back of my lashes. I glance down at my hands before raising my chin making eye contact Beta DuPont. "I never lied or personally attacked the second territory. I have no reason to!"

Luke grabs my shoulder and pushes me into a chair. "Sit," he says sharply. "Let the Beta talk."

Beta DuPont smiles like the cat who got the cream. "I didn't recognize you at first. You've grown into quite a young woman. But the hair and those eyes... We thought you were dead all this time. What you put your mother and brother through. Our family—the pack—has never been the same."

The young man who called me "Grit" scoffs and runs his fingers through his hair.

Alpha Rhineheart growls. "One word, boy, and I will strip you of your title and banish you from our pack!"

"No, Alpha. It's really not his fault. The poor boy is part of this tangled web of lies and manipulation woven together by this horrible monster."

I attempt to stand. I will not let this asshole spread lies about me. But Luke continues to hold me down and tightly squeezes my shoulder. "I can't believe you. Whatever happened to you having my back, too?" I hiss.

He doesn't respond or show any kind of emotion, looking expectedly at the Beta.

"Your Majesty, I'm so ashamed to involve you in this. This really should have been pack business. I tried my best to raise my daughter to be an upstanding member of my pack."

Daughter? What the fuck?!

"She was always a difficult child, telling lies, manipulating young men to do her bidding, and causing fights amongst the pack members. We punished her to correct this behavior, but she ran around the pack and claimed we starved her, beat her, and locked her out of her home. She made us look like monsters when it she was abusing us."

I squirm, trying to wiggle out of Luke's grasp, but he bears down even harder.

"She manipulated the Young Alpha into taking her side, pitting him against his own father, against his best friend, my son, Bart. She used the betrothal contract between the Young Alpha and herself to manipulate him, knowing the contract was binding."

"Betrothed?" my father and I say in unison.

"No fucking way! You're lying! There is no way I am betrothed to anyone!" I scream.

The Young Alpha's eyes avoid mine, and he shakes his head. "The contract is real, Grit," he replies softly.

"What the fuck did you just call me?!" I shout.

"Grit, your name. Come now. I know you never liked it, but don't be so dramatic." Beta DuPont feigns sincerity.

I want to scratch his eyeballs out with my fingernails.

He chuckles. "Your Majesty, I can supply you with the contract, if you like. It was formalized a few months after her birth. It's legal and binding. Of course, it's written under her original name, Grit DuPont."

My father stares at the Beta. "Yes. I want a copy of that contract in my office by the end of the day."

I turn to my father. "No! I am not the horrible monster they claim me to be! I will never mate with anyone who thinks so little of the opposite sex!"

"Grit, I—"

"That is not my name!" I yell at the Young Alpha. Luke squeezes my shoulder. "Let go of me, or you will regret it!"

He ignores me and addresses Beta DuPont. "Why did you think she died?"

"Well, you see, she had made so many problems among the

pack that even her peers began to hate her. She started fights and then cried that she was being bullied. My poor son tried everything to save her from herself. We were told that she had a fight with one of her best friends, uh, Kat, I think. She messed around with Kat's boyfriend behind her back.

"Anyway, a group of friends and peers confronted her about it. According to my son, it was a bad fight. When it was over, she returned home. Bart, my son, said he found her in the bathroom, indulging in wine she stole from my cellar, mutilating herself. She told Bart she planned to kill herself and make it appear like she was murdered.

"Bart tried to stop her and called his friends for help. She's a strong girl, even though she's quite petite. They chased her all the way to the falls, but then he lost track of her. She was missing for—what—a week, almost two. The entire pack searched for her. Then, my son found her body in a ravine near the falls. Her body was so unrecognizable, we could only identify her by the color of her hair.

"My son never recovered. He was so devastated that he couldn't help his sister. My mate never forgave herself for not doing more for her daughter, as well as for me... How do you recover from losing a child?"

"You are not my father, you horrible piece of shit!" I struggle against Luke's restraining grip. I swear I am going to break his fucking hand!

"If she is here," my father asks, "then whose body did you find?"

Beta DuPont shrugs. "Your Majesty, we had no reason to believe it wasn't her." He hesitates for a moment. "She's a very smart girl. She attended senior year courses when she was only a sophomore. She's a musical prodigy. We wanted to place her in a special school for gifted children, but we were so afraid of the trouble she would cause outside of the territory. I can only imagine that she found another child similar in height and weight to look like her.”

I glare at Beta DuPont.

“You murdered a child, Jessica?” Slowly, I turn to look at Luke. My body trembles, and I ball my hands into fists. “You accused my mate of setting up the murder of your best friend, Emily. This makes me wonder if—”

“Don't you dare,” I threaten through clenched teeth. I swing my right arm, gripping Luke's and twisting, releasing his hold on me. I stand and smash my left fist into his face.

I jump on the table and wrap my hands around Beta DuPont's throat and squeeze. He grabs my wrist with both hands, digging into my flesh with his filthy nails, but I don't flinch or release him. I squeeze harder. Kneeling, I lean in closer. I can smell the stench of his rotting breath.

“Listen, you miserable, fat, power-starving, Alpha wannabe. Listen well because I will only say this once. Seven years ago, when your territory suffered from a drought, reducing your crops and slowing your wine production, even though I was advised against it, I bought thirty percent of your business shares. I even convinced my brothers to invest in eight percent and my parents to invest another three. When you and your horrible son pissed everyone off within the LS territory with your assholery and unprofessionalism, I still bought and stocked your wine in my hotels, even when my restaurant manager and concierge threatened to quit if they had to deal with either of you one more time.

“Five years ago, when I discovered that your winery expanded outside of the LS territory, I imported your wines from Rome even when it cost me more money, just so everyone working under me could avoid interacting with you. I jumped in as a silent investor in your whiskey distillery. I fronted thousands of dollars to your startup and recruited other investors and marketers. As if that isn't enough, I buy and stock your whiskey in all of my hotels, restaurants, and clubs. My clubs exclusively use only your whiskeys and wines in our signature drinks. When your son pissed off my friend and business partner, Jacques Gattefosse, he wanted to burn your business to the ground. I convinced him to let it go. I have copies of all of my investments, purchase orders, and more, if you want to challenge me on this."

Beta DuPont's face turns a shade of purple. I ever so slightly loosen my grip to offer him enough air so he doesn't pass out. He swallows, and when I see color return to his cheeks, I lean in and squeeze.

"I sent investigators to your territory to investigate all the attacks you claim were done by the rogues. Do you know what we found instead? There are no rogue attacks. Each attack occurred within your own territory. In fact, the incident with my guard happened when he caught them vandalizing your warehouses. Your pack tortured and nearly killed my guard, chaining and collaring him to a wall in one of the storage closets for three days." I clench my hand around his pudgy neck even harder.

"Jessica..." my father warns.

"The only thing you have on me is that I crossed your territory line to save my guard! When I find that coward son of yours, I will make sure he endures every form of torture he imparted on my guard."

He squirms and digs his fingers into my wrists.

"You need to think carefully about how you want this to go. Unlike you, I have the power to be your salvation, or your destruction." I squeeze his throat one last time before shoving him away from me.

Landing in his chair, he instantly grabs his throat, wheezing and gasping for air.

Large hands pull me off the table. "Enough, Little One. Let us take care of the rest," my father whispers into my ear. "Guards!" he yells. The conference room door crashes open. Anders leads three guards and the twins.

Luke stands off to the side, wiping blood from his nose with the back of his shirt sleeve. He sends me a murderous glare.

Fuck him, traitorous ass. *Glare at me all you want. You deserved that punch.*

Despite all the commotion, Alpha Rhineheart remains seated, staring vacantly in the distance, not even displaying concern for his Beta.

Young Alpha Dimitri looks down at his father. "Aren't you going to do something about this?" he asks. Alpha Rhineheart simply laughs.

Beta DuPont, still wheezing and coughing, croaks, "I want her arrested for murdering an innocent child to fake her own death, murdering two of our pack members, threatening my son's life, and threatening my own."

Luke, still dabbing at his nose, turns toward Beta DuPont and nods. "I agree. An arrest should be made today." Beta DuPont's eyes brighten. I twist out of my father's arms.

Young Alpha Dimitri stands from his seated position. "You can't arrest her. I can testify that everything he said is a lie!"

"She murdered two of our pack members!" Beta DuPont wheezes.

"Enough!" My father's booming voice echoes within the room.

Luke commands, "Guards, arrest this man for the abuse of a minor living in his household and arrest these two for conspiring in the attempted murder of a minor living in the protection of their pack."

I freeze in shocked silence. Wasn't he on their side mere minutes ago?

Luke leans forward, his hulking form hovering over both the Alpha and the Beta. "I know that you lied about everything! You want to test me and ask me how?" His lips curl in a snarl.

"She set it all up! She mutilated herself, slicing her arms, stabbing herself in the leg, and cutting off her eyelashes and her hair. Please, you can't believe her lies!"

Luke punches the Beta. Jeremy catches the Beta before he falls to the floor. Luke replies, "You wouldn't have known any of that unless you were involved. She didn't run to the falls because I found her hanging from a tree just over our territory boundary."

The Beta stammers, "She—she—she planned it. I'm sure of it!"

Luke clasps the Beta by his shirt. "She was dead when I found her. She wasn't just mutilated—she was beaten until her face was unrecognizable, her back torn to shreds by wolves! I had to cut a hole in her throat so she could breathe, to perform CPR. When her heart started to beat again, we still weren't sure she would survive because she nearly bled dry! I carried her barely living body to the clinic. I stood there and watched a team of medical professionals work on her lifeless body, doing everything they could to bring her back to life! Through all of that, her survival was not guaranteed because her little body was so malnourished and unable to heal on its own. I sat next to her bedside while tubes, wires, and machines kept her alive. For two weeks, she laid in a coma, and I prayed for a miracle to bring her back to life, healthy and fully functioning. Do you want to know the best part? When she finally woke up, she had no memory of who she was, of who attacked her, or of her life before she came into ours."

The Beta's face pales, and his eyes widen.

"You set yourself up with all your lies! As much as I want to kill you right now, I want the motherfucker who put his hands on her!" He punches the Beta again. This time, Jeremy steps aside, letting him slam into the wall.

With a menacing glare, Luke sets his eyes on the Young Alpha, who stutters, "I wasn't there! I wasn't there that night. I have proof! I can bring it to you." One of the guards wrestles with him, to restrain him. "I wasn't there! I would never let them hurt her!" He looks to me. "I would never have let them hurt you! You have to believe me!"

Tears trail down my face. I don't know what to believe. I only know what I looked like when I woke up in the clinic.

He shoves into Alexis, knocking him to the side. He tries to circle the table, but Justin crashes into him, taking him down.

"Get them the fuck out of here!" Luke roars.

The Alpha laughs like an insane madman as Anders and another guard hold him. "All this trouble over an unwanted child." He cackles.

I glance at Luke, and we share a look of worry over the Alpha's mental wellbeing. I link my mind with his, but I can't make sense of his jumbled thoughts. A sharp dagger slices through my link, throwing it back at me like a dart. Shit! I slap my hand over my temple and lean forward.

An unfamiliar voice shouts in my head, and an image of an angry teenage boy forms. "They should have left you near the falls, where they found you! They should have thrown you into the water and let you drown!"

The room starts to spin, and the Alpha's maniacal laughter grows louder. Then, he shouts, "I should have left you to die out on the cliff when you were a baby!"

CHAPTER 38

MURDEROUS ALPHA

LUKE

TWO WEEKS AGO

MARCH 14, 2025: 1:24 P.M.

ALPHA KINGS MANSION: CONFERENCE ROOM

I should have stood closer to her. My stupid Alpha ego got in the way. I want to tear apart the Young Alpha and show him that she's mine. He's in *my* territory, and for whatever part he played in hurting her, I will hurt him.

I should never have moved away. When I turn to look at her, she clutches her head and bends over the table. My father barks orders, and the Beta fights to get free. The room erupts into a loud chaotic mess, all while Alpha Rhineheart shouts and laughs.

Before I can reach Jessica, the Alpha breaks out of his restrained hold and transitions into a large chestnut brown wolf. He bounds over the table, knocking down my father, and attacks Jessica.

"No!" Dimitri and I yell at the same time. Justin and Alexis

335

pin the Young Alpha to the ground he frantically fights their restraints.

Jessica raises her arms as the Alpha lands on her, his jaws snapping, teeth tearing into one arm. She's in human form—fragile, breakable. She manages to roll out from under him, army crawling away. He catches her by the ankle and flings her body across the room like a rag doll.

Her scream fills the room. Wolves pounce onto the Alpha's back, and one of the golden wolves, larger than the Alpha, knocks him over. My father enters the fight.

No, no, no! I run toward the two Alphas fighting, growling. I transition midair as I jump onto Alpha Rhineheart's back. He's too strong. His large jaw clamps down on my father's leg, I hear the bone crack followed by his growl of pain.

The Alpha throws off another wolf, but I'm still atop him. I grab onto his haunches, pulling him back, tearing at flesh. That gets his attention. In a flurry of teeth, claws, and vicious snarls, we fight each other, aiming for the jugular.

He's just too damn strong, like he's on steroids. What the hell is this? In human form, he's an empty shell. In wolf form, he's a killing machine. He throws more wolves off him, pulling me by the shoulder he whips me across the room.

He's not interested in killing any one of us. His focus is on Jessica. Free, he stalks toward her, lying unconscious on the floor. A smaller chestnut brown wolf with a hint of gray mixed into its fur joins him.

Dimitri is still in human form, fighting Alexis. Jeremy is mid-shift. A black wolf and another golden wolf, Chris and Elias, race into the room, immediately attacking the Alpha and the other, who I can only assume is the Beta. Shortly, a gray wolf runs in next, all teeth snarling, and immediately shields my father. Joe?

Raising myself to all fours, I enter the fray. Together, we

work to thwart the Beta and Alpha Rhineheart. A large white wolf jumps into the crowd, and steel jaws clamp down on my hind leg. I howl at the searing pain. The Alpha hovers over me, sharp teeth dripping with saliva, eyes glowing with a scarlet violence. A low growl emanates from his chest, he aims for my jugular, Chris slams into him, knocking him over.

Get her out of here! Anders snarls through our mind-link. With my shoulder injured and my hind leg broken, I crawl through the violence and make my way to Jessica.

Her breathing is shallow, but she's alive. Blood drips from a wound on her scalp, and her arm is bent under her at an unnatural angle. I nuzzle her face, but she doesn't move. My own injuries prevent me from carrying or dragging her to safety. I lay down, practically on top of her, protecting her the only way I can for now.

The smaller chestnut-colored wolf approaches me, growling, warning me to get out of his way. I try to stand, but sharp pain forces me back down. He steps forward, and I calculate how to rip out his throat when he lunges forward.

I want to use my magic. I'm sure we all do. But if this asshole survives, it puts all of our lives in danger. I sneer, *I will kill you, motherfucker. Just try it.*

My body tenses in anticipation. A smaller golden wolf with longer, fluffier fur rushes through the door and lands on his back, gripping the scruff of his neck. Anders pulls away from the chaos and helps.

My mother is relentless, tearing into the Beta, all teeth and claws. Anders is just as ferocious, merciless. The two of them kill the Beta. Dark red mats Anders's perfectly white fur, and blood covers my mother's muzzle. She rears up, preparing to jump into the frenzied fight nearby, when Ander blocks her path. She tries to get past him, but he blocks her again.

No! Anders says through our link.

The Beta transitions into human form. Gaping holes distort his throat and abdomen. My mother turns toward the Beta, bends over him, and rips his head off, flinging it across the room. She leaves no room for that motherfucker to survive. In a huff, she leaves the room.

Anders returns to the fight with Alpha Rhineheart. Alexis still wrestles with Dimitri, who shouts, "Let me go! I can help. He's my father!"

I lick Jessica's wound on her scalp and nuzzle her head. The cacophony of snarls, whimpers and yelps closes in on us. She groans slightly. I need to get her out of here.

The Alpha won't cease. He throws Anders and Elias off him. A growl emanates from his chest as he prowls toward us. As other wolves continue to jump on him and grab at his hindquarters, he merely brushes them off like pesky flies.

My heart races. Shit! With my injuries, I'm no match for him. I shift my weight, preparing for another fight as he stalks closer, preparing to sacrifice myself to save her.

In my periphery Dimitri throws Alexis down, punches Justin, and finally transitions into a large chestnut-colored wolf, equally as big as the Alpha. I force myself to stand and roar through the pain. Instead of charging me, the Young Alpha collides into his father, catching him off guard.

They become a blur of sharp canines, fur, and murderous snarls. Claws dig into flesh. Both are strong and unyielding in their fight. The Alpha yelps in pain. Then, silence. The Alpha falls onto his side. Dimitri transitions into human form and falls to his knees.

No one moves, anticipating the Alpha's attack, but it doesn't come. Dimitri is covered in blood, scratches, and open bites. He reaches forward and rests his hand on his father's large wolf head.

Slowly, everyone shifts into their human forms. Alexis,

whose face is a bloody mess, and Justin, who looks just as bad, restrain Dimitri's hands behind his back. He doesn't fight or resist, staring at his father's lifeless form. As the Alpha begins to transition, Dimitri winces, seeing the front of his father's throat torn open.

Dimitri scans the room. "I'm one of you, I'm a guard. Shadow. He's my commanding officer and lawyer. He can vouch for me." Anders frowns. "I didn't train here. He sent me straight to Ryukyu Island eight years ago."

Chris steps forward. "Shadow has been extricated from the guards for his acts of treason. His word means nothing to us."

"One- five- O- five- twenty- one- six." He blurts out, eyes darting back and forth between the leads.

Chris and Elias exchange a glance.

"You sent the warning that Beta DuPont intended to stage a coup against Jessica." My father says, grunting as Joe assists him to his feet. Blood seeps down his chest, and his right leg bends at an awkward angle. His body sways before Joe steps in to support him. Jeremy rushes to bolster him on the other side.

"You're the Sheild?" Elias asks at the same time Chris remarks.

"You're the guards undercover agent."

Dimitri nods, "I requested to keep my true identity hidden. I didn't want my father to find out that I was opposing him."

Anders glares at him with obvious suspicion.

Dimitri glances back at Jessica. I position my wolf to obstruct his line of sight. He closes his eyes briefly before redirecting his focus back to the leads. "My father and his Beta ordered Grit's execution. I made it my mission to avenge her death, even after I learned she was still alive." His eyes fall on his father's lifeless form, his face devoid of emotion, then shifts back to Anders, "I beg you, don't wage a war on my Pack. Not all of them are monsters, like their leaders."

"You expect me to take your word at face value?" Anders snarls and the temperature in the room drops.

"No, but there's a woman in my pack who is willing to vouch for them. Her name is Natalie Fields She said that you know her as Natalia Parker."

A puff of frosty air billows out from between Anders's lips. "Get him some clothes, and place him in containment until we sort this out." He directs to Elias.

I'm the last to transition and gather Jessica into my arms. As Alexis and Justin lead Dimitri out of the room, he stops short and asks, "Is she okay?"

"She's alive." I tell him. He caresses her with his eyes. She moans as I pull her closer into the cradle of my arms and I growl in warning. *Mine.*

He smirks as if he's thinking the same.

CHAPTER 39

WE SHOULDN'T

JESSICA
TWO WEEKS AGO:
MARCH 14, 2025: 4:15 P.M.
ALPHA KINGS MANSION

My head throbs. My shoulder aches. I blink open my eyes and take in my surroundings. It's dark in my bedroom. I slowly sit and slide to the edge of the bed rubbing the back of my neck and then my shoulder.

"Jessica." Luke walks toward me from the sitting area. He kneels in front of me, caressing my face. "Are you okay?"

"Yeah. I'm fine. You know, nine lives and all that," I tease with a breathy laugh.

"Not funny." He scowls.

"It kind of is," I retort. I notice he's not wearing a shirt. Goddess, why is he not wearing a shirt?

As much as I should look the other way, I don't. My eyes peruse his defined muscles ... He has a bite mark on his shoulder. I gingerly trace it. It's already fading. My hand slides

343

down his shoulder, over his pecs, down to his abdomen, and faintly brushes over a thick, ragged scar from five years ago.

Guilt squeezes my heart, reminding me once again why he and I can't be together. I tear my eyes away and look into his face. "Are you okay? Is Dad okay?"

"I'm fine. Dad and the twins are fine. And all the guards. We're all fine." He searches my eyes. "That was a lot of information today. How are you holding up?"

I scoff. "I just woke up. I haven't had time to process it all yet."

He rests his forehead against mine. "I'm here, babe. I'm right here. I'll be here for you while you work through this. You don't need to do this alone."

I drop my eyes, and of course, they land on his scar again. Gently, he pulls me closer, tips my chin up and kisses me. Slow and sensual, his tongue traces my lower lip before he slides in to stroke his tongue with mine.

I should stop this—no, I need to stop this.

He trails one hand down my back and pulls me into him, forcing my knees to part. He rests between my legs. The heat of his body warms my inner thighs. His kiss grows urgent. His fingers slide down my neck, gently over my collarbone, to my breast. I moan as his touch sends a pulsing electrical sensation up my spine, tingling my skin.

Moisture pools between my legs as he sucks on my lower lip, tugging it between his teeth. When he releases it, he kisses my jaw, making his way down my neck, licking my skin.

"I've been so fucking hard for you since this morning." He places my hand over his hardened cock, rubbing my palm against his thick length. He moans as I wrap my fingers around him through the fabric of his pants.

His fingers curl around my... I just realized I'm barely wearing any clothing. Where are my clothes?

Gently, he pushes me back. I brace myself with a hand behind me, indenting the comforter. I have to stop this. I can't...

He pulls down my camisole. "Luke," I whisper. "I... need to..." I moan as he rolls his tongue over my nipple. "I have to leave. The clock says it's four thirty."

He sucks on my nipple and thrusts his hips against my core. "Stay," he whispers. "Stay with me. Make love to me. Talk to me," he murmurs, pleasuring my body.

I lean back even farther, and my free hand reaches for his hair. I shouldn't encourage him. I need to stop. This is so wrong.

He grips my knees with both hands and spreads them wider apart. Sliding one hand up my thigh, he slips under my panties, pushing it to the side, and runs his finger down my slit. He hisses, "So fucking wet for me, babe. It's been too long since I tasted you, been inside of you. Stay." He strokes his tongue up the entrance of my pussy and uses the flat of his tongue to massage my clit. "You taste so fucking good." He does it again, and I fight the urge to press his face harder into my center, to grind my hips against his face. "Don't fight it. Let me love you," he whispers, gently blowing on my clit, making it pulse.

I throw my head back. Gods, I want more, and I almost give in.

"Stay with me, babe..." He licks and sucks, pushing a finger inside. "I want to make love all night long." He inserts a second finger and curls it just so it hits the right spot. I gasp as my insides clench around him. "I want to talk and move past all the crap between us so we can start over." He rolls his tongue over my clit and sucks harder, thrusting his finger in and out of me. "When we're done making love and talking, I want you to be mine. I need you to be mine."

My body freezes, and I close my eyes briefly. I pull his head back by his hair and move away. No, this is a mistake. I let it go too far. I should have stopped him at that first kiss.

Luke grips my legs. "Don't—don't run from me." I shake my head and try to push him off me. "If you don't want to go any further, then we won't. I need to talk. We need to talk." He drags me back into him and wraps his arms around me. "I'm in love with you, Jessica. You were meant to be mine. It started before I brought you down from the tree. I fucked up—I know I fucked up in the beginning. I've been trying to make up for it for years. Please, don't run. We can get past everything, if you just give me a chance to explain."

He's not making sense. Or my brain can't process his words. This is too much. "I need to go. I can't do this right now." I push at his shoulder to release me.

"Please, stay with me so we can talk."

I push harder. This time, he slowly releases me. I move as far away from him as I can without falling off the bed. The pain shining in his eyes makes me feel guilty for allowing this. "I'm sorry, but I can't be with you, Luke."

His pain morphs into anger. "Can't or won't?"

"Both," I whisper.

"If you would just talk to me—you've been avoiding me for three years!" he yells.

"It's too late, Luke. I'm with someone else."

His eyes narrow. "Then call him and end it. I don't share what is mine," he growls. "Tomorrow, we'll talk—however long it takes. I won't give up on you, on us." He stands and abruptly walks toward to the door.

"I'm not yours, Luke. You lost me a long time ago." I don't shout. I don't scream in anger. I simply mutter in a low, toneless voice devoid of any emotion.

He stops. His hands tighten into fists at his sides. Standing in the doorway, he replies, "Tomorrow, Jessica. You promised me tomorrow."

JESSICA
TWO WEEKS AGO:
MARCH 14, 2025: 7 P.M.
ALPHA KINGS MANSION

My thoughts tumble around in my mind while riding into the city. I remember Alpha Agnus's funeral, the truth revealed about Anders being my biological father, the accusations of that dickhead Beta, Young Alpha Dimitri calling me Grit and informing me we were betrothed.

As much as I dislike Territory Two's leaders, I always held a soft spot for that place. I don't recall ever visiting, nor did I ever meet anyone from there. When they encountered financial hardship, I wanted to help—not for the leaders but for those in the pack. I never understood why I felt compelled to aid them. Now, I guess I understand. Apparently, I grew up there.

Then, I think of Luke. Why does he always come at me this way? If he's not after me for some stupid made-up bullshit in his head, he blasts me with declarations of love. I cannot fall down that rabbit hole again. I gave him my heart once. He took it, ripped it apart, and stomped on it.

I still feel his lips against mine, feel his touch. Even when I am so angry with him and I want to dig his eyeballs out with my claws, he still makes me melt, and I want to give him anything he wants, even if it hurts or breaks me.

"What's the deal with you and Luke?" Odyssey asks.

"Stay out of my head, Odyssey."

He chuckles. "Stop thinking about him, then."

"I'm not."

"Sure, you're not."

I glare at Odyssey next to me in the backseat.

"He loves you, Jessica. He really does. You should have seen the way he behaved when we arrived earlier. No one could touch you. He was so badly injured, but he insisted on caring for you first."

Guilt curls its way into my gut. "I don't want to talk about him right now."

"Jessica, you need to talk to him. What you think happened —that's not how it went down. He's been agonizing over it for years."

I fold my arms over my chest. "Why are you taking his side?"

He shrugs. "I'm not taking anyone's side. There's the truth, and there's what you think happened. You need to hear the truth. You deserve to know that truth."

"It doesn't change anything. Can we talk about something else?"

"Fine. Let's talk about why you're doing this tonight. I can't believe you're going through with this, especially after the day you had." I narrow my eyes at him, and he scoffs. "I'm serious. You endured a shitstorm of a day. You don't have to do this. You should be at home with your family, working through all of the new developments."

"Stay out of my head, Odie."

He growls at my nickname. "Whatever you're planning, you don't have to do it. It won't bring her back."

I stare out the window. After a while, I finally respond. "Who says I'm only doing this for her?" I ask quietly.

"I'm not. But your whole plan puts your life at risk. It's suicide. You know it, and I know it."

The hairs at the back of my neck bristle at his insinuation. Electricity crackles in my palms.

He ignores my brewing anger and continues, "You and I have been friends for a long time. I'm not one to pull punches. I'm saying this because I care about what happens to you. What you're planning tonight is dangerous. You need to reconsider."

I clench my jaw and turn away. "What should I do? Hide, like I have been doing my entire life?"

"You're home now. You have the entire guard at your disposal and then some. There's a better way to do this."

"I'm not talking about this anymore." I gaze out the window, ignoring Odyssey for the rest of the trip. When we are close to the venue, I reach for my mask.

Odyssey places his hand over mine. "It's not too late. We can turn around and take you home." I move my hand and adjust my mask into place. He persists, "If we return home, I'm sure Luke will be a very happy guy. Maybe you can finish what he tried to start."

"Stay out of my head!" I shout.

He scrunches his nose. "Well, you could have at least let him get you off."

I give him the finger just before we pull alongside the curb. He laughs and steps out of the car.

The backstage of the runway is a catastrophe. Akiyo meets

me near the doorway. "Just as I predicted." She motions for me to follow her through the chaos. I'm more than a little late. I missed the stage rehearsal and sound check.

Odyssey's and Elijah's eyes bulge and zoom around the room, finding half-naked, tall, beautiful men and women everywhere. Odyssey's cheeks turn pink.

I giggle. "You look as if you've never seen naked shifters before, Odie."

He narrows his eyes, making me laugh even more. Elijah recovers from his initial shock and just keeps walking, back in bodyguard mode.

I stand behind the entrance of the stage and peek through the silk, gauzy fabric, adorned with fake diamonds and pearls. I sneak a look at the VIP section. The guards escort my parents, the twins, and Luke to their seats. Chris, Elias and Anders stayed behind to interrogate our prisoner.

I should have stayed behind as well, but honestly, I really don't want to discover any new revelations. I can barely process everything so far.

All of this—tonight, this runway show—I planned before I learned about my past. I am committed, and I won't turn back on what I aim to do.

The house is full. Cameras are everywhere. Tonight's runway show is streaming around the world. I take one last glance at my family. I didn't think Luke would come. I watch him for a few seconds. He looks sad, unfocused, like the weight of the world rests on his shoulders.

Why must I feel so guilty every time I put my foot down with him? He's done way worse shit to me.

Letting the curtain fall back into place, I roll my shoulders, suck in a deep breath, and slowly let it out. I look over to Odyssey, and he nods. Elijah nods, too. The host starts his opening monologue, the music starts, and a platform carrying the band Raw rises in the center of the stage. Their lead singer, Ray, plays his Stratocaster.

Charlie steps onto the runway from the opposite side with his guitar and sings the opening lines. When I hear the chorus to "Love Me Like I Want To," I approach the stage.

I forget everything about today. I forget that I am the newly named successor of the Whitemore pack, the CEO of W&P Corp, Princess Jessica Langhlan, the person formally known as Grit, or even "G," the rock singer.

I'm me—all of me—heart and soul laid out for everyone to see, to hear. My words, my voice sings for anyone who will listen to my joys, my sadness, my heartache, and my anger.

CHAPTER 41
NOT HERE

LUKE
TWO WEEKS AGO:
MARCH 14, 2025: 8 P.M.
LUNA SOLAR: CONCERT VENUE

I take my seat in the VIP section. I came tonight even after she rejected me in hopes that I could talk to her. She promised me tomorrow, but I know her—she'll invent some excuse to avoid me.

She's been avoiding me for three years. Fuck, we're business partners, and somehow, she avoids direct in-person meetings with me. When we do meet, she's available through video chats, and we are never alone. If I call, she doesn't answer. Her only responses are either in text or email.

But she's home now, and I'm not giving up. I need her to see how much I love her, care about her. I need her to see that I am not that spoiled, vindictive person she believes that I am.

I receive an elbow jab to my ribs and emit a breathy oomph.

"Why are you here if you're going to mope?" Jeremy hisses in my ear.

"I'm not moping. I'm just thinking about everything that happened earlier today."

He chuckles. "You worried that the betrothal contract still holds water?"

No, I'm not fucking thinking of that. Leave it to Jeremy to mention that shit. "Now I am. Thanks," I mutter under my breath.

"Did you see the way he looked at her when they escorted him out of the room?" He glances sideways at me, but I refuse to acknowledge his question. He whistles. "Come on, man. I mean, he killed his own father to protect her."

I want to throttle Jeremy. I don't care if thousands of people in this venue watch us. I *will* hit him. "Can you not talk for the rest of the show? Or here's an idea—switch seats with Justin."

Instead, Jeremy holds out a pamphlet. "She's not sitting here because she's part of the main attraction."

I glance down at the paper he tosses into my lap. A banner across the bottom catches my attention: Special guest model featuring petite line, Princess Jessica Langhlan. Musical guest featuring Raw, Charlie Langhlan, and "G."

What? Princess Jessica has never made a public appearance, ever. Even in photos, they aren't clear enough to capture her facial features. We all share a standing joke that she's actually a ghost. Once, a reporter had the nerve to ask Jeremy if she was ugly, thus the reason for her staying out of the limelight. Jeremy broke the reporter's nose, and our PR guy had a field day calming the media storm.

The lights flash, and everyone quiets in their seats. The host rambles on during his opening. The music starts. Models walk onto the runway. Charlie enters, playing his guitar, and starts to sing.

Then I hear her. My girl makes her way onto the stage. She wears a spectacular faux-leather outfit with a flowing cape. Fake tattoo mesh sleeves cover the scars on her arms. Her long hair is made up in a fancy braid that almost looks like a faux hawk, and her signature choker necklace covers the scar at the base of her throat. That very scar I made to save her life. She sings the chorus along with Charlie.

I become mesmerized. Everything else disappears. I don't hear the crowd screaming for her. I don't see the band. It's only her—singing, dancing, happy, free. Everything she is or isn't melts away when she performs. I hate her mask, though. I always have. I told her many times before—it's a grave injustice to her fans to hide her face. Her face when she sings expresses all her emotions. Her music, the lyrics she writes, acts like her diary, poetically written and composed into a song. It's why her fans love her—they relate to her.

I feel it, too. I know some of her songs were written about me. It hurts how I angered her, betrayed her, broke her heart. My own bleeds just thinking about it. She's written a thousand songs for other artists, but she kept and sang the ones she identified with the most.

She stand between Raw's lead singer, Ray, and Charlie. She slings one arm over Charlie's shoulder as he performs a solo riff. Jealousy runs up my spine. He's my doppelganger in every way, yet their friendship represents so much more than I ever had with her. She loves him, trusts him, believes in him. She smiles at him. I wish I could see more of her face.

A piece of paper flutters from the ceiling and lands near my foot. I look around, but no one moves to retrieve it.

Jessica faces the crowd, belting the lines to a new song. *"You're supposed to protect me, love me, take care of me. Instead, you shatter my soul."*

Jeremy side-eyes me. I bend forward to pick up the paper. When I turn it over, I discover that it's a tarot card, with the picture of Death.

Fear seizes my heart, transporting me back to memories from eight years earlier.

CHAPTER 42

DEATH CARD

LUKE

EIGHT YEARS AGO:
NOVEMBER 14, 2016: 11:55 P.M.
EMERALD PACK TOWN

The recruits and I arrive downtown. My mother, Jessica, and the other girls are shopping. We try not to make it obvious that we're here to watch over them as we approach the little restaurant where my mother likes to eat.

"Luke! Hey, baby. I missed you so much!"

Shit. I forgot Wills, Elaine, and the rest of their crew are here. Elaine crashes into me and tilts her head for a kiss. I turn my head just in time and push her backward to avoid further contact. This girl cannot take a hint. Any kind word, sometimes even a smile, is instantly taken out of context.

Ignoring her, I shake Wills's hand. "Hey, man. What are you doing here?" I ask, feigning ignorance.

He quirks his brow. "I texted you earlier. We all arrived a

day early for the ball. Haven't seen you for a while and wanted to hang out, catch up."

"Ah, yeah, sorry, man. Been busy. Must have missed your text."

"No worries. You're here now. We can hang and catch up later tonight at your place. Just like old times."

How the hell do I always get sucked into their bullshit? The worst part is I never know how to say no.

Darwin clears his throat. "Sorry, man. We're here to grab some lunch, pick up some supplies, and then head back to the training center. We recruits have plans—last hoorah before the ceremony and ball. You're gonna have to catch up later."

Wills narrows his eyes at Darwin. I add, "Sorry, man. Got plans. I didn't know you guys were coming."

His face instantly changes from irritation and suspicion to indifference. "No worries. We already ate, but we can hang until you get your shit. We can catch up tomorrow night." I nod. Elaine pouts, arms crossed over her chest. Wills whispers in her ear.

Cassie, another girl in their group, stares at Liam like he hung the moon and stars. I huff a breathy laugh. Liam adopts his usual pinched expression and tries to ignore her. The other two girls have their hooks into Sodie and Stan. I leave them to their own devices. If they know what's good for them, they'll stay far away from this bunch.

The recruits and I grew closer after Jessica's disappearance. When I first started with the recruits, some kissed my ass while others didn't like me right off the bat. They assumed, because I was the Young Alpha Prince, I would get away with anything.

They were wrong. I was bullied the most, and expectations were much higher than for everyone else. Slowly, over time, many of them dropped out, fed up with Marcus, Boris, and

Dustin's antics. The ones who remained simply kept to themselves.

I look around the recruits intermingled with the preppy kids from my former private school. True friends stand out among the group, and I feel lucky for the opportunity to be among them in the program.

When Wills and Elaine drift farther away, I slap Darwin on the shoulder. "Thanks, man. I appreciate the interception."

"Just doing my job." I raise an eyebrow at him. He smirks. "It's our job to protect *all* of the royal family. My gut instincts say these friends of yours, especially your girlfriend, are nothing but trouble."

I grimace at his reference to Elaine. "She's not my girlfriend, and yeah, those two are always up to something."

He laughs. "I think someone missed the memo 'cause that girl thinks she owns you."

I shudder at the thought. "Right. So, I roped Emily into doing recon for Mission 'Keep the Powers Twins away,'" I chuckle.

Darwin brightens. "Emily?"

"For some reason, Elaine is scared of her."

"I can see that. She's pretty fierce."

Poor dude. I can practically see the hearts floating in his eyes. She will break his heart. Darwin and Emily worked together to hack into some of the government's security systems searching for Jessica. Darwin might not be the best recruit in combat training, but he is wicked smart with computers.

That's how Shadow found him. Darwin was expelled in his territory for hacking into the school's system and changing fellow classmates' grades for a nominal fee. With the rise of technology, Shadow thought we needed more recruits familiar with technical operations.

The leads didn't agree, until we needed him. Darwin was the first person Liam thought of when Emily suggested using the airport and port systems. He not only hacked into the LS territory systems but the Northern A ones as well, and then some. He proved himself, and although we are not best friends, I couldn't be prouder of him that he stuck with it these past two years and finished.

"So, how close are you and Emily?" Darwin finally builds the courage to ask.

"I didn't sleep with her, if that's what you're getting at."

He sighs. "I wasn't, but thanks for the info. I mean, are you close enough to know if she's dating anyone, met her true mate, that kind of thing?"

I internally groan. Emily owes me big for this. I constantly fend off guys interested in her, so much so that sometimes they think it's because I'm in love with her.

"No, man. She's single, as far as I know. But, uh, I wouldn't hold out too much hope. She's, um, picky, and she never gets involved for the long term."

I watch the wheels churn in that big brain of his. "I can live with that. Not sure where I'll go after graduation. A short-term relationship works for me."

I shake my head. "Please don't."

Darwin's eyes narrow. "Why? Thought you two were like family."

I glance around. The other recruits caught up with the girls. Elaine flirts relentlessly, probably trying to gain my attention. "Look. Emily doesn't get involved in relationships because she's betrothed. I'm not supposed to say anything, so keep it to yourself." His eyes widen. "She was betrothed to the Obsidian Alpha's son before she was even born. She knows it. She's fine with it. She's accepted it."

Darwin frowns. "What about what she wants?"

"Sometimes we don't get what we want. I know she's an awesome girl, and you can probably see yourself with her short term or long term. But she won't go there. There's no room for what-ifs."

His shoulders sag. "Alright. Thanks for the heads-up."

I nod. I feel bad for the guy. He really likes her. But this isn't my first rodeo, and until Emily becomes mated, I'm afraid it won't be my last. Maybe I should just tell everyone we're dating. It might be easier to fend them off.

This time, though, I didn't lie to Darwin. The original Blackguard Alpha of the Obsidian Pack created a binding contract to the Obsidian Alpha who migrated to the LS territory after the great war and established the Obsidian Pack territory. Not sure how the Obsidian Alpha came to be here or how they know each other. The contract states that the first female born of the true Blackguard family line, or the Obsidian Alpha family, will be mated with the Alpha child of the same blood origin.

For generations, neither of the families had a female child. When Emily was born, her fate became sealed. Because of it, she was given the best education and sent to the elite private school in the city. Her college education is already paid. She also trained in martial arts and weaponry. She is everything the Obsidian Alpha could ever hope for in a mate for his Alpha son.

Except for one aspect. She doesn't like men. And she doesn't want children. I love Emily, and I am proud of her for accepting the situation. She never complains.

I wouldn't be so compliant. I am grateful for my parents. As the Alpha King, my father could have set up a betrothal contract to ensure our family's bloodline. He didn't. He and my mother are true mates. My brothers and I are the products of true love. Our parents want the same for us—the freedom to find our true mates or at least mate for love.

Elaine flirts with Stan, talking loudly. I roll my eyes. Sometimes, I think Emily has a good deal. At least she can always use the betrothal card to fend off unwanted male callers. I, on the other hand, must deal with manipulative, gold-digging women who only want me for my title.

We finally arrive at my mom's favorite restaurant. They eat lunch at one of the outdoor tables. Nothing appears amiss. Stan also pans the crowd. When he catches me looking at him, he nods. The girls squeal and make a ruckus in front of an old woman who set up a table outside of one of the stores.

Jessica sits quietly with her baseball cap so low, it hides her features. Emily and Sixes talk with their hands, as they do. My mother and Jessica laugh. She looks so petite, compared to the other women at their table. If onlookers didn't know better, she could pass for a young teen, until they see her body.

She takes a bite of food, and her face transforms with pleasure from whatever she just popped into her mouth. I swear I see the goosebumps along her arms. She closes her eyes, relishing the taste.

Damnit! I tear my eyes away. She's eating lunch, for crying out loud. I look up and down the main thoroughfare, but my vision gravitates right back to her.

She smiles and throws a balled-up napkin at Emily. Emily catches it, giggling. Why didn't I talk to Emily first before I jumped to conclusions?

I wouldn't be standing here, pining over a girl who hates my guts, not that I blame her. When I finally told Emily what happened when I came home, she gave me a black eye. I deserved it. I already felt like shit at the dinner table. With Jessica's disappearance and learning about Marcus and his asshole followers, the guilt never really left.

I don't know how to fix it. She won't give me the time of

day. My charm doesn't affect her. I was so wrong. Had I given her a chance to get to know me—the real me—we could have at least been friends.

Laughter erupts from the group. Elaine watches me with narrowed eyes. Crap. How long have I been staring at Jessica? Maybe she'll think I'm looking at Emily. Fuck, I hope so.

The elderly woman sits at her table, holding a deck of cards toward Liam.

"Come on. Give it a try. Maybe it will say we are destined to be together," Cassie purrs in Liam's ear. He grimaces. Cassie is curvy, dressed in the latest fashion, with light brown, wavy hair. She's taken to social media and wants to act or model. She may be pretty, but she's average, nothing special about her looks or her personality.

Sodie slaps Liam on the back. "Just do it. The faster you get it done, the faster she will realize she's not your destiny." Sodie chuckles. Liam motions for the elderly woman to hand him a card. She shuffles the deck, fans it out, and instructs Liam to pick one.

He pulls a card and flips it over. He scowls while everyone starts to laugh and cheer. Cassie bats her fake eyelashes. Liam shows the elderly woman the card.

She smiles. "Ah, the Lovers card. Destined to be together. Joined by fate. True mates." Then, she frowns. "You're fighting it. Why?" She shuffles the cards again and lifts one from the top of the deck. "The King of Cups, reversed," she explains. "If you don't let love in, you will still achieve everything you're destined for, but you will live a lonely and miserable life. The monster within will be unleashed and leave you a very feared man, a man you fight so hard to refrain from becoming." She takes the Lovers card and places it over the King of Cups. "Let love in, and you will gain everything your heart desires. The choice is yours."

Cassie smiles and intertwines her hand with Liam's. He glances at their hands and then at Cassie. "I told you we were destined to be together," she announces.

The old woman cackles. "Oh, sweetheart, it's not you. He knows exactly who it is." A slight reprieve crosses Liam's features before he schools his normal expression.

Cassie huffs. "We'll see about that!" She stomps away and turns back to look at Liam. He doesn't follow.

"Take it. You need the reminder," the old woman says to Liam, handing him the cards.

Elaine intwines her fingers with mine. "Your turn, baby," she sings.

I remove my hand from hers and move toward the table, taking Liam's place. I smile at the woman, flashing her my dimples, and she blushes.

"You're a horrible flirt," she claims.

At least I know it still works. I wink, and she shakes her head.

"You know, that charm will not work on everyone. Sometimes, you need to work a little harder to gain a certain someone's attention," she says with her own wink.

I chuckle. "I hear you, old woman, loud and clear." She smiles, showing her brown and yellow teeth, and fans the cards in front of me. I pull one, but another falls from the deck onto the table. She rests her hand over it, sliding it toward her, but she doesn't place it back into the deck. Gesturing to the card in my hand, I flip it over. The King of Pentacles.

"Ah. You will be a great king when it becomes your turn. But we already knew that. Didn't we? That's not what you want to know. Is it?" She smiles widely, and her eyes shine, like she knows a secret. She retrieves the card that fell and turns it over. The Queen of Wands reversed. She tsks. "You let the influences of others drive you to make a very wrong and hurtful decision."

The blood drains from my face. How could she possibly know that? Am I too late?

"But fear not. There is hope. You cannot rely on charm and that pretty face. You must dig deep and work hard to make things right. It will not happen overnight. Be mindful of those around you. The influences can cause more damage than you know."

She flips another card. The World. She smiles.

"Big changes are coming—some bad, some good. If you handle them well, it can all be yours. Just remember one important thing. It will look nothing like how you think it will. Once you accept that, she can be yours, too."

I frown. I don't understand that last part. She doesn't explain, hands me the cards, and repeats the same message she told Liam.

Elaine pushes me to the side. "Who is she?" she asks, crossing her arms.

The woman laughs and shuffles the deck. One tumbles out, face up. The High Priestess. "Someone very important." She looks at all of us before replacing it back in the stack.

"It's my turn," Elaine whines. I'm not sure why I stay to listen, but my feet seem rooted in place. I wait for Elaine's cards to show.

Elaine looks smug, knowing she's now the center of attention. She thrives on it. Elaine has a cute face and tan-colored hair she styles herself. Like Cassie, she dresses in the latest fashion, but she doesn't have Cassie's curves.

Underneath the carefully applied makeup and clothing, she is the ugliest girl I have ever met. Elaine is shallow, petty, and manipulative, but everyone knows it. Unlike the girl who used me, who hid and lied, Elaine wears her true colors.

Elaine growls, "What the fuck is this?!" She holds the Devil card. Snickers circle around the girls. Wills, her own brother, coughs and covers his smile. "This is not funny, Wills," she screeches.

The old woman smirks. "I don't have to explain this card to you. It's obvious you know what it means. But the divine is giving you a chance... to choose a different path. Jealousy is your one true enemy."

"And where the fuck did you get that from? One of your tacky quotes in those ugly, handmade cards in your store?!"

"Elaine," I warn.

She turns on me with eyes brimming with tears, "This isn't fair. I want another card!"

The woman obliges by shuffling the deck. She pauses before fanning them out. "You may not want the other card. Greed doesn't make you a better person."

Elaine snarls, "I want the other card."

"I will give you another card only if you allow me to say what you need to hear." She raises an eyebrow in anticipation of Elaine's answer.

"Fine," she snaps.

The woman leans forward and fans the cards before her. Elaine pulls a card, and as it did for me, another falls from the deck. The woman palms it.

When Elaine flips her pulled card, she finds Death. She begins panting, and her face turns red.

I side-eye Sodie, who readies to grab her if needed.

"What the fuck," she breathes.

The woman sits back and studies Elaine. "I was going to tell you that you have an opportunity to change, that jealousy will only eat you alive and ruin your life. It won't ruin just your life. Your jealousy will ruin others." She searches Elaine's face. "I'm afraid you already made up your mind, and as a result, someone will die because of you. In fact, many will die because of your jealousy and your greed." The woman frowns. "But maybe, just maybe, you can change."

"I've never been jealous of anyone in my entire life! I think you have it wrong. People are jealous of me!"

The woman sadly shakes her head. "Then you made your choice. I see." She lifts her palm to peek at the fallen card. She hesitates before continuing, "You will meet a great adversary." The woman quickly places the card in the deck.

"Give me back the card!" Elaine screams.

The woman looks down, slides the card back out of the deck, and flips it over. The Fool. "You won't win," she whispers.

Elaine screeches and throws the cards at the woman. "You changed it on purpose. You're trying to make me look like a fool. Well, I have news for you! I don't believe in any of this crap. I make my own destiny! I. Always. Get. What. I. Want!" Elaine turns, hesitates, then turns back, taking the money from the old woman's tip jar and stomps off.

I roll my eyes. The girls follow Elaine. Stan snorts. "She's a piece of work."

Darwin whistles. "That's the definition of crazy. I think we need to tighten security on you," he teases.

My blood runs cold. "I won't lie. She fucking scares the shit out of me," I admit, halfheartedly lightening the mood. I retrieve my wallet and place a fifty in the woman's jar. "Sorry about that. I hope this makes up for what she took."

The other guys follow suit, placing bills in her jar.

The old woman smiles. Crooking her finger, she stops us in our tracks. "I need to show you something." She sets a card on the table. The High Priestess. "This is the card I didn't want to show her, her greatest adversary. You need to protect her. If that girl gets what she wants..."

She bends down and picks up the cards Elaine threw at her.

Without looking at them, she covers the High Priestess with the Death card and then the Devil.

"Let her win, and it will destroy the entire LS territory." The woman's expression is overcome with sadness. Tapping the High Priestess, she cautions, "Protect her. Protect yourselves. Take care of one another."

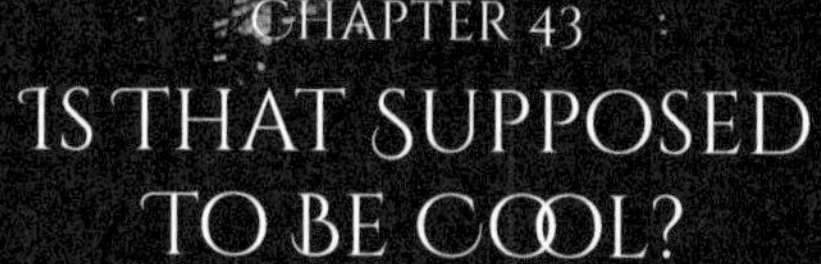

CHAPTER 43
IS THAT SUPPOSED TO BE COOL?

LIAM

EIGHT YEARS AGO:
NOVEMBER 14, 2016: 4:45 P.M.
EMERALD PACK TOWN

We walk through town for hours, watching over Jessica. I swear if this Cassie girl touches me one more time, I just might hit her.

We sit outside at the restaurant Shakti, Emily, Sixes, and Jessica ate at earlier. It's the perfect spot, center of the town. I can keep an eye on both ends of town. The women need to make their way back this way to get to the car. How long does it take to get your hair done?A car passes by, slowly. As it approaches, it halts, then reverses. A young guy sticks his head out of the back window. "Hey, baby. You need a ride?" The girl he calls out to doesn't look back. "Come on, baby. Don't do this to me. I just want to take you for a ride."

The girl scans the sidewalk. "Yeah, baby, you. I'm talking to you, beautiful." She turns around to face the guy. "Holy fuck! Are you mated? No? Good because I'm never letting you out of my sight." He exits the car by climbing through the window.

Does he think that makes him look cool? Or does the passenger door not open?

Sodie stands from his chair and whistles. The girl turns toward us. "Jessica!" he calls.

No fucking way. Jessica? She looks... wow. I blink a few times to make sure it's really her. Her long white-blonde hair is a darker shade of blonde with streaks of purple. She switched her outfit to ripped jeans that barely cover her muscular thighs and a navy-blue long-sleeved crop top that fits snugly over ample breasts. She raises her hand to move a strand of hair off her face, exposing her smooth abdomen that tapers to a narrow waist.

I already knew that her physical features changed after she disappeared. But this ... I can't breathe, and my limbs feel heavy and weak. Regaining my composure, I being to rise and follow the other recruits crossing the street. Cassie grabs my arm and pulls me back down.

I pry her grip off me. "Sorry, girl. I'm already taken."

She snarls, a mixture of anger and disappointment in her expression. Ignoring her I push off my seat and cross the street.

"Hey! What the hell, man. I saw her first!" the guy protests.

Luke and Sodie hover over him, and Darwin and Stan stand in front of Jessica. She looks confused, like she doesn't understand what's happening right now. I make my way through the group, cracking my knuckles, causing the guy to widen his eyes and gradually retreat.

Sodie growls, "Get in the car, my friend."

The guy looks at Sodie, me, Jessica, and then Luke. "Luke,

holy crap. Tell them you know me. What the hell? I just want to talk to the pretty girl."

Luke smiles. "She's off-limits. Get back in the car before the guards break your jaw."

His face reddens. "What? Why? She's not even from here."

Sodie growls again, stepping closer. "She's the princess. Now get in the car." His eyes dart back and forth between the recruits, his mouth opens ready for another protest. I crack my neck and stare him down.

He turns, runs, and jumps through the car window. "Go, go, go," he shouts. The driver peels rubber and speeds out of town.

We all crack up and high five each other. But Jessica does not look amused. She rolls her eyes at Luke and shakes her head at me.

Sodie, still chuckling, says, "Aww, come on, Little One. You know that was funny. The guy practically pissed himself before he jumped through the window."

She tries to hide her smile. "Please don't tell me this is what I can expect when I start bringing dates to the house." She stares at Stan and Darwin.

Darwin shrugs. "Depends. Is that how you're going to dress on a date?"

She shrugs. "Maybe. Since my mother bought my clothes, I assumed this was perfectly acceptable attire." Darwin and Stan laugh.

Dates? Over my fucking dead body.

Luke's idiot friends cross the street as Shakti, Emily, and Sixes depart from one of the shops.

Shakti announces, "Well, I think we'll call it a day." We offer to carry their packages and escort them back to their car.

Jessica refuses to let me take her bags. Why is she being so difficult? She won't even look at me. Wills approaches Jessica, but Emily maneuvers herself to block him. Darwin stands on her other side, and I walk behind them, leaving no room for anyone to reach her. Luke walks with his mother and Sixes in the front.

At the car, Elaine tries to invite herself back to the mansion. "I'm sorry, sweetheart. Our rooms are quite full, and we have so many preparations to complete for the ball tomorrow. Perhaps another time." Elaine is clearly upset with this response, but she smiles and graciously accepts the rejection.

Cassie bumps into me and whispers, "Text me, and I'll sneak over tonight."

"Not interested," I respond. With my attention diverted, Wills manages to move next to Jessica.

"Hi. I'm Wills Powers, Luke's best friend." He holds out his hand. She glances at it but doesn't move to shake it.

Yes, good girl.

"Never heard of you, Luke's best friend," she replies.

He laughs, ignoring her dry tone. "So, are you friends with one of Luke's cousins?"

"Sure," she deadpans.

"I mentioned that I am Luke's best friend, right?" Luke winces at his second declaration. Wills is far from being his best friend. He's just another one of those posers hanging on to Luke's coat tails because of his royal status.

She narrows her eyes. "Is that supposed to earn you brownie points?"

He smirks and rubs the back of his neck. "I was hoping it would."

Deciding to walk away instead of continuing the conversation, Jessica walks toward the car when Wills blocks her path. Her dark eyebrows raise. "Some words of advice. Dropping names doesn't impress anyone." She turns and notices Luke over the roof of the car. "Especially when someone's not quite impressed with your best friend." She pushes him out of the way and climbs into the car.

Wills smiles. "Noted," he says, closing the door after her.

Luke taps the top of the car. "Hey. I'm gonna jump in with them. I'll meet you back at the dorms."

Before I can acknowledge, arms snake around my waist, making my skin crawl.

I run over to the driver's side. "Hey, Xavier. Got room for one more up front?" He nods, and I reach into my pocket and toss the keys to the shuttle at Sodie. I waste no time getting into the passenger seat. Laughter echoes behind me. Sticking my hand out the window, I give them the finger.

CHAPTER 44

I WAS A FOOL

LUKE

EIGHT YEARS AGO:
NOVEMBER 15, 2016: 12:14 A.M.
EMERALD PACK: DAIRY FARM

It's after midnight when I finally return to the house from the dorms. I decide at the last minute that I want to stop by the stables. I haven't spent nearly as much time with Queenie as I had wanted to with the way the week turned out.

That's when I see them. Charlie wraps his arm around Jessica's shoulders. What the hell, Charlie? She's sixteen.

Charlie could have anyone. I mean literally anyone. Why her? Why Jessica? He's almost twenty-one, I think? Anyway, he's older. He's been with so many other women, older, experienced women.

Anger rages inside me. Quietly, I follow them into the barn. I glimpse Jessica's purple-streaked ponytail enter Queenie's stall.

"Words can't describe how I feel right now," Charlie says in a low voice. "It was perfect—so fucking amazingly perfect for our first time."

What the fuck?! I kick something in my path, and it scatters across the walkway. I duck into one of the stalls and crouch against the wall.

Boots approach. "You hear something, Little Bird?" Charlie asks Jessica.

"No," she answers.

"Huh?" His boots walk away, and I breathe a sigh of relief.

"So, when are we going to share our little secret? Do you still want it to be a surprise?" he prompts.

She giggles. "The whole point was to keep it a surprise."

Silence. Images of Jessica kissing Charlie form in my head. Charlie, who virtually has the exact same face as mine. Images barrage me of Jessica straddling Charlie in the corner of the stall, his hands caressing those perfect breasts and that curvaceous ass.

"How do you think everyone will react?" Charlie inquires.

"I don't know. This is all new to me, too," she offers. Queenie joins the conversation. Jessica laughs. "Aww, you want to be included," she coos to Queenie.

"Nah. I think she wants you to know that everyone will be stunned, at first. I think Aunt Shakti will cry. My mother will definitely cry. Emily will be pissed you're holding out on her."

"What makes you think I am holding out on Emily?"

"Wait. She knows?"

"Not all of it. Who do you think came up with the idea?"

I just can't right now. Of course, Emily—fucking Emily—is involved with their little hookup. But why tell anyone? Did he mate her? He couldn't have. Could he?

I need to think this through before I confront them. I can't believe Charlie did this. Just when I thought I knew Jessica, I was a fool.

Lying in bed, staring at the ceiling, I replay their conversation in my mind. While it's not uncommon for some shifters to mate early, we just don't. It's not who we are, unless we find our true mate.

Well, that's a different story. Still, maybe I have it all wrong. Instead of accusing Jessica, I should blame Charlie. Everyone knows he is a fuckboy. Maybe he's using her. No. As much as I want to think badly about Charlie, that's not him. He knows better. He knows when he shouldn't cross the line. It has to be Jessica.

I hear footsteps outside my door. Is she just coming home now? Glancing at the clock on my nightstand, I see it's almost four in the morning. Thanks to her, I haven't slept at all.

I want answers. Fuck lying in this bed, trying to pull reason from my bedroom ceiling. I hop up, storm down the hallway, and crash into Jessica's room.

She gasps, covering a scream with her hand. But she recovers quickly, fear morphing into irritation.

I immediately clutch her by her neck and slam her against the bathroom door. "What the fuck are you doing?" I growl.

"What are you accusing me of this time?" she spits back.

"Everyone said you suffer from insomnia. So, you use your time to hook up?"

She raises a hand to hit me, but I pin it above her head. I press my weight into her so she can't kick me. Her other hand grips my wrist, digging her nails into my skin, but I don't release her.

"Answer me! Are you fucking the men in the guard?" I lean in and trail my nose along her jaw, inhaling.

Her nails pierce my skin. I waver for a moment because I don't smell Charlie on her skin. But I sense a mixture of different male scents. One in particular is most fresh on her—Liam.

A burning sensation creeps up my neck. I tighten my grip on her throat. "You gave Charlie your V-card. Then, you ran to others and ended with Liam. Did you lie to Charlie? Convince him you were a virgin?" I loosen my hold just a fraction before I force her back into the door.

Tears streaming down her face. I'm right. She's just like everyone else. Instead of playing me, she's messing with my best friend, my cousin, and whoever else she was with tonight.

I bring my face closer to hers. She winces, and I smile. She should be afraid of me.

I'm going to teach her a lesson she will never forget, and she will think twice before playing games with anyone else. She might have fooled me twice now, but never again.

I stare down into her face and discover a bruise forming on her jaw. This bruise isn't from me. Releasing my grasp, other bruises spot her neck. Some of them look like bite marks. What the fuck?

An explosion blasts my body away from Jessica and into the wall. I blink up at the ceiling as a fist flies toward my face. I block it, and another comes at me. I'm not fast enough.

It catches me in the eye. I flip over to stand, and a kick lands in my ribs, Knocking me to my knees. Another explosion crashes into me, and I fall flat on my back.

Blinding fury consumes me. I push to my feet and fight back, blocking and throwing punches, using my magic. Someone slams into my middle, and I land on a soft surface. A crack echoes in the air, and whatever I land on collapses beneath me. Suddenly, two hard bodies jump on top of me.

"Enough! What the fuck has gotten into you!" Jeremy's voice shocks me from my rage, enough to comprehend that I'm fighting with my brothers and not Jessica. Hands tighten around my wrists, restraining me.

"I want her out of my house! She's a fucking whore!" I scream.

"What the hell are you talking about?" Justin shouts.

"Ask her! Ask her who she's fucking! She's fucking playing them!"

"Where did you get that idea from?"

I struggle against their restraint. I don't want to answer any more of their questions. I need to find her.

"Calm the fuck down!" Jeremy snarls.

I can't break free so I stop fighting. I take several deep breaths, trying to control my rage.

"Explain!" Justin barks.

The twins think I'm insane. They insist they were with Jessica the entire evening late into the night. But they can't confirm nor deny my suspicions of the conversation I overheard in the barn.

And Liam? I can't justify my suspicions, but she smells like him. His scent is all over her. The twins dismiss it as my being unaware of their friendship. Nothing we say makes any difference, though. The three of us stomp off to our rooms.

CHAPTER 45

MISUNDERSTANDING

LIAM

EIGHT YEARS AGO:

NOVEMBER 15, 2016: 3:39 A.M.

EMERALD PACK TERRITORY

Lightning streaks the sky, but I don't reach her in time. She's walking back to the house when I find her. Her shirt has been ripped open. Bruises discolor her jawline. Bite marks dot her neck and her chest

I want to kill whoever did this to her. I study her face. Her faraway gaze is devoid of emotion. No tears. No anger. No fear. She refuses to make eye contact with me, staring at the ground. She smells like Queenie, which masks the scent of her attacker.

I pull off my hoodie to cover her. She doesn't speak. She won't tell me what happened. I want to shake her. I want to... just hold her in my arms . Even then, she doesn't respond to my touch or murmurs of her safety, of my protection. She won't answer my questions.

She whispers that she wants to get inside. Reluctantly, I let her go.

She enters the house through the back entrance, and I race around to the back to wait for her to flip the light switch three times, our signal she settles for the night. It's also Mm signal to her—I love you—even though she doesn't know what it means.

I watch her drapes close, but I can't bring myself to leave just yet. Sending a quick text to the group that I found her, I keep an eye on the road to make sure the Powers twins don't return to the property.

Sixes replies quickly after they find Wills and Elaine. Fuck. Did they attack Jessica? It had to be them. I will fucking kill them.

Where the hell is Luke? He hasn't responded to any of my messages.

I check the vicinity twice, ensuring no one else lingers. I approach the kitchen entrance of the mansion when Jessica bolts out of the door, chest heaving, sobbing.

She crashes into me, clinging to me like I'm her lifeline.

What the fuck?!

Clutching my shirt, she shakes her head. "It's fine. It's fine. Just a misunderstanding."

I frown. A misunderstanding wouldn't leave her shaking like this. I smell the fear radiating from her. I also smell Luke on her. I urge her to the side so I can enter the house.

Did he attack her again? He confessed to me about the incident the day he met her for the first time—how they fought, how he took it too far because of his own misconceptions. I didn't respond at the time because the twins already reamed his ass. He seemed remorseful, and after talking to him, I thought he was clear of her intentions for a family, for a place to belong and nothing more.

I pinch the bridge of my nose. "Jessica, let me go in there."

"No, please, Liam. The twins are with him. It's fine." She's covering for him, the same way she covered for him the first time.

I raise an eyebrow at her. "Then tell me what happened." Her face ashen, the bruises on her face and neck darkening. At least she's responding to something, but I hate the wild look of fear in her eyes.

"He thinks I gave Charlie my V-card and then met you after."

What? Luke is usually a pretty level-headed guy. Why must he fly off the handle with Jessica? After what she just endured, this shit won't sit well with me. This whole time, he has been home, ignoring our calls and texts. Was he with Elaine? None of this makes sense. I glance at the door. I should go slap some sense into him.

Jessica tugs on my shirt, vehemently shaking her head. I need to get her out of here. I need her to talk to me.

I take Jessica's hand and lead her away from the house to the cliff that overlooks the seventh territory. The sun should rise soon, a beautiful sight as it touches the territory.

When we arrive, I help her climb onto a large rock where I like to sit and think. I situate behind her, to hold her. She doesn't protest.

I won't see her after this, unless I come back to visit. The thought of not seeing my family, my friends, Jessica, finally sinks in.

What if I return home to visit my family and see Jessica on those occasions. What if she has a boyfriend? I draw her closer to me. My chest aches. I don't want her with anyone else but me. But she isn't mine.

Hell, I tried to keep my distance from her. I just couldn't *not* touch her. I wanted to hold her hand, kiss the top of her head, keep her in my arms. But I had to constantly remind myself not to get attached. Marcus, Dustin, and Boris were watching her, watching me.

Pressing my nose against her hair, I take her in and kiss her head. I have longed to do that since she returned, since she was found. I give myself this one last moment before I leave.

She stiffens and leans forward. But I don't pull back. I rest my arms on my knees.

I watch her, no longer admiring the sunrise. Her eyes stare, but she's lost in her thoughts. I wish she would tell me who hurt her. I can't hear her thoughts anymore, and I hate it. I never needed to talk or ask her questions. She never stopped thinking.

She used to study me all the time, when I sat in the corner of the room. I liked it. I liked that she looked at me more than the others. I liked that even though I rarely spoke to her, she felt the most secure with me.

She turns her face, and I trace her scars. They are lighter now, not as raised as they once were. She tenses as my thumb caresses her skin. I lean forward and kiss the scars. "You're still so beautiful," I whisper against her temple and press my lips there.

She turns away. "You shouldn't kiss me or hold me."

Her words stab me in the heart. Shit. "Sorry. I didn't mean to... I just..." Crap. I don't know what to say. I pushed too far. She was just attacked, and here I am, touching her, holding her, kissing her.

She shakes her head. "I don't need your girlfriend coming at me, too. That's all."

"I don't have a girlfriend." Leaning forward, I angle my head to see her face.

"She was all over you in town. I saw the lingerie she bought and planned to meet you tonight." She squeezes her eyes shut. "Oh, gods! I let you kiss me, and you were with her." She inches forward, but I wrap my arms around her waist.

"You mean Cassie?" She nods, keeping her eyes closed. I laugh. "She's not my girlfriend. Did you not see me run and jump in the car as fast as I could to get away from her? Hell, I haven't been able to live that shit down since it happened."

She shakes her head, trying to dismiss my explanation.

"Look at me," I encourage softly, but she won't. I lift my hand, placing two fingers under her chin, and bring her face closer to mine. "Look at me, baby. Open your eyes." She slowly opens them, and I search their depths. "I want you. I wanted to kiss you that first night they moved you to the main house, but I didn't. I was afraid. I didn't want to take advantage of how vulnerable you were, overwhelmed by everything."

She blushes. "Don't lie just to make me feel better," she scoffs and lowers her eyes.

"Make you feel better?"

"I'm ugly, Liam. I was even uglier then, practically bald, with broken teeth and a face full of scars. I was blind, but I could still see what I looked like."

I growl, "Kiss me right now."

She meets my intense gaze, lips slightly parted in shock. Before she protests, I pull her toward me, crashing my lips against hers.

Electricity sparks. Her small hand touches my face, sending flames up my spine and into my chest. I deepen the kiss, taking advantage of her parted lips. I wish I had done this sooner. I hate that I have to leave tonight.

I squeeze her closer, not wanting this to end. But I can't push—she's been through so much. I release her slowly, so slowly, so I can remember this moment forever.

Her face is flushed, her eyes still closed. The tip of her tongue brushes against her lower lip. When she finally opens her eyes, I gauge her reaction. There is no fear, only sadness and an unexpected emotion—love.

My own feelings reflect back at me through the windows to her soul. She doesn't speak, simply leaning into me. I kiss her temple, sigh, and commit her smell to memory.

I want to tell her I love her, but if I do, it will only make leaving harder for both of us. I can't do that to her. We sit in silence for several heartbeats. I hold her and cherish her for as long as she lets me.

I point to a ridge along the horizon of the seventh territory. "See that hill over there?"

She nods.

"Before my mother died, she used to tell me stories about kings and princesses in some foreign place. The first time, she brought me to a place where we could overlook the seventh territory. She told me to close my eyes and imagine it to be a beautiful place full of shifters, a happy place with no crime, where Alphas actually cared about their packs. She made me promise that whenever I found myself unhappy or sad, I would think about my happy place.

"As life got shittier, I couldn't picture that happy place anymore. Instead, I pretended that the hill was a large castle surrounded by dragons and ogres who ate shifters," I admit, clearing my throat nervously, starting to feel uncomfortable that I'm revealing a silly, vulnerable, part of myself.

She reaches up and cups my face with her hand. She rubs her thumb along my jawline and presses her temple against my cheek, giving me the confidence to continue.

"I used to daydream that a princess was locked away in the castle, held against her will as a prisoner. I imagined that I would one day slay all the dragons and kill the ogres. Once inside, I would fight the evil witch and use my magic to burn her to a crisp. I would search the entire castle and rescue the princess from her captivity."

She turns her head to look up at me. "Did you fall in love and live happily ever after?"

I shake my head and smile sadly. "No. You see, in my fantasy, the princess had magical powers beyond anyone's imagination. I just wanted her to bring my parents back from the dead so we could be a happy family and live together in the world my mother imagined. I would repay her by serving as her guard for the rest of my life in gratitude."

Twisting her body, she searches my face with those clear blue eyes.

I avert my gaze. I don't want her pity.

She slides her hand around my neck and pulls me down, gently pressing her lips on mine. Her kiss is sweet, compared to my crushing one earlier.

Breaking our kiss, I confess, "In all my life, I never once thought I would serve as a guard to an actual princess. I will slay all the dragons and ogres and kill the evil witch with my magic for you. I would protect you and keep you safe for the rest of my life."

She rests her forehead against mine. "I know," she whispers. She pulls back to stare at my chest. "I wish you weren't leaving." Turning forward again, she angles her head so I can't see her expression. I pull her body flush against mine and wrap my arms tight around her.

I murmur into her ear, "I don't want to. Leaving you is the last thing I want to do." Her head bobs against my shoulder. "Baby, you asked me if I fell in love with the princess and lived happily ever after. I never imagined it because guys like me don't know how to fall in love or find a happily ever after. Or, I thought that... until I met you. I've fallen in love with you. But a happily ever after just isn't in my cards. That's why I need to leave."

She wipes her face with the sleeve of my hoodie.

I want to promise her that, somehow, I'll figure it out. But those promises are just lies. I don't make promises I can't keep. I tighten my hold on her, not wanting to let her go.

We sit there in silence, wishing I could say or do something to ease the pain that envelops us. I can't think of anything to make it better, and I don't want to make it worse.

Her soft, raspy voice breaks through the melancholy. "Can I kiss you one last time before we go? Before you leave, and I never see you again."

I rest my head against hers and squeeze my eyes shut. Something inside of me breaks. Emotions I never allowed myself to feel flood to the surface. Tears build behind my lids, and I taste them in the back of my throat.

I haven't cried for nearly thirteen years, not since that horrible night my mother died. How? How could I have fallen so hard for this precious, resilient woman, full of magic and unwavering love? How could I have found her, only to lose her at the same time?

"Anything you want," I reply, my voice hoarse, raw with emotion. I lean back to gaze into her beautiful face, into those fucking amazing eyes. My lips tremble. Fear of losing her paralyzes me.

She tilts her chin up, curling her hand in my hair, and pulls me toward her. Pushing away all the angst and regret filtering through my mind, I show her how much I love her by deepening the kiss. I lose myself in her sweet, soft lips.

Our spell finally breaks. As we walk back, I hold her hand, relishing the way it feels in my own. I rub the back of her hand with my thumb. Looking down at our entwined fingers, I remember the first time I held her hand in mine, the night we brought her home from Whitemore plantation. That was the moment, that first touch, when I gave her my heart.

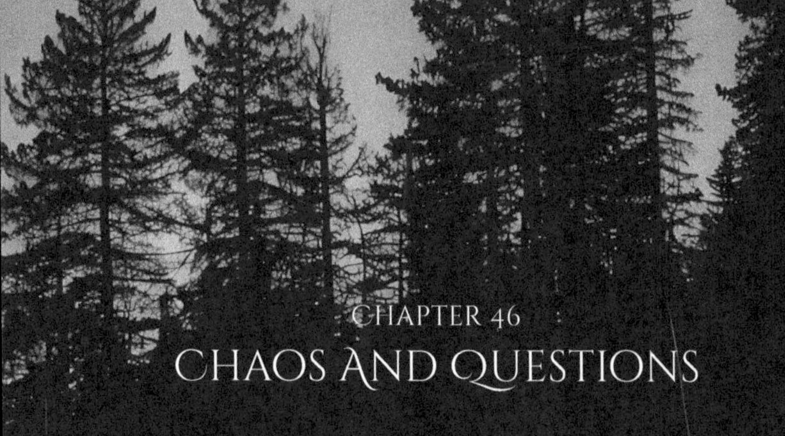

CHAPTER 46
CHAOS AND QUESTIONS

LUKE

EIGHT YEARS AGO:

NOVEMBER 15, 2016: 10 A.M.

ALPHA KINGS MANSION

My growling stomach forces me out of my room and down to the kitchen. I find it bustling with staff and Aunt Tater ordering everyone about. They all are in full prep mode for tonight's ball.

My mother clusters in the group assembling trays of hors d'oeuvres. I kiss her cheek as I pass by. She smiles and immediately grabs a plate for me, piling it with food. "Have a good time celebrating your accomplishments?" she asks and sets the plate in front of me on the kitchen counter.

I did until Jessica ruined my mood. "Yeah, we had a good time hanging out."

"Good." She offers me another small smile. "Time flew by so fast. I will miss you when you leave for school tomorrow."

"I'll miss you, too, Mom." I sit, waiting for her to question me about this morning. But they never come. "Uh, did you see the twins this morning?"

"Yeah. They left with Jessica a couple of hours ago." She holds up a hand. "Before you start, Charlie went with them, along with Sixes and Emily. She's fine. They will be back before the ceremony."

I wasn't planning to ask, but good to know. I really don't care what happens to Jessica anymore. I just want her to stay away from my family, from my friends. I lose my appetite, but I force myself to eat a little while my mother and I engage in small talk. I should enjoy these moments with her before I leave.

Instead, I brood over Jessica. My mother eventually leaves, allowing me to stew alone with my thoughts. Aunt Tater brings me samples of food to try, like when I was a little boy.

"Joe, find Anders! Jessica's room is destroyed. It looks like she was attacked!" Everyone in the kitchen stops and turns toward my mother. "I would get Nathan, but he's busy right now."

Joe doesn't move and starts to laugh. "I'm sorry, Your Majesty. With all the prep work needed this morning, I forgot to inform you that Jessica told me before she left that the twins discovered some new... abilities sometime early this morning. It was quite catastrophic, but she will clean her room when she returns."

"Clean up her room? Joe, it's destroyed. There are scorch marks on the carpet and walls. What exactly can the twins do?"

Joe cracks a smile. "They make things explode."

My mother grimaces. "Of course, they can. If it's not one thing, it's another," she huffs, drumming her fingers on the kitchen counter.

Everyone resumes their tasks. Just a normal day in the life.

This loyal staff has been with my family for years. They know my brothers well.

"I let them leave the house. I should have them return right away."

Joe raises a finger. "They were fine when they left. They didn't leave a path of destruction in their wake. I'm sure they'll be fine. I also sent a message to Anders before my attention went elsewhere."

My mother sighs.

"I can straighten the room, Mom."

She shakes her head. "It's fine. I'll take care of it tomorrow."

"No, really. I can clean what I can before I head over to the graduation ceremony."

"Thank you, sweetheart. Your brothers should be the ones to clean their mess."

No, Jessica should clean it up, I think. But I don't want my mother to suffer for it.

I haven't seen the twins, Emily, Sixes, or Charlie. The ceremony will start soon. I'm still in a mood, but it lessened somewhat over the course of the day.

Sodie places his hand on my shoulder. "Can you and I talk in private?" He furrows his brow, and his mouth is set in a firm line.

"Sure." We move to a more secluded area.

"So, what's the deal? You haven't answered your phone or responded to any texts after you left last night," he claims.

I pat my pockets to locate my phone. I'm sure I grabbed it before I left. "Shit. I must have left it at the dorms."

He raises an eyebrow. "No, I don't think so. Stan and I had cleanup duty this morning. Didn't come across it."

Where the hell is my phone?

"I guess that explains why you went MIA. Anyway, have you seen Jessica at all today?"

"No, I haven't." Not exactly a lie.

He nods. "Your girlfriend and Cassie arrived not too long after you left. They gave us hell, trying to round them up. Your girlfriend disappeared after we tossed her friend off the property. We searched but couldn't find her."

"So, what? You thought I went MIA because I was with her?"

Sodie shrugs.

"I'm not that desperate for pussy," I retort.

He shakes his head. "Nah, that's not it. Liam found Jessica with fucking bruises on her face, neck, and arms. But she refused to tell him what happened. Charlie insists she didn't look like that when he left her early this morning, sometime after midnight, not quite one in the morning."

But Jessica didn't come home until a few hours later. She was probably with Liam, then. "So, when did Liam find her with bruises?"

Sodie frowns. "Close to four a.m."

I stare at Sodi. His eyes narrow, and head tilts. His breathing is even, heartbeat steady. He's not lying or covering for Liam. He's studying me. "You think I attacked Jessica?"

He doesn't deny it, and his eye contact never wavers. "We think if Elaine saw Jessica with Charlie and thought it was you, she could have attacked Jessica."

Heat rises in my face. "And what exactly were Charlie and Jessica doing to stir up crazy notions in Elaine's head?"

"I may not know your friend or her brother, but something isn't right about those two. I'm sure if she simply saw the two of you standing next to each other, she would attack Jessica first and ask questions later."

He's not wrong—Elaine is crazy. We all witnessed firsthand how she can fly off the handle. Did Sodie just confirm what I overheard between them? "So, everyone knows about Jessica and Charlie, except for me?"

Sodie scrunches his face. "Don't say it like that, man. It was supposed to be a surprise. Anyway, I healed Jessica, so the bruises are gone. I think we should keep a close eye on her tonight. She won't tell us who attacked her. We can't point the finger at Marcus or Dustin because they were locked in their rooms all night. Boris is back home. Darwin confirmed it through the airport surveillance. I haven't spoken to the twins yet, and I'm not sure if she said anything to them."

"If I hear anything, I will let you guys know."

Satisfied with my answer, he squeezes my shoulder.

Everyone arrives moments before the ceremony. Jessica presents each of us with our guard rings and pins. When she reaches me in the line, fear glimmers in her eyes, and her hand tremble.

Who the hell attacked her? Why won't she tell anyone? Was she really even attacked?

When the ceremony is over, we all migrate to the ballroom. "Luke! You look so handsome!" Elaine yells, waving frantically. She's surrounded by her minions and Wills. I smile and allow them to hug me. Elaine attempts a kiss, but I turn my head. Her lips land on my cheek.

"Hey, man. You didn't tell us yesterday that beauty is your sister." Wills elbows me in the ribs, which are still tender.

"Nothing to tell. She's not my sister. She's adopted," I reply.

Elaine whirls around. "Adopted? Isn't she too old? I thought people adopt babies."

I give Elaine a bored look. "Children can be adopted at

different ages," I answer, trying to stifle the impulse to roll my eyes. What an idiot.

She rests her hands on her hips. "What the hell does that mean?"

Wills grabs her arm. "Relax. Father is here. Don't make a scene." Wills grimaces before feigning a sincere apology. "She's just feeling a little threatened. She's convinced she saw you flirting with her last night."

Last night? I recall my conversation with Sodie.

"No, I said she was flirting with him." Elaine grumbles.

Cassie crosses her arms over her chest. "I thought you said you found Luke and were with him after I got kicked off the property?" Cassie questions Elaine.

Elaine smirks. "Jealous?"

I sigh and turn to leave. Enough of their bullshit. I'm not in the mood to correct her.

"Oh, baby, you left your phone behind." Elaine holds up my phone. She walks over to me and places it in my hand.

I grab her wrist. "Where the hell did you find my phone?"

She arches her eyebrows and sneers, sending shivers up my spine. Then, smiling for her performance, she says, "Don't worry. I won't tell anyone about our secret spot." She leans in closer. "I left you some pictures to remember me by."

I release her and turn as Jessica and Emily pass us. Emily scrunches her nose and glares daggers at me.

I seize the opportunity to greet one of the guests. Confused as hell, I don't have time to inquire about Jessica's whereabouts for those missing hours.

As the night wears on, guilt eats away at me. At some point, I tell Sodie that Elaine returned my phone, insinuating I left it behind after a secret hookup. He gives my phone to Darwin to check it out for spyware or a tracking device.

I avoid Wills and Elaine as much as possible. Cassie still guns for Liam, but he does a good job dodging her.

I find my father on the balcony, talking to someone. I haven't seen him all day, on purpose, and I hate it. I leave tomorrow. Otherwise, all we have are phone calls to check in. I won't be here.

He sees me approach and inclines his head, acknowledging me. "If you will excuse me, I would like to take this opportunity to bond with my son," he explains to our guest. They leave, congratulating me on their way inside.

My father pulls me into a big bear hug. "So proud of you, son. You'll make a great Alpha King one day." Guilt and self-loathing consume me. Why does Jessica bring out the worst in me? "Want to tell me what's on your mind?" he asks.

I lean on the balcony railing, not sure what to say. Should I come clean and tell him what I know about Jessica? I already tried once. He didn't listen then. My temper gets the best of me. "Why did you have to introduce her as your daughter? As my sister?"

"Luke, I thought we were past this. Can you—"

"Nathan," my mother calls behind us. We both turn. Jessica stands next to her.

Great. This is just great. She looks ready to cry at any moment.

"Is everything okay?" my father asks.

"Yes. Jessica is going to play the piano. Alpha Agnus insisted on it. Come on. We'll find front-row seats." My mother turns toward me. "You too, Luke."

Sitting next to Liam, I look around the room. "Where are my brothers?" I wonder.

Liam's eyes remain glued to Jessica, who stands next to the piano. "I haven't seen them for a bit," he answers. Sodie leans in from Liam's other side and whispers.

My father takes the stage and introduces Jessica again before she sits at the piano. Her hands shake. Everyone is quiet in the ballroom, waiting for her to begin, except for rude and loud snickering in the back.

I glance over my shoulder and discover Elaine and her friends. Liam uses his fingers to let out a whistle, cheering for Jessica. Sodie shouts and starts clapping. The entire room follow suite, encouraging her to play.

She looks at Liam, or is it Sodie? From where I sit, I can't tell. She closes her eyes, emits a slow breath, and her fingers begin to move over the keys, smooth, like she's done this a million times before.

I haven't heard this particular piece before. Sheet music rests on the ledge in front of her, but her eyes are still closed. My mouth falls open in awe. I'm transfixed as she moves with the music, and her facial features no longer appear taut or scared. Her entire being lights from within and burns around her so brightly that an ethereal beauty starts to shine.

As her piece comes to an end, she seamlessly transitions into another song. My heart stops when she opens her mouth and starts to sing. Her voice is strong, with a slight rasp. It's sexy. She enthralls me now by everything she gives. I don't move a muscle. I don't even breathe.

We all sit in wonder that such substantial presence could come from her petite frame. The entire room stands, enraptured by her amazing talent. I want to bottle it and never let it out of my possession.

She immediately plays the next song. A guitar sounds from the far end of the stage. Charlie emerges, singing along with her. They are meant for each other, the way they blend their voices.

Collective sighs echo behind me, witnesses of a love story

unfolding. They sing one more song together, and when it ends, Charlie waves Jessica over.

She stands from her seat, and they hug. The entire ballroom erupts with whistles and cheers. For the first time in my life, I want to be Charlie. I want that perfectly beautiful girl to look at me that way—all smiles and blushes, eyes shining with admiration.

When the ballroom quiets, Charlie speaks into the microphone. "I told you our mothers were going to cry." He points at our mothers, dabbing their eyes with tissues.

My mind races back to that conversation in the barn. Sharp pain stabs through my heart. My throat constricts. I close my eyes.

"Last night, Jessica and I sang together for the first time. I was amazed at how well we did, how perfect we sounded. We have a little surprise for all of you. This is an original song Jessica and I wrote together." Charlie strums his guitar. "Ready, Little Bird?"

I want to disappear. The fear in her eyes at the ceremony haunts me. The words from the elderly woman in town yesterday ring in my ears. "*Don't let the influence of others affect you.*" That is exactly what I did, not once but twice.

My night continues to get worse. After Jessica and Charlie sing their duets, she announces that she wrote a special song for the guards as a thank you for everything. She uses the words "protect" and "care."

I run my hand over my face, more uncomfortable than I have ever felt.

She motions her arms, shooing Charlie off the stage. "This song is called 'Armor.' Ready, boys? One, two, three." Music swells from behind her. As she sings, the curtains open. Jeremy plays the drums, and Justin strums the bass. A mixture of their friends and young men from our pack who work on the dairy fill in as her makeshift band.

She sings two verses when a female voice joins her. Someone else has taken over, not once missing a beat. "Sammy Cane," Jessica introduces. The winner of the song contest that hit the mainstream only a month ago, walks along the stage and sings Jessica's song.

Jessica points at our table with a big smile and clasps her hands together in a big thank you. She repeats the gesture to Charlie and Ean. Another song starts to play. Jessica adds, "I didn't forget about all the badass women in my life, too. This one is called 'Unstoppable Women.'"

Sammy insists they sing it together. As the song ends, a different beat blends the song. Sammy Cane introduces The Kittens, a popular girl group. The lead singer shares, "The next few songs are originals written by the very beautiful, very talented, your very own Princess Jessica Langhlan."

I look over at my mother and Aunt Tater, who jump up and down. I chuckle at the excitement and beaming smiles on their faces. Everyone stands from their seats, clapping and dancing. Everyone enjoys themselves.

And I feel like absolute shit. I watch Jessica from afar, dancing with Emily and Sixes and a slew of men who now want her attention.

That burning sensation starts up the back of my neck again. "That's called jealousy, Young Alpha Prince."

"Alpha Agnus, enjoying the ball?" I bow my head in respect.

Her eyes narrow, and she growls from deep in her chest. I try not to cringe, as guilt roils in the pit of my stomach. Did Jessica tell her about me? How poorly I treated her? She lifts her cane and whacks me in the abdomen, hard, causing me to pitch forward.

I clear my throat and slowly straighten. Sweat beads on my forehead. I am thankful she didn't aim any lower.

"Get your shit together, young man. Stop behaving like them." She points her cane to Wills and Elaine. Alpha Agnus steps closer. "Continue to act like them, and you will suffer for it." As abruptly as she appeared, she walks away, leaving me to stare at her retreating back. She's right, though.

Gazing around the ballroom, I think about how long I waited for this day. From the first moment I attended a guard ceremony, I couldn't wait to be among those graduating. I became enamored by the men dressed in their formal wear, taking their oath, vowing to protect my family.

When Elias and Charlie graduated, I was so proud. And now, my opportunity to prove I am worthy to wear the crest of a guard, I let shit from the past influence my actions, my feelings, toward someone innocent. I don't deserve to be here.

I take one last look at the dance floor. Emily and Sixes dance with the recruits. Jessica is probably mixed in there, but she's so short that I can't see her clearly.

"Hey, man. Can we talk?" Wills walks up to me from the side with a guilty expression. Normally, I would brush him off, but something tells me what he has to say isn't good.

CHAPTER 47

UNFINISHED BUSINESS

LIAM

EIGHT YEARS AGO:
NOVEMBER 15, 2016: NIGHT OF THE BALL
ALPHA KINGS MANSION: BALLROOM

I leave the dance floor in search of Luke. I need to talk to him before I leave. I need to ensure he has his shit straight and stops fighting with Jessica. I search everywhere for him, even outside of the ballroom, to no avail. I find the rest of the recruits and Ean lingering by the balcony entrance.

"You were planning to let them threaten you, hold your life over your head?" Emily shouts, her hands fisted at her sides. She stand just a few feet in front of Jessica. Jessica meets Emily's angry glare with her own steely-eyed gaze.

I glance at Ean. "What the hell did I miss?"

He shrugs. "Not exactly sure, but I think the Greystones had a word with Jessica. Elaine Powers got involved. Emily broke her nose and the other one who had her hooks in you earlier."

My spine stiffens, and my palms tingle. "Are you fucking kidding me?" The rage builds. If Marcus laid a hand on her...

Ean shakes his head and places a hand on my shoulder. "Calm down. This is why we didn't look for you. Uncle Nathan and the leads are handling it. You need to focus on you right now."

Focus on me? How the fuck am I supposed to do that when nothing is resolved?

Jessica steps forward, closing the distance between her and Emily. "Yes! If it means protecting all of you, then yes! If it means that I die so that you can live, then yes! You each mean something to someone, your family, to me. My life, my protection, is not worth losing any of you. I'm just a stray, some poor girl who should have died anyway. No one misses me from where I came from. No one cares that I'm not home. There's no missing child reported. No one on the news is crying for me. I am not worth putting your lives at stake."

I wince at her words. After our moment early this morning, how can she possibly still feel that way?

"You're wrong!" Emily yells and tears streak down her face.

"I love all of you. If I have to sacrifice my own happiness or my life for all of you, then that's what I will do," Jessica admits.

"You're an idiot!" Emily bites.

Shock and pain flash across Jessica's face before she replies, "I never said I wasn't one."

I press my lips together to keep from laughing out loud. I didn't expect that out of her mouth.

Emily, however, isn't amused. "No, you're an idiot because you think no one would hurt if something happened to you! How the hell do you think we all felt when you went missing?! We didn't just sit around and wait for you to come back. We worried. We cried. We searched. We banded together. We fucking lost sleep. Your mother was devastated. Your father was ready to start a war! Anders prepared to kill anyone who hurt you. My father, my brothers, Charlie, Uncle Chris, all the guards would have been right there with him, too. You have no idea how it affected all of us, especially me!" She grabs Jessica by the arm and pulls her into a ferocious hug. "You are our fucking family, too!"

Jessica buries her face into Emily's shoulder and wraps her arms around her. Emotions and tears on everyone's faces say a lot about this woman, who appeared one stormy night and tornadoed her way into our hearts.

I shake my head. My sister and my girl—so different and yet so similar. She will always be *my* girl, will always be *my* family.

Ean bumps my shoulder. "We got this. Xavier is ready when you are. No rush. All of your belongings are packed in the car."

"Thank you."

"I'm not one for sentiment, but should you change your mind, you will always be welcomed back home. You're our family, too."

I crack a thin smile and hold out my hand to him.

He looks down at it and frowns. Gripping my forearm, he pulls me into a hug. "Brother, safe travels, and keep in touch. Don't forget family always has each other's back."

I slap him on the back and nod. Pulling back, I guess it's my time to go. I turn for one last look at my girl, who cries in Emily's arms. She lifts her head as if she can sense my stare. I mouth the words, "I love you."

Then, I quickly turn away, not waiting for her response, for her rejection, for her tears. Because I fear I will tear her from Emily and kiss her senseless until I convince myself I shouldn't leave.

I still need to find Luke. I walk down the hall leading to the private quarters and offices when I hear loud voices.

"Luke, calm down!" Nathan booms in his commanding tone.

"Calm down?! They threatened her. We can't just let this go!"

"We aren't. However, we must proceed cautiously with the Alpha from Territory Six. Now, he has Territory Three involved. Our hands are tied."

"This is bullshit. We can't let them get away with this kind of crap, not just because of Jessica, but for everyone else they hurt. We have to stop them!"

"I completely agree, but as the Alpha King, I can't simply execute every asshole who exists. What they do in their own territory is out of my hands."

"This was done on our territory! You're going to stand behind political bullshit?!"

Good for Luke. I give him credit for his stance. I'm not sure what I would do if in his shoes. I know what I *want* to do.

I turn to leave, knowing Luke won't exit that room until he reaches a satisfactory outcome. He will do what's right by Jessica—well, I hope so. My mind wanders back to when she ran out of the mansion, scared and frantic and still reassuring me it was fine. I still want to discuss it with Luke, but for now, I'll leave it alone.

Maybe I should talk to Sodie before I go. He wasn't on the balcony when I left, so I search for him. I find him outside on the phone.

"No! You fucked up, twice! You were supposed to keep her there. How the hell did you let her escape?!"

What the hell? Is he referring to Jessica?

"All I know is that when you get into the recruit program, you do your job. There's been a change in plans. I won't be here like I planned, which is why you were supposed to take her—"

Take her? Was he part of Jessica's kidnapping? We never

really figured who was responsible. Hell, so much shit remains unfinished. How can I leave her now? How can I keep her safe if I am not here to protect her?

"She won't remember you. She doesn't even remember me."

Remember him? From her past, before she came here?

"Stop sniveling. I can't help you. I'm already in enough shit! Well, figure it out. You're on your own. I'm done talking." He disconnects the call and pockets his phone.

I retreat deeper into the shadows and watch him leave. I debate whether to follow and confront him. A hand on my shoulder stops me before take a step. Adopting a defensive stance, I whip around.

"Whoa! I didn't mean to startle you," Shadow says. His hands raise in front of him in a nonthreatening manner.

I loosen my posture, slightly, not completely lowering my guard.

He inclines his head toward Sodie. "I think you and I need to talk."

I cock my head to the side, glancing at Sodie's figure growing smaller in the distance.

"Relax. I heard the same one-sided conversation. We should find some place a little more private. You're going to have to trust me, especially if you want to help me keep her safe."

CHAPTER 48

I'M GOING TO KILL HER

LUKE

TWO WEEKS AGO:
MARCH 14, 2025: 9:45 P.M.
LUNA SOLAR CITY: CONCERT VENUE

Silence wakes me from my trip down memory lane. I look up from the piece of paper in my hand. The models still sashay down the runway. Murmurs grow louder from the onlookers. Then, I hear Jessica's voice.

She steps onto the stage. Gasps swirl all around me. She's not wearing her mask. No music plays in the background, no gimmicks, just her own voice. There is no mistaking that she's "G."

What the hell is she doing? As much as I wanted to see her face while she sang, today, of all days, isn't the right time. I crinkle the paper in my hand and glance around the venue again. Guards are posted everywhere. Is this enough?

My brothers' expressions mirror my own, depicting both worry and anger. My father's face slowly turns red, and my mother's eyebrows arch in surprise, I swear they could disappear into her hairline.

I want to jump onto the stage and throttle her. Why would she take this risk? Dammit!

The music starts to play in the background. She moves, and a male model dances with her, strategically removing her trench coat. As the song comes to an end the model throws her coat off to the side she's wearing nothing but barely there lingerie.

Justin slaps his hands over his eyes. Jeremy claps the sides of his head, squeezing his eyes shut, and moans, "Please tell me when this is fucking over!"

I cover my mouth as I snarl, "I'm going to kill her!"

CHAPTER 49

NO TURNING BACK

JESSICA
TWO WEEKS AGO:
MARCH 14, 2025: 11:11 P.M.
LUNA SOLAR CITY: CONCERT VENUE

I need some fresh air. Rampant thoughts run through my head. My throat closes, and it's harder to breathe. Doubt settles in my chest, although it's way too late for that now. I set everything in motion. There is no turning back.

A growl breaks through the silence I sought. A tingling sensation creeps up my neck, a warning sign that I am not safe here alone. Shit. I thought I hid deep enough in the alleyway that no one could see me. I strain my ears to listen for footsteps. There are none. Either he's flying or he knows how to sneak up on his victim. Besides, I can't see too well in the dark due to night blindness thanks to the trauma I endured eight years ago.

I feel their presence. Soon, they'll overpower me.

I hold my breath and stand still, waiting for the right moment. The soft whisper of rubber brushing against concrete prompts me to move. I swing around with an open palm, intending to strike him in the carotid artery, but my arm is blocked. I lash out with my other hand, but that one is blocked, too.

Large arms wraps around me. I spin clockwise to escape my attacker when these stupid heels cause my ankle to wobble.

That's all it takes, a fraction of a second. An arm snakes around my waist. I use my elbow to jab, and he grunts as it connects with his hard muscular chest. His grip slightly loosens. Twisting the opposite way with an open hand, I strike down toward his arm.

He releases his hold around my waist to block my strike, catching me by surprise. He's a trained fighter.

Taking advantage of my surprise, his large hand grips me around the throat, and he slams me against the wall of the building. He presses his large body against mine, so I can't kick or knee him in the junk. He snakes his free arm around my waist, lifting me off the ground so I'm almost level to his height. He brings his face close to mine, so close his breath warms my face.

"What the hell are you thinking? Do you have any idea of the potential dangers you will face?" His masculine scent surrounds me, clean fresh cologne with an underlying hint of campfire smoke. Liam.

He doesn't wait for an answer. His lips crash into mine. His tongue coaxes my lips apart so he can slide his tongue in against mine. He deepens the kiss, pressing his hard muscular body closer.

I lift my arm, but he clasps my wrist, pinning it above my head. Releasing my neck, he runs his hand down my other arm and raises it as well, pinning me to the wall with his body.

He doesn't stop kissing me, and I don't want him to. I wrap my legs around his waist, my dress tearing in the process.

He softly moans and grinds his hips into me. He grasps both of my wrists in one hand so he can caress the length of my body, which tingles with electricity and heat. I want more.

He breaks our kiss and rests his forehead against mine. "Baby, you fucking drive me crazy. I don't know if I want to strangle you or fuck you right now."

I slowly lick his bottom lip. "Fuck me," I whisper, bringing my lips closer to his. "Right here, right now." I need it. I need him.

He groans and kisses me again, deeper, harder. With his free hand, he pulls my dress up higher and slide his fingers between my legs. "I can smell your arousal." He slips into my panties, inserting one finger between my already slick folds.

I tip my head back and moan.

"Already so fucking wet." He releases my wrists, and I wrap my arms around his neck. He grinds his hardened cock into my center, making my toes curl. He licks and nips at my neck, slipping another finger into me. "Are these the same panties that every man in the venue just saw you in?"

I push my hips forward and bite his lip. "Yes."

He sneers. Pulling his fingers out of me, he tears my panties off in his fist. My hips jerk forward with the force, and I whimper. "Then I don't feel bad about ruining these." He tosses them over his shoulder, igniting them in a burst of flames, and pulls me against him. The material of his pants grinds against my clit.

I want them off. I want him inside of me. I reach down to undo his belt.

He chuckles. "My greedy girl. Always my girl," he murmurs against the sensitive spot on my neck.

"Please," I whisper. He slides his hand down my chest, cups my breast and gently squeezes. I finally manage to open his pants and search for what I need. Curling my fingers around his thick, hard cock, I rub my hand down and then back up.

"Fuck..." He bites my hardened nipple through my dress. Readjusting our position, he holds me firmly against the wall.

I pull my dress up higher to give him more access. He slides the head of his cock against the slit of my opening, torturing me, playing with me, until I pant and plead.

He finally enters me, in slow tortuous increments. Then, pulling back out almost completely, he slams his hips forward, burying himself deep inside. He captures my whimper with an open-mouthed kiss. He grinds into me, pushing me further into the wall.

"Do you know how many men must be fucking their mates right now, pretending that they are you?" He pulls back and pumps into me again. "How many men are fisting their cocks, wishing it was your pussy wrapped around them?"

I moan as he slides in and out of me, slow and deep. "Please, just fuck me. I can't..." He tortures me, punishing me, holding back.

He nips at my lip and laugh. "Oh, baby, I'll give you what you want, but I'm going to punish you first for showing the whole fucking world what is mine." He cants his hips. I try to push forward with my own, but he holds me firmly in place.

Nibbling and teasing my lips, he won't even give me his mouth, pulling away every time I try to kiss him deeper. I dig the heels of my shoes into his ass.

"Say it, baby, and I will give you what you want." He grinds into me slowly, rolling his hips to his own melodic pace.

I gasp at the delicious friction he creates. "Please," I whimper.

He pulls my strapless dress down, releasing my breast, and licks my nipple. I grip his hair. He teases, giving me just a taste. I growl in frustration. I want him to ravish me, take me hard. He licks his way back up my neck, and when he reaches my lips, he smiles, continuing to work his hips in slow circles. I bite his lip, but still, he doesn't give in.

"Say it." His jaw clenches, and his chest heaves with desire, with need. His muscles tremble beneath my touch. He's torturing himself, too.

I can play this game. Biting my bottom lip, trying to hold back my smile, I rotate my own hips, thrusting against his when he circles back around.

His breath hitches. His mouth slightly parts. I capture his lower lip, sucking it in between my teeth, sliding my hand from his hair to his neck, his chest, his abs. I love the way his muscles twitch from my touch through his dress shirt. Reaching down, I move my dress out of the way to watch as he glides his hard cock in and out of my pussy.

Inching my hands lower, I flick my clit. I look at him through my thickened lashes and massage my clit with my fingers. Leaning my head back against the wall, my eyes roll back, humming as I relish the pleasure.

"Fuck," he whispers. I grin because I know I won. He smashes his lips into mine, shoving his tongue in time with his thrashing hips. My back slams into the wall with his every move. One large hand squeezes my breast, while the other holds me in the air.

He breaks our kiss to suck at the sensitive spot on my neck. Groaning, his pace quickens, filling the silence of the alleyway with our breathy moans and the sounds of our bodies slamming into each other.

"Say it, baby." He releases my breast and removes my hand over my clit, sucking my fingers before he replaces my arm around his neck. "Say you're mine."

Tightening my hold, I writhe under him. He hovers his

mouth over mine, and I finally give him what he wants, sighing, "Forever."

He pounds into me harder. His fingers dig into the back of my thighs. Canting my hips forward, I meet him thrust for thrust. My clit throbs, aching. I need more. I want more.

He repositions his arms, inserts one hand between us, and massage my clit with his thumb. "That's it, baby. I know exactly what you need." He increases his hard, penetrating thrusts. I start to tremble. "Fuck, yes, right there. Come for me, baby." He slams into me, again and again, taking my mouth with his.

Lightning flashes behind my eyelids. My body thrums in pleasure, and my pussy clenches around his thick length. Dropping my head onto his shoulder, I cry out as a strong wave of ecstasy rips through my core. He follows right behind me, burying his face in the nape of my neck, and emits his own cry of release.

His hips slow their rhythm. He presses his lips tenderly against my own. "I missed you," he murmurs.

Chapter 50

SO MANY EMOTIONS

LIAM

TWO WEEKS AGO:

MARCH 14, 2025: 10:33 P.M.

LUNA SOLAR CITY: CONCERT VENUE

I watch the show from afar with a slew of emotions running through me—pride, awe, admiration, and love. Watching Jessica sing as her alter ego 'G,' then watching her as herself walking the runway in her designer clothing. With everything she endured these past three years, I am so damn proud she took this leap—that is, until she comes out without her mask.

Jealousy overwhelm me, especially when that male model removes her trench coat. I want to jump up on the stage and kill him.

The man to my left starts to grope his mate, and the one on my right adjusts his pants, breathing hard. I itch to grab him by the throat and inform him that his hard-on is for my girl. If he wants to keep it, he needs to control his shit.

Sure, other models flaunt around in less clothing, but I only have eyes for her. I'm a cocky bastard, and my ego is pretty big. I always think everyone is after my girl. Instead of losing my temper, I clench my hands to my sides.

During the closing song of the night, Jessica steps out surrounded by other models, all faux-leather dresses in different styles similar to what a submissive or a dominant would wear. Akiyo moves alongside her, harmonizing with her. Her song is seductive, powerful, and dangerous—all about women being viewed as submissive, but they have power. They are in control and fearless.

The backdrop suddenly flashes a picture of Emily. I know exactly what my girl is doing, sending a big fuck-you message to the Resistance. She is done hiding, and if they want her, they need to come get her. Fear and fury grip my gut.

I move just as the song ends, intending to seek her out before anyone else finds her. It's been so long since I last saw her. I miss her so fucking much. The sight of her alone drives me over the edge.

I find her in the alley. I catch her scent, and I am done. I can't even finish what I intended to, which is get her the fuck out of here and tear her ass apart for her performance. When she urges me to fuck her, how the hell can I say no?

The irrational part of my brain still wants to punish her for risking her life, for torturing me. I make her plead and pant, struggling for more of what only I can give her. Be damned that we fuck up against a wall in the middle of an alleyway. I've taken her in worse places when she drives me absolutely crazy.

And Jessica knows exactly how to turn the tables on me. I cave, giving her exactly what she wants. But I want it, too. We remain in our postcoital bliss, smashed against the wall, unmoving, catching our breath, breathing in each other's scents.

I miss her so much. It kills me that I have to stay away.

She finally breaks the silence between us. "How long are you staying this time?"

I wince at her words. They no longer carry an undertone of irritation or sadness. No, Jessica accepted our way long ago. She never questions it, never fights it, although sometimes I wish she would. More specifically, my ego needs reassurance that she still wants me as much as I still want her.

I gently kiss her lips. "A couple of days." I slide out of her and guide her down onto her feet. Once she's steady, I cup her face in both of my hands and kiss her again. I search her face and find hints of sadness and worry that weren't there before.

She steps back to adjust her clothing, avoiding my gaze. I stare at her, adjusting my pants and tucking in my shirt. "Talk to me, baby. What's going on?"

"A lot has happened since I saw you last. It's been one hell of a day."

"Okay. Come back with me to the hotel, and I promise we can talk first before I bury myself inside of you for the next forty hours," I tease, trying to lighten the mood. I hate seeing her fight some internal turmoil.

She shakes her head. "I'm staying, Liam."

I frown. She never turns me away. What the hell? No point in arguing with her or cajoling her into coming with me. I know my girl, but I also know one way to convince her.

I step closer and grab the front of her dress. Part of her red bodice peeks out beneath the fabric. " I change my mind. I'm going to take you to the hotel, rip this off you, burn it like those panties you were wearing, and then bury myself inside of you for the next two days." With my hand in her hair, I expose her neck and lick from the base up to her ear. "You can tell me everything that's been going on as I ravish your body and pump my hard cock in and out of that sweet pussy of yours." I press my body against hers.

She tugs both of my wrists, and I immediately let go. "No, Liam. I'm staying," she repeats softly, no fight behind her words.

I step back to allow her some space. "Okay. Then, we'll stay." Reaching for her again, she retreats. She pretends to fix her dress and hair. Slow tendrils of fear weave their way along my spine.

We've been here before. She behaved this way when she chose someone else. Not just anyone, my former best friend. I close my eyes, forcing the thought away. My fear of losing her makes me paranoid.

"Baby, talk to me. Don't push me away. We can stay, or we can go. I don't care. I just want to be with you. I'm here for you." I tip her chin, forcing her to meet my eye.

She covers her forehead with a hand. "Liam," she breathes my name, and her face crumples. "Alpha Agnus passed. She named me her successor, but that's not the worst part. The seventh territory comes with the title."

I inhale sharply. As a female successor, she must be mated to keep her position as Alpha. It's a common tradition but rarely implemented due to so few female Alphas named. A young female Alpha like Jessica, especially in the LS territory, will be forced to mate, or she will be challenged to the death for her position. The Whitemore pack is small. No one would make a big deal if their Alpha is unmated. No one would really care, but adding the seventh territory into the mix—shifters have fought and died over that territory.

There's a reason why it remains vacant, why it's been protected for years by the Alpha King. Her life is in danger more now than it ever has been.

Thinking back on her performance, she did that on purpose.

Fear couples with panic, clenching my chest in a vise. A flurry of different possibilities race through my mind. I involuntarily step back, as if someone punched me in the gut.

A flicker of hurt crosses her features. She thinks I'm rejecting her. She turns and says more forcefully, "I'm staying here."

I grab her arm. "Wait. You didn't give me a chance to—"

"What were you thinking, Exposing yourself like that?!" We both pivot toward the booming voice at the entrance of the alleyway. I step in front of Jessica as Luke stomps toward us. His nostrils flare, no doubt smelling our recent coupling still lingering in the air.

Jessica tries to come around me, but I grip her arm, holding her back.

"Is he the one you're with?" he snarls, eyes flaring wide, his face reddening. He glares at me now, but I refuse to move.

I peer over my shoulder at Jessica. She won't look at him. Her cheeks flush.

"You selfish bastard, still stringing her along after all this time?" he spits.

My head jerks forward to face him. This is long overdue. We might have entered a short truce between us for Emily, but I'll never forgive him for what he did. He took Jessica from me. "Stringing her along? We would still be together if not for you!" I accuse.

"Together?!" he shouts. "I had nothing to do with what happened. You had an obligation, a responsibility to your pack that you ran from."

I cut off his bullshit. "There are no rules that forbid us from being together. If you want to talk about rules, how about we review the legal documentation that states you're her older adoptive brother. But that hasn't stopped you! As soon as you got rid of me, you made your move."

He closes the space between us, getting in my face. "You had your chance to come back for her, to write to her, call her, text her. You're the one who chose to ghost her. I stood by and watched her fall apart, waiting for you to return. I'm the one who—"

"Enough!" Jessica yells, forcing her way between us.

"Did you tell her why you never came back?" Luke sneers.

I issue a low warning growl.

He barks with laughter. "You never told her. Did you?"

I glance down at Jessica, her hand resting on my chest. The electricity crackles from her palms, but it's nothing compared to the pain wrapped around my heart.

She asks, "Tell me what?" I don't answer her right away. "Tell me what, Liam?" Her hand trembles. I can't bring myself to say it. She turns toward Luke. Motherfucker actually has the balls to look remorseful. "Tell me!" she shouts, sending small shocks into my body.

"He's betrothed, Jessica." More shocks shoot from her hands, and he clears his throat. "The invitation to his mating ceremony is dated for one week from today."

She lowers her head and drops both of her hands from our chests. I don't know what to say. I don't know how to fix this. I squeeze my eyes shut, waiting for the execution. Her heels click on the pavement.

Luke offers, "Let me take you home."

Of course, he will act as her savior. I can't watch her leave with him.

"Luke!" she screams. "Stop it. Just stop! You're not any better than him!" I open my eyes as she shoves him away. "You're mated. Or did you forget? You mated the most horrible piece-of-shit woman on the planet. Elaine made my life miserable for years. Now, you expect me to—what? Choose you? Be with you after you chose her over me?"

I look at Luke, his shoulders droop, he squeezes his eyes close.

She whirls around to face me. "I already knew that you were betrothed, but for some stupid idiotic reason, I still let you in." She comes closer, tears streaking down her face. "So why visit this time, huh? One last goodbye fuck, or maybe a proposal to continue on as your side piece? No, wait!" She snaps her fingers. "You weren't planning on saying anything. Just disappear like you always do, without a word, and leave me wondering if I will ever see you again. Then, you'll show up, just when I finally feel like moving on again."

I grind my teeth and clench my fists at my sides. I can't force the right words out of my mouth. The pain around my heart intensifies, and yet I can't utter a fucking word.

She raises an eyebrow. "I have loved you for eight years, and you have nothing to say?" She looks down at her hands. "That's fine because I have one last thing to say to both of you. I'm done. I'm done playing these games." She raises her chin, her tears glinting in the moonlight. "I don't choose either of you. So, please, just leave me the fuck alone!"

She turns, but I won't let her walk away.

I can explain. I will fix this. I ignore Luke and rush after her. His footsteps echo behind me, but I don't care. I need to stop her.

I catch up to her, grabbing her arm and turning her to face me. "Please just listen, Jessica. Don't leave, not like this." Desperate, I cup her face, bringing her close to me, resting my forehead against hers. I see how much she hurts, and I want to take it away.

She pushes me, but I won't let her go. She starts to fight me.

Luke interferes, pulling me from her. I turn on him. Everything—all of this, losing her—happened because of him. I hit him in the face, knocking him back. He comes right back with a punch to my ribs and one to my jaw.

Thunder booms over our heads. We both stop mid-fight, covering our ears.

Clutching Luke's shirt, she cries, "Go home, Luke! I don't want to see you. I don't want you in my life!"

He wipes blood from his lips and sneers at her. "That's a bit hard, given the circumstances. Don't you think?"

Through gritted teeth, she adds, "I've managed to make it work for three years. I'm pretty sure I can do it for the rest of my life!" The anger in his eyes morphs into despair as she walks toward me.

I move to wrap my arm around her waist.

She holds up her hand. "Liam, go home. I'm pretty sure your fiancée must be wondering where you are." She glares, ice blue eyes I once compared to a warm sky, now hard and cold. With a warning rumble, she walks out of my life, taking my heart with her again.

CHAPTER 51

TIRED OF HIDING

JESSICA
PRESENT DAY:
MARCH 31, 2025

I sob after telling Christian about that night after the fashion show. He hands me a box of tissues and sits next to me. I can't stop crying. It's so late. Carmen never returns, so he calls a wrap on the interview for the day and escorts me back to my room.

I refused to let myself think about Liam after I walked away that night, likely why it hits so hard rehashing it. I assume by now he's mated. Chris and Elias, with the rest of their family, left for his mating ceremony. Liam is like a son to Elias, and I can't begrudge him that. The same reason I won't let my family choose me over Luke.

I flop on my bed and glare at the ceiling, angrier at myself than anyone else. Turning over, I bury my face in my pillow and start to cry again.

A small part of me always hoped he would at least call, send an email or text, but in typical Liam fashion, he vanished into radio silence. More tears fall. I was so stupid to love him, to believe he would choose me, fight for us, help me when I need him the most.

My bed dips, and a gentle hand strokes my hair. Sixes says, "That was a rough one."

I wipe my face and nod.

"Why are you doing this?" she asks.

I roll onto my back, avoiding her gaze. "Time to move on. And because I make crappy choices in men, I may as well go through the process like I'm choosing a business partner."

She snorts. "If you're looking for a business partner, then why not choose Jacques? You two have a bunch of businesses together, not to mention you're probably the only person in his life who stayed by his side for so long."

"He's the wrong species," I grumble.

"Now you're just being a speciest," she teases.

I chuckle. "Is that even a word?"

"Yes, I'm pretty sure it is," she retorts.

"Besides, he doesn't have a pack. I need a mate who will merge packs with mine."

She blows a raspberry. "Stupid political bullshit."

I face her and rest my head in my hand. "I need to protect my pack. It doesn't matter what I want anymore. The other option is I don't mate and someone challenges me until I die or start an all-out war." I blink up at her. "You think about it and let me know which option is better," I mock.

She lies beside me, placing an arm behind her head, and stares at the ceiling. "What about that Henry guy you chat with online?"

I frown. "Henry? I don't know Henry that well, and we don't chat online."

She hums. "I see the way your face lights up when he sends a text or an email."

"He's not real. He's a fantasy I mostly built up in my head. Besides, I think he's just a lonely, old guy, which is why he spends so much time sending emails and text messages."

She rolls her eyes. "I read some of those texts. Remember? And I saw the pictures of his abs and his..." She blushes without finishing her sentence. "Anyway, he did not look nor sound like an old guy."

I roll my eyes. "Can we not talk about Henry?" I ask dryly.

"Let me guess. You embarked on a destructive warpath and ended it with Henry after everything with Liam and Luke."

"No..."

"I'm pretty sure that is exactly what happened. You went down the 'I don't deserve anything good or things that make me happy' spiral."

I cross my arms over my chest and pout. "I did not."

She shakes her head. "What am I going to do with you? I thought we worked past all of that."

I sigh. "I still have my moments." I rub my face. I know she's right, but I just don't want to hear it right now. "Can we talk about something else?"

We both gaze at the ceiling, looking for answers.

My bedroom door open, and Carmen walks in. She stands at the foot of my bed. "Your parents are adamant that they have the day tomorrow to conduct their own background checks. I prefer that filming starts tomorrow to stay on schedule."

I slide to the edge of the bed and slowly stand. "Let's go talk to my parents, then." She eyes me suspiciously, assuming I have no sway over my parents. Smiling, I push past her and leave the room.

My parents are absolutely livid. The producers threw another five men into the lineup, on top of the eight I already knew about. I just didn't tell them I knew. Carmen didn't know about the changes the producers made, which I find odd, seeing as she is in charge of making all the arrangements. The producers claim it was a last-minute decision to boost ratings and planned on informing Carmen tonight.

I insist that, even with the changes, we move forward with the meet-and-greet tomorrow evening. The sooner we start, the sooner I can move on with my life and focus on my duties as the Alpha and whatever other disasters that ensue. I assure my parents that all will be fine, and Anders can perform his checks tonight and all day tomorrow until the meeting.

Carmen flips through the pages on her clipboard. Setting it back in her lap, she rests her forearms over it, clasps her hands, and addresses me. "I'm sorry we need to continue at this late hour. Life in front of the camera is not always easy. I appreciate you being amenable and a team player. I understand you have been through quite a lot these past two weeks, especially with all the unwanted attention from the reporters and paparazzi. I just wanted to check in and see how you're doing with all of that."

Since I revealed myself as both princess and "G," the media ran with my big reveal. I became an overnight sensation. An anonymous source leaked that I was originally from Territory Two, I came to live with and was adopted by the royal family, and, hours following, I became the successor for not only the Whitemore territory but the seventh territory as well. They even included pictures of when I was in a coma and proof of my abuse. The media portrayed me as a living, breathing, fairy tale princess.

And without warning, the media turned on me. I transformed from a real-life Cinderella to a sneaky, manipulative, evil witch. Past news clips resurfaced, and entertainment series spread rumors of my affair with Luke as "G," as well as an affair with Jacques. Questions were raised.

Is she manipulating the royal family for her title? Did she con Alpha Agnus into naming her as the successor? Why did she always wear a mask when she performed as "G?" Did Young Alpha Prince Luke Langhlan know he was having sex with his own sister? Was Jessica Langhlan responsible for the terrible breakup between the Young Alpha Prince Luke Langhlan and Elaine Powers?

Then, the accusations started. Princess Jessica Langhlan conned the royal family into adopting her. Sources from Territory Two state she was a horrible child, a monster. Quotes from artists who wish to remain anonymous claim "G" is difficult to work with. "G" is almost banned from the music industry for being eccentric. Princess Jessica Langhlan used the royal family's money to buy businesses, and profits weren't returned to the pack.

Reporters and news channels televised this information and more rumors and speculations of how I came to live with the royal family. Magazines, social media, bloggers, you name it, had a field day. Of course, most of it is fake news. No one does a good job at really digging into a story and finding the truth anymore. Opinions and gossip are misconstrued as fact. People who don't know any better believe it all. If it's on the news, it must be real. Right?

When I made the announcement I would be the next star of *A Game of Heart's Desire*, the media circus exploded. Gary, my PR guy, handles everything. As much as I dislike him and he dislikes me, I have to hand it to him. He is very good at his job. I also should give props to my lawyer, Reggie. I need to remember to give them both a raise before this is over.

"Yes, I learned over the years that people can be cruel. The media enjoys its own form of bullying. Sometimes, I don't know which is worse—taking a beating or dealing with the aftermath of cruel words and false accusations. I knew when I signed up for the show that I would face challenges. I just hope that those who really know me believe the truth, believe me. And I hope there are some good journalists out there who know how to search for real information."

Carmen narrows her eyes.

I shake my head and chuckle at her expression. I admit she's pretty good at reading people. "What? Did that sound too scripted? You can thank my PR guy. He wrote it. I've been spewing this shit for the past week. I figured you can use the clip somewhere in editing."

"Can you just be real with me about this whole thing? Share your true feelings on all of this? It's a lot, and it can weigh on a person's emotions and mental wellness."

How real does she want me to be? I glance at the camera. Christian was given the rest of the night off. My parents are busy with the background checks. It's just me and Carmen.

I sigh. "You want to know what I really think about all of this media crap? The truth is I don't think much about it. It really doesn't bother me, not in the way you think it should."

Her brows raise. "What does that mean?"

I cross my legs, fold my arms in front of me, and grin. "It doesn't bother me because I'm the one who started the media frenzy."

Her eyes widen, and she leans back in her chair. "Care to elaborate on that?"

"Sure. Revealing myself as 'G' wasn't accidental. It was planned. I gave Stancy Danton, the famous gossip journalist, front-row seats to the fashion show. I also gave her the exclusive backstory on Princess Jessica Langhlan. Where or how she found those pictures, I'm not sure. I don't even have copies of those."

Carmen blinks repeatedly, stunned. "You're the anonymous source?" she asks.

I grin. "Yes, Stancy and I discussed at length how we would control the narrative before someone else spun it unfavorably. To get ahead of the gossip and bad press, we brought up old articles, gossip blogs, news clips, and reports. You can thank Beta DuPont for the inspiration to paint such a horrible picture of myself. I gave Stancy permission to spread some of the lies Beta DuPont was spewing. It all took off from there. Everyone loves a good story. Everyone loves gossip."

She shakes her head. "You're doing this all for the attention?"

"Yes and no. I want the attention, but not for the reasons you may think. I don't need money or fame. I don't need to portray myself as the victim, and I am sure as shit am not evil or manipulative—well, in most aspects of my life.."

"Why, then?"

I think for a moment before I answer. "I want the bastards who have been hunting me for most of my life, the ones who hunt magic wielders, use them for sex trafficking and medical experiments, and kill them for no other reason than their abilities to wield magic. I want the ones who forced the white wolf species to become nearly extinct and the survivors to go into hiding." My voice cracks. I swallow my rage.

"Jessica, you're putting a target on your back. You can't do this alone. You're trying to start a war—you're just one person. This is dangerous. This is suicide."

I clench my fist in my lap. "They started this war out of selfishness and greed. And they've gotten away with it for centuries." The threat of tears burns behind my eyes. "They could have won if they only focused on killing me. But they didn't. They killed my best friend! They attacked my family! I will not stop until I take down their leader, even if it means killing myself in the process."

I hold Carmen's gaze, unwilling to back down. If she decides to pack up and abandon ship, then so be it. I will find another way. I already planted the seeds outside of this show, and I'm not afraid of finding other avenues. She has no idea what I've been doing the past three years, no idea what I am truly capable of. No one knows, and I much prefer to keep it that way.

Recognizing the determination in my eyes, Carmen nods. "Okay. Okay." She blows out a long breath and glances at her clipboard. "I think we should take five and probably resume your interview from where you left off with Christian."

I wipe the tears from my face when I hear a click. Turning toward the noise, Carmen's hand moves away from the camera.

"I had you figured all wrong. Didn't I?"

I don't answer her. She's either on my side or she's with them. I did my research on her, finding nothing significant, no glaring warnings.

She rests her elbows on the arms of the chair and steeples her hands in front of her mouth. "You're either going to make or break my career. You know that?"

"Figured as much. It's why I requested you. What I still don't understand is why you chose a career in reality TV when you've won so many awards as an investigative journalist."

She drops her hands away from her face. "I really did underestimate you."

I smile. "I told you from the very beginning, I'm good at hiding out in the open. It's a requirement when you're one of the last of your kind and you spend your entire life simply trying to stay alive."

LUKE
TWO WEEKS AGO:
MARCH 17, 2025: 9:22 A.M.
ALPHA KINGS MANSION: CONFERENCE ROOM

After Jessica leaves us in the alley, she disappears for two days. She won't answer her phone. No one knows where she is. The media goes crazy, highlighting her on every news channel. The paparazzi and reporters camp out in front of our home, Whitemore plantation, and our hotel in the city. My parents, including Anders, practically climb the walls with worry. Has she been captured or hurt physically?

I'm sure she harbors some emotional damage after the day she had. The twins keep trying to reach her. She won't respond to their calls or those from the guards to whom she is especially close.

Sixes finally admits that she knows where she went and reassures everyone that she is fine.

On the morning of the third day, she finally responds to Jeremy's text and tells him she's on her way home. When she arrives, we all wait for her in the conference room. Before she can even sit at the table, both my parents, Anders, and the twins lay into her.

I sit quietly. She never once addresses what happened between her and me, and I won't bring it up. Sometimes, our parents and family just don't need to know. If she would talk to me, I hope to clarify my actions. I want to start over. But for now, other matters require our attention first.

Anders slams his fist on the table, drawing my attention back to the argument. Jessica refuses to back down, even with sound reason. Some part of me feels that she has every right to be upset. So many secrets were kept from her, meant to protect her. Even her becoming mated is designed to protect her. She is so damned stubborn. She honestly believes she doesn't need a mate.

Maybe she doesn't.

She's successful in her own right, independent, and able to protect herself. But she doesn't understand that she needs a mate and the backing of his pack to protect her pack.

I glance over at my brothers, red-faced. My mother looks on the verge of tears. My father's jaw tenses as he grinds his teeth. Everyone is wearing casual clothing, faded jeans and plain t-shirts. But the intensity of the meeting makes it feel like we should have worn something more appropriate for business or war.

With palms planted on the table, Jessica stands, leaning forward, and mirrors Anders's stance. Ice crystals form around his hands.

I pinch the bridge of my nose and sigh. "Jessica, knock it off!" I yell. Somehow in the heat of this argument, I think they all forgot I was even sitting here. Jessica is the last one to turn those clear, icy blue eyes on me. Her oversized sweater slides down her shoulder. Wayward strands fall into her face.

A growl escapes her lips. Fuck it, so much for sweet talk. She always responds better when we fight anyway.

"Sit your fucking ass down, and listen," I bark.

Her eyes narrow, and she sneers, "Fuck you! What makes you think I will listen to anything you have to say?!"

I lean over the table. "Stop acting like a brat and sit down!"

Thunder rumbles in the distance. "A brat? You think I'm acting like a brat!"

"As a matter of a fact, I do." I clench my jaw.

"This is my life, Luke. I don't need a man to help me lead a pack!"

"No one said you couldn't. This is about laws and rules. This is about protecting you *and* your pack."

"*I* can protect my pack. I can teach them how to protect themselves, if that's what they need!"

"Yeah. Right. You'll teach a bunch of geriatrics and pediatrics how to fight a war, if that's what your stubborn ass brings to them. You, out of all of us sitting here, know this pack. Haven't you taken a good look at them? There are no young adults, no warriors among them. If an Alpha shows up with his pack and decides to take you out, what about them? What about their lives and their families? You would rather leave them vulnerable for your own selfish reasons?"

Her spine softens, and she lowers her gaze. She knows I'm right. This pack she acquired comprises elderly men and women, too old to learn how to fight, and the younger ones are just too young. I never really understood why there were no teenagers or young adults in the pack. I assumed they all left for school or jobs, but none of them returned. Where are the young parents to the children?

She drops herself into her chair with an exasperated sigh. She rubs her hands against the worn fabric of her jeans. I can hardly suppress a chuckle at the sight of the chucks she's wearing. Between the twins and me, we must of have bought her numerous identical pairs of those shoes. Because she simply won't wear anything else. Between her chucks and hoodies, she considers both to be her security blanket.

"He's right, Jessica," my mother agrees.

"We would never ask you to consider Alpha Agnus's decree if it wasn't for your safety and the safety of your pack," my father adds, rubbing his temples.

"I don't want to be mated," Jessica whispers.

Anders slowly takes his seat. "We know that, but your pack is too small. There are only a couple of hundred shifters in total, not enough to build a small army, not enough to protect you from what's coming."

Jessica leans her forehead on her clasped hands.

I recline in my seat and rest one hand on the table. Maybe I can change her perspective by making it appear like a business transaction. "There is one solution," I offer. Everyone around the table turns toward me. My eyes remain on Jessica. "If you mate me, we can combine our packs. The Emerald Pack will include the Emerald Guards. This will solve—"

"Are you out of your fucking mind!" she roars, flying out of her seat. A torrent of wind whips her hair, and a clap of thunder erupts above our heads. The twins duck, sneaking peeks at the ceiling. "I would rather mate with that sexist asshole from Territory Two than mate you!"

My father stands. "Enough!" The veins at his temples pop out. "There isn't another option, Jessica!"

"There is always another option!" she growls.

"You are already a part of this pack, a part of the guards.

This makes sense! Whatever your reasons are, you must put them aside and—"

"No! I will not mate with Luke! Not. Now. Not. Ever!"

My heart deflates. Does she hate me so much that she's willing to mate with a man she has no memory of, a man who could possibly be involved in her attack all those years ago? We still don't have all the answers, or at least I don't. Anger and jealousy burn in the back of my throat. I stand to reply when my father holds up his hand.

"Jessica, if you will not accept this proposal, then you will mate with the Territory Two Alpha. I have the contract on my desk. He couriered it over yesterday."

Her face scrunches, as if in pain, and her eyes shine with unshed tears. "No!"

"Then you will accept Luke's proposal."

"No, I will not be his second mate!"

I close my eyes briefly. She still doesn't know the truth. She hasn't read any of my letters.

"You don't have a choice!"

She glares at my father defiantly, tipping her chin slightly. "I have choices. Everyone has a choice." She turns her icy blue eyes toward me, piercing my heart.

I didn't have a choice. I wish she knew that.

"I'm giving you two choices, Jessica. Now, choose!" My father's roar should scare anyone, but Jessica shifts her heated stare back to him.

"No!"

He straightens his spine, his Alpha energy building, forcing everyone out of their seats to step back, including myself.

Jessica holds her stance. "No!" she answers in a low tone, balling her fists at her sides.

"Choose!" The command is harsh. He pushes his power

further. I have never seen my father do this before. I heard of it, but I have never bore the brunt of such power.

Her face cringes, and a single tear trails down her cheek. I want to stop him, but an invisible force keeps me rooted in place. The twins take another step back. My mother starts to object, and he raises a hand to stop her. She drops her chin and bows.

"Choose!" His roar shakes our surroundings.

Jessica lifts her chin higher, and perspiration beads on her upper lip and at her hairline. "No!"

My father fists his hands. "Jessica, you will be mated, and you will choose either Luke or the Territory Two Alpha!" More energy bursts from him. My body trembles wanting to fall to my knees. I hate that she's being forced to decide. At the same time, I hope she chooses me. I close my eyes, waiting for her answer.

The air shifts. I look at her through my lashes, not able to lift my head from the pressure of my father's influence. Jessica's eyes and her posture change. Her facial features and hands relax. A touch of red flashes deep within her irises, and a different energy emanates from her body, swirling around her, pushing back on my father's own Alpha powers.

My father's eyes widen. Wind billows her long white-blonde locks around her, and she begins to levitate.

"No." Her voice echoes in the room. Her body rises, her power pushing harder against my father's. We all fall to our knees, bowing our heads. The air crackles from their collective energy.

My father falls into his chair.

"If I must choose a mate, it will be on my terms. My. Choice." The last word reverberates against the walls, layering her voice.

My father's head lowers, but he doesn't submit easily. "But you will mate."

"Yes," she concedes.

He nods, and at the same time, their powers retract. We all take a breath of relief. I slowly get to my feet, helping one of my brothers to stand.

Jessica's feet touch the floor. The swirling wind dies. Regret crosses her features as she surveys the room. She steps back, shaking her head. Choking back a sob, she runs out the door.

I move to follow her. With every new situation, a new magic power emerges, and with each new power, she always freaks out, panicked that she will accidentally hurt someone.

"Luke, stop." I brace myself on the frame of the door. "Let her be. She needs time to find her bearings," my father says.

Anders approaches my father. "Are you okay?"

He waves him off, and they both laugh. Did I miss something? My brothers turn to each other, confusion etched in their faces. Glad to know I'm not the only one out of the joke.

Jeremy elbows Justin. "I think she broke them," he mutters. Justin nods, eyes still wide as Anders and my father chuckle.

My mother wraps her arms around herself. "Did you have to push her so hard?" she asks.

My father sighs. "I know you didn't like it, sweetheart. It was hard for me, too." She curls into his lap, and he rests his head against hers.

Anders uprights a chair and drops into it, blowing out a long breath. Running his hand through his hair, he finally speaks. "She knocked you on your ass. I don't know if I am proud as hell... or terrified."

Jeremy grumbles, "I hate it when you three talk in code."

Justin sits next to Jeremy. "What the hell is so funny?" Warily, I take the seat opposite everyone. My parents watch Anders, waiting for him to answer.

"I needed to test her," my father admits. "We knew she was always a natural Alpha, but your mother felt there was more to

Jessica than just inherited Alpha powers and white wolf magic. To test that theory, I took advantage of her heightened emotional state." He shakes his head, smirking. "But I didn't expect that." My mother mirrors his smile.

I clear my throat. "I don't understand. What the hell did she do?"

"I told you. A mother knows her child," my mother declares.

"I'm her fucking biological father, and I didn't see that coming." Anders runs a hand through his hair.

"Can you three please get to the damn point!" Justin bellows.

"Yeah, I'm not getting any younger here," Jeremy chimes in.

"Only a true royal-blooded Alpha can challenge another royal-blooded Alpha, and a young one barely of age just knocked the Alpha King on his ass," my mother answers proudly.

My head snaps up, and I make eye contact with my father. He smiles and nods.

"That doesn't make sense. Jessica is adopted," Jeremy mumbles.

"Think about it!" I snap. I watch him intently and wait for realization to strike.

The twins both bolt upright and, in unison, exclaim, "She's the prophecy!"

"Alpha Agnus, Jessica's biological great-grandmother, is of the original white wolf bloodline. This whole time, I thought she acquired her title from her mate, who passed away. This entire time, she was the true owner of Territory Seven. She was never just any white wolf species. She would have been the queen, if she hadn't hidden her true identity," I explain.

"If Alpha Agnus was supposed to be the true queen, doesn't that make Anders the rightful king?" Justin asks.

Anders shakes his head. "The history books omitted the fact

that the original White Wolf Alpha was a female. Only the women in my family line hold the title of queen and are born with that kind of powerful magic. But not every female..." He trails off and rubs his forehead. "Not every female has that kind of power. We were not the line of the direct queen."

Jeremy frowns. "I don't follow."

My father clarifies, "Alpha Agnus's mother wasn't the trueborn Alpha Queen. It was supposed to be her older sister, who allegedly was murdered or executed, depending on who tells the story."

"So, your family line of three, maybe four, generations of women never possessed the true Alpha Queen's powers until now?" I ask.

Anders gazes out the window. "Yes."

"The original queen's declarations are coming to fruition," my father says softly. Anders nods his concurrence.

"Declarations?" Justin prompts.

"On the day of her death, she declared that she would return to take her rightful place as queen and seek revenge for being wronged, for her kind from being wronged. A few decades later, the great war happened. Some say the Resistance grew scared and was determined to kill every female in the royal bloodline. Then, the prophecy came to light, and they began the white hunt," my mother explains.

Silence settles over us as we ponder this new revelation.

"Holy crap, Luke. Looks like you're out of a job," Jeremy snickers.

Our bloodline was only meant to hold this space as royals temporarily. I'm not sure how or when that agreement was made, but it's why the secret of the true ruler of Territory Seven was kept in our family.

My Jessica is the rightful queen, a true Alpha Princess. I should be angry, considering I have been groomed and prepared for the position of Alpha King my entire life. I push my tongue up against the roof of my mouth, tasting this new reality. A slow smile forms because it is not bitter at all. I never really wanted the title, and the idea of being free of it thrills me. "Jessica is the rightful ruler of the entire Luna Solar territory, the true Alpha Queen," I announce to the group.

Anders nods and whispers, "If history doesn't repeat itself."

LUKE
TWO WEEKS AGO:
MARCH 17, 2025: 1:32 P.M.
EMERALD PACK TERRITORY

A couple of hours later, Jessica still hasn't returned to the manor, even though my brothers try to convince me to let her be. I ignore them and set out to look for her anyway. I follow her scent and her tracks and find her sitting on a large boulder at the cliff 's edge, overlooking the seventh territory.

Her legs are crossed in front of her, and her eyes are closed, chin tilted toward the sun. I quietly step closer so I don't disturb her. I enjoy seeing her calm, at peace.

Trails of dried tears streak down her face. Is she crying over what happened earlier today, or is she crying over him? This was their meeting spot. I only know because I saw them come here together once. I remember the looks on their faces, how happy she seemed, how in love she looked. She never looked at me that way.

I want to punch something. No, I want to shake her and ask why? Why him and not me? Why can't she love me the same way that I love her? But I already know the answers. She did—once—even though some part of her held back a little. She loved me, and then fucking Elaine happened.

My hands clench in front of me. If Elaine wasn't already rotting in jail for the rest of her life, I would hunt her down myself and kill her. Glancing back at Jessica, I lower my first, sadness deflating my anger. I can't force her to take me back. I can't force her to love me again. Defeated, I turn to leave.

A twig snaps under my foot. Birds fly from a low-lying tree branch, and bird shit plops on my shoulder. I close my eyes, wrinkling my nose. Fucking great! Giggles echo behind me.

"You think that's funny?" I ask, turning to face her. She covers her mouth, hiding her smile, but then she laughs even harder. I snort. In a few quick strides, I reach her as she stands on the boulder. "You didn't answer my question."

She clears her throat, trying to stop smiling. I miss that smile. "Well, I was planning on attacking you for spying, but I think the birds did me a solid." She bursts into more giggles.

I can't help but smile at her. An idea hits me. Narrowing my eyes, I lunge forward and grab her by the legs, swinging her upper body over my shoulder, right on top of the bird shit.

"Oh, ewww," she screeches. I chuckle. I think the birds did me a solid, too. She pounds my back. "Put me down, Luke!" I slap her ass. "Dammit, Luke! Put me down!"

I ignore her and race into the forest. Trees and brush part, creating a clear pathway, and I keep running. Her legs try to kick free from my grasp, but I hold firm.

"Luke, this isn't funny. Put me down!"

When I reach my destination, I set her on her feet. Roots and vines from the ground surface, twining around her legs and arms. She fights the bindings, but they are too strong for her. I finally have her right where I always wanted to bring her. This time, she can't run, and she will listen to me.

"Luke, let me go!" Fear flashes in her eyes.

I caress my fingers down her cheek and grip her neck, bringing her forehead to mine. Her breathing quickens, and she struggles more. "I just want you to listen. I won't hurt you."

Her eyes dart between my own, seeking confirmation. The roots and vines turn her as I turn. I point to a low-lying tree branch above us. She gasps. A bit of rope still hangs from the branch, evidence of where we found her.

I pull her to me and kiss the top of her head. "It was Queenie who led me here. Something spooked her, and she ran. Every time we got near her, she ran again. She never behaved that way before. It was almost like she was leading us directly to you. When she reached this very spot, she started whining, snorting, and stamping the ground. The rain fell in heavy sheets, and lightning struck through the sky above where we stand right now.

"When the second flash hit, Queenie reared up, waving her legs in the air. That's when I saw you, hanging from the tree. At first, we didn't know what the hell we were looking at. I brought you down using my magic. In that moment, I didn't care about keeping my magic a secret or that I wasn't alone. The rope barely hung by a few threads. It was easy to break. We couldn't administer CPR because your neck and face were so swollen. I found a knife on the ground and used it to make a hole in your throat. Well, you heard the rest of it the other day."

Waving my hand in the air, the vines release her.

"Something deep inside of me screamed that there was still some spark of life inside of you. Everyone thought I was crazy, but I refused to let you die."

CHAPTER 54

I HATE YOU

JESSICA
TWO WEEKS AGO:
MARCH 17, 2025: 1:52 P.M.
EMERALD PACK TERRITORY

I search his deep emerald eyes. As bad as our relationship has been, I still miss looking into them.

What am I doing? I break eye contact and push him away. Without looking at him, I ask, "When you say us, you mean the twins and Duck?"

He hesitates briefly before he answers. "Anders and Liam were also among us. Queenie nearly plowed Anders down when she ran through the training facility and Liam was with me when Queenie took off."

I picture a stern-faced Anders nearly mowed over by a thousand-pound animal. I smile at the image in my head. "I'm the reason they sent you to the academy. I took you away from your family." No wonder he was so mad at me when he returned home. In his eyes, I really was a thief, pushing him out to take his place.

He shrugs. "It didn't go down like you think. It was challenging keeping my magic abilities a secret. With the Resistance still pursuing magic wielders, I realized that sooner or later, I would make a mistake and become their target. When our parents and Anders mentioned sending me away, I wanted to go. I had little control over my magic and I didn't want to inadvertently harm you or anyone else."

I frown at his admission. So, if his anger toward me wasn't the reason for him leaving, why was he so mad? I study him. Then a thought crosses my mind, "How is it that you are the only one in the family capable of wielding magic before I met you?"

He lifts his gaze to the piece of rope still hanging from the tree, then turns to the forest of Territory Two. "Because I met you before you were..."

"How?" I stare at the back of his head. He refuses to look back at me.

A blush of red creeps up his neck as he reminisces, "I was fifteen back then, and this girl I really liked betrayed me. I returned home from school for the weekend, filled with all this rage and heartache. I just wanted to...I don't know, escape. I shifted and went for a run. I ignored all the warnings to stay away from the Ruby Falls Pack Territory. I underestimated how ruthless the Ruby Pack could be. I ran right into a trap, and before I knew it, I was lying there, caught in a homemade net. A group of teenagers, close to my age or perhaps a bit older, gathered around me, teasing, taunting, and threatening to kill me for trespassing."

He turns those emerald green eyes back to me, "You showed up, wearing your school uniform, and started throwing rocks at them. I can't remember exactly what you said, but it was enough to make them angry and chase after you. The more I struggled, the net tightened making it impossible for me to shift into human form. I lay there tangled in the net for what felt like ages as the forest darkened. Then you returned alone, with bruises on your face and arms. I felt like a stupid idiot, for getting into this mess and I remember wishing that I had magic to free myself instead of relying on you. While you were cutting away at the net, your hands started to glow, this white luminescent light settled over me. The twine of the net just fell away, and I was free. After you urged me to leave and never return. It took me a while to see, how the trees and brush parted for me as I ran back home. That's when I understood that you had given me magic."

I scowl at his confession, "This whole time" I shake my head in disbelief, "You knew where I came from and you kept this a secret from me!"

He squeezes his eyes shut and shakes his head, "I kept it from everyone."

Angry tears start to form, "I don't know what makes me angrier finding out that Anders is my biological father or learning that you knew something about my past and didn't tell me." I cover my face with my hands and scream in frustration. "Why does everyone think they have the right to keep secrets from me?! This is my life! Do you have any idea what it has been like for me? Not knowing where I came from, how I ended up with magic. How I ended up almost dead!"

He takes a step forward, I retreat a step back. "It wasn't meant to hurt you. At the time, we thought the less you knew would keep you safe and I never intended to keep these secrets from you for as long as I have."

"What a crock of fucking shit!" I spit out. He takes another step forward and reaches out, "Don't you dare touch me or use your magic on me!" I growl in warning.

He drops his arm to his side and dips his chin. "Jessica, just wait, please. I—"

Ignoring his plea, I twist around, instantly shifting into my wolf form, and run through the forest as fast as my four legs will take me. As I near the forest's edge, a massive, powerful wolf collides with me, sending me tumbling to the ground. I quickly regain my footing, but Luke is already on the attack. I growl defiantly, refusing to back down. I brace myself for his impact. We tumble together, crashing into the bushes scattered across the forest floor. I rake my claws against him and sink my teeth into his shoulder. He lets out a piercing whine, and we break apart.

He lunges for me, snarling. I snap my jaws, and he places an enormous paw over my head, pinning me to the ground. He uses all his weight to hold me under him.

Damnit, Jessica, stop fighting me! His loud voice shouts through our mind-link.

Get off of me, Asshole! I roar.

Shift! He commands. I try to wiggle free, but I can't escape. *Jessica, shift!*

I know it's pointless, but I continue to writhe and squirm. *Get off me!* I snap my jaw aiming for his leg, but it's just out of reach.

"Jessica, there are fucking paparazzi everywhere. If they see you in wolf form, it will be all over the damn news! The public can't know you're a white wolf! Not until you're mated, and your pack is secure.

I stop struggling beneath him. *Get off me. If I shift, you'll crush me.*

Stop fucking around and just shift! Damnit, Jessica! Now! I cringe at the harsh tone ringing in my head. Reluctantly, I shut my eyes and transition into my human form. As I gradually open my eyes, I anticipate encountering Luke's wolf. Instead, his human face and completely bare body hovers above mine.

His chest heaves, and so does mine. "I went back for you. I found this little campsite nestled in the forest, and I recognized your scent. I would leave you little gifts and notes asking for you to meet me or at least tell me if you needed help. You never replied."

I glare at him, "Why were you so cruel to me when we first met."

"When my father told me that they adopted you, I immediately thought you were manipulating me and my family. Because I knew you were from Territory Two and even though we don't have proof, we know they have an association with the Resistance." He expels a breath and rests his forehead against mine. "I was a stupid teenage kid, that had gotten his heart broken for the first time. I promised myself that I would never allow anyone to take advantage of me like that again. I became overly distrustful, and second guessed everyone's intentions. I know that I fucked up, and I caused you pain."

He moves his face closer. "I love you, and I've spent years trying to atone for my past actions. I never intended to keep those secrets from you, but not all of them were mine to share." I squeeze my eyes shut and turn my head away from him. "Look at me, please," he whispers softly in my ear.

"This doesn't change things between us, Luke." Before I can push him off, his lips crash into mine, his tongue invades the open space.

His hand skims down my body, tiny electrical pricks ghost across my skin. His erection presses against my thigh. He pulls back slightly, nipping at my lips. "Tell me you don't feel this," he whispers as he glides his hand over my breast. "Tell me you don't want me as much as I want you." His lips meet mine, and he raises my leg to hook around his waist. "You can't lie to me. I smell your arousal. I feel it in your kisses." He lifts his body, just enough for the cool breeze to tickle my skin.

My skin instantly misses his warmth. I miss him, his scent, his kisses, his touch. I curl my hands around his biceps. In my head, I mean to push him away, but my traitorous body pulls him closer. I kiss him, allowing his tongue to plunge deep into my mouth.

He smiles softly against my lips, moaning as my hips grind into his erection. Meeting my eyes, he implores, "Don't toy with me, Jessica. I don't think my heart can survive you abandoning me again."

I turn my head. "I can't be with you."

His expression falls, and he slams his fist into the ground near my head. Jolted by his sudden reaction, I push against him and try to maneuver out from underneath him, but he pins me with his weight.

"Stop lying!" he spits "You still have feelings for him, don't you?" When I don't answer him, me moves off me and swings his arm, punching the air. "How can you fucking still want him? How can you excuse him for abandoning you, for betraying you? But you refuse to forgive me!"

I sit up and cross my arms to cover my nakedness. Tears stream down my face as I shake my head. "This isn't about Liam or Shadow. This is about what you did to *me*!" I yell. I rise to my feet. I have to get out of here.

"I am just as much a victim in all of this," he yells back.

"A victim?! You want to call yourself a victim?" I shove him, rage consuming me. I laugh. "You were in her bed, naked!" I shove him again, but he regains his stance. "Elaine answered the door naked with your mate mark, fresh and dripping with blood!" I scream and punch him so hard he falls back. Gripping my arm at the last moment, he takes me down with him. "You didn't just fuck her! You mated her!"

Luke wraps his arms around my waist and flips me on my back. I attempt another punch, and he restrains my hands above my head. But he doesn't reply. Years of hurt and anger that I was holding back takes over. I want to hurt him the same way he hurt me.

"I hate you for making me love you! I hate you for breaking my heart! I hate you because you mated her! I hate her for taking my best friend away from me, and I hate you for letting her!" I narrow my eyes, hating the tears that spill from my eyes. "I. Hate. You."

He presses his face in the crook of my neck, and drops of moisture trickle down my damp skin. We both pause, no longer fighting, panting, crying.

In a gravelly tone, he says, "I lost Emily, too, Jessica. I hate myself every day, knowing I lost both of you, and there was nothing I could do to stop it." He adjusts so that I lay on top of him.

I seize the opportunity of freedom and sprint all the way back to the manor.

Once inside my room, I lean against the door, catching my breath, and force the sobs escaping my throat to stop. I immediately start packing. I need to leave. I know Luke. Even after everything I said, he won't stop. We'll just fight some more or end up fucking and then fight again.

My door bangs open, and Luke stalks over to me. He wears sweatpants, the bastard. "We aren't done talking!"

"I have nothing more to say. Get out of my room!" He reaches for me, to pull me to him. "Just stop!" I yell, yanking my arm back.

He combs his fingers through his hair. "I can't keep doing this."

"Good! Now get out!" I bark. His jaw tenses, and his hands fist at his sides. From my bag, I retrieve a manila envelope. I planned to leave this for him when I left. I guess it's now or never. "Here." I slap the envelope into his chest.

He catches it before it falls to the floor. "What the hell is this?" he asks, removing the documents to read them.

In the two days that I hid from everyone, I collected paperwork for our businesses and signed everything over to him. "What the fuck is this?!" he roars.

Continuing to pack, searching for clothes, I answer quietly, "I meant what I said."

He glances up from the papers in his hand. "I did this for you!"

"I know, and that is why I'm giving it to you."

"I don't want this without you!" His voice cracks, heavy with emotion.

"I want you to take it," I whisper. I can't look at him. If I do, I might change my mind, and I can't afford that.

He shakes the agreements. "You hate me so much, you're willing to give all of this away?" He tosses the documents onto my bed. "Sell it! Sell all of it!"

I shake my head, and he turns to leave.

Stopping just before the door, he states, "I'm done, Jessica. It's obvious there's no in-between for us. I tried. I really tried, but you won't hear me out."

My mouth opens, but I can't form the words. Besides, there is no point in twisting the metaphorical knife any further.

His energy shifts, pushing against my skin. "You leave me no choice." he threatens.

More tears burn in the back of my throat. I lower my head in submission. If I continue to fight him, it fixes nothing. It only ever leads to more fighting. I gaze up at him through wet lashes.

His face contorts with fury. "I want you out of my house. I want you off my territory, and I never want to see you again!" His last word holds such force that the windows rattle. On his way out of the room, he punches the door off its hinges.

I crumble to my knees and sob.

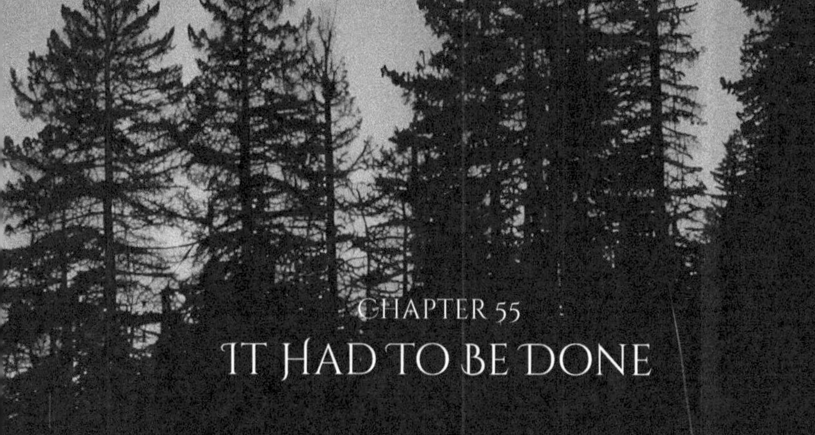

LUKE

TWO WEEKS AGO:
MARCH 17, 2025: 3:45 P.M.
ALPHA KINGS MANSION

I watch from my bedroom window as Jessica climbs into her new SUV, taking the pieces of my broken heart with her. I grip the windowsill to prevent myself from running after her. I commit to my decision, and as much as it pains me, I must stay the course. What other choice do I have? She hates me. She fucking hates me.

Footsteps approach from down the hall. "It's done," I tell them.

They walk into my room. "I know. We all heard." My father sighs. "I told you I would take care of it."

I shake my head. "She needs you and Mom. It's better this way." To extricate her from the pack and remove the people she loves in her life would destroy her. I don't want that. I also can't see my mother going along with it. She cried when my father and Anders decided to remove her from the pack. It wasn't to hurt either one of them but to force Jessica to understand her situation. She also needs to be on her own, to lead her pack and rebuild it.

Gentle hands rest on my shoulders. "You were protecting me. Weren't you?" my mother asks.

"I can assure you, it was purely selfish."

She scoffs. "I know a liar when I see one." She leans in closer. "It's my superpower. Remember?"

My hands tremble, so I grip the windowsill tighter. "I was trying to tell her the truth. I don't want any more secrets lingering between us, but she..." I pause, swallowing the surge of emotion. "She gave me the businesses we built together." I sniff. Her handing me those documents felt like a piece of my heart was ripped out. It was such a final gesture, one for which I wasn't prepared. She ended everything about us. She submitted to my hurt and my rage and didn't even fight back. She is truly done with me.

"She signed over the hotel business to you?" My mother asks. I nod in response not trusting the steadiness of my voice. She releases my shoulder and turns to my father. "Nathan?"

"Just the hotel business?" he asks.

"No. All of them—the clubs and restaurants. She signed over everything to me."

"Where are the documents?" my mother inquires.

I shrug. I threw them on her bed, hoping she would take them back. She could have taken them with her, destroyed them, I hope. "I told her to sell them."

My mother leaves my room and returns with the envelope. "Nathan, she left everything to Luke and the twins."

"What?" we gasp in unison. I turn to face my parents.

"It's all right here. All her businesses with the boys, she gave it all to them!"

My father grabs the papers and studies them. "Luke, this is more than your joint business. She left you and the twins her personal businesses."

What the hell is she doing?

My mother cries, "Nathan, she's going after the Resistance."

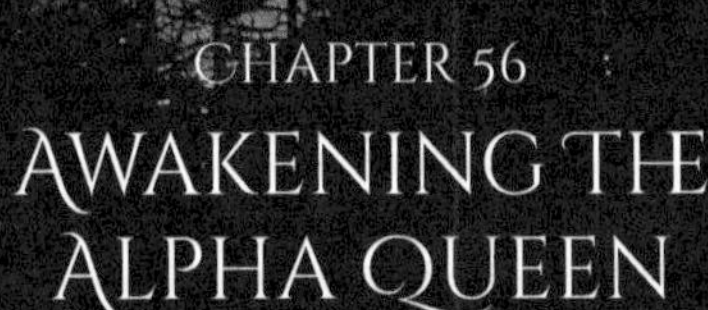

CHAPTER 56

AWAKENING THE ALPHA QUEEN

JESSICA
TWO WEEKS AGO:
MARCH 17, 2025: 5:45 P.M.
WHITEMORE PLANTATION

When Joe and Xavier exit the car, they retrieve several bags from the back of the SUV. "What's all of this?" I ask Joe.

"Sixes will make arrangements to have the rest of your things delivered." I look around at the bags. Those are not mine.

"Whose bags are these?"

Xavier continues to unload the car. "Us," he answers, nonchalant.

I turn from Joe to Xavier and back again. "Your bags?"

Xavier nods.

"I don't understand."

"We no longer work for the royal family," Joe explains briefly.

"No. You can't do that. They need you. You've been there for years."

Joe shakes his head. "Our loyalties lie with Anders. You are Anders's daughter, so our loyalties lie with you."

"Joe, I can't ask that of you."

"You didn't have to," Anders says. "They came here on their own. Why don't the two of you find a place to set your belongings, and I'll meet you in front of the pack hall." he suggests to the two men.

"What are you doing here?" I ask Anders.

He shrugs. "I moved back home." He lowers his gaze. "I wanted to live near you. I hope that's okay."

I tsk. "This place is more yours than mine. You shouldn't feel as if you need to ask."

"It's not mine. It's yours. It was left to you. And thank you for allowing me to live here. I needed a place to stay, now that I no longer work for the Emerald Guard."

My eyes widen. "What the hell are you talking about?! Anders, you cannot leave the guard! They need you!"

"My daughter needs me more, and besides that, I hoped that the Alpha Princess would hire me as her new head guard."

My jaw drops. Did I just enter a crazy town? "Have you lost your mind? Anders, there are no guards to lead! Were you not involved in that argument several hours ago?"

He chuckles. "Okay. Maybe I am getting ahead of myself just a little. Why don't you come with me?" He motions for me to follow him. Narrowing my eyes, I reluctantly do.

As we approach the pack hall, the entire Whitemore pack and at least twenty-five Emerald guards gather outside, including Sixes.

What's happening? I ask her through our link.

She smiles. *You'll see.*

Miller walks away from the pack toward me. He rests his hand at my back and hurries me along until I stand in front of everyone. He raises his hand for everyone's attention. They quiet down. Some of the pack members hush the younger children.

"Princess Jessica G. Langhlan," Miller boasts, "you have been named as successor by our Alpha Agnus Whitemore, the sixth-generation Alpha of the original Quartz Pack, ruler of the seventh territory. Do you accept this position?"

I scan the crowd before me. I must look like a hot mess in an oversized hoodie and yoga pants, not to mention I spent the last two hours bawling my eyes out. Who in their right mind would want an Alpha who can't keep their shit together? We're doing this? Now? Couldn't Anders have let me use the bathroom first?

Can you stop overthinking everything and just say yes? Odyssey chastises in my head. I look among the guards and find him with the pack.

What are you doing here?

Answer the question.

Fine! I clear my throat and turn to Miller. "Yes." I cringe at the intensity of my voice ringing out.

Soft lines crinkle around his eyes in amusement before he nods his approval. "Is there anyone here who disagrees with this decision made by our former Alpha? State your concerns now and rise to challenge."

I swallow. Challenge? Anders simply stares ahead. After a few moments of silence, no one speaks. No one issues a challenge.

Miller continues. "Very well. If there will be no challenges, for those of you who do not want to live under the leadership of the Alpha Princess Jessica Langhlan, you may choose to leave and live out the remainder of your existence without a pack. Do so now."

No one moves. Not even the children utter a peep. I continue to survey the crowd.

"Very good. Now swear your allegiance to your new Alpha Princess Jessica G. Langhlan."

Everyone, from the entire pack to the guards, including Anders, Sixes, and Miller, fall to one knee and place their right hand over their hearts. With a determined look, they lock eyes with me as I observe each shifter. Tears begin to well as I navigate the rows. Friends I formed through my bond with Alpha Agnus. Pieces of my chosen family. Brothers I acquired through the guard recruitment program. We trained together, fought side by side. I would do anything for them, even cross enemy territory borders to rescue them. My eyes rests on Alexis. His smile radiates pride and reassurance. In unison, they all recite, "We swear to you our loyalty, faith, and allegiance for as long as you shall live." They bow their heads in submission.

My heart swells from their unwavering loyalty and love. An electrical pulse begins in my solar plexus. With the next beat, a radiant white light erupts from my core, elevating me slightly off the ground. I take a deep breath and close my eyes, allowing the light to envelope me completely.

Alpha Agnus's voice echoes in my mind. *Welcome home, Alpha Queen of the Lunar Solar Realm, Alpha to the white wolf shifters. Make us proud.*

A surge of white light emanates from my hands and my feet, rising up and out through the top of my head. Like a beacon, light shoots skyward.

A clap of thunder erupts, and flashes of lightning illuminate the sky. Raindrops cascade onto my face as more lightning strikes, and the deep rumbles of thunder persists. The wind swirls around me, lifting me higher until I hover above the pack and gently spin in a small circle.

A torrent of varying emotions fill my soul. Memories of ancestors past surge through my mind—love, trust, faith, betrayal, heartache, pain, and death. So much death, so much loss, so much anguish. I silently vow to bring down the leader of the Resistance. The agony will cease with me.

A distant rumble trembles the earth. The raindrops intensify, becoming harder as they strike against my skin and ground. I whirl faster in the escalating wind. The thunder delivers its muted whispers and intensifies in resonant power. Lightning draws nearer, streaking across the sky.

Then, everything halts.

My feet return to the ground. The sun shines bright, blessing everything under its warm rays. The harsh winds return to a gentle breeze, caressing my skin and filling the air with a sweet floral scent. Birds start to sing as if in approval. I drop my arms to my sides and slowly open my eyes.

Wide eyes stare back at me. Looking to Odyssey, I ask, *Did that just really happen?*

His expression bewildered, he answers, *That shit really fucking happened.*

Everyone remains in their kneeling position. "Is everyone okay?" I wince at my weak, insecure tone, waiting for them to stand and run for the hills.

Heads turn, back and forth, checking on their neighbors and the children within their clutches. Yet no one stands.

Miller clears his throat. "Princess, uh, Alpha Princess, you need to direct us to stand."

"Oh, uh…" I think back to the Alpha King, how he commands the room when everyone is around him at conferences and meetings. I square my shoulders, lift my chin, and proclaim, "You may rise." My voice shakes, but everyone stands.

Miller announces that dinner will take place in the pack hall tonight. Anders rests a hand on my shoulder. "Don't worry. You will get used to it. Think of it like bossing around a board member in a conference room."

"I don't boss anyone around," I reply.

"No, but when it comes to business, you have command. I've seen it. You're a natural. This too will come to you naturally. Speaking of business..." He walks toward the twenty-five guards, plus Xavier and Joe. "Your new pack members." He waves toward them. I raise my eyebrows. "Alpha Princess, these men and women have voluntarily joined your pack, sworn their allegiance to you, and would like a position as members of your guard."

"Didn't you swear your allegiance to the Emerald Pack as guards?"

Odyssey and Alexis step forward. "We resigned," Alexis offers.

Anders lifts a hand to stop my protest. "There are over 300 guards in the Emerald Pack and then some, some training now as we speak. This was their choice. These are the ladies and gentlemen who could be here today. As time goes on, I am sure there will be more."

My brow furrows in confusion. Sixes was born into the Emerald Pack, and she is a direct descendant of the royal bloodline. She can't just leave the Emerald Pack. Can she?

This is my choice. I belong with you. Her voice whispers in my head.

Tears prick behind my eyes, and my lungs expel a long breath of acceptance. *Okay.* Forcing the tears back, I touch Anders's arm. "As a former head guard, who among here do you think will qualify as the next head guard?" I ask. He quirks an eyebrow at me.

Alexis chokes in shock, startled by my question. *What are you doing?* Odyssey exclaims in my head.

Relax. I'm just messing with him.

Please don't. He's still my boss, and I've seen him pissed.

"Oh, I thought you were retiring. No?" I chuckle.

Entwining my arm with Anders's, we shift to face the former guards of the Emerald pack together. "This, ladies and gentlemen, is the Quartz pack head guard, Anders Knight. He will oversee your positions within the guard."

He lifts his chin, and the guards, with a fisted right hand placed over their hearts, dip their heads in respect.

"Shall I leave you to it then?" He nods. Before I walk away, I turn. "Oh, I have one request. I need one of your guards to be my assistant."

Anders smiles. "Sixes will be your assistant. Joe will be your head of the household. Xavier will be your driver. Odyssey will be the second in command. Alexis the third in command. Does that meet with your approval?"

I smile. "It does." I look over the group. "Thank you. You have no idea how much this means to me."

After the festivities, I take a stroll from the pack hall to my home. Alpha Agnus's house appears exactly as it did eight years ago. With its rusty iron roof, the sagging porch, boarded-up lower floor windows and the chipped, nearly brown, white paint on the exterior walls. Most of the homes I just passed by seem just as rundown. I don't know how much money is in the pack account or even if there are enough funds to accommodate all the new pack members, but I would like start by renovating their homes. Heading to the office to review the business accounts and anything else I need to learn about my new pack.

I switch on the light, it flickers twice before it remains lit. The large Mahogony desk in the center of the room is cluttered with piles of untouched documents. The crumbling shelves that hold books are covered in dust and spider webs. I let out a sigh. When I use to come here frequently, I would clean for her and ensure her home was tidy. I haven't been here for three years. It's obvious no one else was available to handle the upkeep and cleaning. I locate a trash can and start clearing up the desk.

Several hours later, pages and numbers blur. A knock at the door startles me. It slowly opens, and Sixes winces. "It's seven am! Don't tell me you were up all night working on pack business."

I glance back down at the papers in front of me. "Then, I won't."

She wrinkles her nose. "Are you going over the financials?"

"Yeah. I honestly thought I was walking into a stable but moderately low financial situation. But..." She comes around the desk to peek at my numbers, which I transferred to a software program that Justin designed.

She whistles. "I did not see that coming."

"Me, either."

She cocks her head to the side and taps her thumb against her leg. I can see the wheels turning in her head. "Have you broken down the numbers—what you can use for housing, repairs, pack allowances, the school?" I click a button and show it to her. She laughs. "Damn."

"What do you think?" I ask.

She puffs out a breath. "I think we should upgrade the place. There is more than enough money for it. I think the pack will appreciate it. Build new homes for the existing pack members with larger families, and fix the current ones for the new single members. Build a training facility for the guards. Maybe even upgrade the tea plantation, work on marketing. With that kind of money, the opportunities are endless."

"I was thinking the same thing. I also have the entire seventh territory. We can expand into that area, even look at other business opportunities for the pack."

She bobs her head, as if listening to a beat only she can hear.

"It's like a blank canvas. I even put money aside for investments, and I..." I almost say I will talk to Justin to start a stock market portfolio, but then I remember I'm not supposed to talk to him anymore. "I also have my own money that I can use to expand into other business ventures, if I need."

Sixes studies me. "Yeah. We can sit down and work on a plan. I think we should start with upgrading the place and finding you a mate."

I don't want to fight about the mate thing anymore so I hum in noncommittal agreement.

"Oh, shoot! I forgot. The reason I came in here was to let you know you have a guest. He's waiting in the dining room."

"He?"

"Yeah, so go get ready. Please wear something presentable."

"Seriously? This is my home."

She rolls her eyes. "Yes, but you are an Alpha now. You know what? Forget it. I'm going to lay out some clothes for you to wear. I planned to send your things down so they should arrive today." She's out the door before I can respond.

When I finally make my way to the dining room, freshly showered and dressed like an Alpha according to Sixes in a lavender long sleeved silk blouse and high waisted dark wash jeans complete with high heeled ankle boots. Gary, my parents' public relations guy, sits at the table. He's maybe my parents age, if I had to guess. His dark blonde hair is slicked back with some greasy hair product. He's dressed in navy slacks, a light blue, short sleeved, collared button-down shirt, no jacket, the knot of his tie sits high against his throat. I envision myself tightening his tie choking him with it until his eyes bulge out. I had to get dressed up for him. Really? He frowns into his cup.

"Good morning, Gary. Is there something wrong with your coffee?"

He doesn't even bother to look up at me and grumbles. "I'm just sitting here, wondering why I'm drinking coffee out of a teacup."

I sigh and plop down in a chair opposite him. "I just got here, Gary. The previous Alpha didn't drink coffee."

"She could have at least had a cup for the coffee drinkers who stopped by."

"Except she never offered it. Why are you here, Gary?"

"I'm here at the request of your parents. I was told to meet them here. I guess I arrived early. You should try it sometime." Begrudgingly, he sips his coffee.

"Gary, if you continue to talk down to me like I'm some prepubescent, lazy-ass teenager, I will hand you a paper cup with your coffee in it and shove—"

"Sweetheart!" My mother's voice rings through the dining room. "How was your first night in your territory?"

I narrow my eyes at Gary and stand to greet my mother. She draws me in for a hug. "Good. Everything has gone well. I didn't expect to see you," I admit.

She kisses my cheek. "Don't worry about Luke."

"Gary, you're early as usual. Thank you for coming," my father says as he walks in.

I glance behind him. There are no guards.

"I told them to take a break," he explains. Then, he hugs me. "Plenty of guards to go around."

"The paparazzi weren't a problem?"

"No. I'm a recluse Alpha King—too boring for them to waste their time."

Gary clears his throat. "I'm happy for this little reunion, but time is of the essence here. Thanks to the Princess revealing her alter ego 'G' and an anonymous source who spilled the "tea" regarding the Princess's past, I now have to develop a media control plan."

"Wait. You want me to do what?" I shout.

"Well, you agreed to move forward with finding a mate, so we thought this would be a suitable alternative," my mother explains, sipping her tea.

"So, the three of you—four, if you include Gary—get to choose random men who I date, and I pick one and mate them before midnight on my birthday?"

"They're not random men," Anders counters.

"We know them and approve of them," my father adds.

Gary shrugs. "You have had two proposals and shut both of them down so I think your parents' alternative is good."

"First of all, Gary, the betrothal contract is null and void, according to my lawyer, because, for one, there is no birth certificate of a Grit DuPont. Grit DuPont was never born or existed on the LS or anywhere else in the world. Two, they were dumb enough to fake a death certificate. So, in either case, Grit DuPont does not exist. I am not obligated to fulfill that contract. And Luke... that's personal and none of your business."

"Sorry to burst your pink twinkling bubble, Princess. There is a shitshow of crap going on just outside the territory boundary. Your life is my business, especially if you need me to clean up what you started," he sneers.

Fuck him. I'll give him a pink princess bubble. "You know what, Gary? Because you hate your job so much, why don't we just save you some time and paste my crappy life on some reality TV show for a tell-all? While we're at it, just throw in the men I need to meet so the entire world can see just how incapable I am of choosing a mate for myself! At least that way, you don't have to lift a finger and do what you actually get paid for."

This time, Gary frowns and leans back in his chair. "Actually, that might work. I can make the arrangements."

"No, Gary! I was being sarcastic, suggesting I want to get rid of your ass!"

He laughs, snapping his fingers and wagging his index finger at me. "I'll be right back. Let me make some phone calls." He leaps from his chair and exits the back door.

"You're fired!" I yell after him, even though I'm pretty sure he can't hear me.

My parents chuckle. "I know he has an attitude, Little One, but he's really great at his job. Or I wouldn't have kept him around as long as I have," my father defends.

"Attitude? More like a personality disorder," I scoff.

Gary returns shortly, crashing through the door with a bag hitched over his shoulder and a huge smile from ear to ear.

"What the hell is that?" I ask, gesturing to his satchel.

"You, Alpha Princess, are going to be the new star attraction on the popular reality TV dating show, *A Game of Heart's Desire*!" he exclaims, clapping his hands together.

"The hell I am!" I shout, standing from my chair.

He laughs. "Oh, yes, you are. This was, after all, your suggestion." He waggles his eyebrows. "And whether you like it or not, you and I will be spending quite a bit of time together. Filming starts in less than two weeks."

ACKNOWLEDGMENTS

To Aunty Cindy Lei and Uncle Reed: Thank you for reading the very rough drafts. Providing constructive criticism and honest feedback. For pushing me to continue to write because I left you hanging on the last chapter. For talking me back down when I had it up to Uncle Reed and felt like giving up. (Aunty Cindy understands what this means.)

To my mama: For introducing me to the supernatural and spiritual side of life. For allowing me to read books from a young age that ignited that crazy and wild imagination inside of my brain.

To the Paper Raven Books Team: Thank you for putting on a retreat. It was the stepping stone I needed to make my dream come alive. For coaching me along the way, helping me to get out of my head. Answering all my ridiculous questions. Every single one of you are amazing.

To my son: For helping me to imagine up different magical powers my characters needed to wield. Making sure one of the villains in my story has a badass scar on their face and giving me ideas for plot twists along the way. One day, when you're an adult and you read and understand what your mother actually wrote, I hope you will find it humorous that you had a part in it.

Last but not least, to my hubby: For having my back. For standing by my side in silent support with every dream, goal, or journey I set out on. For letting me do my thing no matter how crazy or time-consuming it is. For taking the kids out of the house when I needed to focus on writing. For listening to me go on and on about the fictitious characters in my head, the crazy plots I dreamed up, and most of all for reading the book even though it's not your thing. Thank you for being the inspiration to many of the MMCs in my book. I love you more than you think I do.

About the Author

Meet Lilinoe K. Russell, a true island soul hailing from the beautiful Hawaii Island. Growing up in the charming town of Honoka'a, where the population barely tipped 2,000, Lilinoe was immersed in a captivating blend of cultures and traditions, thanks to the town's proximity to the Sugar plantation and the Paniolo (Cowboy) lifestyle.

In the heart of this tight-knit community, she found herself spellbound by the rich narratives shared by the kupuna (elders). Their tales, woven with the threads of history, myths, and legends of Hawaii, along with stories from diverse cultures, formed the tapestry of her upbringing.

Lilinoe has always had a soft spot for stories that flirt with the supernatural, brimming with magic and mystery. And who could forget the spine-tingling obake (ghost) stories—her second-favorite indulgence! These tales, passed down through the generations, have become an integral part of her very being.

Fueled by the inspiration drawn from these enchanting stories, Lilinoe harbored a lifelong dream of becoming a writer. Now, the time has come for her to unfurl her own tales, continuing the legacy of storytelling ingrained deep within her bones. Get ready to embark on a journey through Lilinoe's imagination, where magic, mystery, and the echoes of ancient stories come to life.

To stay up to date on all things Lilinoe Russel.
Scan this QR code:

www.ingramcontent.com/pod-product-compliance
Lightning Source LLC
Chambersburg PA
CBHW070301310726

48976CB00005B/1518

9798990779044